THE HISTORY OF
MR. POLLY

&

THE WAR
IN THE AIR

THE HISTORY OF MR. POLLY

and

THE WAR IN THE AIR

by

H. G. WELLS

ODHAMS PRESS LIMITED
LONDON, W.C. 2

Printed in Great Britain

THE HISTORY OF
MR. POLLY

CONTENTS

CHAPTER ONE

BEGINNINGS AND THE BAZAAR

§ 1

"HOLE!" said Mr. Polly, and then for a change, and with greatly increased emphasis: "*'Ole!*" He paused, and then broke out with one of his private and peculiar idioms. "Oh! *Beastly* Silly Wheeze of a hole!"

He was sitting on a stile between two threadbare-looking fields, and suffering acutely from indigestion.

He suffered from indigestion now nearly every afternoon in his life, but as he lacked introspection he projected the associated discomfort upon the world. Every afternoon he discovered afresh that life as a whole, and every aspect of life that presented itself, was "beastly." And this afternoon, lured by the delusive blueness of a sky that was blue because the March wind was in the east, he had come out in the hope of snatching something of the joyousness of spring. The mysterious alchemy of mind and body refused, however, to permit any joyousness in the spring.

He had had a little difficulty in finding his cap before he came out. He wanted his cap—the new golf cap—and Mrs. Polly must needs fish out his old soft brown felt hat. "*'Ere's* your 'at," she said, in a tone of insincere encouragement.

He had been routing among the piled newspapers under the kitchen dresser, and had turned quite hopefully and taken the thing. He put it on. But it didn't feel right. Nothing felt right. He put a trembling hand upon the crown and pressed it on his head, and tried it askew to the right, and then askew to the left.

Then the full sense of the offered indignity came home to him. The hat masked the upper sinister quarter of his face, and he spoke with a wrathful eye regarding his wife from under the brim. In a voice thick with fury he said, "I s'pose you'd like me to wear that silly Mud Pie for ever, eh? I tell you I won't. I'm sick of it. I'm pretty near sick of everything, comes to that. . . . Hat!"

He clutched it with quivering fingers. "Hat!" he repeated. Then he flung it to the ground, and kicked it with extraordinary fury across the kitchen. It flew up against the door and dropped to the ground with its ribbon band half off.

"Shan't go out!" he said, and sticking his hands into his jacket pockets, discovered the missing cap in the right one.

There was nothing for it but to go straight upstairs without a word, and out, slamming the shop door hard.

"Beauty!" said Mrs. Polly at last to a tremendous silence, picking up and dusting the rejected headdress. "Tantrums,"

she added, " I 'aven't patience." And moving with the slow
reluctance of a deeply offended woman, she began to pile together the simple apparatus of their recent meal, for trans-
portation to the scullery sink.

The repast she had prepared for him did not seem to her to
justify his ingratitude. There had been the cold pork from
Sunday, and some nice cold potatoes, and Rashdall's Mixed
Pickles, of which he was inordinately fond. He had eaten
three gherkins, two onions, a small cauliflower head, and
several capers, with every appearance of appetite, and indeed
with avidity ; and then there had been cold suet pudding
to follow, with treacle, and then a nice bit of cheese. It was
the pale, hard sort of cheese he liked ; red cheese he declared
was indigestible. He had also had three big slices of grayish
baker's bread, and had drunk the best part of the jugful of
beer. . . . But there seems to be no pleasing some people.

"Tantrums!" said Mrs. Polly at the sink, struggling with
the mustard on his plate, and expressing the only solution of
the problem that occurred to her.

And Mr. Polly sat on the stile and hated the whole scheme
of life—which was at once excessive and inadequate of him.
He hated Fishbourne, he hated Fishbourne High Street, he
hated his shop and his wife and his neighbours—every blessed
neighbour—and with indescribable bitterness he hated himself.

" Why did I ever get in this silly Hole ? " he said. " Why did
I ever ? "

He sat on the stile, and looked with eyes that seemed blurred
with impalpable flaws at a world in which even the spring buds
were wilted, the sunlight metallic, and the shadows mixed
with blue-black ink.

To the moralist I know he might have served as a figure of
sinful discontent, but that is because it is the habit of moralists
to ignore material circumstances—if, indeed, one may speak
of a recent meal as a circumstance—seeing that Mr. Polly was
circum. Drink, indeed, our teachers will criticise nowadays
both as regards quantity and quality, but neither church nor
state nor school will raise a warning finger between a man and
his hunger and his wife's catering. So on nearly every day in
his life Mr. Polly fell into a violent rage and hatred against the
outer world in the afternoon, and never suspected that it was
this inner world to which I am with such masterly delicacy
alluding, that was thus reflecting its sinister disorder upon
the things without. It is a pity that some human beings are
not more transparent. If Mr. Polly, for example, had been
transparent, or even passably translucent, then perhaps he
might have realised, from the Laocoon struggle he would have
glimpsed, that indeed he was not so much a human being as a
civil war.

Wonderful things must have been going on inside Mr. Polly.
Oh ! wonderful things. It must have been like a badly managed

industrial city during a period of depression ; agitators, acts of violence, strikes, the forces of law and order doing their best, rushings to and fro, upheavals, the *Marseillaise,* tumbrils, the rumble and the thunder of the tumbrils. . . .

I do not know why the east wind aggravates life to unhealthy people. It made Mr. Polly's teeth seem loose in his head, and his skin feel like a misfit, and his hair a dry stringy exasperation. . . .

Why cannot doctors give us an antidote to the east wind ?

" Never have the sense to get your hair cut till it's too long," said Mr. Polly, catching sight of his shadow, " you blighted, desgenerated Paintbrush ! Ugh ! " and he flattened down the projecting tails with an urgent hand.

§ 2

Mr. Polly's age was exactly thirty-seven years and a half. He was a short, compact figure, and a little inclined to a localised embonpoint. His face was not unpleasing ; the features fine, but a trifle too large about the lower half of his face, and a trifle too pointed about the nose to be classically perfect. The corners of his sensitive mouth were depressed. His eyes were ruddy brown and troubled, and the left one was round with more of wonder in it than its fellow. His complexion was dull and yellowish. That, as I have explained, on account of those civil disturbances. He was, in the technical sense of the word, clean-shaved, with a small fallow patch under the right ear and a cut on the chin. His brow had the little puckerings of a thoroughly discontented man, little wrinklings and lumps, particularly over his right eye, and he sat with his hands in his pockets, a little askew on the stile, and swung one leg.

" Hole ! " he repeated presently.

He broke into a quavering song : " Roöötten Beëëastly Silly Hole ! "

His voice thickened with rage, and the rest of his discourse was marred by an unfortunate choice of epithets.

He was dressed in a shabby black morning coat and vest ; the braid that bound these garments was a little loose in places. His collar was chosen from stock and with projecting corners, what was called in those days a " wing-poke " ; that and his tie, which was new and loose and rich in colouring, had been selected to encourage and stimulate customers—for he dealt in gentleman's outfitting. His golf cap, which was also from stock and aslant over his eye, gave his misery a desperate touch. He wore brown leather boots—because he hated the smell of blacking.

Perhaps after all it was not simply indigestion that troubled him.

Behind the superficialities of Mr. Polly's being moved a larger and vaguer distress. The elementary education he had acquired had left him with the impression that arithmetic was a fluky science and best avoided in practical affairs, but even the absence of bookkeeping and a total inability to distinguish between capital and interest, could not blind him for ever to the fact that the little shop in the High Street was not paying. An absence of returns, a constriction of credit, a depleted till—the most valiant resolves to keep smiling could not prevail for ever against these insistent phenomena. One might bustle about in the morning before dinner and in the afternoon after tea and forget that huge dark cloud of insolvency that gathered and spread in the background, but it was part of the desolation of these afternoon periods, those gray spaces of time after meals when all one's courage had descended to the unseen battles of the pit, that life seemed stripped to the bone and one saw with a hopeless clearness.

Let me tell the history of Mr. Polly from the cradle to these present difficulties.

"First the infant, mewling and puking in its nurse's arms."

There had been a time when two people had thought Mr. Polly the most wonderful and adorable thing in the world, had kissed his toe-nails, saying "myum, myum!" and marvelled at the exquisite softness and delicacy of his hair, had called to one another to remark the peculiar distinction with which he bubbled, had disputed whether the sound he had made was just da, da, or truly and intentionally dadda, had washed him in the utmost detail, and wrapped him up in soft warm blankets, and smothered him with kisses. A regal time that was, and four-and-thirty years ago ; and a merciful forgetfulness barred Mr. Polly from ever bringing its careless luxury, its autocratic demands and instant obedience, into contrast with his present condition of life. These two people had worshipped him from the crown of his head to the soles of his exquisite feet. And also they had fed him rather unwisely, for no one had ever troubled to teach his mother anything about the mysteries of a child's upbringing—though, of course, the monthly nurse and the charwoman gave some valuable hints—and by his fifth birthday the perfect rhythms of his nice new interior were already darkened with perplexity. . . .

His mother died when he was seven. He began only to have distinctive memories of himself in the time when his education had already begun.

I remember seeing a picture of Education—in some place. I think it was Education, but quite conceivably it represented the Empire teaching her Sons, and I have a strong impression that it was a wall-painting upon some public building in Manchester or Birmingham or Glasgow, but very possibly I am mistaken about that. It represented a glorious woman, with a wise and fearless face, stooping over her children, and pointing them to far horizons. The sky displayed the pearly

warmth of a summer dawn, and all the painting was marvellously bright as if with the youth and hope of the delicately
beautiful children in the foreground. She was telling them,
one felt, of the great prospect of life that opened before them,
of the splendours of sea and mountain they might travel and
see, the joys of skill they might acquire, of effort and the pride of
effort, and the devotions and nobilities it was theirs to achieve.
Perhaps even she whispered of the warm triumphant mystery
of love that comes at last to those who have patience and un-
blemished hearts. . . . She was reminding them of their great
heritage as English children, rulers of more than one-fifth of
mankind, of the obligation to do and be the best that such a
pride of empire entails, of their essential nobility and knight-
hood, and of the restraints and charities and disciplined
strength that is becoming in knights and rulers. . . .

The education of Mr. Polly did not follow this picture very
closely. He went for some time to a National School, which
was run on severely economical lines to keep down the rates,
by a largely untrained staff ; he was set sums to do that he did
not understand, and that no one made him understand ; he
was made to read the Catechism and Bible with the utmost
industry and an entire disregard of punctuation or significance ;
caused to imitate writing copies and drawing copies ; given
object-lessons upon sealing-wax and silkworms and potato-
bugs and ginger and iron and such-like things ; taught various
other subjects his mind refused to entertain ; and afterwards,
when he was about twelve, he was jerked by his parents to
" finish off " in a private school of dingy aspect and still
dingier pretensions, where there were no object-lessons, and
the studies of bookkeeping and French were pursued (but never
effectually overtaken) under the guidance of an elderly gentleman, who wore a nondescript gown and took snuff, wrote
copperplate, explained nothing, and used a cane with remarkable dexterity and gusto.

Mr. Polly went into the National School at six, and he left
the private school at fourteen, and by that time his mind
was in much the same state that you would be in, dear reader,
if you were operated upon for appendicitis by a well-meaning,
boldly enterprising, but rather overworked and underpaid
butcher boy, who was superseded towards the climax of the
operation by a left-handed clerk of high principles but in-
temperate habits—that is to say, it was in a thorough mess.
The nice little curiosities and willingness of a child were in a
jumbled and thwarted condition, hacked and cut about—the
operators had left, so to speak, all their sponges and ligatures
in the mangled confusion—and Mr. Polly had lost much of his
natural confidence, so far as figures and sciences and languages
and the possibilities of learning things were concerned. He
thought of the present world no longer as a wonderland of
experiences, but as geography and history, as the repeating

of names that were hard to pronounce, and lists of products and populations and heights and lengths, and as lists and dates —oh! and Boredom indescribable. He thought of religion as the recital of more or less incomprehensible words that were hard to remember, and of the Divinity as of a limitless Being having the nature of a schoolmaster and making infinite rules, known and unknown, rules that were always ruthlessly enforced, and with an infinite capacity for punishment and most horrible of all to think of—limitless powers of espial. (So to the best of his ability he did not think of that unrelenting eye.) He was uncertain about the spelling and pronunciation of most of the words in our beautiful but abundant and perplexing tongue—that especially was a pity, because words attracted him, and under happier conditions he might have used them well—he was always doubtful whether it was eight sevens or nine eights that was sixty-three (he knew no method for settling the difficulty), and he thought the merit of a drawing consisted in the care with which it was " lined in." " Lining in " bored him beyond measure.

But the indigestions of mind and body that were to play so large a part in his subsequent career were still only beginning. His liver and his gastric juice, his wonder and imagination kept up a fight against the things that threatened to overwhelm soul and body together. Outside the regions devastated by the school curriculum he was still intensely curious. He had cheerful phases of enterprise, and about thirteen he suddenly discovered reading and its joys. He began to read stories voraciously, and books of travel, provided they were also adventurous. He got these chiefly from the local institute, and he also " took in " irregularly, but thoroughly, one of those inspiring weeklies that dull people used to call " penny dreadfuls," admirable weeklies crammed with imagination that the cheap boys' " comics " of to-day have replaced. At fourteen, when he emerged from the valley of the shadow of education, there survived something—indeed it survived still, obscured and thwarted, at five-and-thirty—that pointed not with a visible and prevailing finger like the finger of that beautiful woman in the picture, but pointed nevertheless to the idea that there was interest and happiness in the world. Deep in the being of Mr. Polly, deep in that darkness, like a creature which has been beaten about the head and left for dead but still lives, crawled a persuasion that over and above the things that are jolly and " bits of all right," there was beauty, there was delight ; that somewhere—magically inaccessible, perhaps, but still somewhere—were pure and easy and joyous states of body and mind.

He would sneak out on moonless winter nights and stare up at the stars, and afterwards find it difficult to tell his father where he had been.

He would read tales about hunters and explorers, and

imagine himself riding mustangs as fleet as the wind across the prairies of Western America, or coming as a conquering and adored white man into the swarming villages of Central Africa. He shot bears with a revolver—a cigarette in the other hand— and made a necklace of their teeth and claws for the chief's beautiful young daughter. Also he killed a lion with a pointed stake, stabbing through the beast's heart as it stood over him.

He thought it would be splendid to be a diver and go down into the dark-green mysteries of the sea.

He led stormers against well-nigh impregnable forts, and died on the ramparts at the moment of victory. (His grave was watered by a nation's tears.)

He rammed and torpedoed ships, one against ten.

He was beloved by queens in barbaric lands, and reconciled whole nations to the Christian faith.

He was martyred, and took it very calmly and beautifully— but only once or twice after the Revivalist week. It did not become a habit with him.

He explored the Amazon, and found, newly exposed by the fall of a great tree, a rock of gold.

Engaged in these pursuits he would neglect the work im- mediately in hand, sitting somewhat slackly on the form and projecting himself in a manner tempting to a schoolmaster with a cane. . . . And twice he had books confiscated.

Recalled to the realities of life, he would rub himself or sigh as the occasion required, and resume his attempts to write as good as copperplate. He hated writing ; the ink always crept up his fingers, and the smell of ink offended him. And he was filled with unexpressed doubts. *Why* should writing slope down from right to left ? *Why* should down-strokes be thick and up-strokes thin ? *Why* should the handle of one's pen point over one's right shoulder ?

His copy-books towards the end foreshadowed his destiny and took the form of commercial documents. " *Dear Sir,*" they ran, " *Referring to your esteemed order of the 26th ult., we beg to inform you,*" and so on.

The compression of Mr. Polly's mind and soul in the educa- tional institutions of his time was terminated abruptly by his father, between his fourteenth and fifteenth birthday. His father—who had long since forgotten the time when his son's little limbs seemed to have come straight from God's hand, and when he had kissed five minute toe-nails in a rapture of loving tenderness—remarked——

" It's time that dratted boy did something for a living."

And a month or so later Mr. Polly began that career in business that led him at last to the sole proprietorship of a bankrupt outfitter's shop—and to the stile on which he was sitting.

§ 3

Mr. Polly was not naturally interested in hosiery and gentlemen's outfitting. At times, indeed, he urged himself to a spurious curiosity about that trade, but presently something more congenial came along and checked the effort. He was apprenticed in one of those large, rather low-class establishments which sell everything from pianos and furniture to books and millinery, a department store, in fact the Port Burdock Drapery Bazaar at Port Burdock, one of the three townships that are grouped round the Port Burdock naval dockyards. There he remained six years. He spent most of the time inattentive to business, in a sort of uncomfortable happiness, increasing his indigestion.

On the whole he preferred business to school; the hours were longer, but the tension was not nearly so great. The place was better aired, you were not kept in for no reason at all, and the cane was not employed. You watched the growth of your moustache with interest and impatience, and mastered the beginnings of social intercourse. You talked and found there were things amusing to say. Also you had regular pocket-money, and a voice in the purchase of your clothes, and presently a small salary. And there were girls ! And friendship ! In the retrospect Port Burdock sparkled with the facets of quite a cluster of remembered jolly times.

(" Didn't save much money, though," said Mr. Polly.)

The first apprentices' dormitory was a long, bleak room with six beds, six chests of drawers and looking-glasses, and a number of boxes of wood or tin ; it opened into a still longer and bleaker room of eight beds, and this into a third apartment with yellow-grained paper and American cloth tables, which was the dining-room by day, and the men's sitting and smoking room after nine. Here Mr. Polly, who had been an only child, first tasted the joys of social intercourse. To begin with, there were attempts to bully him on account of his refusal to consider face-washing a diurnal duty, but two fights with the apprentices next above him established a useful reputation for choler, and the presence of girl apprentices in the shop somehow raised his standard of cleanliness to a more acceptable level. He didn't, of course, have very much to do with the feminine staff in his department, but he spoke to them casually as he traversed foreign parts of the Bazaar, or got out of their way politely, or helped them to lift down heavy boxes, and on such occasions he felt their scrutiny. Except in the course of business or at meal-times the men and women of the establishment had very little opportunity of meeting; the men were in their rooms and the girls in theirs. Yet these feminine creatures, at once so near and so remote, affected him profoundly. He would watch them going to and fro, and marvel secretly at the beauty of their hair, or the roundness of their necks, or the warm softness of their cheeks, or the delicacy of their hands. He would fall into passions for them at dinner-time, and try to show devotions by his manner of passing the bread and margarine at tea. There was a very fair-haired, fair-skinned apprentice in the adjacent haberdashery to whom he said " good morning " every morning, and for a period it seemed to him the most significant event in his day. When she said, " I do hope it will be fine to-morrow," he felt it marked an epoch. He had had no sisters, and was innately disposed to worship womankind. But he did not betray as much to Platt and Parsons.

To Platt and Parsons he affected an attitude of seasoned depravity towards the creatures. Platt and Parsons were his contemporary apprentices in departments of the drapery shop, and the three were drawn together into a close friendship by the fact that all their names began with P. They decided they were the three P's, and went about together of an evening with the bearing of desperate dogs. Sometimes when they had money they went into public houses and had drinks. Then they would become more desperate than ever and walk along the pavement under the gas-lamps arm in arm singing. Platt had a good tenor voice and had been in a church choir, and so he led the singing. Parsons had a serviceable bellow, which roared and faded and roared again very wonderfully. Mr. Polly's share was an extraordinary lowing noise, a sort of flat recitative which he called " singing seconds." They would have sung catches if they had known how to do it, but as it was they sang melancholy music-hall songs about dying soldiers and the old folks far away.

They would sometimes go into the quieter residential quarters of Port Burdock, where policemen and other obstacles were infrequent, and really let their voices soar like hawks, and feel very happy. The dogs of the district would be stirred to hopeless emulation, and would keep it up for long after the three P's had been swallowed up by the night. One jealous brute of an Irish terrier made a gallant attempt to bite Parsons, but was beaten by numbers and solidarity.

The three P's took the utmost interest in each other, and found no other company so good. They talked about everything in the world ; and would go on talking in their dormitory after the gas was out, until the other men were reduced to throwing boots. They skulked from their departments in the slack hours of the afternoon to gossip in the packing-room of the warehouse. On Sundays and Bank Holidays they went for long walks together, talking.

Platt was white-faced and dark, and disposed to undertones and mystery, and a curiosity about society and the *demi-monde*. He kept himself *au courant* by reading a penny paper of infinite suggestion called *Modern Society*. Parsons was of an ampler build, already promising fatness, with curly hair and a lot of rolling, rollicking, curly features, and a large, blob-shaped nose. He had a great memory, and a real interest in literature. He knew great portions of Shakespear and Milton by heart, and would recite them at the slightest provocation. He read everything he could get hold of, and if he liked it he read it aloud ; it did not matter who else liked it. At first Mr. Polly was disposed to be suspicious of this literature, but he was carried away by Parsons' enthusiasm. The three P's went to a performance of " Romeo and Juliet " at the Port Burdock Theatre Royal, and hung over the gallery fascinated. After that they made a sort of password of, " Do you bite your thumbs at Us, Sir ? " To which the countersign was, " We bite our Thumbs."

For weeks the glory of Shakespear's Verona lit Mr. Polly's life. He walked as though he carried a sword at his side, and swung a mantle from his shoulders. He went through the grimy streets of Port Burdock with his eye on the first-floor windows—looking for balconies. A ladder in the yard flooded his mind with romantic ideas. Then Parsons discovered an Italian writer, whose name Mr. Polly rendered as " Bocashieu " ; and after some excursions into that author's remains, the talk of Parsons became infested with the word " amours," and Mr. Polly would stand in front of his hosiery fixtures trifling with paper and string, and thinking of perennial picnics under dark olive-trees in the everlasting sunshine of Italy.

And about that time it was that all three P's adopted turn-down collars and large, loose, artistic silk ties, which they tied very much on one side, and wore with an air of defiance ; and a certain swashbuckling carriage.

And then came the glorious revelation of that great Frenchman whom Mr. Polly called " Rabooloose." The three P's thought the birth-feast of Gargantua the most glorious piece of writing in the world—and I am not certain they were wrong ; and on wet Sunday evenings, when there was danger of hymn-singing, they would get Parsons to read it aloud.

Towards the several members of the Y. M. C. A. who shared the dormitory, the three P's always maintained a sarcastic and defiant attitude.

" We have got a perfect right to do what we like in our corner," Platt maintained. " You do what you like in yours."

" But the language," objected Morrison, the white-faced, earnest-eyed improver, who was leading a profoundly religious life under great difficulties.

" *Language*, man ! " roared Parsons ; " why, it's *LITERA-TURE !* "

" Sunday isn't the time for Literature."

" It's the only time we've got. And besides——"

The horrors of religious controversy would begin. . . .

Mr. Polly stuck loyally by the three P's, but in the secret places of his heart he was torn. A fire of conviction burned in Morrison's eyes and spoke in his urgent, persuasive voice. He lived the better life manifestly : chaste in word and deed, industrious, studiously kindly. When the junior apprentice had sore feet and homesickness, Morrison washed the feet and comforted the heart ; and he helped other men to get through with their work when he might have gone early— a superhuman thing to do. No one who has not worked for endless days of interminable hours, with scarce a gleam of rest or liberty between the toil and the sleep, can understand how superhuman. Polly was secretly a little afraid to be left alone with this man and the power of the spirit that was in him. He felt watched.

Platt, also struggling with things his mind could not contrive to reconcile, said, " That confounded hypocrite."

" He's no hypocrite," said Parsons ; " he's no hypocrite, O' Man. But he's got no blessed *Joy de Vive*—that's what's wrong with him. Let's go down to the Harbour Arms and see some of those blessed old captains getting drunk."

" Short of sugar, O' Man," said Mr. Polly, slapping his trouser pocket.

" Oh, *carm* on," said Parsons ; " always do it on tuppence for a bitter."

" Lemme get my Pipe on," said Platt, who had recently taken to smoking with great ferocity. " Then I'm with you."

(Pause and struggle.)

" Don't ram it down, O' Man," said Parsons, watching with knitted brows ; " don't ram it down. Give it Air. Seen my stick, O' Man ? Right O."

And, leaning on his cane, he composed himself in an attitude of sympathetic patience towards Platt's incendiary efforts.

§ 4

Jolly days of companionship they were for the incipient bankrupt on the stile to look back upon.

The interminable working hours of the Bazaar had long since faded from his memory—except for one or two conspicuous rows and one or two larks—but the rare Sundays and holidays shone out like diamonds among pebbles. They shone with the mellow splendour of evening skies reflected in calm water, and athwart them all went old Parsons bellowing an interpretation of life, gesticulating, appreciating, and making appreciate, expounding books, talking of that mystery of his, the " Joy de Vive."

There were some particularly splendid walks on Bank Holidays. The three P's would start on Sunday morning early, and find a room in some modest inn and talk themselves asleep, and return singing through the night, or having an " argy bargy " about the stars, on Monday evening. They would come over the hill out of the pleasant English countryside in which they had wandered and see Port Burdock spread out below, a network of interlacing street-lamps and shifting tram-lights against the black, beacon-gemmed immensity of the harbour waters.

" Back to the collar, O' Man," Parsons would say. There is no satisfactory plural to " O' Man," so he always used it in the singular.

" Don't mention it," said Platt.

And once they got a boat for the whole summer day, and rowed up past the moored ironclads and the black old hulks and the various shipping of the harbour, past a white troop-ship, and past the trim front and the slips and interesting vistas of the dockyard to the shallow channels and rocky, weedy wildernesses of the upper harbour. And Parsons and Mr. Polly had a great dispute and quarrel that day as to how far a big gun could shoot.

The country over the hills behind Port Burdock is all that an old-fashioned, scarcely disturbed English countryside should be. In those days the bicycle was still rare and costly, and the motor-car had yet to come and stir up rural serenities. The three P's would take footpaths haphazard across fields, and plunge into unknown winding lanes between high hedges of honeysuckle and dogrose. Greatly daring, they would follow green bridle-paths through primrose-studded under-growths, or wander waist-deep in the bracken of beech woods. About twenty miles from Port Burdock there came a region of hop-gardens and hoast-crowned farms ; and farther on, to be reached only by cheap tickets on Bank Holiday times, was a sterile ridge of very clean roads and red sandpits and pines, and gorse and heather. The three P's could not afford to buy bicycles, and they found boots the greatest item of their skimpy expenditure. They threw appearances to the winds at last, and got ready-made working-men's hobnails. There was much discussion and strong feeling over this step in the dormitory, and the three P's were held to have dero-gated from the dignity of the emporium.

There is no countryside like the English countryside for those who have learned to love it ; its firm yet gentle lines of hill and dale, its ordered confusion of features, its deer parks and downland, its castles and stately houses, its hamlets and old churches, its farms and ricks and great barns and ancient trees, its pools and ponds and shining threads of rivers, its flower-starred hedgerows, its orchards and wood-land patches, its village greens and kindly inns. Other country-sides have their pleasant aspects, but none such variety, none that shine so steadfastly throughout the year. Picardy is pink-and-white and pleasant in the blossom-time ; Burgundy goes on with its sunshine and wide hillsides and cramped vineyards, a beautiful tune repeated and repeated ; Italy gives salitas and wayside chapels, and chestnuts and olive-orchards ; the Ardennes has its woods and gorges—Touraine and the Rhineland, the wide Campagna with its distant Apennines, and the neat prosperity and mountain backgrounds of South Germany all clamour their especial merits at one's memory. And there are the hills and fields of Virginia, like an England grown very big and slovenly, the woods and big river sweeps of Pennsylvania, the trim New England landscape, a little bleak and rather fine, like the New England mind, and the wide, rough country roads and hills and woodland of New York State. But none of these change scene and character in three miles of walking, nor have so mellow a sunlight nor so diversified a cloudland nor confess the perpetual refreshment of the strong soft winds that blow from off the sea, as our mother England does.

It was good for the three P's to walk through such a land and forget for a time that indeed they had no footing in it all, that they were doomed to toil behind counters in such places as Port Burdock for the better part of their lives. They would forget the customers and shop-walkers and department buyers and everything, and become just happy wanderers in a world of pleasant breezes and song-birds and shady trees.

The arrival at the inn was a great affair. No one, they were convinced, would take them for drapers, and there might be a pretty serving-girl or a jolly old landlady, or what Parsons called a " bit of character " drinking in the bar.

There would always be weighty inquiries as to what they could have, and it would work out always at cold beef and pickles, or fried ham and eggs and shandygaff, two pints of beer and two bottles of ginger-beer foaming in a huge round-bellied jug.

The glorious moment of standing lordly in the inn doorway and staring out at the world, the swinging sign, the geese upon the green, the duck-pond, a waiting wagon, the church-tower, a sleepy cat, the blue heavens, with the sizzle of the frying audible behind one ! The keen smell of the bacon ! The trotting of feet bearing the repast ; the click and clatter as the tableware is finally arranged ! A clean white cloth ! " Ready, Sir ! " or " Ready, Gentlemen ! " Better hearing that than " Forward, Polly ! Look sharp ! "

The going in ! The sitting down ! The falling to !

" Bread, O' Man ? "

" Right-o ! Don't bag all the crust, O' Man."

Once a simple-mannered girl in a pink print dress stayed and talked with them as they ate ; led by the gallant Parsons they professed to be all desperately in love with her, and courted her to say which she preferred of them, it was so manifest she did prefer one and so impossible to say which it was held her there, until a distant maternal voice called her away. Afterwards, as they left the inn, she waylaid them at the orchard corner and gave them, a little shyly, three yellow-green apples—and wished them to come again some day, and vanished, and reappeared looking after them as they turned the corner, waving a white handkerchief. All the rest of that day they disputed over the signs of her favour, and the next Sunday they went there again.

But she had vanished, and a mother of forbidding aspect afforded no explanations.

If Platt and Parsons and Mr. Polly live to be a hundred, they will none of them forget that girl as she stood with a pink flush upon her, faintly smiling and yet earnest, parting the branches of the hedgerows and reaching down, apple in hand. . . .

And once they went along the coast, following it as closely as possible, and so came at last to Fishbourne, that eastern-most suburb of Brayling and Hampstead-on-the-Sea.

Fishbourne seemed a very jolly little place to Mr. Polly that afternoon. It has a clean sandy beach, instead of the mud and pebbles and coaly defilements of Port Burdock, a row of six bathing-machines, and a shelter on the Parade in which the three P's sat after a satisfying but rather expensive lunch that had included celery. Rows of verandahed villas proffered apartments ; they had feasted in a hotel with a porch painted white, and gay with geraniums above ; and the High Street, with the old church at the head, had been full of an agreeable afternoon stillness.

" Nice little place for business," said Platt sagely from behind his big pipe.

It stuck in Mr. Polly's memory.

§ 5

Mr. Polly was not so picturesque a youth as] Parsons. He lacked richness in his voice, and went about in those days with his hands in his pockets looking quietly speculative.

He specialised in slang and the misuse of English, and he played the rôle of an appreciative stimulant to Parsons. Words attracted him curiously, words rich in suggestion, and he loved a novel and striking phrase. His school training had given him little or no mastery of the mysterious pronunciation of English, and no confidence in himself. His schoolmaster indeed had been both unsound and variable. New words had terror and fascination for him ; he did not acquire them, he could not avoid them, and so he plunged into them. His only rule was not to be misled by the spelling. That was no guide anyhow. He avoided every recognised phrase in the language, and mispronounced everything in order that he should be suspected of whim rather than of ignorance.

" Sesquippledan," he would say, " Sesquippledan verboo-juice."

" Eh ? " said Platt.

" Eloquent Rapsodooce."

" Where ? " asked Platt.

" In the warehouse, O' Man. All among the tablecloths and blankets. Carlyle. He's reading aloud. Doing the High Froth. Spuming ! Windmilling ! Waw, waw ! It's a sight worth seeing. He'll bark his blessed knuckles one of these days on the fixtures, O' Man."

He held an imaginary book in one hand and waved an eloquent gesture. " So too shall every Hero inasmuch as notwithstanding for evermore come back to Reality," he parodied the enthusiastic Parsons, " so that in fashion and thereby, upon things and not *under* things articulariously He stands."

" I should laugh if the Governor dropped on him," said Platt. " He'd never hear him coming."

" The O' Man's drunk with it—fair drunk," said Polly. " *I* never did. It's worse than when he got on to Raboloose."

CHAPTER TWO

THE DISMISSAL OF PARSONS

§ 1

SUDDENLY Parsons got himself dismissed.

He got himself dismissed under circumstances of peculiar violence, that left a deep impression on Mr. Polly's mind. He wondered about it for years afterwards, trying to get the rights of the case.

Parson's apprenticeship was over ; he had reached the status of an Improver, and he dressed the window of the Manchester department. By his own standards he dressed it wonderfully. " Well, O' Man," he used to say, " there's one thing about my position here—I *can* dress a window."

And when trouble was under discussion he would hold that " little Fluffums "—which was the apprentices' name for Mr. Garvace, the senior partner and managing director of the Bazaar—would think twice before he got rid of the only man in the place who could make a windowful of Manchester goods *tell*.

Then, like many a fellow artist, he fell a prey to theories.

" The art of window-dressing is in its infancy, O' Man—in its blooming Infancy. All balance and stiffness like a blessed Egyptian picture. No Joy in it, no blooming Joy ! Conventional. A shop-window ought to get hold of people, *grip* 'em as they go along. It stands to reason. Grip ! "

His voice would sink to a kind of quiet bellow. " *Do* they grip ? "

Then, after a pause, a savage roar : " *Naw !* "

" He's got a Heavy on," said Mr. Polly. " Go it, O' Man ; let's have some more of it."

" Look at old Morrison's dress-stuff windows ! Tidy, tasteful, correct, I grant you, but Bleak ! " He let out the word reinforced to a shout : " Bleak ! "

" Bleak ! " echoed Mr. Polly.

" Just pieces of stuff in rows, rows of tidy little puffs, perhaps one bit just unrolled, quiet tickets."

" Might as well be in church, O' Man," said Mr Polly.

" A window ought to be exciting," said Parsons ; " it ought to make you say, ' 'El-*lo* ! ' when you see it."

He paused, and Platt watched him over a snorting pipe.

" Rockcockyo," said Mr. Polly.

" We want a new school of window-dressing," said Parsons, regardless of the comment. " A New School ! The Port Burdock school. Day after to-morrow I change the Fitzallan Street stuff. This time it's going to be a change. I mean to have a crowd or bust ! "

And as a matter of fact he did both.

His voice dropped to a note of self-reproach. " I've been timid, O' Man. I've been holding myself in. I haven't done myself Justice. I've kept down the simmering, seething, teeming ideas. . . . All that's over now."

" Over," gulped Polly.

" Over for good and all, O' Man."

§ 2

Platt came to Polly, who was sorting up collar-boxes. " O' Man's doing his Blooming Window."

" What window ? "

" What he said."

Polly remembered.

He went on with his collar-boxes with his eye on his senior, Mansfield. Mansfield was presently called away to the counting-house, and instantly Polly shot out by the street door, and made a rapid transit along the street front past the Manchester window, and so into the silk-room door. He could not linger long, but he gathered joy, a swift and fearful joy, from his brief inspection of Parsons' unconscious back. Parsons had his tail-coat off, and was working with vigour ; his habit of pulling his waistcoat straps to their utmost brought out all the agreeable promise of corpulence in his youthful frame. He was blowing excitedly and running his fingers through his hair, and then moving with all the swift eagerness of a man inspired. All about his feet and knees were scarlet blankets, not folded, not formally unfolded, but—the only phrase is— shied about. And a great bar sinister of roller towelling stretched across the front of the window on which was a ticket, and the ticket said in bold, black letters : " *LOOK !* "

So soon as Mr. Polly got into the silk department and met Platt he knew he had not lingered nearly long enough outside

" Did you see the boards at the back ? " said Platt.

Mr. Polly hadn't. "The High Egrugious is fairly On," he said, and dived down to return by devious subterranean routes to the outfitting department.

Presently the street door opened and Platt, with an air of intense devotion to business, assumed to cover his adoption of that unusual route, came in and made for the staircase down to the warehouse. He rolled up his eyes at Polly. " Oh, Lor ! " he said, and vanished.

Irresistible curiosity seized Polly. Should he go through the shop to the Manchester department or risk a second transit outside ?

He was impelled to make a dive at tne street door.

" Where are you going ? " asked Mansfield.

" Lill dog," said Polly, with an air of lucid explanation, and left him to get any meaning he could from it.

Parsons was worth the subsequent trouoie. Parsons really was extremely rich. This time Polly stopped to take it in.

Parsons had made a huge asymmetrical pile of thick white-and-red blankets twisted and rolled to accentuate their woolly softness heaped up in a warm disorder with large window tickets inscribed in blazing red letters : Cosey Comfort at Cut Prices," and " Curl up and Cuddle below Cost." Regardless of the daylight he had turned up the electric light on that side of the window to reflect a warm glow upon the head, and behind, in pursuit of contrasted bleakness, he was now hanging long strips of gray silesia and chilly-coloured linen dustering.

It was wonderful, but——

Mr. Polly decided that it was time he went in. He found Platt in the silk department, apparently on the verge of another plunge into the exterior world. " Cosey Comfort at Cut Prices," said Polly. " Allittritions Artful Aid."

He did not dare go into the street for the third time, and he was hovering feverishly near the window when he saw the governor, Mr. Garvace—that is to say, the managing director of the Bazaar—walking along the pavement after his manner, to assure himself all was well with the establishment he guided.

Mr. Garvace was a short, stout man, with that air of modest pride that so often goes with corpulence, choleric and decisive in manner, and with hands that looked like bunches of fingers. He was red-haired and ruddy, and after the custom of such complexions, hairs sprang from the tip of his nose. When he wished to bring the power of the human eye to bear upon an assistant, he projected his chest, knitted one brow, and partially closed the left eyelid.

An expression of speculative wonder overspread the countenance of Mr. Polly. He felt he must *see*. Yes, whatever happened, he must *see*.

" Want to speak to Parsons, Sir," he said to Mr. Mansfield, and deserted his post hastily, dashed through the intervening

departments, and was in position behind a pile of Bolton
sheeting as the governor came in out of the street.

"What on earth do you think you are doing with that
window, Parsons ? " began Mr. Garvace.

Only the legs of Parsons and the lower part of his waistcoat
and an intervening inch of shirt were visible. He was standing
inside the window on the steps, hanging up the last strip of his
background from the brass rail along the ceiling. Within, the
Manchester shop-window was cut off by a partition rather like
the partition of an old-fashioned church pew from the general
space of the shop. There was a panelled barrier, that is to say,
with a little door like a pew door in it. Parsons' face appeared,
staring with round eyes at his employer.

Mr. Garvace had to repeat his question.

"Dressing it, Sir—on new lines."

"Come out of it," said Mr. Garvace.

Parsons stared, and Mr. Garvace had to repeat his command.

Parsons, with a dazed expression, began to descend the steps
slowly.

Mr. Garvace turned about. "Where's Morrison ? Morrison ! "

Morrison appeared.

"Take this window over," said Mr. Garvace, pointing his
bunch of fingers at Parsons. "Take all this muddle out and
dress it properly."

Morrison advanced, and hesitated.

"I beg your pardon, Sir," said Parsons, with an immense
politeness, " but this is *my* window."

"Take it all out," said Mr. Garvace, turning away.

Morrison advanced. Parsons shut the door with a click that
arrested Mr. Garvace.

"Come out of that window," he said. "You can't dress it.
If you want to play the fool with a window——"

"This window's All Right," said the genius in window-
dressing, and there was a little pause.

"Open the door and go right in," said Mr. Garvace to
Morrison.

"You leave that door alone, Morrison," said Parsons.

Polly was no longer even trying to hide behind the stack of
Bolton sheetings. He realised he was in the presence of forces
too stupendous to heed him.

"Get him out," said Mr. Garvace.

Morrison seemed to be thinking out the ethics of his position.
The idea of loyalty to his employer prevailed with him. He
laid his hand on the door to open it ; Parsons tried to disengage
his hand. Mr. Garvace joined his effort to Morrison's. Then
the heart of Polly leaped, and the world blazed up to wonder
and splendour. Parsons disappeared behind the partition for
a moment, and reappeared instantly, gripping a thin cylinder
of rolled huckaback. With this he smote at Morrison's head.
Morrison's head ducked under the resounding impact, but he

clung on and so did Mr. Garvace. The door came open, and then Mr. Garvace was staggering back, hand to head, his autocratic, his sacred baldness, smitten. Parsons was beyond all control— a strangeness, a marvel. Heaven knows how the artistic struggle had strained that richly endowed temperament. " Say I can't dress a window, you thundering old Humbug," he said, and hurled the huckaback at his master. He followed this up by pitching first a blanket, then an armful of silesia, then a window support out of the window into the shop. It leaped into Polly's mind that Parsons hated his own effort and was glad to demolish it. For a crowded second his attention was concentrated upon Parsons, infuriated, active, like a figure of earthquake with its coat off, shying things headlong.

Then he perceived the back of Mr. Garvace and heard his gubernatorial voice crying to no one in particular and everybody in general, " Get him out of the window. He's mad. He's dangerous. Get him out of the window."

Then a crimson blanket was for a moment over the head of Mr. Garvace, and his voice, muffled for an instant, broke out into unwonted expletive.

Then people had arrived from all parts of the Bazaar. Luck, the ledger clerk, blundered against Polly and said, " Help him ! " Somerville from the silks vaulted the counter, and seized a chair by the back. Polly lost his head. He clawed at the Bolton sheeting before him, and if he could have detached a piece he would certainly have hit somebody with it. As it was he simply upset the pile. It fell away from Polly, and he had an impression of somebody squeaking as it went down. It was the sort of impression one disregards. The collapse of the pile of goods just sufficed to end his subconscious efforts to get something to hit somebody with, and his whole attention focussed itself upon the struggle in the window. For a splendid instant Parsons towered up over the active backs that clustered about the shop-window door, an active whirl of gesture, tearing things down and throwing them, and then he went under. There was an instant's furious struggle, a crash, a second crash, and the crack of broken plate glass. Then a stillness and heavy breathing.

Parsons was overpowered. . . .

Polly, stepping over scattered pieces of Bolton sheeting, saw his transfigured friend with a dark cut, that was not at present bleeding, on the forehead, one arm held by Somerville and the other by Morrison.

" You—you—you—you annoyed me," said Parsons, sobbing for breath.

§ 3

There are events that detach themselves from the general stream of occurrences and seem to partake of the nature of revelations. Such was this Parsons affair. It began by seeming

grotesque ; it ended disconcertingly. The fabric of Mr. Polly's
daily life was torn, and beneath it discovered depths and terrors.

Life was not altogether a lark.

The calling in of a policeman seemed at the moment a
pantomime touch. But when it became manifest that Mr.
Garvace was in a fury of vindictiveness, the affair took on a
different complexion. The way in which the policeman made
a note of everything and aspirated nothing impressed the
sensitive mind of Polly profoundly. Polly presently found
himself straightening up ties to the refrain of " 'E then 'It
you on the 'Ead—'Ard."

In the dormitory that night Parsons became heroic. He
sat on the edge of the bed with his head bandaged, packing
very slowly and insisting over and over again, " He ought
to have left my window alone, O' Man. He didn't ought to
have touched my window."

Polly was to go to the police-court in the morning as a witness.
The terror of that ordeal almost over-shadowed the tragic fact
that Parsons was not only summoned for assault, but
" swapped," and packing his box. Polly knew himself well
enough to know he would make a bad witness. He felt sure of
one fact only—namely, that " 'E then 'It 'Im on the 'Ead—
'Ard." All the rest danced about in his mind now, and how it
would dance about on the morrow Heaven only knew. Would
there be a cross-examination ? Is it perjoocery to make a slip ?
People did sometimes perjuice themselves. Serious offence.

Platt was doing his best to help Parsons and inciting public
opinion against Morrison. But Parsons would not hear of
anything against Morrison. " He was all right, O' Man—
according to his lights," said Parsons. " It isn't him I complain
of."

He speculated on the morrow. " I shall 'ave to pay a fine,"
he said. " No good trying to get out of it. It's true I hit him.
I hit him "—he paused and seemed to be seeking an exquisite
accuracy. His voice sank to a confidential note—" on the
head—about here."

He answered the suggestion of a bright junior apprentice
in a corner of the dormitory. " What's the Good of a Cross
summons," he replied, " with old Corks the chemist and Mottis-
head the house agent and all that lot on the Bench ? Humble
Pie, that's my meal to-morrow, O' Man. Humble Pie."

Packing went on for a time.

" But, Lord ! what a Life it is ! " said Parsons, giving his
deep notes scope. " Ten-thirty-five a man trying to do his
Duty, mistaken perhaps, but doing his best ; ten-forty,
Ruined. Ruined ! " He lifted his voice to a shout : " Ruined ! "
and dropped it to " Like an earthquake."

" Heated altaclation," said Polly.

" Like a blooming earthquake," said Parsons, with the
notes of a rising wind.

He meditated gloomily upon his future, and a colder chill invaded Polly's mind. " Likely to get another crib, ain't I ? —with assaulted the guv'nor on my reference. . . . I suppose, though, he won't give me refs. Hard enough to get a crib at the best of times," said Parsons.

" You ought to go round with a show, O' Man," said Mr. Polly.

Things were not so dreadful in the police-court as Mr. Polly had expected. He was given a seat with other witnesses against the wall of the court, and after an interesting larceny case Parsons appeared and stood, not in the dock, but at the table. By that time Mr. Polly's legs, which had been tucked up at first under his chair out of respect to the court, were extended straight before him, and his hands were in his trousers pockets. He was inventing names for the four magistrates on the bench, and had got to " the Grave and Reverend Signor with the palatial Boko," when his thoughts were recalled to gravity by the sound of his name. He rose with alacrity, and was fielded by an expert policeman from a brisk attempt to get into the vacant dock. The clerk to the Justices repeated the oath with incredible rapidity.

" Right-o," said Mr. Polly, but quite respectfully, and kissed the book.

His evidence was simple and quite audible after one warning from the superintendent of police to " speak up." He tried to put in a good word for Parsons by saying he was " naturally of a choleric disposition," but the start and the slow grin of enjoyment upon the face of " the Grave and Reverend Signor with the palatial Boko " suggested that the word was not so good as he had thought it. The rest of the bench was frankly puzzled, and there were hasty consultations.

" You mean 'E as a 'Ot temper," said the presiding magistrate.

" I mean 'E as a 'Ot temper," replied Polly, magically incapable of aspirates for the moment.

" You don't mean 'E ketches cholera ? "

" I mean—he's easily put out."

" Then why can't you say so ? " said the presiding magistrate.

Parsons was bound over.

He came for his luggage while every one was in the shop, and Garvace would not let him invade the business to say good-bye. When Mr. Polly went upstairs for margarine and bread and tea, he slipped on into the dormitory at once to see what was happening further in the Parsons case. But Parsons had vanished. There was no Parsons, no trace of Parsons. His cubicle was swept and garnished. For the first time in his life Polly had a sense of irreparable loss.

A minute or so after Platt dashed in.

" Ugh ! " he said, and then discovered Polly. Polly was

leaning out of the window, and did not look round. Platt
went up to him.

" He's gone already," said Platt. " Might have stopped to
say good-bye to a chap."

There was a little pause before Polly replied. He thrust his
finger into his mouth and gulped.

" Bit on that beastly tooth of mine," he said, still not
looking at Platt. " It's made my eyes water something chronic.
Any one might think I'd been Piping my Eye, by the look of
me."

CHAPTER THREE

CRIBS

§ I

PORT BURDOCK was never the same place for Mr. Polly
after Parsons had left it. There were no chest notes in
his occasional letters, and little of the " Joy de Vive "
got through by them. Parsons had gone, he said, to London,
and found a place as warehouseman in a cheap outfitting
shop near St. Paul's Churchyard, where references were not
required. It became apparent as time passed that new interests
were absorbing him. He wrote of Socialism and the rights of
man, things that had no appeal for Mr. Polly. He felt strangers
had got hold of his Parsons, were at work upon him, making
him into some one else, something less picturesque. . . . Port
Burdock became a dreariness full of faded memories of Parsons
and work a bore. Platt revealed himself alone as a tiresome
companion, obsessed by romantic ideas about intrigues and
vices and " society women."

Mr. Polly's depression manifested itself in a general slackness. A certain impatience in the manner of Mr. Garvace
presently got upon his nerves. Relations were becoming
strained. He asked for a rise of salary to test his position
and gave notice to leave when it was refused.

It took him two months to place himself in another situation,
and during that time he had quite a disagreeable amount of
loneliness, disappointment, anxiety, and humiliation.

He went at first to stay with a married cousin who had a
house at Easewood. His widowed father had recently given
up the music and bicycle shop (with the post of organist at
the parish church) that had sustained his home, and was
living upon a small annuity as a guest of his cousin, and
growing a little tiresome on account of some mysterious
internal discomfort that the local practitioner diagnosed as
imagination. He had aged with unusual rapidity and become
excessively irritable, but the cousin's wife was a born manager,
and contrived to get along with him. Our Mr. Polly's status

was that of a guest pure and simple ; but after a fortnight of congested hospitality, in which he wrote nearly a hundred variants of :

Sir,—Reffering to your advt. in the " Christian World " for an Improver in Gents' outfitting, I beg to submit myself for the situation. Have had six years' experience. . . .

and upset a penny bottle of ink over a toilet cover and the bedroom carpet, his cousin took him for a walk and pointed out the superior advantages of apartments in London from which to swoop down upon the briefly yawning vacancy.

" Helpful," said Mr. Polly ; " very helpful, O' Man, indeed. I might have gone on here for weeks," and packed.

He got a room in an institution that was partly a benevolent hostel for men in his circumstances and partly a high-minded but forbidding coffee-house, and a centre for Pleasant Sunday Afternoons. Mr. Polly spent a critical but pleasant Sunday afternoon in a back seat inventing such phrases as :

" Soulful Owner of the Exorbiant Largenial Development." An Adam's Apple being in question.

" Earnest Joy."

" Exultant, Urgent Loogoobuosity."

A manly young curate, marking and misunderstanding his preoccupied face and moving lips, came and sat by him, and entered into conversation with the idea of making him feel more at home. The conversation was awkward and disconnected for a minute or so, and then suddenly a memory of the Port Burdock Bazaar occurred to Mr. Polly, and with a baffling whisper of " Lill dog," and a reassuring nod, he rose up and escaped, to wander out relieved and observant into the varied London streets.

He found the collection of men he met waiting about in wholesale establishments in Wood Street and St. Paul's Church-yard (where they interview the buyers who have come up from the country) interesting and stimulating, but far too strongly charged with the suggestion of his own fate to be really joyful. There were men in all degrees between confidence and distress, and in every stage between extravagant smartness and the last stages of decay. There were sunny young men full of an abounding and elbowing energy before whom the soul of Polly sank into hate and dismay. " Smart Juniors," said Polly to himself, " full of Smart Juniosity. The Shove-acious Cult." There were hungry-looking individuals of thirty-five or so, that he decided must be " Proletelerians "—he had often wanted to find some one who fitted that attractive word. Middle-aged men, " too old at Forty," discoursed in the waiting-rooms on the outlook in the trade ; it had never been so bad, they said, while Mr. Polly wondered if " Dejuiced " was a permissible epithet. There were men with an overweening sense of their importance, manifestly annoyed and angry to find themselves still disengaged, and inclined to suspect a plot, and men so faint-hearted one was terrified to imagine their behaviour when it came to an interview. There was a fresh-faced young man with an unintelligent face who seemed to think himself equipped against the world beyond all misadventure by a collar of exceptional height, and another who introduced a note of gaiety by wearing a flannel shirt and a check suit of remarkable virulence. Every day Mr. Polly looked round to mark how many of the familiar faces had gone, and the deepening anxiety (reflecting his own) on the faces that remained, and every day some new type joined the drifting shoal. He realised how small a chance his poor letter from Easewood ran against this hungry cluster of competitors at the fountainhead.

At the back of Mr. Polly's mind while he made his observations was the disagreeable flavour of the dentist's parlour. At any moment his name might be shouted, and he might have to haul himself into the presence of some fresh specimen of employer, and to repeat once more his passionate protestation of interest in the business, his possession of capacity for zeal—zeal on behalf of any one who would pay him a salary of twenty-six pounds a year.

The prospective employer would unfold his ideals of the employee. " I want a smart, willing young man, thoroughly willing, who won't object to take trouble. I don't want a slacker, the sort of fellow who has to be pushed up to his work and held there. I've got no use for him."

At the back of Mr. Polly's mind, and quite beyond his control, the insubordinate phrasemaker would be proffering such combinations as " Chubby Chops," or " Chubby Charmer," as suitable for the gentleman, very much as a hat salesman proffers hats.

" I don't think you'd find much slackness about *me*, Sir," said Mr. Polly brightly, trying to disregard his deeper self.

" I want a young man who means getting on."

" Exactly, Sir. Excelsior."

" I beg your pardon ? "

" I said excelsior, Sir. It's a sort of motto of mine. From Longfellow. Would you want me to serve through ? "

The chubby gentleman explained and reverted to his ideals, with a faint air of suspicion. " Do *you* mean getting on ? " he asked.

" I hope so, Sir," said Mr. Polly.

" Get on or get out, eh ? "

Mr. Polly made a rapturous noise, nodded appreciation, and said indistinctly, " *Quite* my style."

" Some of my people have been with me twenty years," said the employer. " My Manchester buyer came to me as a boy of twelve. You're a Christian ? "

" Church of England," said Mr. Polly.

" H'm," said the employer, a little checked. " For good all round business work, I should have preferred a Baptist. Still——"

He studied Mr. Polly's tie, which was severely neat and businesslike, as became an aspiring outfitter. Mr. Polly's conception of his own pose and expression was rendered by that uncontrollable phrasemonger at the back as " Obsequies Deference."

" I am inclined," said the prospective employer in a conclusive manner, " to look up your reference."

Mr. Polly stood up abruptly.

" Thank you," said the employer, and dismissed him.

" Chump chops ! How about chump chops ? " said the phrasemonger with an air of inspiration.

" I hope then to hear from you, Sir," said Mr. Polly in his best salesman manner.

" If everything is satisfactory," said the prospective employer.

§ 2

A man whose brain devotes its hinterland to making odd phrases and nicknames out of ill-conceived words, whose conception of life is a lump of auriferous rock to which all the value is given by rare veins of unbusinesslike joy, who reads Boccaccio and Rabelais and Shakespear with gusto, and uses " Stertoraneous Shover " and " Smart Junior " as terms of bitterest opprobrium, is not likely to make a great success under modern business conditions. Mr. Polly dreamt always of picturesque and mellow things, and had an instinctive hatred of the strenuous life. He would have resisted the spell of ex-President Roosevelt, or General Baden Powell, or Mr. Peter Keary, or the late Dr. Samuel Smiles quite easily —I doubt if even Mr. St. Loe Strachey could have inspired him ; and he loved Falstaff and Hudibras and coarse laughter, and the Old England of Washington Irving and the memory of Charles the Second's courtly days. His progress was necessarily slow. He did not get rises ; he lost situations ; there was something in his eye employers did not like ; he would have lost his places oftener if he had not been at times an exceptionally brilliant salesman, rather carefully neat, and a slow but very fair window-dresser.

He went from situation to situation, he invented a great wealth of nicknames, he conceived enmities and made friends —but none so richly satisfying as Parsons. He was frequently, but mildly and discursively, in love ; and sometimes he thought of that girl who had given him a yellow-green apple. He had an idea amounting to a flattering certainty whose youthful freshness it was had stirred her to self-forgetfulness. And sometimes he thought of Fishbourne sleeping prosperously in the sun. And he had moods of discomfort and lassitude and ill-temper, due to the beginnings of indigestion.

Various forces and suggestions came into his life and swayed him for longer and shorter periods.

He went to Canterbury and came under the influence of Gothic architecture. There was a blood affinity between Mr. Polly and the Gothic; in the Middle Ages he would, no doubt, have sat upon a scaffolding and carved out penetrating and none-too-flattering portraits of church dignitaries upon the capitals; and when he strolled, with his hands behind his back, along the cloisters behind the cathedral, and looked at the rich grass-plot in the centre, he had the strangest sense of being at home—far more than he had ever been at home before. " Portly capons," he used to murmur to himself, under the impression that he was naming a characteristic type of mediæval churchman.

He liked to sit in the nave during the service, and look through the great gates at the candles and choristers, and listen to the organ-sustained voices, but the transepts he never penetrated because of the charge for admission. The music and the long vista of the fretted roof filled him with a vague and mystical happiness that he had no words, even mispronounceable words, to express. But some of the smug monuments in the aisles got a wreath of epithets ; " metrorious urnfuls," " funererial claims," " dejected angelosity," for example. He wandered about the precincts and speculated about the people who lived in the ripe and cosey houses of grey stone that cluster there so comfortably. Through green doors in high stone walls he caught glimpses of level lawns and blazing flower-beds ; mullioned windows revealed shaded reading-lamps and disciplined shelves of brown bound books. Now and then a dignitary in gaiters would pass him (" Portly capon "), or a drift of white-robed choir-boys cross a distant arcade and vanish in a doorway, or the pink and cream of some girlish dress flit like a butterfly across the cool still spaces of the place. Particularly he responded to the ruined arches of the Benedictine's Infirmary and the view of Bell Harry Tower from the school-building. He was stirred to read the " Canterbury Tales," but he could not get on with Chaucer's old-fashioned English, it fatigued his attention, and he would have given all the story-telling very readily for a few adventures on the road. He wanted these nice people to live more and yarn less. He appreciated the wife of Bath very keenly. He would have liked to have known that woman.

At Canterbury too, he first, to his knowledge, saw Americans. His shop did a good class trade in Westgate Street, and he would see them go by on the way to stare at Chaucer's " Chequers " and then turn down Mercery Lane to Prior Goldstone's gate. It impressed him that they were always in a kind of quiet hurry, and very determined and methodical people—much more so than any English he knew.

" Cultured Rapacacity," he tried.

" Vorocious Return to the Heritage."

He would expound them incidentally to his attendant apprentices. He had overheard a little lady putting her view to a friend near the Christchurch gate. The accent and intonation had hung in his memory, and he would reproduce them more or less accurately. " Now, does this Marlowe monument really and truly *matter* ? " he had heard the little lady inquire. " We've no time for side shows and second-rate stunts, Mamie. We want just the Big Simple Things of the place, just the Broad Elemental Canterbury Prahposition. What is it saying to us ? I want to get right hold of that, and then have tea in the very room where Chaucer did, and hustle to get that four-eighteen train back to London. . . ."

He would go over these specious phrases, finding them full of an indescribable flavour. " Just the Broad Elemental Canterbury Prahposition," he would repeat. . . .

He would try to imagine Parsons confronted with Americans. For his own part, he knew himself to be altogether inadequate. . . .

Canterbury was the most congenial situation Mr. Polly ever found during these wander years, albeit a very desert so far as companionship went.

§ 3

It was after Canterbury that the universe became really disagreeable to Mr. Polly. It was brought home to him not so much vividly as with a harsh ungainly insistence that he was a failure in his trade. It was not the trade he ought to have chosen, though what trade he ought to have chosen was by no means clear.

He made great but irregular efforts, and produced a forced smartness that, like a cheap dye, refused to stand sunshine. He acquired a sort of parsimony also, in which acquisition he was helped by one or two phases of absolute impecuniosity. But he was hopeless in competition against the naturally gifted, the born hustlers, the young men who meant to get on.

He left the Canterbury place very regretfully. He and another commercial gentleman took a boat one Sunday afternoon at Sturry-on-the-Stour, when the wind was in the west, and sailed it very happily eastward for an hour. They had never sailed a boat before, and it seemed a simple and wonderful thing to do. When they turned, they found the river too narrow for tacking, and the tide running out like a sluice. They battled back to Sturry in the course of six hours (at a shilling the first hour and sixpence for each hour afterwards), rowing a mile in an hour and a half or so, until the turn of the tide came to help them, and then they had a night walk to Canterbury, and found themselves remorselessly locked out.

The Canterbury employer was an amiable, religious-spirited man, and he would probably not have dismissed Mr. Polly if that unfortunate tendency to phrase things had not shocked him. "A Tide's a Tide, Sir," said Mr. Polly, feeling that things were not so bad. "I've no lune-attic power to alter *that*."

It proved impossible to explain to the Canterbury employer that this was not a highly disrespectful and blasphemous remark.

"And besides, what good are you to me this morning, do you think?" said the Canterbury employer, "with your arms pulled out of their sockets?"

So Mr. Polly resumed his observations in the Wood Street warehouses once more, and had some dismal times. The shoal of fish waiting for the crumbs of employment seemed larger than ever.

He took counsel with himself. Should he "chuck" the outfitting? It wasn't any good for him now, and presently, when he was older and his youthful smartness had passed into the dullness of middle age, it would be worse. What else could he do?

He could think of nothing. He went one night to a music-hall and developed a vague idea of a comic performance; the comic men seemed violent rowdies, and not at all funny; but when he thought of the great pit of the audience yawning before him, he realised that his was an altogether too delicate talent for such a use. He was impressed by the charm of selling vegetables by auction in one of those open shops near London Bridge, but admitted upon reflection his general want of technical knowledge. He made some inquiries about emigration, but none of the colonies were in want of shop assistants without capital. He kept up his attendance in Wood Street.

He subdued his ideal of salary by the sum of five pounds a year, and was taken into a driving establishment in Clapham, which dealt chiefly in ready-made suits, fed its assistants in an underground dining-room, and kept open until twelve on Saturdays. He found it hard to be cheerful there. His fits of indigestion became worse, and he began to lie awake at night and think. Sunshine and laughter seemed things lost for ever picnics, and shouting in the moonlight.

The chief shop-walker took a dislike to him and nagged him. "Nar, then, Polly!" "Look alive, Polly!" became the burden of his days. "As Smart a chap as you could have," said the chief shop-walker, "but no *Zest*. No *Zest!* No *Vim!* What's the matter with you?"

During his night vigils Mr. Polly had a feeling. . . . A young rabbit must have very much the feeling when, after a youth of gambolling in sunny woods and furtive jolly raids upon the growing wheat and exciting triumphant bolts before ineffectual casual dogs, it finds itself at last for a long night of floundering effort and perplexity in a net—for the rest of its life.

He could not grasp what was wrong with him. He made

enormous efforts to diagnose his case. Was he really just a "lazy slacker" who ought to "buck up"? He couldn't find it in him to believe it. He blamed his father a good deal—it is what fathers are for—in putting him to a trade he wasn't happy to follow, but he found it impossible to say what he ought to have followed. He felt there had been something stupid about his school, but just where that came in he couldn't say. He made some perfectly sincere efforts to "buck up" and "shove" ruthlessly. But that was infernal—impossible. He had to admit himself miserable with all the misery of a social misfit, and with no clear prospect of more than the most incidental happiness ahead of him. And for all his attempts at self-reproach and self-discipline he felt at bottom that he wasn't at fault.

As a matter of fact all the elements of his troubles had been adequately diagnosed by a certain high-browed, spectacled gentleman living at Highbury, wearing a gold pince-nez, and writing for the most part in the beautiful library of the Climax Club. This gentleman did not know Mr. Polly personally, but he had dealt with him generally as " one of those ill-adjusted units that abound in a society that has failed to develop a collective intelligence and a collective will for order commensurate with its complexities."

But phrases of that sort had no appeal for Mr. Polly.

CHAPTER FOUR

MR. POLLY AN ORPHAN

§ 1

THEN a great change was brought about in the life of Mr. Polly by the death of his father. His father died suddenly—the local practitioner still clung to his theory that it was imagination he suffered from, but compromised in the certificate with the appendicitis that was then so fashionable—and Mr. Polly found himself heir to a debatable number of pieces of furniture in the house of his cousin near Easewood Junction, a family Bible, an engraved portrait of Garibaldi and a bust of Mr. Gladstone, an invalid gold watch, a gold locket formerly belonging to his mother, some minor jewellery and bric-a-brac, a quantity of nearly valueless old clothes, and an insurance policy and money in the bank amounting altogether to the sum of three hundred and fifty-five pounds.

Mr. Polly had always regarded his father as an immortal, as an eternal fact ; and his father, being of a reserved nature in his declining years, had said nothing about the insurance policy. Both wealth and bereavement therefore took Mr. Polly by surprise, and found him a little inadequate. His mother's death had been a childish grief and long forgotten, and the

strongest affection in his life had been for Parsons. An only
child of sociable tendencies turns his back a good deal upon
home ; and the aunt who had succeeded his mother was an
economist and furniture-polisher, a knuckle-rapper and sharp
silencer : no friend for a slovenly little boy. He had loved other
little boys and girls transitorily ; none had been frequent and
familiar enough to strike deep roots in his heart ; and he had
grown up with a tattered and dissipated affectionateness that
was becoming wildly shy. His father had always been a
stranger, an irritable stranger with exceptional powers of intervention and comment, and an air of being disappointed about
his offspring. It was shocking to lose him ; it was like an unexpected hole in the universe, the writing of " Death " upon the
sky ; but it did not at first tear Mr. Polly's heart-strings so much
as rouse him to a pitch of vivid attention.

He came down to the cottage at Easewood in response to an
urgent telegram, and found his father already dead. His
Cousin Johnson received him with much solemnity, and
ushered him upstairs to look at a stiff, straight, shrouded form
with a face unwontedly quiet and, it seemed by reason of its
pinched nostrils, scornful.

" Looks peaceful," said Mr. Polly, disregarding the scorn to
the best of his ability.

" It was a merciful relief," said Mr. Johnson.

There was a pause.

" Second—second Departed I've ever seen—not counting
mummies," said Mr. Polly, feeling it necessary to say something.

" We did all we could."

" No doubt of it, O' Man," said Mr. Polly.

A second long pause followed, and then, to Mr. Polly's
great relief, Johnson moved towards the door.

Afterwards Mr. Polly went for a solitary walk in the evening
light, and as he walked, suddenly his dead father became real
to him. He thought of things far away down the perspective of
memory—of jolly moments when his father had skylarked with
a wildly excited little boy ; of a certain annual visit to the
Crystal Palace pantomime, full of trivial glittering incidents
and wonders; of his father's dread back while customers were in
the old, minutely known shop. It is curious that the memory
which seemed to link him nearest to the dead man was the
memory of a fit of passion. His father had wanted to get a
small sofa up the narrow winding staircase from the little
room behind the shop to the bedroom above, and it had
jammed. For a time his father had coaxed, and then groaned
like a soul in torment, and given way to blind fury ; had
sworn, kicked, and struck at the offending piece of furniture,
and finally, with an immense effort, wrenched it upstairs, with
considerable incidental damage to lath and plaster and one
of the casters. That moment when self-control was altogether

torn aside, the shocked discovery of his father's perfect
humanity, had left a singular impression on Mr. Polly's queer
mind. It was as if something extravagantly vital had come
out of his father and laid a warmly passionate hand upon his
heart. He remembered that now very vividly, and it became
a clue to endless other memories that had else been dispersed
and confusing.

A weakly wilful being, struggling to get obdurate things
round impossible corners—in that symbol Mr. Polly could
recognise himself and all the trouble of humanity.

He hadn't had a particularly good time, poor old chap ;
and now it was all over—finished. . . .

Johnson was the sort of man who derives great satisfaction
from a funeral ; a melancholy, serious, practical-minded man of
five-and-thirty, with great powers of advice. He was the up-line
ticket clerk at Easewood Junction, and felt the responsibilities
of his position. He was naturally thoughtful and reserved,
and greatly sustained in that by an innate rectitude of body
and an overhanging and forward inclination of the upper part
of his face and head. He was pale but freckled, and his dark
grey eyes were deeply set. His lightest interest was cricket, but
he did not take that lightly. His chief holiday was to go to a
cricket-match, which he did as if he was going to church ;
and he watched critically, applauded sparingly, and was
darkly offended by any unorthodox play. His convictions
upon all subjects were taciturnly inflexible. He was an obstinate
player of draughts and chess, and an earnest and persistent
reader of the *British Weekly*. His wife was a pink, short,
wilfully smiling, managing, ingratiating, talkative woman,
who was determined to be pleasant, and take a bright, hopeful,
view of everything, even when it was not really bright and
hopeful. She had large, blue, expressive eyes and a round face,
and she always spoke of her husband as Harold. She addressed
sympathetic and considerate remarks about the deceased to Mr.
Polly in notes of brisk encouragement. " He was really quite
cheerful at the end," she said several times, with congratulatory
gusto ; " quite cheerful."

She made dying seem almost agreeable.

Both these people were resolved to treat Mr. Polly very well,
and to help his exceptional incompetence in every possible way ;
and after a simple supper of ham and bread and cheese and
pickles and cold apple tart and small beer had been cleared
away, they put him into the armchair almost as though he was
an invalid, and sat on chairs that made them look down upon
him, and opened a directive discussion of the arrangements
for the funeral. After all, a funeral is a distinct social opportunity, and rare when you have no family and few relations,
and they did not want to see it spoiled and wasted.

" You'll have a hearse, of course," said Mrs. Johnson ; " not
one of them combinations, with the driver sitting on the coffin.

Disrespectful, I think they are, I can't fancy how people can bring themselves to be buried in combinations." She flattened her voice in a manner she used to intimate æsthetic feeling. " I *do* like them glass hearses," she said. " So refined and nice they are."

" Podger's hearse you'll have," said Johnson conclusively ; " it's the best in Easewood."

" Everything that's right and proper," said Mr. Polly.

" Podger's ready to come and measure at any time," said Johnson.

" Then you'll want a mourner's carriage or two, according to whom you're going to invite," said Mr. Johnson.

" Didn't think of inviting any one," said Mr. Polly.

" Oh, you'll *have* to ask a few friends," said Mr. Johnson. " You can't let your father go to his grave without asking a few friends."

" Funerial baked meats, like," said Mr. Polly.

" Not baked ; but of course you'll have to give them something. Ham and chicken's very suitable. You don't want a lot of cooking, with the ceremony coming into the middle of it. I wonder who Alfred ought to invite, Harold ? Just the immediate relations. One doesn't want a Great Crowd of People, and one doesn't want not to show respect."

" But he hated our relations—most of them."

" He's not hating them *now*," said Mr. Johnson ; " you may be sure of that. It's just because of that I think they ought to come, all of them—even your Aunt Mildred."

" Bit vulturial, isn't it ? " said Mr. Polly unheeded.

" Wouldn't be more than twelve or thirteen people if they *all* came," said Mr. Johnson.

" We could have everything put out ready in the back room, and the gloves and whisky in the front room ; and while we were all at the—ceremony, Bessie could bring it all into the front room on a tray, and put it out nice and proper. There'd have to be whisky, and sherry-or-port for the ladies. . . ."

" Where'll you get your mourning ? " asked Johnson abruptly.

Mr. Polly had not yet considered this by-product of sorrow. " Haven't thought of it yet, O' Man."

A disagreeable feeling spread over his body, as though he was blackening as he sat. He hated black garments.

" I suppose I must *have* mourning," he said.

" *Well !* " said Johnson, with a solemn smile.

" Got to see it through," said Mr. Polly indistinctly.

" If I were you," said Johnson, " I should get ready-made trousers. That's all you really want. And a black satin tie, and a top hat with a deep mourning band. And gloves."

" Jet cuff-links he ought to have—as chief mourner," said Mrs. Johnson.

" Not obligatory," said Johnson.

" It shows respect," said Mrs. Johnson.

" It shows respect, of course," said Johnson.

And then Mrs. Johnson went on with the utmost gusto to the details of the " casket," while Mr. Polly sat more and more deeply and droopingly into the armchair, assenting with a note of protest to all they said. After he had retired for the night he remained for a long time perched on the edge of the sofa, which was his bed, staring at the prospect before him. " Chasing the o' man about to the last," he said.

He hated the thought and elaboration of death as a healthy animal must hate it. His mind struggled with unwonted social problems.

" Got to put 'em away somehow, I suppose," said Mr. Polly. " Wish I'd looked him up a bit more while he was alive."

§ 2

Bereavement came to Mr. Polly before the realisation of opulence and its anxieties and responsibilities. That only dawned upon him on the morrow—which chanced to be Sunday—as he walked with Johnson before church time about the tangle of struggling building enterprise that constituted the rising urban district of Easewood. Johnson was off duty that morning, and devoted the time very generously to the admonitory discussion of Mr. Polly's worldly outlook.

" Don't seem to get the hang of the business somehow," said Mr. Polly. " Too much blooming hum-bug in it for my way of thinking."

" If I were you," said Mr. Johnson, " I should push for a first-class place in London—take almost nothing and live on my reserves. That's what I should do."

" Come the Heavy," said Mr. Polly.

" Get a better-class reference."

There was a pause. " Think of investing your money ? " asked Johnson.

" Hardly got used to the idea of having it yet, O' Man."

" You'll have to do something with it. Give you nearly twenty pounds a year if you invest it properly."

" Haven't seen it yet in that light," said Mr. Polly defensively.

" There's no end of things you could put it into."

" It's getting it out again I shouldn't feel sure of. I'm no sort of Fiancianier. Sooner back horses."

" I wouldn't do that if I were you."

" Not my style, O' Man."

" It's a nest-egg," said Johnson.

Mr. Polly made an indeterminate noise.

" There's building societies," Johnson threw out in a speculative tone. Mr. Polly, with detached brevity, admitted there were.

" You might lend it on mortgage," said Johnson. " Very safe form of investment."

" Shan't think anything about it—not till the o' man's underground," said Mr. Polly, with an inspiration.

They turned a corner that led towards the junction.

" Might do worse," said Johnson, " than put it into a small shop."

At the moment this remark made very little appeal to Mr. Polly. But afterwards it developed. It fell into his mind like some obscure seed and germinated.

" These shops aren't in a bad position," said Johnson.

The row he referred to gaped in the late painful stage in building before the healing touch of the plasterer assuages the roughness of the brickwork. The space for the shop yawned an oblong gap below, framed above by an iron girder ; " Windows and fittings to suit tenant," a board at the end of the row promised ; and behind was the door space and a glimpse of stairs going up to the living-rooms above. " Not a bad position," said Johnson, and led the way into the establishment. " Room for fixtures there," he said, pointing to the blank wall.

The two men went upstairs to the little sitting-room (or best bedroom it would have to be) above the shop. Then they descended to the kitchen below.

" Rooms in a new house always look a bit small," said Johnson.

They came out of the house again by the prospective back door, and picked their way through builder's litter across the yard space to the road again. They drew nearer the junction to where a pavement and shops already open and active formed the commercial centre of Easewood. On the opposite side of the way the side door of a flourishing little establishment opened, and a man and his wife and a small boy in a sailor suit came into the street. The wife was a pretty woman in brown, with a floriferous straw hat, and the group was altogether very Sundayfied and shiny and spick and span. The shop itself had a large plate-glass window whose contents were now veiled by a buff blind on which was inscribed in scrolly letters: " Rymer, Pork Butcher and Provision Merchant," and then with voluptuous elaborations, " The World Famed Easewood Sausage."

Greetings were exchanged between Mr. Johnson and this distinguished comestible.

" Off to church already ? " said Johnson.

" Walking across the fields to Little Dorington," said Mr. Rymer.

" Very pleasant walk," said Johnson.

" Very," said Mr. Rymer.

" Hope you'll enjoy it," said Mr. Johnson.

" That chap's done well," said Johnson, *sotto voce*, as they went on. " Came here with nothing—practically, four years ago. And as thin as a lath. Look at him now !

" He's worked hard, of course," said Johnson, improving the occasion.

Thought fell between the cousins for a space.

" Some men can do one thing," said Johnson, " and some another. . . . For a man who sticks to it there's a lot to be done in a shop."

§ 3

All the preparations for the funeral ran easily and happily under Mrs. Johnson's skilful hands. On the eve of the sad occasion she produced a reserve of black sateen, the kitchen steps, and a box of tin tacks, and decorated the house with festoons and bows of black in the best possible taste. She tied up the knocker with black crape, and put a large bow over the corner of the steel engraving of Garibaldi, and swathed the bust of Mr. Gladstone that had belonged to the deceased with inky swathings. She turned round the two vases that had views of Tivoli and the Bay of Naples, so that these rather brilliant landscapes were hidden and only the plain blue enamel showed, and she anticipated the long contemplated purchase of a table-cloth for the front room, and substituted a violet-purple cover for the now very worn and faded raptures and roses in plushette that had hitherto done duty there. Everything that loving consideration could do to impart a dignified solemnity to her little home was done.

She had released Mr. Polly from the irksome duty of issuing invitations, and as the moments of assembly drew near she sent him and Mr. Johnson out into the narrow, long strip of garden at the back of the house, to be free to put a finishing touch or so to her preparations. She sent them out together because she had a queer little persuasion at the back of her mind that Mr. Polly wanted to bolt from his sacred duties, and there was no way out of the garden except through the house.

Mr. Johnson was a steady, successful gardener, and particularly good with celery and peas. He walked slowly along the narrow path down the centre, pointing out to Mr. Polly a number of interesting points in the management of peas, wrinkles neatly applied and difficulties wisely overcome, and all that he did for the comfort and propitiation of that fitful but rewarding vegetable. Presently a sound of nervous laughter and raised voices from the house proclaimed the arrival of the earlier guests, and the worst of that anticipatory tension was over.

When Mr. Polly re-entered the house he found three entirely strange young women with pink faces, demonstrative manners, and emphatic mourning engaged in an incoherent conversation with Mrs. Johnson. All three kissed him with great gusto after the ancient English fashion. " These are your Cousins

Larkins," said Mrs. Johnson. "That's Annie" (unexpected hug and smack), "that's Miriam" (resolute hug and smack), "and that's Minnie" (prolonged hug and smack).

"Right-o," said Mr. Polly, emerging a little crumpled and breathless from the hearty introduction. "I see."

"Here's Aunt Larkins," said Mrs. Johnson, as an elderly and stouter edition of the three young women appeared in the doorway.

Mr. Polly backed rather faint-heartedly, but Aunt Larkins was not to be denied. Having hugged and kissed her nephew resoundingly, she gripped him by the wrists and scanned his features. She had a round, sentimental, freckled face. "I should 'ave known 'im anywhere," she said, with fervour.

"Hark at Mother!" said the cousin called Annie. "Why, she's never set eyes on him before."

"I should 'ave known 'im anywhere," said Mrs. Larkins, "for Lizzie's child. You've got her eyes! It's a Resemblance! And as for never seeing 'im—I've *dandled* him, Miss Imperence. I've dandled him."

"You couldn't dandle him now, Ma!" Miss Annie remarked, with a shriek of laughter.

All the sisters laughed at that. "The things you say, Annie!" said Miriam, and for a time the room was full of mirth.

Mr. Polly felt it incumbent upon him to say something. "*My* dandling days are over," he said.

The reception of this remark would have convinced a far more modest character than Mr. Polly that it was extremely witty.

Mr. Polly followed it up by another one almost equally good. "My turn to dandle," he said, with a sly look at his aunt, and convulsed every one.

"Not me," said Mrs. Larkins, taking his point, "*thank* you," and achieved a climax.

It was queer, but they seemed to be easy people to get on with anyhow. They were still picking little ripples and giggles of mirth from the idea of Mr. Polly dandling Aunt Larkins when Mr. Johnson, who had answered the door, ushered in a stooping figure, who was at once hailed by Mrs. Johnson as "Why! Uncle Pentstemon!" Uncle Pentstemon was rather a shock. His was an aged rather than venerable figure. Time had removed the hair from the top of his head and distributed a small dividend of the plunder in little bunches carelessly and impartially over the rest of his features; he was dressed in a very big, old frock-coat and a long, cylindrical top-hat, which he had kept on; he was very much bent, and he carried a rush basket, from which protruded coy intimations of the lettuces and onions he had brought to grace the occasion. He hobbled into the room, resisting the efforts of Johnson to divest him of his various encumbrances, halted, and surveyed the company with an expression of profound hostility, breathing hard. Recognition quickened in his eyes.

" *You* here ? " he said to Aunt Larkins, and then, " You *would* be. . . . These your gals ? "

" They are," said Aunt Larkins, " and better gals——"

" That Annie ? " asked Uncle Pentstemon, pointing a horny thumb-nail.

" Fancy your remembering her name ! "

" She mucked up my mushroom bed, the baggage ! " said Uncle Pentstemon ungenially, " and I give it to her to rights. Trounced her I did—fairly. *I* remember her. Here's some green stuff for you, Grace. Fresh it is, and wholesome. I shall be wanting the basket back, and mind you let me have it. . . . Have you nailed him down yet ? Ah ! You always was a bit in front of what was needful."

His attention was drawn inward by a troublesome tooth, and he sucked at it spitefully. There was something potent about this old man that silenced every one for a moment or so. He seemed a fragment from the ruder agricultural past of our race, like a lump of soil among things of paper. He put his packet of earthy vegetables very deliberately on the new violet table-cloth, removed his hat carefully, and dabbled his brow, and wiped out his hat brim with an abundant crimson-and-yellow pocket-handkerchief.

" I'm glad you were able to come, Uncle," said Mrs. Johnson.

" Oh, I *came*," said Uncle Pentstemon, " I *came*."

He turned on Mrs. Larkins. " Gals in service ? " he asked.

" They aren't, and they won't be," said Mrs. Larkins.

" No," he said, with infinite meaning, and turned his eye on Mr. Polly.

" You Lizzie's boy ? " he said.

Mr. Polly was spared much self-exposition by the tumult occasioned by further arrivals.

" Ah ! here's May Punt ! " said Mrs. Johnson, and a small woman dressed in the borrowed mourning of a large woman, and leading a very small, fair-haired, sharp-nosed, observant little boy—it was his first funeral—appeared, closely followed by several friends of Mrs. Johnson who had come to swell the display of respect, and who left only vague, confused impressions upon Mr. Polly's mind. (Aunt Mildred, who was an unexplained family scandal, had declined Mrs. Johnson's hospitality to the relief of every one who understood—as Mrs. Johnson intimated—though who understood, and what, as my head master used to say, Mr. Polly could form no idea.)

Everybody was in profound mourning, of course—mourning in the modern English style, with the dyer's handiwork only too apparent, and hats and jackets of the current cut. There was very little crape, and the costumes had none of the goodness and specialization and genuine enjoyment of mourning for mourning's sake that a similar Continental gathering would have displayed. Still that congestion of strangers in black sufficed to stun and confuse Mr. Polly's impressionable mind.

It seemed to him much more extraordinary than anything he had expected.

" Now, gals," said Mrs. Larkins, " see if you can help," and the three daughters became confusingly active between the front room and the back.

" I hope every one'll take a glass of sherry and a biscuit," said Mrs. Johnson. " We don't stand on ceremony," and a decanter appeared in the place of Uncle Pentstemon's vegetables.

Uncle Pentstemon had refused to be relieved of his hat ; he sat stiffly down on a chair against the wall, with that venerable head-dress between his feet, watching the approach of any one jealously. " Don't you go squashing my hat," he said. Conversation became confused and general. Uncle Pentstemon addressed himself to Mr. Polly.

" You're a little chap," he said ; " a puny little chap. I never did agree to Lizzie marrying him, but I suppose bygones must be bygones now. I suppose they made you a clerk or something."

" Outfitter," said Mr. Polly.

" I remember. Them girls pretend to be dressmakers."

" They *are* dressmakers," said Mrs. Larkins across the room.

" I *will* take a glass of sherry," he remarked ; and then mildly to Mr. Polly, " They 'old to it, you see."

He took the glass Mrs. Johnson handed him, and poised it critically between a horny finger and thumb. " You'll be paying for this," he said to Mr. Polly. " Here's *to* you. . . . Don't you go treading on my hat, young woman. You brush your skirts against it and you take a shillin' off its value. It ain't the sort of 'at you see nowadays."

He drank noisily.

The sherry presently loosened everybody's tongue, and the opening coldness passed.

" There ought to have been a *post-mortem*," Polly heard Mrs. Punt remarking to one of Mrs. Johnson's friends, and Miriam and another were lost in admiration of Mrs. Johnson's decorations. " So very nice and refined," they were both repeating at intervals.

The sherry and biscuits were still being discussed when Mr. Podger, the undertaker, arrived, a broad, cheerfully sorrowful, clean-shaven little man, accompanied by a melancholy-faced assistant. He conversed for a time with Johnson in the passage outside. The sense of his business stilled the rising waves of chatter and carried off every one's attention in the wake of his heavy footsteps to the room above.

§ 4

Things crowded upon Mr. Polly. Every one, he noticed, took sherry with a solemn avidity, and a small portion was administered sacramentally even to the Punt boy. There followed a distribution of black kid gloves, and much trying-on and humouring of fingers. " *Good* gloves," said one of Mrs. Johnson's friends. " There's a little pair there for Willie," said Mrs. Johnson triumphantly. Every one seemed gravely content with the amazing procedure of the occasion. Presently Mr. Podger was picking Mr. Polly out as Chief Mourner to go with Mrs. Johnson, Mrs. Larkins, and Annie in the first mourning carriage.

" Right-o," said Mr. Polly, and repented instantly of the alacrity of the phrase.

" There'll have to be a walking-party," said Mrs. Johnson cheerfully. " There's only two coaches. I dare say we can put in six in each, but that leaves three over."

There was a generous struggle to be pedestrian, and the two other Larkins girls, confessing coyly to tight new boots and displaying a certain eagerness, were added to the contents of the first carriage.

" It'll be a squeeze," said Annie.

" *I* don't mind a squeeze," said Mr. Polly.

He decided privately that the proper phrase for the result of that remark was " Hysterial catechunations."

Mr. Podger re-entered the room from a momentary super-vision of the bumping business that was now proceeding down the staircase.

" Bearing up," he said cheerfully, rubbing his hands to-gether. " Bearing up ! "

That stuck very vividly in Mr. Polly's mind, and so did the close-wedged drive to the churchyard, bunched in between two young women in confused dull and shiny black, and the fact that the wind was bleak and that the officiating clergyman had a cold, and sniffed between his sentences. The wonder of life ! The wonder of everything ! What had he expected that this should all be so astoundingly different ?

He found his attention converging more and more upon the Larkins cousins. The interest was reciprocal. They watched him with a kind of suppressed excitement and became risible with his every word and gesture. He was more and more aware of their personal quality. Annie had blue eyes, and a red, attractive mouth, a harsh voice, and a habit of extreme liveliness that even this occasion could not suppress ; Minnie was fond, extremely free about the touching of hands and such-like endearments ; Miriam was dark and quieter than her sisters and regarded him earnestly. Mrs. Larkins was very happy in her daughters, and they had the naïve affec-tionateness of those who see few people and find a strange cousin a wonderful outlet. Mr. Polly had never been very much kissed, and it made his mind swim. He did not know for the life of him whether he liked or disliked all or any of the Larkins cousins. It was rather attractive to make them laugh anyhow ; they laughed at anything.

There they were tugging at his mind, and the funeral tugging at his mind too, and the sense of himself as Chief Mourner in a brand-new silk hat with a broad mourning band. He watched the ceremony and missed his responses, and strange feelings twisted at his heart-strings.

§ 5

Mr. Polly walked back to the house because he wanted to be alone. Miriam and Minnie would have accompanied him, but finding Uncle Pentstemon beside the Chief Mourner they went on in front.

" You're wise," said Uncle Pentstemon.

" Glad you think so," said Mr. Polly, rousing himself to talk.

" I likes a bit of walking before a meal," said Uncle Pentstemon, and made a kind of large hiccup. " That sherry rises," he remarked. " Grocer's stuff, I expect."

He went on to ask how much the funeral might be costing, and seemed pleased to find Mr. Polly didn't know.

" In that case," he said impressively, " it's pretty certain to cost more'n you expect, my boy."

He meditated for a time. " I've seen a mort of undertakers," he declared ; " a mort of undertakers."

The Larkins girls attracted his attention.

" Lets lodgin's and chars," he commented. " Leastways she goes out to cook dinners. And *look* at 'em ! Dressed up to the nines. If it ain't borryd clothes, that is. And they goes out to work at a factory ! "

" Did you know my father much, Uncle Pentstemon ? " asked Mr. Polly.

" Couldn't stand Lizzie throwin' herself away like that," said Uncle Pentstemon, and repeated his hiccup on a larger scale.

" That *weren't* good sherry," said Uncle Pentstemon, with the first note of pathos Mr. Polly had detected in his quavering voice.

The funeral in the rather cold wind had proved wonderfully appetising, and every eye brightened at the sight of the cold collation that was now spread in the front room. Mrs. Johnson was very brisk, and Mr. Polly, when he re-entered the house, found the party sitting down.

" Come along, Alfred," cried the hostess cheerfully. " We can't very well begin without you. Have you got the bottled beer ready to open, Bessie ? Uncle, you'll have a drop of whisky, I expect."

" Put it where I can mix for myself ; I can't bear wimmin's mixing," said Uncle Pentstemon, placing his hat very carefully out of harm's way on the bookcase.

There were two cold boiled chickens, which Johnson carved with great care and justice, and a nice piece of ham, some

brawn, and a steak-and-kidney pie, a large bowl of salad and
several sorts of pickles, and afterwards some cold apple tart,
jam roll, and a good piece of Stilton cheese, lots of bottled
beer, some lemonade for the ladies, and milk for Master Punt :
a very bright and satisfying meal. Mr. Polly found himself
seated between Mrs. Punt, who was much preoccupied with
Master Punt's table manners, and one of Mrs. Johnson's school
friends, who was exchanging reminiscences with Mrs. Johnson
of school-days and news of how various common friends had
changed and married. Opposite him was Miriam and another
of the early Johnson circle, and also he had brawn to carve,
and there was hardly room for the helpful Bessie to pass
behind his chair, so that altogether his mind would have been
amply distracted from any mortuary broodings, even if a
wordy warfare about the education of the modern young
woman had not sprung up between Uncle Pentstemon and
Mrs. Larkins, and threatened for a time, in spite of a word or
so in season from Johnson, to wreck all the harmony of the
sad occasion.

The general effect was after this fashion :

First an impression of Mrs. Punt on the right, speaking in a
refined undertone : " You didn't, I suppose, Mr. Polly, think
to 'ave you poor dear father *post-mortemed* ? "

Lady on the left side, breaking in : " I was just reminding
Grace of the dear dead days beyond recall."

Attempted reply to Mrs. Punt : " Didn't think of it for a
moment. Can't give you a piece of this brawn, can I ?"

Fragment from the left : " Grace and Beauty they used to
call us, and we used to sit at the same desk."

Mrs. Punt, breaking out suddenly : "Don't *swaller* your
fork, Willie—You see, Mr. Polly, I used to have a young gentleman, a medical student, lodging with me——"

Voice from down the table with a large softness : " 'Am,
Elfred ? I didn't give you very much 'am."

Bessie became evident at the back of Mr. Polly's chair,
struggling wildly to get past. Mr. Polly did his best to be
helpful. " Can you get past ? Lemme sit forward a bit. Urr-
oo ! Right-o ! "

Lady to the left going on valiantly and speaking to every
one who cared to listen, while Mrs. Johnson beamed beside
her : " There she used to sit as bold as brass, and the fun she
used to make of things no one *could* believe—knowing her
now. She used to make faces at the mistress through the—— "

Mrs. Punt, keeping steadily on : " The contents of the
stummik at any rate *ought* to be examined."

Voice of Mrs. Johnson : " Elfrid, pass the mustid down."

Miriam, leaning across the table : " Elfrid ! "

" Once she got us all kept in. The whole school ! "

Miriam, more insistently : " Elfrid ! "

Uncle Pentstemon, raising his voice defiantly : " Trounce

'er again I would if she did as much now. That I would.
Dratted mischief ! "

Miriam, catching Mr. Polly's eye : " Elfrid ! This lady
knows Canterbury. I been telling her you been there."

Mr. Polly : " Glad you know it."

The lady, shouting : " I like it."

Mrs. Larkins, raising her voice : " I won't 'ave my girls
spoken of, not by nobody, old *or* young."

POP ! imperfectly located.

Mr. Johnson, at large : " *Ain't* the beer up ! It's the 'eated
room."

Bessie : " 'Scuse me, Sir, passing so soon again, but——"
Rest inaudible. Mr. Polly, accommodating himself : " Urr-oo !
Right ? Right-o ! "

The knives and forks, probably by some secret common
agreement, clash and clatter together, and drown every other
sound.

" Nobody 'ad the least idea 'ow 'E died—nobody. . . .
Willie, don't *golp* so. You ain't in a 'urry, are you ? You don't
want to ketch a train, or anything—golping like that ! "

" D'you remember, Grace, 'ow one day we 'ad writing
lesson. . . ."

" Nicer girls no one ever 'ad—though I say it who shouldn't."

Mrs. Johnson, in a shrill, clear, hospitable voice: " Harold,
won't Mrs. Larkins 'ave a teeny bit more fowl ? "

Mr. Polly was rising to the situation. " Or some brawn,
Mrs. Larkins ? " Catching Uncle Pentstemon's eye: " Can't
send *you* some brawn, Sir ? "

" Elfrid ! "

Loud hiccup from Uncle Pentstemon, momentary consternation, followed by giggle from Annie.

The narration at Mr. Polly's elbow pursued a quiet but
relentless course. " Directly the new doctor came in, he said,
' Everything must be took out and put in spirits—everything.' "

Willie—audible ingurgitation.

The narration on the left was flourishing up to a climax.
" Ladies, she sez, dip their pens *in* their ink and keep their
noses out of it."

" Elfrid ! " persuasively.

" Certain people may cast snacks at other people's daughters,
never having had any of their own, though two poor souls
of wives dead and buried through their goings on——"

Johnson, ruling the storm : " We don't want old scores dug
up on such a day as this——"

" Old scores you may call them, but worth a dozen of them
that put them to their rest, poor dears."

" Elfrid ! " with a note of remonstrance.

" If you choke yourself, my lord, not another mouthful
do you 'ave. No nice puddin' ! Nothing ! "

" And kept us in, she did, every afternoon for a week ! "

It seemed to be the end, and Mr. Polly replied, with an air of being profoundly impressed, " Really ! "

" Elfrid ! " a little disheartened.

" And then they 'ad it ! They found he'd swallowed the very key to unlock the drawer——"

" Then don't let people go casting snacks ! "

" *Who's* casting snacks ? "

" Elfrid ! This lady wants to know, 'ave the Prossers left Canterbury ? "

" No wish to make myself disagreeable, not to God's 'umblest worm——"

" Alf, you aren't very busy with that brawn up there ! "

And so on for the hour.

The general effect upon Mr. Polly at the time was at once confusing and exhilarating ; but it led him to eat copiously and carelessly, and long before the end, when after an hour and a quarter a movement took the party, and it pushed away its cheese-plates and rose sighing and stretching from the remains of the repast, little streaks and bands of dyspeptic irritation and melancholy were darkening the serenity of his mind.

He stood between the mantel-shelf and the window—the blinds were up now—and the Larkins sisters clustered about him. He battled with the oncoming depression, and forced himself to be extremely facetious about two noticeable rings on Annie's hand. " They ain't real," said Annie coquettishly. " Got 'em out of a prize packet."

" Prize packet in trousers, I expect," said Mr. Polly, and awakened inextinguishable laughter.

" Oh, the Things you say ! " said Minnie, slapping his shoulder.

Something he had quite extraordinarily forgotten came into his head.

" Bless my heart ! " he cried, suddenly serious.

" What's the matter ? " asked Johnson.

" Ought to have gone back to shop three days ago. They'll make no end of a row ! "

" Lor, you *are* a treat ! " said Cousin Annie, and screamed with laughter at a delicious idea. " You'll get the Chuck," she said.

Mr. Polly made a convulsive grimace at her.

" I'll die ! " she said. " I don't believe you care a bit."

Feeling a little disorganised by her hilarity and a shocked expression that had come to the face of Cousin Miriam, he made some indistinct excuse and went out through the back room and scullery into the little garden. The cool air and a very slight drizzle of rain was a relief—anyhow. But the black mood of the replete dyspeptic had come upon him. His soul darkened hopelessly. He walked with his hands in his pockets down the path between the rows of exceptionally cultured peas, and unreasonably, overwhelmingly, he was smitten by sorrow for his father. The heady noise and muddle and confused excitement of the feast passed from him like a curtain drawn away. He thought of that hot and angry and struggling creature who had tugged and sworn so foolishly at the sofa upon the twisted staircase, and who was now lying still and hidden at the bottom of a wall-sided, oblong pit, beside the heaped gravel that would presently cover him. The stillness of it ! the wonder of it ! the infinite reproach ! Hatred for all these people—all of them—possessed Mr. Polly's soul.

" Hen-witted gigglers," said Mr. Polly.

He went down to the fence, and stood with his hands on it, staring away at nothing. He stayed there for what seemed a long time. From the house came a sound of raised voices that subsided, and then Mrs. Johnson calling for Bessie.

"Gowlish gusto," said Mr. Polly. " Jumping it in. Funererial Games. Don't hurt him, of course. Doesn't matter to *him*. . . ."

Nobody missed Mr. Polly for a long time.

When at last he reappeared among them his eye was almost grim, but nobody noticed his eye. They were looking at watches, and Johnson was being omniscient about trains. They seemed to discover Mr. Polly afresh just at the moment of parting, and said a number of more or less appropriate things. But Uncle Pentstemon was far too worried about his rush basket, which had been carelessly mislaid, he seemed to think with larcenous intentions, to remember Mr. Polly at all. Mrs. Johnson had tried to fob him off with a similar but inferior basket—his own had one handle mended with string according to a method of peculiar virtue and inimitable distinction known only to himself—and the old gentleman had taken her attempt as the gravest reflection upon his years and intelligence. Mr. Polly was left very largely to the Larkins trio. Cousin Minnie became shameless, and kept kissing him good-bye—and then finding out it wasn't time to go. Cousin Miriam seemed to think her silly, and caught Mr. Polly's eye sympathetically. Cousin Annie ceased to giggle, and lapsed into a nearly sentimental state. She said with real feeling that she had enjoyed the funeral more than words could tell.

CHAPTER FIVE

ROMANCE

§ 1

Mr. Polly returned to Clapham from the funeral celebrations prepared for trouble, and took his dismissal in a manly spirit.

" You've merely antiseparated me by a hair," he said politely.

And he told them in the dormitory that he meant to take a little holiday before his next crib, though a certain inherited reticence suppressed the fact of the legacy.

" You'll do that all right," said Ascough, the head of the boot-shop. " It's quite the fashion just at present. Six Weeks in Wonderful Wood Street. They're running excursions. . . . "

" A little holiday " ; that was the form his sense of wealth took first—it made a little holiday possible. Holidays were his life, and the rest merely adulterated living. And now he might take a little holiday and have money for railway fares and money for meals, and money for inns. But— He wanted some one to take the holiday with.

For a time he cherished a design of hunting up Parsons, getting him to throw up his situation, and going with him to Stratford-on-Avon and Shrewsbury, and the Welsh mountains and the Wye, and a lot of places like that, for a really gorgeous, careless, illimitable old holiday of a month. But, alas ! Parsons had gone from the St. Paul's Churchyard outfitter's long ago, and left no address.

Polly tried to think he would be almost as happy wandering alone, but he knew better. He had dreamt of casual encounters with delightfully interesting people by the wayside— even romantic encounters. Such things happened in Chaucer and " Bocashiew " ; they happened with extreme facility in Mr. Richard le Gallienne's very detrimental book, "The Quest of the Golden Girl," which he had read at Canterbury ; but he had no confidence they would happen in England—to him.

When, a month later, he came out of the Clapham side door at last into the bright sunshine of a fine London day, with a dazzling sense of limitless freedom upon him, he did nothing more adventurous than order the cabman to drive to Waterloo, and there take a ticket to Easewood.

He wanted—what *did* he want most in life ? I think his distinctive craving is best expressed as fun—fun in companionship. He had already spent a pound or two upon three select feasts to his fellow assistants, sprat suppers they were, and there had been a great and very successful Sunday pilgrimage to Richmond, by Wandsworth and Wimbledon's open common, a trailing garrulous company walking about a solemnly happy host, to wonderful cold meat and salad at the Roebuck, a bowl of punch, punch ! and a bill to correspond ; but now it was a week-day, and he went down to Easewood with his bag and portmanteau in a solitary compartment, and looked out of the window upon a world in which every possible congenial seemed either toiling in a situation or else looking for one with a gnawing and hopelessly preoccupying anxiety. He stared out of the window at the exploitation roads of suburbs and rows of houses all very much alike, either emphatically and impatiently TO LET, or full of rather busy unsocial people.

Near Wimbledon he had a glimpse of golf-links, and saw two elderly gentlemen, who, had they chosen, might have been gentlemen of grace and leisure, addressing themselves to smite hunted little white balls great distances with the utmost bitterness and dexterity. Mr. Polly could not understand them.

Every road, he remarked as freshly as though he had never observed it before, was bordered by inflexible palings or iron fences or severely disciplined hedges. He wondered if perhaps abroad there might be beautifully careless, unenclosed highroads. Perhaps after all the best way of taking a holiday is to go abroad.

He was haunted by the memory of what was either a half-forgotten picture or a dream ; a carriage was drawn up by the wayside and four beautiful people, two men and two women graciously dressed, were dancing a formal ceremonious dance, full of bows and curtseys, to the music of a wandering fiddler they had encountered. They had been driving one way and he walking another—a happy encounter with this obvious result. They might have come straight out of happy Theleme, whose motto is : " Do what thou wilt." The driver had taken his two sleek horses out ; they grazed unchallenged ; and he sat on a stone clapping time with his hands while the fiddler played. The shade of the trees did not altogether shut out the sunshine, the grass in the wood was lush and full of still daffodils, the turf they danced on was starred with daisies.

Mr. Polly, dear heart ! firmly believed that things like that could and did happen—somewhere. Only it puzzled him that morning that he never saw them happening. Perhaps they happened south of Guilford ! Perhaps they happened in Italy. Perhaps they ceased to happen a hundred years ago. Perhaps they happened just round the corner—on week-days when all good Mr. Pollys are safely shut up in shops. And so dreaming of delightful impossibilities until his heart ached for them, he was rattled along in the suburban train to Johnson's discreet home and the briskly stimulating welcome of Mrs. Johnson.

§ 2

Mr. Polly translated his restless craving for joy and leisure into Harold Johnsonese by saying that he meant to look about him for a bit before going into another situation. It was a decision Johnson very warmly approved. It was arranged that Mr. Polly should occupy his former room and board with the Johnsons in consideration of a weekly payment of eighteen shillings. And the next morning Mr. Polly went out early and reappeared with a purchase, a safety bicycle which he proposed to study and master in the sandy lane below the Johnsons' house. But over the struggles that preceded his mastery it is humane to draw a veil.

And also Mr. Polly bought a number of books ; Rabelais for his own, and " The Arabian Nights," the works of Sterne, a pile of " Tales from Blackwood," cheap in a second-hand book-shop, the plays of William Shakespear, a second-hand copy of Belloc's " Path to Rome," an odd volume of " Purchas his Pilgrimes " and " The Life and Death of Jason."

" Better get yourself a good book on bookkeeping," said Johnson, turning over perplexing pages.

A belated spring, to make up for lost time, was now advancing with great strides. Sunshine and a stirring wind were poured out over the land, fleets of towering clouds sailed upon urgent tremendous missions across the blue sea of heaven, and presently Mr. Polly was riding a little unstably along unfamiliar Surrey roads, wondering always what was round the next corner, and marking the blackthorn and looking out for the first white flower-buds of the may. He was perplexed and distressed, as indeed are all right-thinking souls, that there is no may in early May.

He did not ride at the even pace sensible people use, who have marked out a journey from one place to another, and settled what time it will take them. He rode at variable speeds, and always as though he was looking for something that missing left life attractive still, but a little wanting in significance. And sometimes he was so unreasonably happy he had to whistle and sing, and sometimes he was incredibly, but not at all painfully, sad. His indigestion vanished with air and exercise, and it was quite pleasant in the evening to stroll about the garden with Johnson and discuss plans for the future. Johnson was full of ideas. Moreover, Mr. Polly had marked the road that led to Stamton, that rising popular suburb ; and as his bicycle legs grew strong his wheel, with a sort of inevitableness, carried him towards a row of houses in a back street in which his Larkins cousins made their home together.

He was received with great enthusiasm.

The street was a dingy little street, a *cul-de-sac* of very small houses in a row, each with an almost flattened bow window and a blistered brown door with a black knocker. He poised his bright new bicycle against the window, and knocked and stood waiting, and felt himself in his straw hat and black serge suit a very pleasant and prosperous-looking figure. The door was opened by Cousin Miriam. She was wearing a blueish print dress that brought out a kind of sallow warmth in her skin, and although it was nearly four o'clock in the afternoon her sleeves were tucked up, as if for some domestic task, above her elbows, showing her rather slender but very shapely yellowish arms. The loosely pinned bodice confessed a delicately rounded neck.

For a moment she regarded him with suspicion and a faint hostility, and then recognition dawned in her eyes.

"Why!" she said, "it's Cousin Elfrid!"

"Thought I'd look you up," he said.

"Fancy you coming to see us like this!" she answered.

They stood confronting one another for a moment, while Miriam collected herself for the unexpected emergency.

"Exploratious menanderings," said Mr. Polly, indicating the bicycle.

Miriam's face betrayed no appreciation of the remark.

"Wait a moment," she said, coming to a rapid decision, "and I'll tell Ma."

She closed the door on him abruptly, leaving him a little surprised in the street. "Ma!" he heard her calling, and a swift speech followed, the import of which he didn't catch. Then she reappeared. It seemed but an instant, but she was changed; the arms had vanished into sleeves, the apron had gone, a certain pleasing disorder of the hair had been at least reproved.

"I didn't mean to shut you out," she said, coming out upon the step. "I just told Ma. How are you, Elfrid? You *are* looking well. I didn't know you rode a bicycle. Is it a new one?"

She leaned upon his bicycle. "Bright it is!" she said. "What a trouble you must have to keep it clean!"

Mr. Polly was aware of a rustling transit along the passage, and of the house suddenly full of hushed but strenuous movement.

"It's plated mostly," said Mr. Polly.

"What d'you carry in that little bag thing?" she asked, and then branched off to: "We're all in a mess to-day, you know. It's my cleaning-up day to-day. I'm not a bit tidy, I know, but I *do* like to 'ave a go in at things now and then. *They'd* leave everything, I believe. If I let 'em. . . . You got to take us as you find us, Elfrid. Mercy we wasn't all out." She paused. She was talking against time. "I *am* glad to see you again," she repeated.

"Couldn't keep away," said Mr. Polly gallantly. "Had to come over and see my pretty cousins again."

Miriam did not answer for a moment. She coloured deeply. "You *do say* things!" she said.

She stared at Mr. Polly, and his unfortunate sense of fitness made him nod his head towards her, regard her firmly with a round brown eye, and add impressively: "I don't say *which* of them."

Her answering expression made him realise for an instant the terrible dangers he trifled with. Avidity flared up in her eyes. Minnie's voice came happily to dissolve the situation.

"'Ello, Elfrid!" she said from the door-step.

Her hair was just passably tidy, and she was a little effaced by a red blouse, but there was no mistaking the genuine brightness of her welcome.

He was to come in to tea, and Mrs. Larkins, exuberantly genial in a floriferous but dingy flannel dressing-gown, appeared to confirm that. He brought in his bicycle and put it in a narrow, empty, dingy passage, and every one crowded into a small, untidy kitchen, whose table had been hastily cleared of the debris of the midday repast.

" You must come in 'ere," said Mrs. Larkins, " for Miriam's turning out the front room. I never did see such a girl for cleanin' up. Miriam's 'Oliday's a scrub. You've caught us on the 'Op, as the sayin' is, but Welcome all the same. Pity Annie's at work to-day ; she won't be 'ome till seven."

Miriam put chairs and attended to the fire ; Minnie edged up to Mr. Polly and said, " I *am* glad to see you again, Elfrid," with a warm contiguous intimacy that betrayed a broken tooth. Mrs. Larkins got out tea-things, and descanted on the noble simplicity of their lives, and how he " mustn't mind our simple ways." They enveloped Mr. Polly with a geniality that intoxicated his amiable nature ; he insisted upon helping to lay the things, and created enormous laughter by pretending not to know where plates and knives and cups ought to go. " Who'm I going to sit next ? " he said, and developed voluminous amusement by attempts to arrange the plates so that he could rub elbows with all three. Mrs. Larkins had to sit down in the windsor chair by the grandfather clock (which was dark with dirt, and not going) to laugh at her ease at his well-acted perplexity.

They got seated at last, and Mr. Polly struck a vein of humour in telling them how he learned to ride the bicycle. He found the mere repetition of the word " wabble " sufficient to produce almost inextinguishable mirth.

" No foreseeing little accidentulous misadventures," he said, " none whatever."

(Giggle from Minnie.)

" Stout elderly gentleman—shirt-sleeves—large straw wastepaper basket sort of hat—starts to cross the road—going to the oil-shop—prodic refreshment of oil-can—— "

" Don't say you run 'im down," said Mrs. Larkins, gasping. " Don't say you run 'im down, Elfrid ! "

" Run 'im down ! Not me, Madam ; I never run anything down. Wabble. Ring the bell. Wabble, wabble—— "

(Laughter and tears.)

" No one's going to run him down. Hears the bell ! Wabble. Gust of wind. Off comes the hat smack into the wheel. Wabble. *Lord ! what's* going to happen ? Hat across the road, old gentleman after it, bell, shriek. He ran into me. Didn't ring his bell, hadn't *got* a bell—just ran into me. Over I went clinging to his venerable head. Down he went with me clinging to him. Oil-can blump, blump into the road."

(Interlude while Minnie is attended to for crumb in the windpipe.)

" Well, what happened to the old man with the oil-can ? "
said Mrs. Larkins.

" We sat about among the debreece and had a bit of an
argument. I told him he oughtn't to come out wearing such a
dangerous hat—flying at things. Said if he couldn't control
his hat, he ought to leave it at home. High old jawbacious
argument we had, I tell you. " I tell you, Sir— " " I tell
you, Sir." Waw-waw-waw. Infuriacious. But that's the sort
of thing that's constantly happening, you know—on a bicycle.
People run into you, hens, and cats, and dogs, and things.
Everything seems to have its mark on you ; everything."

" *You* never run into anything."

" Never. Swelpme," said Mr. Polly very solemnly.

" Never, 'E say ! " squealed Minnie. " Hark at 'im ! " and
relapsed into a condition that urgently demanded back-
thumping. " Don't be so silly," said Miriam, thumping hard.

Mr. Polly had never been such a social success before. They
hung upon his every word—and laughed. What a family they
were for laughter ! And he loved laughter. The background
he apprehended dimly ; it was very much the sort of background his life had always had. There was a threadbare
table-cloth on the table, and the slop-basin and teapot did
not go with the cups and saucers, the plates were different
again, the knives worn down, the butter lived in a greenish
glass dish of its own. Behind was a dresser hung with spare
and miscellaneous crockery, with a work-box and an untidy
work-basket ; there was an ailing musk-plant in the window,
and the tattered and blotched wall-paper was covered by
bright-coloured grocers' almanacs. Feminine wrappings hung
from pegs upon the door, and the floor was covered with a
varied collection of fragments of oil-cloth. The windsor chair
he sat in was unstable—and presently afforded material for
humour. " Steady, old nag," he said ; " Whoa, my friskiacious
palfrey ! "

" The things he says ! You never know what he won't say
next ! "

§ 3

" You ain't talkin' of goin' ! " cried Mrs. Larkins.

" Supper at eight."

" Stay to supper with *us*, now you '*ave* come over," said
Mrs. Larkins, with corroborating cries from Minnie. " 'Ave a
bit of a walk with the gals, and then come back to supper.
You might all go and meet Annie while I straighten up, and
lay things out."

" You're not to go touching the front room, mind," said
Miriam.

" *Who's* going to touch yer front room ? " said Mrs. Larkins,
apparently forgetful for a moment of Mr. Polly.

Both girls dressed with some care while Mrs. Larkins sketched the better side of their characters, and then the three young people went out to see something of Stamton. In the streets their risible mood gave way to a self-conscious propriety that was particularly evident in Miriam's bearing. They took Mr. Polly to the Stamton wreckery-ation ground—that at least was what they called it — with its handsome custodian's cottage, its asphalt paths, its Jubilee drinking-fountain, its clumps of wallflower and daffodils, its charmingly artistic notice-boards with green borders and " art " lettering, and so to the new cemetery and a distant view of the Surrey hills, and round by the gas-works to the canal, to the factory that presently disgorged a surprised and radiant Annie.

" 'El-*lo* ! " said Annie.

It is very pleasant to every properly constituted mind to be a centre of amiable interest for one's fellow creatures ; and when one is a young man conscious of becoming mourning and a certain wit, and the fellow creatures are three young and ardent and sufficiently expressive young women who dispute for the honour of walking by one's side, one may be excused a secret exaltation. They did dispute.

" I'm going to 'ave 'im now," said Annie. " You two've been 'aving 'im all the safternoon. Besides, I've got something to say to 'im."

She had something to say to him. It came presently.

" I say," she said abruptly. " I *did* get them rings out of a prize packet."

" What rings ? " asked Mr. Polly.

" What you saw at your poor father's funeral. You made out they meant something. They didn't—straight."

" Then some people have been very remiss about their chances," said Mr. Polly, understanding.

" They haven't had any chances," said Annie. " I don't believe in making oneself too free with people."

" Nor me," said Mr. Polly.

" I may be a bit larky and cheerful in my manner," Annie admitted. " But it don't *mean* anything. I ain't that sort."

" Right-o," said Mr. Polly.

§ 4

It was past ten when Mr. Polly found himself riding back towards Easewood in a broad moonlight, and with a little Japanese lantern dangling from his handle-bar, making a fiery circle of pinkish light on and roundabout his front wheel. He was mightily pleased with himself and the day. There had been four-ale to drink at supper mixed with ginger beer, very free and jolly in a jug. No shadow fell upon the agreeable excitement of his mind until he faced the anxious and reproachful face of Johnson, who had been sitting up for him, smoking and trying to read the odd volume of " Purchas his

Pilgrimes "—about the monk who went into Sarmatia and saw those limitless Tartar carts that carried tents.

" Not had an accident, Elfrid ? " said Johnson.

The weakness of Mr. Polly's character came out in his reply.

" Not much," he said. " Pedal got a bit loose in Stamton, O' Man. Couldn't ride it ; so I looked up the cousins while I waited."

" Not the Larkins lot ? "

" Yes."

Johnson yawned hugely, and asked for and was given friendly particulars.

" Well," he said, " better get to bed. I been reading that book of yours ; rum stuff. Can't make it out quite. Quite out of date, I should say, if you asked me."

" That's all right, O' Man," said Mr. Polly.

" Not a bit of use for anything that I can see."

" Not a bit."

" See any shops in Stamton ? "

" Nothing to speak of," said Mr. Polly. " Goo' night, O' Man."

Before and after this brief conversation his mind ran on his cousins very warmly and prettily in the vein of high spring. Mr. Polly had been drinking at the poisoned fountains of English literature, fountains so unsuited to the needs of a decent clerk or shopman, fountains charged with the dangerous suggestion that it becomes a man of gaiety and spirit to make love gallantly and rather carelessly. It seemed to him that evening to be handsome and humorous and practicable to make love to all his cousins. It wasn't that he liked any of them particularly, but he liked something about them. He liked their youth and femininity, their resolute high spirits, and their interest in him.

They laughed at nothing and knew nothing, and Minnie had lost a tooth, and Annie screamed and shouted ; but they were interesting, intensely interesting.

And Miriam wasn't so bad as the others. He had kissed them all, and had been kissed in addition several times by Minnie—" oscoolatory exercises."

He buried his nose in his pillow and went to sleep—to dream of anything rather than getting on in the world, as a sensible young man in his position ought to have done.

§ 5

And now Mr. Polly began to lead a double life. With the Johnsons he professed to be inclined, but not so conclusively inclined as to be inconvenient, to get a shop for himself— to be, to use the phrase he preferred, " looking for an opening." He would ride off in the afternoon upon that research, remarking that he was going to " cast a strategetical eye " on Chertsey or Weybridge. But if not all roads, still a great majority of them led by however devious ways to Stamton, and to laughter and increasing familiarity. Relations developed with Annie and Minnie and Miriam. Their various characters were increasingly interesting. The laughter became perceptibly less abundant, something of the fizz had gone from the first opening, still these visits remained wonderfully friendly and upholding. Then back he would come to grave but evasive discussions with Johnson.

Johnson was really anxious to get Mr. Polly " into something." His was a reserved, honest character, and he would really have preferred to see his lodger doing things for himself than receive his money for housekeeping. He hated waste, anybody's waste, much more than he desired profit. But Mrs. Johnson was all for Mr. Polly's loitering. She seemed much the more human and likeable of the two to Mr. Polly.

He tried at times to work up enthusiasm for the various avenues to well-being his discussion with Johnson opened. But they remained disheartening prospects. He imagined himself wonderfully smartened up, acquiring style and value in a London shop ; but the picture was stiff and unconvincing. He tried to rouse himself to enthusiasm by the idea of his property increasing by leaps and bounds, by twenty pounds a year or so, let us say, each year, in a well-placed little shop, the corner shop Johnson favoured. There was a certain picturesque interest in imagining cutthroat economies, but his heart told him there would be little in practising them.

And then it happened to Mr. Polly that real Romance came out of dreamland into his life, intoxicated and gladdened him with sweetly beautiful suggestions—and left him. She came and left him as that dear lady leaves so many of us, alas ! not sparing him one jot or one tittle of the hollowness of her retreating aspect.

It was all the more to Mr. Polly's taste that the thing should happen as things happen in books.

In a resolute attempt not to get to Stamton that day, he had turned due southward from Easewood towards a country where the abundance of bracken jungles, lady's smock, stitchwort, bluebells, and grassy stretches by the wayside under shady trees does much to compensate the lighter type of mind for the absence of promising " openings." He turned aside from the road, wheeled his machine along a faintly marked attractive trail through bracken until he came to a heap of logs against a high old stone wall with a damaged coping and wallflower plants already gone to seed. He sat down, balanced the straw hat on a convenient lump of wood, lit a cigarette, and abandoned himself to agreeable musings and the friendly observation of a cheerful little brown-and-gray bird his stillness presently encouraged to approach him.

" This is All Right," said Mr. Polly softly to the little brown-and-gray bird. " Business—later."

He reflected that he might go on in this way for four or five years, and then be scarcely worse off than he had been in his father's lifetime.

" Vile Business," said Mr. Polly.

Then Romance appeared. Or to be exact, Romance became audible.

Romance began as a series of small but increasingly vigorous movements on the other side of the wall, then a voice murmuring, then as a falling of little fragments on the other side and as ten pink finger-tips, scarcely apprehended before Romance became startlingly and emphatically a leg, remained for a time a fine, slender, actively struggling limb, brown-stockinged, and wearing a brown toe-worn shoe, and then. . . . A handsome, red-haired girl wearing a short dress of blue linen was sitting astride the wall, panting, considerably disarranged by her climbing, and as yet unaware of Mr. Polly. . . .

His fine instincts made him turn his head away and assume an attitude of negligent contemplation, with his ears and mind alive to every sound behind him.

" Goodness ! " said a voice, with a sharp note of surprise.

Mr. Polly was on his feet in an instant. " Dear me ! Can I be of any assistance ? " he said, with deferential gallantry.

" I don't know," said the young lady, and regarded him calmly with clear blue eyes. " I didn't know there was any one here," she added.

" Sorry," said Mr. Polly, " if I am intrudacious. I didn't know you didn't want me to be here."

She reflected for a moment on the word.

" It isn't that," she said, surveying him. " I oughtn't to get over the wall," she explained. " It's out of bounds ; at least in term time. But this being holidays—— "

Her manner placed the matter before him.

" Holidays is different," said Mr. Polly.

" I don't want to actually *break* the rules," she said.

" Leave them behind you," said Mr. Polly, with a catch of the breath, " where they are safe." And marvelling at his own wit and daring, and indeed trembling within himself, he held out a hand for her.

She brought another brown leg from the unknown, and arranged her skirt with a dexterity altogether feminine.

" I think I'll stay on the wall," she decided. " So long as some of me's in bounds—— "

She continued to regard him with an irresistible smile of satisfaction. Mr. Polly smiled in return.

" You bicycle ? " she said.

Mr. Polly admitted the fact, and she said she did too.

" All my people are in India," she explained. " It's beastly rot—I mean it's frightfully dull being left here alone."

" All *my* people," said Mr. Polly, " are in heaven ! "

" I say ! "

" Fact," said Mr. Polly. " Got nobody."

" And that's why—" She checked her artless comment on his mourning. " I say," she said in a sympathetic voice, " I *am* sorry. I really am. Was it a fire, or a ship—or something ? "

Her sympathy was very delightful. He shook his head. " The ordinary tables of mortality," he said. " First one, and then another."

Behind his outward melancholy, delight was dancing wildly.

" Are *you* lonely ? " asked the girl.

Mr. Polly nodded.

" I was just sitting there in melancholic rectrospectatiousness," he said, indicating the logs ; and again a swift thoughtfulness swept across her face.

" There's no harm in our talking," she reflected.

" It's a kindness. Won't you get down ? "

She reflected, and surveyed the turf below and the scene around, and him.

" I'll stay on the wall," she said, " if only for bounds' sake."

She certainly looked quite adorable on the wall. She had a fine neck and pointed chin that was particularly admirable from below, and pretty eyes and fine eyebrows are never so pretty as when they look down upon one. But no calculation of that sort, thank Heaven, was going on beneath her ruddy shock of hair.

§ 6

" Let's talk," she said, and for a time they were both tongue-tied.

Mr. Polly's literary proclivities had taught him that under such circumstances a strain of gallantry was demanded. And something in his blood repeated that lesson.

" You make me feel like one of those old knights," he said, " who rode about the country looking for dragons and beautiful maidens and chivalresque adventures."

" Oh ! " she said. " Why ? "

" Beautiful maiden," he said.

She flushed under her freckles with the quick bright flush those pretty red-haired people have. " Nonsense " she said.

" You are. I'm not the first to tell you that. A beautiful maiden imprisoned in an enchanted school."

" *You* wouldn't think it enchanted."

" And here am I—clad in steel. Well, not exactly, but my fiery war-horse is, anyhow. Ready to absquatulate all the dragons, and rescue you."

She laughed, a jolly laugh, that showed delightfully gleaming teeth. " I wish you could *see* the dragons," she said, with great enjoyment. Mr. Polly felt they were a sun's distance from the world of every day.

" Fly with me ! " he dared.

She stared for a moment, and then went off into peals of laughter. " You *are* funny ! " she said. " Why, I haven't known you five minutes."

" One doesn't—in this medevial world. My mind is made up, anyhow."

He was proud and pleased with his joke, and quick to change his key neatly. " I wish one could," he said.

" I wonder if people ever did."

" If there were people like you."

" We don't even know each other's names," she remarked, with a descent to matters of fact.

" Yours is the prettiest name in the world."

" How do you know ? "

" It must be—anyhow."

" It *is* rather pretty, you know. It's Christabel."

" What did I tell you ? "

" And yours ? "

" Poorer than I deserve. It's Alfred."

" *I* can't call you Alfred."

" Well, Polly."

" It's a girl's name ! "

For a moment he went out of tune. " I wish it was," he said, and could have bitten out his tongue at the Larkins sound of it.

" I shan't forget it," she remarked consolingly.

" I say," she said, in the pause that followed, " why are you riding about the country on a bicycle ? "

" I'm doing it because I like it."

She sought to estimate his social status on her limited basis of experience. He stood leaning with one hand against the wall, looking up at her and tingling with daring thoughts. He was a littleish man, you must remember, but neither mean-looking nor unhandsome in those days, sunburnt by his holiday and now warmly flushed. He had an inspiration to simple speech that no practised trifler with love could have bettered. " There *is* love at first sight," he said, and said it sincerely.

She stared at him with eyes round and big with excitement.

" I think," she said slowly, and without any signs of fear or retreat, " I ought to get back over the wall."

" It needn't matter to you," he said ; " I'm just a nobody. But I know you are the best and most beautiful thing I've ever spoken to." His breath caught against something. " No harm in telling you that," he said.

" I should have to go back if I thought you were serious," she said after a pause, and they both smiled together.

After that they talked in a fragmentary way for some

time. The blue eyes surveyed Mr. Polly with kindly curiosity
from under a broad, finely modelled brow, much as an exceptionally intelligent cat might survey a new sort of dog. She
meant to find out all about him. She asked questions that
riddled the honest knight in armour below, and probed ever
nearer to the hateful secret of the shop and his normal servi-
tude. And when he made a flourish and mispronounced a
word, a thoughtful shade passed like the shadow of a cloud
across her face.

"Boom !" came the sound of a gong.

"Lordy !" cried the girl, and flashed a pair of brown legs
at him and was gone.

Then her pink finger-tips reappeared, and the top of her red
hair. "Knight," she cried from the other side of the wall.
"Knight there !"

"Lady !" he answered.

"Come again to-morrow."

"At your command. But——"

"Yes ?"

"Just one finger."

"What do you mean ?"

"To kiss."

The rustle of retreating footsteps and silence. . . .

But after he had waited next day for twenty minutes she
reappeared, a little out of breath with the effort to surmount
the wall, and head first this time. And it seemed to him she
was lighter and more daring and altogether prettier than the
dreams and enchanted memories that had filled the interval.

§ 7

From first to last their acquaintance lasted ten days, but
into that time Mr. Polly packed ten years of dreams.

"He don't seem," said Johnson, "to take a serious interest
in anything. That shop at the corner's bound to be snapped
up if he don't look out."

The girl and Mr. Polly did not meet on every one of those
ten days ; one was Sunday and she could not come, and on
the eighth the school reassembled and she made vague excuses.
All their meetings amounted to this, that she sat on the wall,
more or less in bounds as she expressed it, and let Mr. Polly
fall in love with her and try to express it below. She sat in a
state of irresponsible exaltation, watching him, and at intervals prodding a vivisecting point of encouragement into him,
with that strange passive cruelty which is natural and proper
in her sex and age.

And Mr. Polly fell in love, as though the world had given
way beneath him and he had dropped through into another,
into a world of luminous clouds and of a desolate, hopeless
wilderness of desiring and of wild valleys of unreasonable
ecstasy, a world whose infinite miseries were finer and in some

inexplicable way sweeter than the purest gold of the daily life, whose joys—they were indeed but the merest remote glimpses of joy—were brighter than a dying martyr's vision of heaven. Her smiling face looked down upon him out of the sky, her careless pose was the living body of life. It was senseless, it was utterly foolish, but all that was best and richest in Mr. Polly's nature broke like a wave and foamed up at the girl's feet, and died, and never touched her. And she sat on the wall and marvelled at him, and was amused, and once, suddenly moved and wrung by his pleading, she bent down rather shamefacedly and gave him a freckled, tennis-blistered little paw to kiss. And she looked into his eyes and suddenly felt a perplexity, a curious swimming of the mind that made her recoil and stiffen, and wonder afterwards and dream. . . .

And then with some instinct of self-protection she went and told her three best friends, great students of character all, of this remarkable phenomenon she had discovered on the other side of the wall.

" Look here," said Mr. Polly. " I'm wild for the love of you ! I can't keep up this gesticulatious game any more. I'm not a Knight. Treat me as a human man. You may sit up there smiling, but I'd die in torments to have you mine for an hour. I'm nobody and nothing. But look here ! Will you wait for me five years ? You're just a girl yet, and it wouldn't be hard."

" Shut up ! " said Christabel, in an aside he did not hear, and something he did not see touched her hand.

" I've always been just dilletentytating about till now, but I could work. I've just woke up. Wait till I've got a chance with the money I've got."

" But you haven't got much money ! "

" I've got enough to take a chance with, some sort of chance. I'd find a chance. I'll do that, anyhow. I'll go away. I mean what I say. I'll stop trifling and shirking. If I don't come back it won't matter. If I do——"

Her expression had become uneasy. Suddenly she bent down towards him.

" Don't ! " she said in an undertone.

" Don't—what ? "

" Don't go on like this ! You're different. Go on being the knight who wants to kiss my hand as his—what did you call it ? " The ghost of a smile curved her face. " Gurdrum ! "

" But——"

Then through a pause they both stared at each other, listening.

A muffled tumult on the other side of the wall asserted itself.

" Shut *up*, Rosie ! " said a voice.

" I tell you I will see ! I can't half hear. Give me a leg up ! "

" You Idiot ! He'll see you. You're spoiling everything."

The bottom dropped out of Mr. Polly's world. He felt as people must feel who are going to faint.

" You've got some one——" he said, aghast.

She found life inexpressible to Mr. Polly. She addressed some unseen hearers. " You filthy little Beasts ! " she cried, with a sharp note of agony in her voice, and swung herself back over the wall and vanished. There was a squeal of pain and fear, and a swift, fierce altercation.

For a couple of seconds he stood agape.

Then a wild resolve to confirm his worst sense of what was on the other side of the wall made him seize a log, put it against the stones, clutch the parapet with insecure fingers, and lug himself to a momentary balance on the wall.

Romance and his goddess had vanished.

A red-haired girl with a pigtail was wringing the wrist of a schoolfellow, who shrieked with pain and cried, " Mercy ! mercy ! O-o-o ! Christabel ! "

" You Idiot ! " cried Christabel. " You giggling Idiot ! "

Two other young ladies made off through the beech-trees from this outburst of savagery.

Then the grip of Mr. Polly's fingers gave, and he hit his chin against the stones and slipped clumsily to the ground again, scraping his cheek against the wall, and hurting his shin against the log by which he had reached the top. Just for a moment he crouched against the wall.

He swore, staggered to the pile of logs, and sat down.

He remained very still for some time, with his lips pressed together.

" Fool ! " he said at last. " You Blithering Fool ! " and began to rub his shin as though he had just discovered his bruises.

Afterwards he found his face was wet with blood—which was none the less red stuff from the heart because it came from slight abrasions.

CHAPTER SIX

MIRIAM

§ 1

IT is an illogical consequence of one human being's ill-treatment that we should fly immediately to another, but that is the way with us. It seemed to Mr. Polly that only a human touch could assuage the smart of his humiliation. Moreover, it had, for some undefined reason, to be a feminine touch, and the number of women in his world was limited.

He thought of the Larkins family—the Larkins whom he had not been near now for ten long days. Healing people they

seemed to him now—healing, simple people. They had good
hearts, and he had neglected them for a mirage. If he rode
over to them he would be able to talk bosh, and laugh, and
forget the whirl of memories and thoughts that was spinning
round and round so unendurably in his brain.

"Law!" said Mrs. Larkins, "come in! You're quite a
stranger, Elfrid!"

"Been seeing to business," said the unveracious Polly.

"None of 'em ain't at 'ome, but Miriam's just out to do a
bit of shopping. Won't let me shop, she won't, because I'm
so keerless. She's a wonderful manager, that girl. Minnie's
got some work at the carpet place. 'Ope it won't make 'er ill
again. She's the loving delikit sort, is Minnie. . . . Come
into the front parlour. It's a bit untidy, but you got to take
us as you find us. Wot you been doing to your face?"

"Bit of a scraze with the bicycle," said Mr. Polly.

"'Ow?"

"Trying to pass a carriage on the wrong side, and he drew
up and ran me against a wall."

Mrs. Larkins scrutinised it. "You ought to 'ave some one
look after your scrazes," she said. "That's all red and rough.
It ought to be cold-creamed. Bring your bicycle into the
passage and come in."

She "straightened up a bit." That is to say, she increased
the dislocation of a number of scattered articles, put a work-
basket on the top of several books, swept two or three dogs'-
eared numbers of *The Lady's Own Novelist* from the table into
the broken armchair, and proceeded to sketch together the
tea-things with various such interpolations as : "Law, if I
ain't forgot the butter!" All the while she talked of Annie's
good spirits and cleverness with her millinery, and of Minnie's
affection, and Miriam's relative love of order and management.
Mr. Polly stood by the window uneasily, and thought how
good and sincere was the Larkins' tone. It was well to be
back again.

"You're a long time finding that shop of yours," said Mrs.
Larkins.

"Don't do to be too precipitous," said Mr. Polly.

"No," said Mrs. Larkins, "once you got it you got it.
Like choosing a 'usband. You better see you got it good. I
kept Larkins 'esitating two years, I did, until I felt sure of
him. A 'ansom man 'e was, as you can see by the looks of the
girls, but 'ansom is as 'ansom does. You'd like a bit of jam
to your tea, I expect? I 'ope they'll keep *their* men waiting
when the time comes. I tell them if they think of marrying,
it only shows they don't know when they're well off. Here's
Miriam!"

Miriam entered with several parcels in a net, and a peevish
expression. "Mother," she said, "you might 'ave prevented
my going out with the net with the broken handle. I've been

cutting my fingers with the string all the way 'ome." Then she discovered Mr. Polly and her face brightened.

" 'Ello, Elfrid ! " she said. " Where you been all this time ? "

" Looking round," said Mr. Polly.

" Found a shop ? "

" One or two likely ones. But it takes time."

" You've got the wrong cups, Mother."

She went into the kitchen, disposed of her purchases, and returned with the right cups. " What you done to your face, Elfrid ? " she asked, and came and scrutinised his scratches. " All rough it is."

He repeated his story of the accident, and she was sympathetic in a pleasant, homely way.

" You *are* quiet to-day," she said, as they sat down to tea.

" Meditatious," said Mr. Polly.

Quite by accident he touched her hand on the table, and she answered his touch.

" Why not ? " thought Mr. Polly, and looking up, caught Mrs. Larkins' eye and flushed guiltily. But Mrs. Larkins, with unusual restraint, said nothing. She made a grimace, enigmatical, but in its essence friendly.

Presently Minnie came in with some vague grievance against the manager of the carpet-making place about his method of estimating piece-work. Her account was redundant, defective, and highly technical, but redeemed by a certain earnestness. " I'm never within sixpence of what I reckon to be," she said. " It's a bit too 'ot." Then Mr. Polly, feeling that he was being conspicuously dull, launched into a description of the shop he was looking for and the shops he had seen. His mind warmed up as he talked.

" Found your tongue again," said Mrs. Larkins.

He had. He began to embroider the subject and work upon it. For the first time it assumed picturesque and desirable qualities in his mind. It stimulated him to see how readily and willingly they accepted his sketches. Bright ideas appeared in his mind from nowhere. He was suddenly enthusiastic.

" When I get this shop of mine, I shall have a cat. Must make a home for a cat, you know."

" What, to catch the mice ? " said Mrs. Larkins.

" No—sleep in the window. A venerable signor of a cat. Tabby. Cat's no good if it isn't tabby. Cat I'm going to have, and a canary ! Didn't think of that before, but a cat and a canary seem to go, you know. Summer weather I shall sit at breakfast in the little room behind the shop, sun streaming in the window to rights, cat on a chair, canary singing, and— Mrs. Polly. . . . "

" 'Ello ! " said Mrs. Larkins.

" Mrs. Polly frying an extra bit of bacon. Bacon singing, cat singing, canary singing, kettle singing. Mrs. Polly——"

" But who's Mrs. Polly going to be ? " said Mrs. Larkins.

" Figment of imagination, M'am," said Mr. Polly.   " Put in to fill up picture. No face to figure—as yet. Still, that's how it will be, I can assure you. I think I must have a bit of garden. Johnson's the man for a garden, of course," he said, going off at a tangent, " but I don't mean a fierce sort of garden.   Earnest industry.   Anxious moments.   Fervous digging. Shan't go in for that sort of garden, M'am. No ! Too much Backache for me. My garden will be just a patch of 'sturtiums and sweetpea. Red-bricked yard, clothes-line. Trellis put up in odd time.   Humorous wind-vane.   Creeper up the back of the house."

" Virginia creeper ? " asked Miriam.

" Canary creeper," said Mr. Polly.

" You *will* 'ave it nice," said Miriam desirously.

" Rather," said Mr. Polly.   " Ting-a-ling-a-ling. Shop ! "

He straightened himself up, and they all laughed.

" Smart little shop," he said.   " Counter. Desk. All complete. Umbrella-stand. Carpet on the floor. Cat asleep on the counter. Ties and hose on a rail over the counter. All right."

" I wonder you don't set about it right off," said Miriam.

" Mean to get it exactly right, M'am," said Mr. Polly.

" Have to have a Tom-cat," said Mr. Polly, and paused for an expectant moment.   " Wouldn't do to open shop one morning, you know, and find the window full of kittens. Can't sell kittens. . . ."

When tea was over he was left alone with Minnie for a few minutes, and an odd intimation of an incident occurred that left Mr. Polly rather scared and shaken. A silence fell between them—an uneasy silence. He sat with his elbows on the table looking at her.   All the way from Easewood to Stamton his erratic imagination had been running upon neat ways of proposing marriage. I don't know why it should have done, but it had. It was a kind of secret exercise that had not had any definite aim at the time, but which now recurred to him with extraordinary force. He couldn't think of anything in the world that wasn't the gambit to a proposal. It was almost irresistibly fascinating to think how immensely a few words from him would excite and revolutionise Minnie. She was sitting at the table with a work-basket among the tea-things, mending a glove in order to avoid her share of clearing away.

" I like cats," said Minnie, after a thoughtful pause. " I'm always saying to Mother, I wish we 'ad a cat. But we couldn't 'ave a cat 'ere—not with no yard."

" Never had a cat myself," said Mr. Polly. " No ! "

" I'm fond of them," said Minnie.

" I like the look of them," said Mr. Polly. " Can't exactly call myself fond."

" I expect I shall get one some day. When about you get your shop."

" I shall have my shop all right before long," said Mr. Polly.
" Trust me. Canary-bird and all."

She shook her head. " I shall get a cat first," she said.
" You never mean anything you say."

" Might get 'em together," said Mr. Polly, with his sense
of a neat thing outrunning his discretion.

" Why ! 'ow do you mean ? " said Minnie, suddenly alert.

" Shop and cat thrown in," said Mr. Polly in spite of himself, and his head swam, and he broke out into a cold sweat
as he said it.

He found her eyes fixed on him with an eager expression.
" Mean to say— ? " she began, as if for verification. He sprang
to his feet, and turned to the window. " Little dog ! " he said,
and moved doorward hastily. " Eating my bicycle tyre, I
believe," he explained. And so escaped.

He saw his bicycle in the hall and cut it dead.

He heard Mrs. Larkins in the passage behind him as he
opened the front door.

He turned to her. " Thought my bicycle was on fire," he
he said. " Outside. Funny fancy ! All right reely. Little dog
outside. . . . Miriam ready ? "

" What for ? "

" To go and meet Annie."

Mrs. Larkins stared at him. " You're stopping for a bit of
supper ! "

" If I may," said Mr. Polly.

" You're a rum un," said Mrs. Larkins, and called :
" Miriam ! "

Minnie appeared at the door of the room looking infinitely
perplexed. " There ain't a little dog anywhere, Elfrid," she
said.

Mr. Polly passed his hand over his brow. " I had a most
curious sensation. Felt exactly as though something was up
somewhere. That's why I said Little Dog. All right now."

He bent down and pinched his bicycle tyre.

" You was saying something about a cat, Elfrid," said
Minnie.

" Give you one," he answered, without looking up. " The
very day my shop is opened."

He straightened himself up and smiled reassuringly.

" Trust me," he said.

§ 2

When, after imperceptible manœuvres by Mrs. Larkins, he
found himself starting circuitously through the inevitable
recreation-ground with Miriam to meet Annie, he found himself quite unable to avoid the topic of the shop that had now
taken such a grip upon him. A sense of danger only increased
the attraction. Minnie's persistent disposition to accompany
them had been crushed by a novel and violent and pungently

expressed desire on the part of Mrs. Larkins to see her do something in the house sometimes. . . .

" You really think you'll open a shop ? " said Miriam.

" I hate cribs," said Mr. Polly, adopting a moderate tone. " In a shop there's this drawback and that, but one *is* one's own Master."

" That wasn't all talk ? "

" Not a bit of it.

" After all," he went on, " a little shop needn't be so bad."

" It's a 'ome," said Miriam.

" It's a home."

Pause.

" There's no need to keep accounts and that sort of thing if there's no assistant. I dare say I could run a shop all right if I wasn't interfered with."

" I should like to see you in your shop," said Miriam. " I expect you'd keep everything tremendously neat."

The conversation flagged.

" Let's sit down on one of those seats over there past that notice-board," said Miriam, " where we can see those blue flowers."

They did as she suggested, and sat down in a corner where a triangular bed of stock and delphinium brightened the asphalted traceries of the recreation-ground.

" I wonder what they call those flowers," she said. " I always like them. They're handsome."

" Delphicums and larkspurs," said Mr. Polly. " They used to be in the park at Port Burdock.

" Floriferous corner," he added approvingly.

He put an arm over the back of the seat, and assumed a more comfortable attitude. He glanced at Miriam, who was sitting in a lax, thoughtful pose, with her eyes on the flowers. She was wearing her old dress. She had not had time to change, and the blue tones of her old dress brought out a certain warmth in her skin, and her pose exaggerated whatever was feminine in her rather lean and insufficient body, and rounded her flat chest delusively. A little line of light lay across her profile. The afternoon was full of transfiguring sunshine, children were playing noisily in the adjacent sand-pit, some Judas-trees were abloom in the villa gardens that bordered the recreation-ground, and all the place was bright with touches of young summer colour. It all merged with the effect of Miriam in Mr. Polly's mind.

Her thought found speech. " One did ought to be happy in a shop," she said, with a note of unusual softness in her voice.

It seemed to him that she was right. One did ought to be happy in a shop. Folly not to banish dreams that made one ache of townless woods and bracken tangles and red-haired linen-clad figures sitting in dappled sunshine upon grey and crumbling walls and looking queenly down on one with clear blue eyes. Cruel and foolish dreams they were, that ended in one's being laughed at and made a mock of. There was no mockery here.

" A shop's such a respectable thing to be," said Miriam thoughtfully.

" *I* could be happy in a shop," he said.

His sense of effect had made him pause.

" If I had the right company," he added.

She became very still.

Mr. Polly swerved a little from the conversational ice-run upon which he had embarked.

" I'm not such a blooming Geezer," he said, " as not to be able to sell goods a bit. One has to be nosey over one's buying, of course. But I shall do all right."

He stopped, and felt falling, falling through the aching silence that followed.

" If you get the right company," said Miriam.

" I shall get that all right."

" You don't mean you've got some one—— ? "

He found himself plunging.

" I've got some one in my eye this minute," he said.

" Elfrid ! " she said, turning to him. " You don't mean—— "

Well, *did* he mean ? " I do ! " he said.

" Not reely ! " She clenched her hands to keep still.

He took the conclusive step.

" Well, you and me, Miriam, in a little shop, with a cat and a canary—" He tried too late to get back to a hypothetical note. " Just suppose it ! "

" You mean," said Miriam, " you're in love with me, Elfrid ? "

What possible answer can a man give to such a question but " Yes ! "

Regardless of the public park, the children in the sand-pit, and every one, she bent forward and seized his shoulder and kissed him on the lips. Something lit up in Mr. Polly at the touch. He put an arm about her and kissed her back, and felt an irrevocable act was sealed.

He had a curious feeling that it would be very satisfying to marry and have a wife—only somehow he wished it wasn't Miriam. Her lips were very pleasant to him, and the feel of her in his arm.

They recoiled a little from each other, and sat for a moment flushed and awkwardly silent. His mind was altogether incapable of controlling its confusions.

" I didn't dream," said Miriam, " you cared—Sometimes I thought it was Annie, sometimes Minnie—— "

"Always I liked you better than them," said Mr. Polly.

" I loved you, Elfrid," said Miriam, " since ever we met at your poor father's funeral. Leastways I *would* have done if

I had thought— You didn't seem to mean anything you said.

" I can't believe it ! " she added.

" Nor I," said Mr. Polly.

" You mean to marry me and start that little shop ? "

" Soon as ever I find it," said Mr. Polly.

" I had no more idea when I came out with you—— "

" Nor me."

" It's like a dream."

They said no more for a little while.

" I got to pinch myself to think it's real," said Miriam. ' What they'll do without me at 'ome I can't imagine. When I tell them—— "

For the life of him Mr. Polly could not tell whether he was fullest of tender anticipations or regretful panic.

" Mother's no good at managing—not a bit. Annie don't care for housework, and Minnie's got no 'ead for it. What they'll do without me I can't imagine."

" They'll have to do without you," said Mr. Polly, sticking to his guns.

A clock in the town began striking.

" Lor ! " said Miriam, " we shall miss Annie, sitting 'ere and love-making."

She rose and made as if to take Mr. Polly's arm. But Mr. Polly felt that their condition must be nakedly exposed to the ridicule of the world by such a linking, and evaded her movement.

Annie was already in sight before a flood of hesitation and terrors assailed Mr. Polly.

" Don't tell any one yet a bit," he said.

" Only Mother," said Miriam firmly.

§ 3

Figures are the most shocking things in the world. The pettiest little squiggles of black, looked at in the right light ; and yet consider the blow they can give you upon the heart. You return from a careless holiday abroad, and turn over the page of a newspaper, and against the name of the distant, vague-conceived railway, in mortgages upon which you have embarked the bulk of your capital, you see, instead of the familiar, persistent 95–6 (varying at most to 93 *ex div.*), this slightly richer arrangement of marks, $76\frac{1}{2}$–$78\frac{1}{2}$.

It is like the opening of a pit just under your feet.

So, too, Mr. Polly's happy sense of limitless resources was obliterated suddenly by a vision of this tracery :

" 298 "

instead of the

" 350 "

he had come to regard as the fixed symbol of his affluence.

It gave him a disagreeable feeling about the diaphragm, akin in a remote degree to the sensation he had when the perfidy of the red-haired schoolgirl became plain to him. It made his brow moist.

" Going down a Vorterex," he whispered.

By a characteristic feat of subtraction he decided that he must have spent sixty-two pounds.

" Funererial baked meats," he said, recalling possible items.

The happy dream in which he had been living, of long, warm days, of open roads, of limitless, unchecked hours, of infinite time to look about him, vanished like a thing enchanted. He was suddenly back in the hard old economic world, that exacts work, that limits range, that discourages phrasing and dispels laughter. He saw Wood Street and its fearful suspenses yawning beneath his feet.

And also he had promised to marry Miriam, and on the whole rather wanted to.

He was distraught at supper. Afterwards, when Mrs. Johnson had gone to bed with a slight headache, he opened a conversation with Johnson.

" It's about time, O' Man, I saw about doing something," he said. " Riding about and looking at shops all very debonairious, O' Man, but it's time I took one for keeps."

" What did I tell you ? " said Johnson.

" How do you think that corner shop of yours will figure out ? " Mr. Polly asked.

" You're really meaning it ? "

" If it's a practable proposition, O' Man. Assuming it's practable, what's your idea of the figures ? "

Johnson went to the chiffonier, got out a letter, and tore off the back sheet. " Let's figure it out," he said, with solemn satisfaction. " Let's see the lowest you could do it on."

He squared himself to the task, and Mr. Polly sat beside him like a pupil, watching the evolution of the grey, distasteful figures that were to dispose of his little hoard.

" What running expenses have we got to provide for ? " said Johnson, wetting his pencil. " Let's have them first. Rent ? . . . "

At the end of an hour of hideous speculations, Johnson decided, " It's close ; but you'll have a chance."

" M'm," said Mr. Polly. " What more does a brave man want ? "

" One thing you can do quite easily. I've asked about it."

" What's that, O' Man ? " said Mr. Polly.

" Take the shop without the house above it."

" I suppose I might put my head in to mind it," said Mr. Polly, " and get a job with my body."

" Not exactly that. But I thought you'd save a lot if you stayed on here—being all alone, as you are."

" Never thought of that, O' Man," said Mr. Polly, and reflected silently upon the needlessness of Miriam.

" We were talking of eighty pounds for stock," said Johnson. " Of course seventy-five is five pounds less, isn't it ? Not much else we can cut."

" No," said Mr. Polly.

" It's very interesting, all this," said Johnson, folding up the half-sheet of paper and unfolding it. " I wish sometimes I had a business of my own instead of a fixed salary. You'll have to keep books, of course."

" One wants to know where one is."

" I should do it all by double entry," said Johnson. " A little troublesome at first, but far the best in the end."

" Lemme see that paper," said Mr. Polly, and took it with the feeling of a man who takes a nauseating medicine, and scrutinised his cousin's neat figures with listless eyes.

" Well," said Johnson, rising and stretching, " Bed ! Better sleep on it, O' Man."

" Right-o ! " said Mr. Polly, without moving ; but indeed he could as well have slept upon a bed of thorns.

He had a dreadful night. It was like the end of the annual holiday, only infinitely worse. It was like a newly arrived prisoner's backward glance at the trees and heather through the prison gates. He had to go back to harness, and he was as fitted to go in harness as the ordinary domestic cat. All night Fate, with the quiet complacency, and indeed at times the very face and gestures, of Johnson, guided him towards that undesired establishment at the corner near the station. " O Lord ! " he cried, " I'd rather go back to cribs. I *should* keep my money, anyhow." Fate never winced.

" Run away to sea," whispered Mr. Polly ; but he knew he wasn't man enough. " Cut my blooming throat."

Some braver strain urged him to think of Miriam, and for a little while he lay still. . . .

" Well, O' Man ? " said Johnson, when Mr. Polly came down to breakfast, and Mrs. Johnson looked up brightly. Mr. Polly had never felt breakfast so unattractive before.

" Just a day or so more, O' Man, to turn it over in my mind," he said.

" You'll get the place snapped up," said Johnson.

There were times in those last few days of coyness with his destiny when his engagement seemed the most negligible of circumstances ; and times—and these happened for the most part at nights, after Mrs. Johnson had indulged everybody in a Welsh rarebit—when it assumed so sinister and portentous an appearance as to make him think of suicide. And there were times too when he very distinctly desired to be married, now that the idea had got into his head, at any cost. Also he tried to recall all the circumstances of his proposal time after time, and never quite succeeded in recalling what had brought the thing off. He went over to Stamton with a becoming frequency, and kissed all his cousins, and Miriam especially, a great deal, and found it very stirring and refreshing. They all appeared to know; and Minnie was tearful but resigned. Mrs. Larkins met him, and indeed enveloped him, with unwonted warmth, and there was a big pot of household jam for tea. And he could not make up his mind to sign his name to anything about the shop, though it crawled nearer and nearer to him, though the project had materialised now to the extent of a draft agreement, with the place for his signature indicated in pencil.

One morning, just after Mr. Johnson had gone to the station, Mr. Polly wheeled his bicycle out into the road, went up to his bedroom, packed his long white night-dress, a comb, and a tooth-brush in a manner that was as offhand as he could make it, informed Mrs. Johnson, who was manifestly curious, that he was " off for a day or two to clear his head," and fled forthright into the road, and mounting, turned his wheel towards the tropics and the equator and the south coast of England, and indeed more particularly to where the little village of Fishbourne slumbers and sleeps.

When he returned, four days later, he astonished Johnson beyond measure by remarking, so soon as the shop project was reopened, " I've took a little contraption at Fishbourne, O' Man, that I fancy suits me better."

He paused, and then added in a manner if possible even more offhand, " Oh, and I'm going to have a bit of a nuptial over at Stamton—with one of the Larkins cousins."

" Nuptial ! " said Johnson.

" Wedding-bells, O' Man. Benedictine collapse."

On the whole Johnson showed great self-control. " It's your own affair, O' Man," he said, when things had been more clearly explained ; " and I hope you won't feel sorry when it's too late."

But Mrs. Johnson was first of all angrily silent, and then reproachful. " I don't see what we've done to be made fools of like this," she said. " After all the trouble we've 'ad to make you comfortable and see after you—out late, and sitting up, and everything ; and then you go off as sly as sly, without a word, an' get a shop behind our backs, as though you thought we meant to steal your money. I 'aven't patience with such deceitfulness, and I didn't think it of you, Elfrid. And now the letting season's 'arf gone by, and what I shall do with that room of yours I've no idea. Frank is frank, and fair play fair play ; so *I* was told, any'ow, when I was a girl. Just as long as it suits you to stay 'ere you stay 'ere, and then it's off and no thank you whether we like it or not. Johnson's too easy with you. 'E sits there and doesn't say a word ; and night after night 'e's been adding up and subtracting, and multiplying and dividing, and suggesting

and thinkin' for you, instead of seeing to his own affairs."
She paused for breath.

"Unfortunate amoor," said Mr. Polly apologetically and
indistinctly. " Didn't expect it myself."

§ 4

Mr. Polly's marriage followed with a certain inevitableness.
He tried to assure himself that he was acting upon his
own forceful initiative, but at the back of his mind was the
completest realisation of his powerlessness to resist the gigantic
social forces he had set in motion. He had got to marry under
the will of society, even as in times past it had been appointed
for other sunny souls under the will of society that they
should be led out by serious and unavoidable fellow creatures
and ceremoniously drowned or burnt or hung. He would
have preferred infinitely a more observant and less conspicuous
rôle, but the choice was no longer open to him. He did his
best to play his part, and he procured some particularly neat
check trousers to do it in. The rest of his costume, except
for some bright yellow gloves, a grey-and-blue mixture tie,
and that the broad crape band was changed for a livelier
piece of silk, were the things he had worn at the funeral of his
father. So nearly akin are human joy and sorrow.

The Larkins sisters had done wonders with grey sateen.
The idea of orange-blossom and white veils had been abandoned reluctantly on account of the expense of the cabs. A
novelette in which the heroine had stood at the altar in " a
modest going-away dress " had materially assisted this decision.
Miriam was frankly tearful, and so, indeed, was Annie, but
with laughter as well to carry it off. Mr. Polly heard Annie
say something vague about never getting a chance because
of Miriam always sticking about at home like a cat at a mouse-
hole, that became, as people say, food for thought. Mrs.
Larkins was from the first flushed, garrulous, and wet and
smeared by copious weeping; an incredibly soaked and
crumpled and used-up pocket-handkerchief never left the
clutch of her plump red hand. " Goo' girls all of them," she
kept on saying in a tremulous voice; " such Goo'-Goo'-Goo'
girls ! " She wetted Mr. Polly dreadfully when she kissed him.
Her emotion affected the buttons down the back of her bodice,
and almost the last filial duty Miriam did before entering
on her new life was to close that gaping orifice for the eleventh
time. Her bonnet was small and ill-balanced, black adorned
with red roses, and first it got over her right eye until Annie
told her of it, and then she pushed it over her left eye and
looked ferocious for a space, and after that baptismal kissing
of Mr. Polly the delicate millinery took fright and climbed
right up to the back part of her head and hung on there by a
pin, and flapped piteously at all the larger waves of emotion
that filled the gathering. Mr. Polly became more and more

aware of that bonnet as time went on, until he felt for it like
a thing alive. Towards the end it had yawning fits.

The company did not include Mrs. Johnson, but Johnson
came with a pervading surreptitiousness and backed against
walls and watched Mr. Polly with doubt and speculation in
his large grey eye, and whistled noiselessly and doubtfully
on the edge of things. He was, so to speak, to be best man
sotto voce. A sprinkling of girls in gay hats from Miriam's
place of business appeared in church, great nudgers all of
them, but only two came on afterwards to the house. Mrs.
Punt brought her son with his ever-widening mind—it was
his first wedding ; and a Larkins uncle, a Mr. Voules, a licensed
victualler, very kindly drove over in a high-hung dog-cart
from Somershill with a plump, well-dressed wife, to give the
bride away. One or two total strangers drifted into the church
and sat down observantly in distant seats.

This sprinkling of people seemed only to enhance the cool
brown emptiness of the church, the rows and rows of empty
pews, disengaged Prayer-Books, and abandoned hassocks. It
had the effect of a preposterous misfit. Johnson consulted
with a thin-legged, short-skirted verger about the disposition
of the party. The officiating clergy appeared distantly in
the doorway of the vestry putting on his surplice, and relapsed
into a contemplative cheek-scratching that was manifestly
habitual. Before the bride arrived, Mr. Polly's sense of the
church found an outlet in whispered criticisms of ecclesiastical
architecture with Johnson. " Early Norman arches, eh ? "
he said, " or Perpendicular."

" Can't say," said Johnson.

" Telessated pavements all right."

" It's well laid anyhow."

" Can't say I admire the altar. Scrappy rather with those
flowers."

He coughed behind his hand and cleared his throat. At
the back of his mind he was speculating whether flight at this
eleventh hour would be criminal or merely reprehensible bad
taste. A murmur from the nudgers announced the arrival of
the bridal party.

The little procession from a remote door became one of the
enduring memories of Mr. Polly's life. The verger had bustled
to meet it and arrange it according to tradition and morality.
In spite of Mrs. Larkins' impassioned " Don't take her from
me yet ! " he made Miriam go first with Mr. Voules, the brides-
maids followed, and then himself, hopelessly unable to dis-
entangle himself from the whispering maternal anguish of
Mrs. Larkins. Mrs. Voules, a compact, rounded woman with
a square, expressionless face, imperturbable dignity, and a
dress of considerable fashion, completed the procession.

Mr. Polly's eyes fell first upon the bride ; the sight of her
filled him with a curious stir of emotion. Alarm, desire, affection,

respect—and a queer element of reluctant dislike, all played their part in that complex eddy. The grey dress made her a stranger to him, made her stiff and commonplace; she was not even the rather drooping form that had caught his facile sense of beauty when he had proposed to her in the recreation-ground. There was something, too, that did not please him in the angle of her hat; it was, indeed, an ill-conceived hat with large, aimless rosettes of pink and grey. Then his mind passed to Mrs. Larkins and the bonnet that was to gain such a hold upon him; it seemed to be flag-signalling as she advanced, and to the two eager, unrefined sisters he was acquiring.

A freak of fancy set him wondering where and when in the future a beautiful girl with red hair might march along some splendid aisle— Never mind! He became aware of Mr. Voules.

He became aware of Mr. Voules as a watchful, blue eye of intense forcefulness. It was the eye of a man who has got hold of a situation. He was a fat, short, red-faced man, clad in a tight-fitting tail-coat of black-and-white check, with a coquettish bow tie under the lowest of a number of crisp little red chins. He held the bride under his arm with an air of invincible championship, and his free arm flourished a grey top-hat of an equestrian type. Mr. Polly instantly learnt from that eye that Mr. Voules knew all about his longing for flight. Its azure-rimmed pupil glowed with disciplined resolution. It said : " I've come to give this girl away, and give her away I will. I'm here now, and things have to go on all right. So don't think of it any more "—and Mr. Polly didn't. A faint phantom of a certain " lill dog " that had hovered just beneath the threshold of consciousness vanished into black impossibility. Until the conclusive moment of the service was attained the eye of Mr. Voules watched Mr. Polly relentlessly, and then instantly he relieved guard, and blew his nose into a voluminous and richly patterned handkerchief, and sighed and looked round for the approval and sympathy of Mrs. Voules, and nodded to her brightly, like one who has always foretold a successful issue to things. Mr. Polly felt at last like a marionette that has dropped off its wire. But it was long before that release arrived.

He became aware of Miriam breathing close to him.

" Hallo ! " he said, and feeling that was clumsy and would meet the eye's disapproval : " Grey dress—suits you no end."

Miriam's eyes shone under her hat-brim.

" Not reely ! " she whispered.

" You're all right," he said, with the feeling of the eye's observation and criticism stiffening his lips. He cleared his throat.

The verger's hand pushed at him from behind. Some one was driving Miriam towards the altar-rail and the clergyman.

" We're in for it," said Mr. Polly to her sympathetically.
" Where ? Here ? Right-o."

He was interested for a moment or so in something indescribably habitual in the clergyman's pose. What a lot of weddings he must have seen ! Sick he must be of them !

" Don't let your attention wander," said the eye.

" Got the ring ?" whispered Johnson.

" Pawned it yesterday," answered Mr. Polly, with an attempt at lightness, and then had a dreadful moment under that pitiless scrutiny while he felt in the wrong waistcoat pocket. . . .

The officiating clergy sighed deeply, began, and married them wearily and without any hitch.

" D'bloved we gath'd gether sighto' Gard 'n face this con'gation join gather Man Wom Ho Mat'mony whichis on'bl state stooted by Gard in times mans in'cency. . . . "

Mr. Polly's thoughts wandered wide and far, and once again something like a cold hand touched his heart, and he saw a sweet face in sunshine under the shadow of trees.

Some one was nudging him. It was Johnson's finger diverting his eyes to the crucial place in the Prayer-Book to which they had come.

" Wiltou lover, cumfer, oner keeper sickness and health ? . . ."

" *Say, ' I will '.*"

Mr. Polly moistened his lips. " I will," he said hoarsely.

Miriam, nearly inaudible, answered some similar demand.

Then the clergyman said : " Who gi's Wom mad't this man ? "

" Well, *I'm* doing that," said Mr. Voules in a refreshingly full voice, and looking round the church.

" Pete arf me," said the clergyman to Mr. Polly. " Take thee Mirum wed wife—— "

" Take thee Mi'm wed' wife," said Mr. Polly.

" Have hold this day ford."

" Have hold this day ford."

" Betworse, richypoo'."

" Bet worse, richypoo'. . . . "

Then came Miriam's turn.

" Lego hands," said the clergyman, " gothering ? No ! on book. So ! Here ! Pete arf me ' Wis ring Ivy wed '."

" Wis ring Ivy wed—— "

So it went on, blurred and hurried, like the momentary vision of a very beautiful thing seen through the smoke of a passing train. . . .

" Now, my boy," said Mr. Voules at last, gripping Mr. Polly's elbow tightly, " you've got to sign the registry and there you are ! Done ! "

Before him stood Miriam, a little stiffly, the hat with a slight rake across her forehead, and a kind of questioning hesitation in her face. Mr. Voules urged him past her.

It was astounding. She was his wife !

And for some reason Miriam and Mrs. Larkins were sobbing, and Annie was looking grave. Hadn't they, after all, wanted him to marry her ? Because if that was the case—— !

He became aware for the first time of the presence of Uncle Pentstemon in the background but approaching, wearing a tie of a light mineral-blue colour, and grinning and sucking enigmatically and judicially round his principal tooth.

§ 5

It was in the vestry that the force of Mr. Voules' personality began to show at its true value. He seemed to open out, like the fisherman's Ginn from the pot, and spread over everything directly the restraints of the ceremony were at an end.

" Ceremony," he said to the clergyman, " excellent, excellent." He also shook hands with Mrs. Larkins, who clung to him for a space, and kissed Miriam on the cheek. " First kiss for me," he said, " anyhow."

He led Mr. Polly to the register by the arm, and then got chairs for Mrs. Larkins and his wife. He then turned on Miriam. " Now, young people," he said. " One ! or *I* shall again."

" That's right," said Mr. Voules. " Same again, Miss."

Mr. Polly was overcome with modest confusion, and turning, found a refuge from this publicity in the arms of Mrs. Larkins. Then in a state of profuse moisture he was assaulted and kissed by Annie and Minnie, who were immediately kissed upon some indistinctly stated grounds by Mr. Voules, who then kissed the entirely impassive Mrs. Voules, and smacked his lips and remarked, " Home again safe and sound." Then, with a strange harrowing cry, Mrs. Larkins seized upon and bedewed Miriam with kisses. Annie and Minnie kissed each other, and Johnson went abruptly to the door of the vestry and stared into the church, no doubt with ideas of sanctuary in his mind. " Like a bit of a kiss round sometimes," said Mr. Voules, and made a kind of hissing noise with his teeth, and suddenly smacked his hands together with great *éclat* several times. Meanwhile the clergyman scratched his cheek with one hand and fiddled the pen with the other, and the verger coughed protestingly.

" The dog-cart's just outside," said Mr. Voules.   " No walking home to-day for the bride, M'am."

" Not going to drive us ? " cried Annie.

" The happy pair, Miss. *Your* turn soon."

" Get out ! " said Annie. " I shan't marry—ever."

" You won't be able to help it. You'll have to do it, just to disperse the crowd." Mr. Voules laid his hand on Mr. Polly's shoulder. " The bridegroom gives his arm to the bride. Hands across, and down the middle. Prump, Prump, Perump-pump-pump-pump-perump."

Mr. Polly found himself and the bride leading the way towards the western door.

Mrs. Larkins passed close to Uncle Pentstemon, sobbing too earnestly to be aware of him. "Such a goo'-goo'-goo' girl," she sobbed.

"Didn't think I'd come, did you?" said Uncle Pentstemon; but she swept past him, too busy with the expression of her feelings to observe him.

"She didn't think I'd come, I lay," said Uncle Pentstemon, a little foiled, but effecting an auditory lodgment upon Johnson.

"I don't know," said Johnson, uncomfortable. "I suppose you were asked. How are you getting on?"

"I was *arst*," said Uncle Pentstemon, and brooded for a moment.

"I goes about seeing wonders," he added, and then in a sort of enhanced undertone, "One of 'er girls gettin' married. That's what I means by wonders. Lord's goodness! Wow!"

"Nothing the matter?" asked Johnson.

"Got it in the back for a moment. Going to be a change of weather, I suppose," said Uncle Pentstemon. "I brought 'er a nice present, too, what I got in this passel. Vallyble old tea-caddy that uset' be my mother's. What I kep' my baccy in for years and years—till the hinge at the back got broke. It ain't been no use to me particular since, so thinks I, drat it! I may as well give it to 'er as not. . . ."

Mr. Polly found himself emerging from the western door.

Outside, a crowd of half a dozen adults and about fifty children had collected, and hailed the approach of the newly wedded couple with a faint, indeterminate cheer. All the children were holding something in little bags, and his attention was caught by the expression of vindictive concentration upon the face of a small, big-eared boy in the foreground. He didn't for the moment realise what these things might import. Then he received a stinging handful of rice in the ear, and a great light shone.

"Not yet, you young fool," he heard Mr. Voules saying behind him, and then a second handful spoke against his hat.

"Not yet," said Mr. Voules, with increasing emphasis, and Mr. Polly became aware that he and Miriam were the focus of two crescents of small boys, each with the light of massacre in his eyes and a grubby fist clutching into a paper bag for rice, and that Mr. Voules was warding off probable discharges with a large red hand.

The dog-cart was in charge of a loafer, and the horse and the whip were adorned with white favours, and the back seat was confused, but not untenable, with hampers. "Up we go," said Mr. Voules. "Old birds in front and young ones behind." An ominous group of ill-restrained rice-throwers followed them up as they mounted.

" Get your handkerchief for your face," said Mr. Polly to his bride, and took the place next the pavement with considerable heroism, held on, gripped his hat, shut his eyes, and prepared for the worst.   " Off ! " said Mr. Voules, and a concentrated fire came stinging Mr. Polly's face.

The horse shied, and when the bridegroom could look at the world again it was manifest the dog-cart had just missed an electric tram by a hair's breadth, and far away outside the church railings the verger and Johnson were battling with an active crowd of small boys for the life of the rest of the Larkins family.   Mrs. Punt and her son had escaped across the road, the son trailing and stumbling at the end of a remorseless arm ; but Uncle Pentstemon, encumbered by the tea-caddy, was the centre of a little circle of his own, and appeared to be dratting them all very heartily.   Remoter, a policeman approached with an air of tranquil unconsciousness.

" Steady, you idiot, stead-y ! " cried Mr. Voules ; and then over his shoulder, " I brought that rice. I like old customs.— Whoa ! stead-y."

The dog-cart swerved violently, and then, evoking a shout of groundless alarm from a cyclist, took a corner, and the rest of the wedding-party was hidden from Mr. Polly's eyes.

§ 6

" We'll get the stuff into the house before the old gal comes along," said Mr. Voules, " if you'll hold the hoss."

" How about the key ? " asked Mr. Polly.

" I got the key, coming."

And while Mr. Polly held the sweating horse and dodged the foam that dripped from its bit, the house absorbed Miriam and Mr. Voules altogether. Mr. Voules carried in the various hampers he had brought with him, and finally closed the door behind him.

For some time Mr. Polly remained alone with his charge in the little blind alley outside the Larkins' house, while the neighbours scrutinised him from behind their blinds.   He reflected that he was a married man, that he must look very like a fool, that the head of a horse is a silly shape and its eye a bulger ; he wondered what the horse thought of him, and whether it really liked being held and patted on the neck, or whether it only submitted out of contempt.   Did it know he was married ?   Then he wondered if the clergyman had thought him much of an ass, and whether the individual lurking behind the lace curtains of the front room next door was a man or a woman.   A door opened over the way, and an elderly gentleman in a kind of embroidered fez appeared smoking a pipe, with a quiet, satisfied expression. He regarded Mr. Polly for some time with mild but sustained curiosity. Finally he called : " Hi ! "

" Hallo ! " said Mr. Polly.

" You needn't 'old that 'orse," said the old gentleman.

" Spirited beast," said Mr. Polly.   " And "—with some
faint analogy to ginger beer in his mind—" he's up to-day."

" 'E won't turn 'isself round," said the old gentleman,
" any'ow.   And there ain't no way through for 'im to go."

" *Verbum sap*," said Mr. Polly, and abandoned the horse
and turned to the door.   It opened to him just as Mrs. Larkins
on the arm of Johnson, followed by Annie, Minnie, two friends,
Mrs. Punt and her son, and at a slight distance Uncle Pentstemon, appeared round the corner.

" They're coming," he said to Miriam, and put an arm
about her and gave her a kiss.

She was kissing him back, when they were startled violently
by the shying of two empty hampers into the passage.   Then
Mr. Voules appeared holding a third.

" Here !   you'll have plenty of time for that presently,"
he said ;   " get these hampers away before the old girl comes.
I got a cold collation here to make her sit up.   My eye ! "

Miriam took the hampers, and Mr. Polly, under compulsion
from Mr. Voules, went into the little front room.   A profuse
pie and a large ham had been added to the modest provision
of Mrs. Larkins, and a number of select-looking bottles
shouldered the bottle of sherry and the bottle of port she had
got to grace the feast.   They certainly went better with the
iced wedding-cake in the middle.   Mrs. Voules, still impassive,
stood by the window regarding these things with faint approval.

" Makes it look a bit thicker, eh ? " said Mr. Voules, and blew
out both cheeks, and smacked his hands together violently
several times.   " Surprise the old girl no end."

He stood back and smiled and bowed with arms extended
as the others came clustering at the door.

" Why, Un-cle Voules ! " cried Annie, with a rising note.

It was his reward.

And then came a great wedging and squeezing and crowding into the little room.   Nearly every one was hungry, and
eyes brightened at the sight of the pie and the ham and the
convivial array of bottles.   " Sit down, every one," cried Mr.
Voules.   " Leaning against anything counts as sitting, and
makes it easier to shake down the grub ! "

The two friends from Miriam's place of business came into
the room among the first, and then wedged themselves so
hopelessly against Johnson in an attempt to get out again
to take off their things up-stairs, that they abandoned the
attempt.   Amid the struggle Mr. Polly saw Uncle Pentstemon
relieve himself of his parcel by giving it to the bride." Here ! "
he said, and handed it to her.   " Weddin'-present," he explained, and added with a confidential chuckle, " *I* never
thought I'd 'ave to give one—ever."

" Who says steak-and-kidney pie ? " bawled Mr. Voules.
" Who says steak-and-kidney pie ?   You 'ave a drop of old

Tommy, Martha.   That's what you want to steady you. . . .

" Sit down, every one, and don't all speak at once. Who says steak-and-kidney pie ? . . . "

" Vocificeratious," whispered Mr. Polly. " Convivial vociferations."

" Bit of 'am with it," shouted Mr. Voules, poising a slice of ham on his knife. " Any one 'ave a bit of 'am with it ? Won't that little man of yours, Mrs. Punt—won't 'e 'ave a bit of 'am ? . . . "

" And now, ladies and gentlemen," said Mr. Voules, still standing and dominating the crammed roomful, "now you got your plates filled, and something I can warrant you good in your glasses, wot about drinking the 'ealth of the bride ? "

" Eat a bit fust," said Uncle Pentstemon, speaking with his mouth full, amidst murmurs of applause. " Eat a bit fust."

So they did, and the plates clattered and the glasses clinked.

Mr. Polly stood shoulder to shoulder with Johnson for a moment. " In for it," said Mr. Polly cheeringly. " Cheer up, O' Man, and peck a bit. No reason why *you* shouldn't eat, you know."

The Punt boy stood on Mr. Polly's boots for a minute, struggling violently against the compunction of Mrs. Punt's grip.

" Pie," said the Punt boy, " Pie ! "

" You sit 'ere and 'ave 'am, my lord ! " said Mrs. Punt, prevailing. " Pie you can't 'ave and you won't."

" Lor' bless my heart, Mrs. Punt ! " protested Mr. Voules, " let the boy 'ave a bit if he wants it—wedding and all ! "

" You 'aven't 'ad 'im sick on your 'ands, Uncle Voules," said Mrs. Punt. " Else you wouldn't want to humour his fancies as you do. . . . "

" I can't help feeling it's a mistake, O' Man," said Johnson, in a confidential undertone. " I can't help feeling you've been Rash. Let's hope for the best."

" Always glad of good wishes, O' Man," said Mr. Polly. " You'd better have a drink or something. Anyhow, sit down to it."

Johnson subsided gloomily, and Mr. Polly secured some ham and carried it off, and sat himself down on the sewing-machine on the floor in the corner to devour it. He was hungry, and a little cut off from the rest of the company by Mrs. Voules' hat and back, and he occupied himself for a time with ham and his own thoughts. He became aware of a series of jangling concussions on the table. He craned his neck, and discovered that Mr. Voules was standing up and leaning forward over the table in the manner distinctive of after-dinner speeches, tapping upon the table with a black bottle. " Ladies and gentlemen," said Mr. Voules, raising his glass solemnly in the empty desert of sound he had made, and paused for a second or so. " Ladies and gentlemen—the Bride." He searched his mind for some suitable wreath of speech, and brightened at last with discovery. " Here's luck to her ! " he said at last.

" Here's Luck ! " said Johnson hopelessly but resolutely, and raised his glass. Everybody murmured, " Here's Luck."

" Luck ! " said Mr. Polly, unseen in his corner, lifting a forkful of ham.

" That's all right," said Mr. Voules, with a sigh of relief at having brought off a difficult operation. " And now, who's for a bit more pie ? "

For a time conversation was fragmentary again. But presently Mr. Voules rose from his chair again, and produced a silence by renewed hammering ; he had subsided with a contented smile after his first oratorical effort. " Ladies and gents," he said, " fill up for a second toast : the happy Bridegroom ! " He stood for half a minute searching his mind for the apt phrase that came at last in a rush. " Here's (hic) luck to *him*," said Mr. Voules.

" Luck to him ! " said every one ; and Mr. Polly, standing up behind Mrs. Voules, bowed amiably, amidst enthusiasm.

" He may say what he likes," said Mrs. Larkins, " he's *got* luck. That girl's a treasure of treasures, and always has been ever since she tried to nurse her own little sister being but three at the time and fell the full flight of stairs from top to bottom, no hurt that any outward eye 'as ever seen but always ready and helping, always tidying and busy. A treasure I must say, and a treasure I will say, giving no more than her due. . . . "

She was silenced altogether by a rapping sound that would not be denied. Mr. Voules had been struck by a fresh idea, and was standing up and hammering with the bottle again.

" The third Toast, ladies and gentlemen," he said ; " fill up, please. The Mother of the Bride. I—er . . . Uoo . . . 'Ere ! . . . Ladies and gem, 'Ere's Luck to 'er ! . . . "

§ 7

The dingy little room was stuffy and crowded to its utmost limit, and Mr. Polly's skies were dark with the sense of irreparable acts. Everybody seemed noisy and greedy, and doing foolish things. Miriam, still in that unbecoming hat—for presently they had to start off to the station together—sat just beyond Mrs. Punt and her son, doing her share in the hospitalities, and ever and again glancing at him with a deliberately encouraging smile. Once she leant over the back of the chair to him and whispered cheeringly, " Soon be together now." Next to her sat Johnson, profoundly silent, and then Annie, talking vigorously to a friend. Uncle Pentstemon was eating voraciously opposite, but with a kindling eye for Annie. Mrs. Larkins sat next Mr. Voules. She was unable to eat a mouthful, she declared, it would choke her ; but ever and again Mr. Voules wooed her to swallow a little drop of liquid refreshment.

There seemed a lot of rice upon everybody, in their hats and hair and the folds of their garments.

Presently Mr. Voules was hammering the table for the fourth time in the interests of the Best Man. . . .

All feasts come to an end at last, and the break-up of things was precipitated by alarming symptoms on the part of Master Punt. He was taken out hastily after a whispered consultation ; and since he had got into the corner between the fireplace and the cupboard, that meant every one moving to make way for him. Johnson took the opportunity to say, "Well, so long," to any one who might be listening, and disappeared. Mr. Polly found himself smoking a cigarette and walking up and down outside in the company of Uncle Pentstemon, while Mr. Voules replaced bottles in hampers, and prepared for departure, and the womenkind of the party crowded up-stairs with the bride. Mr. Polly felt taciturn, but the events of the day had stirred the mind of Uncle Pentstemon to speech. And so he spoke, discursively and disconnectedly, a little heedless of his listener, as wise old men will.

"They do say," said Uncle Pentstemon, "one funeral makes many. This time it's a wedding. But it's all very much of a muchness. . . .

"'Am *do* get in my teeth nowadays," said Uncle Pentstemon, "I can't understand it. 'Tisn't like there was nubblicks or strings or such in 'am. It's a plain food, sure-ly.

"You *got* to get married," said Uncle Pentstemon, resuming his discourse. "That's the way of it. Some has. Some hain't. I done it long before I was your age. It hain't for me to blame you. You can't 'elp being the marrying sort any more than me. It's nat'ral—like poaching, or drinking, or wind on the stummik. You can't 'elp it, and there you are ! As for the good of it, there ain't no particular good in it as I can see. It's a toss-up. The hotter come, the sooner cold ; but they all gets tired of it sooner or later. . . . I hain't no grounds to complain. Two I've 'ad and buried, and might 'ave 'ad a third, and never no worrit with kids—never. . . .

"You done well not to 'ave the big gal. I will say that for ye. She's a gad-about grinny, she is, if ever was. A gad-about grinny. Mucked up my mushroom-bed to rights, she did, and I 'aven't forgot it. Got the feet of a centipede, she 'as—all over everything, and neither with your leave nor by your leave. Like a stray 'en in a pea-patch. Cluck ! cluck ! Trying to laugh it off. *I* laughed 'er off, I did. Dratted lumpin' baggage ! . . ."

For a while he mused malevolently upon Annie, and routed out a reluctant crumb from some coy sitting-out place in his tooth.

"Wimmin's a toss-up," said Uncle Pentstemon. "Prize

packets they are, and you can't tell what's in 'em till you took 'em 'ome and undone 'em. Never was a bachelor married yet that didn't buy a pig in a poke. Never! Marriage seems to change the very natures in 'em through and through. You can't tell what they won't turn into—nohow."

" I seen the nicest girls go wrong," said Uncle Pentstemon, and added with unusual thoughtfulness, " Not that I mean *you* got one of that sort."

He sent another crumb on to its long home with a sucking, encouraging noise.

" The wust sort's the grizzler," Uncle Pentstemon resumed. " If ever I'd 'ad a grizzler, I'd up and 'it 'er on the 'ead with sumpthin' pretty quick. I don't think I *could* abide a grizzler," said Uncle Pentstemon. " I'd liefer 'ave a lump-about like that other gal. I would indeed. I lay I'd make 'er stop laughing after a bit for all 'er airs. And mind where her clumsy great feet went. . . .

" A man's got to tackle 'em, whatever they be," said Uncle Pentstemon, summing up the shrewd observation of an old-world lifetime. " Good or bad," said Uncle Pentstemon, raising his voice fearlessly, " a man's got to tackle 'em."

§ 8

At last it was time for the two young people to catch the train for Waterloo *en route* for Fishbourne. They had to hurry, and as a concluding glory of matrimony they travelled second class, and were seen off by all the rest of the party except the Punts, Master Punt being now beyond any question unwell.

" Off ! " The train moved out of the station.

Mr. Polly remained waving his hat and Mrs. Polly her handkerchief until they were hidden under the bridge. The dominating figure to the last was Mr. Voules. He had followed them along the platform, waving the equestrian grey hat and kissing his hand to the bride.

They subsided into their seats.

" Got a compartment to ourselves, anyhow," said Mrs. Polly, after a pause.

Silence for a moment.

" The rice 'e must 'ave bought. Pounds and pounds ! "

Mr. Polly felt round his collar at the thought.

" Ain't you going to kiss me, Elfrid, now we're alone together ? "

He roused himself to sit forward, hands on knees, cocked his hat over one eye, and assumed an expression of avidity becoming to the occasion.

" Never ! " he said. " Ever ! " and feigned to be selecting a place to kiss with great discrimination.

" Come here," he said, and drew her to him.

" Be careful of my 'at," said Mrs. Polly, yielding awkwardly.

CHAPTER SEVEN

THE LITTLE SHOP AT FISHBOURNE

§ 1

FOR fifteen years Mr. Polly was a respectable shopkeeper in Fishbourne.

Years they were in which every day was tedious, and when they were gone it was as if they had gone in a flash. But now Mr. Polly had good looks no more. He was, as I have described him in the beginning of this story, thirty-seven, and fattish in a not very healthy way, dull and yellowish about the complexion, and with discontented wrinkles round his eyes. He sat on the stile above Fishbourne and cried to the heavens above him : " Oh, Roöötten Beëëastly Silly Hole ! " And he wore a rather shabby black morning coat and vest, and his tie was richly splendid, being from stock, and his gold cap aslant over one eye.

Fifteen years ago, and it might have seemed to you that the queer little flower of Mr. Polly's imagination might be altogether withered and dead, and with no living seed left in any part of him. But, indeed, it still lived as an insatiable hunger for bright and delightful experiences, for the gracious aspect of things, for beauty. He still read books when he had a chance—books that told of glorious places abroad and glorious times, that wrung a rich humour from life, and contained the delight of words freshly and expressively grouped. But, alas ! there are not many such books, and for the newspapers and the cheap fiction that abounded more and more in the world, Mr. Polly had little taste. There was no epithet in them. And there was no one to talk to, as he loved to talk. And he had to mind his shop.

It was a reluctant little shop from the beginning.

He had taken it to escape the doom of Johnson's choice, and because Fishbourne had a hold upon his imagination. He had disregarded the ill-built, cramped rooms behind it in which he would have to lurk and live, and the relentless limitations of its dimensions, the inconvenience of an underground kitchen that must necessarily be the living-room in winter—the narrow yard behind giving upon the yard of the Royal Fishbourne Hotel—the tiresome sitting and waiting for custom, the restricted prospects of trade. He had visualised himself and Miriam first as at breakfast on a clear, bright, winter morning, amidst a tremendous smell of bacon, and then as having muffins for tea. He had also thought of sitting on the beach on Sunday afternoons, and of going for a walk in the country behind the town and picking marguerites and poppies. But, in fact, Miriam and he were usually extremely cross at breakfast, and it did not run to muffins at tea And she didn't think it looked well, she said, to go trapesing about the country on Sundays.

It was unfortunate that Miriam never took to the house from the first. She did not like it when she saw it, and liked it less as she explored it. "There's too many stairs," she said, "and the coal being indoors will make a lot of work."

"Didn't think of that," said Mr. Polly, following her round.

"It'll be a hard house to keep clean," said Miriam.

"White paint's all very well in its way," said Miriam, "but it shows the dirt something fearful. Better 'ave 'ad it nicely grained."

"There's a kind of place here," said Mr. Polly, "where we might have some flowers in pots."

"Not me," said Miriam. "I've 'ad trouble enough with Minnie and 'er musk. . . ."

They stayed for a week in a cheap boarding-house before they moved in. They had bought some furniture in Stamton, mostly second-hand, but with new cheap cutlery and china and linen, and they supplemented this from the Fishbourne shops. Miriam, relieved from the hilarious associations of home, developed a meagre and serious quality of her own, and went about with knitted brows pursuing some ideal of "'aving everything right." Mr. Polly gave himself to the arrangement of the shop with a certain zest, and whistled a great deal, until Miriam appeared and said that it went through her head. So soon as he had taken the shop he had filled the window with aggressive posters, announcing in no measured terms that he was going to open ; and, now he was getting his stuff put out, he was resolved to show Fishbourne what window-dressing could do. He meant to give them boater straws, imitation Panamas, bathing-dresses with novelties in stripes, light flannel shirts, summer ties, and ready-made flannel trousers for men, youths, and boys. Incidentally he watched the small fishmonger over the way, and had a glimpse of the china-dealer next door, and wondered if a friendly nod would be out of place. And on the first Sunday in this new life he and Miriam arrayed themselves with great care, he in his wedding-funeral hat and coat and she in her going-away dress, and went processionally to church—a more respectable-looking couple you could hardly imagine—and looked about them.

Things began to settle down next week into their places. A few customers came, chiefly for bathing-suits and hat-guards, and on Saturday night the cheapest straw hats and ties, and Mr. Polly found himself more and more drawn towards the shop door and the social charm of the street. He found the china-dealer unpacking a crate at the edge of the pavement, and remarked that it was a fine day. The china-dealer gave a reluctant assent, and plunged into the crate in a manner that presented no encouragement to a loquacious neighbour.

" Zealacious commerciality," whispered Mr. Polly to that unfriendly back view. . . .

§ 2

Miriam combined earnestness of spirit with great practical incapacity. The house was never clean nor tidy, but always being frightfully disarranged for cleaning or tidying up, and she cooked because food had to be cooked, and with a sound moralist's entire disregard of the quality or the consequences. The food came from her hands done rather than improved, and looking as uncomfortable as savages clothed under duress by a missionary with a stock of out-sizes. Such food is too apt to behave resentfully, rebel, and work Obi. She ceased to listen to her husband's talk from the day she married him, and ceased to unwrinkle the kink in her brow at his presence, giving herself up to mental states that had a quality of preoccupation. And she developed an idea, for which, perhaps, there was legitimate excuse, that he was lazy. He seemed to stand about a great deal, to read —an indolent habit—and presently to seek company for talking. He began to attend the bar-parlour of the God's Providence Inn with some frequency, and would have done so regularly in the evening if cards, which bored him to death, had not arrested conversation. But the perpetual foolish variation of the permutations and combinations of two-and-fifty cards taken five at a time, and the meagre surprises and excitements that ensue, had no charm for Mr. Polly's mind, which was at once too vivid in its impressions and too easily fatigued.

It was soon manifest the shop paid only in the most exacting sense, and Miriam did not conceal her opinion that he ought to bestir himself and " do things," though what he was to do was hard to say. You see, when you have once sunken your capital in a shop you do not very easily get it out again. If customers will not come to you cheerfully and freely, the law sets limits upon the compulsion you may exercise. You cannot pursue people about the streets of a watering-place, compelling them either by threats or importunity to buy flannel trousers. Additional sources of income for a trades-man are not always easy to find. Wintershed, at the bicycle and gramophone shop to the right, played the organ in the church, and Clamp of the toy-shop was pew-opener and so forth ; Gambell, the greengrocer, waited at table and his wife cooked, and Carter, the watchmaker, left things to his wife while he went about the world winding clocks ; but Mr. Polly had none of these arts, and wouldn't, in spite of Miriam's quietly persistent protests, get any other. And on summer evenings he would ride his bicycle about the country, and if he discovered a sale where there were books, he would as often as not waste half the next day in going again to acquire a job lot of them haphazard, and bring them home tied about with string, and hide them from Miriam under the counter in the shop. That is a heart-breaking thing for any wife with a serious investigatory turn of mind to discover. She was always thinking of burning these finds, but her natural turn for economy prevailed with her.

The books he read during those fifteen years! He read everything he got except theology, and, as he read, his little unsuccessful circumstances vanished and the wonder of life returned to him ; the routine of reluctant getting up, opening shop, pretending to dust it with zest, breakfasting with a shop egg underdone or overdone, or a herring raw or charred, and coffee made Miriam's way, and full of little particles, the return to the shop, the morning paper, the standing, standing at the door saying " How do ! " to passers-by, or getting a bit of gossip, or watching unusual visitors, all these things vanished as the auditorium of a theatre vanishes when the stage is lit. He acquired hundreds of books at last—old, dusty books, books with torn covers and broken covers, fat books whose backs were naked string, and glue—an inimical litter to Miriam.

There was, for example, the voyages of La Perouse, with many careful, explicit woodcuts and the frankest revelations of the ways of the eighteenth-century sailorman, homely, adventurous, drunken, incontinent, and delightful, until he floated, smooth and slow, with all sails set and mirrored in the glassy water, until his head was full of the thought of shining kindly, brown-skinned women, who smiled at him and wreathed his head with unfamiliar flowers. He had, too, a piece of a book about the lost palaces of Yucatan, those vast terraces buried in primordial forest, of whose makers there is now no human memory. With La Perouse he linked " The Island Nights' Entertainments," and it never palled upon him that in the dusky stabbing of the " Island of Voices " something poured over the stabber's hands " like warm tea." Queer, incommunicable joy it is, the joy of the vivid phrase that turns the statement of the horridest fact to beauty.

And another book which had no beginning for him was the second volume of the travels of the Abbés Huc and Gabet. He followed those two sweet souls from their lessons in Thibetan under Sandura the Bearded (who called them donkeys, to their infinite benefit, and stole their store of butter) through a hundred misadventures to the very heart of Lhasa ; and it was a thirst in him that was never quenched to find the other volume and whence they came, and who in fact they were. He read Fenimore Cooper and " Tom Cringle's Log " side by side with Joseph Conrad, and dreamt of the many-hued humanity of the East and West Indies until his heart ached to see those sun-soaked lands before he died. Conrad's prose had a pleasure for him that he was never able to define, a peculiar, deep-coloured effect. He found, too, one day, among a pile of soiled sixpenny books at Port Burdock, to which place he sometimes rode on his ageing bicycle, Bart Kennedy's " A Sailor Tramp," all written in vivid jerks, and had for ever after a kindlier and more understanding eye for every burly rough who slouched through Fishbourne High Street. Sterne he read with a wavering appreciation and some perplexity, but except for the " Pickwick Papers," for some reason that I do not understand, he never took at all kindly to Dickens. Yet he liked Lever, and Thackeray's " Catherine," and all Dumas until he got to the " Vicomte de Bragelonne." I am puzzled by his insensibility to Dickens, and I record it, as a good historian should, with an admission of my perplexity. It is much more understandable that he had no love for Scott. And I suppose it was because of his ignorance of the proper pronunciation of words that he infinitely preferred any prose to any metrical writing.

A book he browsed over with a recurrent pleasure was Waterton's " Wanderings in South America." He would even amuse himself by inventing descriptions of other birds in the Watertonian manner, new birds that he invented, birds with peculiarities that made him chuckle when they occurred to him. He tried to make Rusper, the ironmonger, share this joy with him. He read Bates, too, about the Amazon ; but when he discovered that you could not see one bank from the other, he lost, through some mysterious action of the soul that again I cannot understand, at least a tithe of the pleasure he had taken in that river. But he read all sorts of things ; a book of old Keltic stories collected by Joyce charmed him, and Mitford's " Tales of Old Japan," and a number of paper-covered volumes, " Tales from Blackwood," he had acquired at Easewood, remained a stand-by. He developed a quite considerable acquaintance with the plays of William Shakespear, and in his dreams he wore cinque cento or Elizabethan clothes, and walked about a stormy, ruffling, taverning, teeming world. Great land of sublimated things, thou World of Books, happy asylum, refreshment, and refuge from the world of every day ! . . .

The essential thing of those fifteen long years of shop-keeping is Mr. Polly, well athwart the counter of his rather ill-lit shop, lost in a book, or rousing himself with a sigh to attend to business.

And meanwhile he got little exercise ; indigestion grew with him until it ruled all his moods ; he fattened and deteriorated physically, great moods of distress invaded and darkened his skies, little things irritated him more and more, and casual laughter ceased in him. His hair began to come off until he had a large bald space at the back of his head. Suddenly, one day it came to him—forgetful of those books and all he had lived and seen through them—that he had been in his shop for exactly fifteen years, that he would soon be forty, and that his life during that time had not been worth living, that it had been in apathetic and feebly hostile and critical company, ugly in detail and mean in scope, and that it had brought him at last to an outlook utterly hopeless and grey.

§ 3

I have already had occasion to mention, indeed I have quoted, a certain high-browed gentleman living at Highbury, wearing a golden *pince-nez*, and writing for the most part in that very beautiful room, the library of the Climax Club. There he wrestles with what he calls " social problems " in a bloodless but at times, I think one must admit, an extremely illuminating manner. He has a fixed idea that something called a collective " intelligence " is wanted in the world, which means in practice that you and I and everyone have to think about things frightfully hard and pool the results, and oblige ourselves to be shamelessly and persistently clear and truthful, and support and respect (I suppose) a perfect horde of professors and writers and artists and ill-groomed, difficult people, instead of using our brains in a moderate and sensible manner to play golf and bridge (pretending a sense of humour prevents our doing anything else with them), and generally taking life in a nice, easy, gentlemanly way, confound him ! Well, this dome-headed monster of intellect alleges that Mr. Polly was unhappy entirely through that.

" A rapidly complicating society," he writes, " which, as a whole, declines to contemplate its future or face the intricate problems of its organisation, is in exactly the position of a man who takes no thought of dietary or regimen, who abstains from baths and exercise and gives his appetites free play. It accumulates useless and aimless lives, as a man accumulates fat and morbid products in his blood ; it declines in its collective efficiency and vigour, and secretes discomfort and misery. Every phase of its evolution is accompanied by a maximum of avoidable distress and inconvenience and human waste. . . .

" Nothing can better demonstrate the collective dullness of our community, the crying need for strenuous, intellectual renewal, than the consideration of that vast mass of useless, uncomfortable, under-educated, under-trained, and altogether pitiable people we contemplate when we use that inaccurate and misleading term, the Lower Middle Class. A great proportion of the lower middle class should properly be assigned to the unemployed and the unemployable. They are only not that, because the possession of some small hoard of money, savings during a period of wage-earning, an insurance policy or such like capital, prevents a direct appeal to the rates. But they are doing little or nothing for the community in return for what they consume ; they have no understanding of any relation of service to the community, they have never been trained nor their imaginations touched to any social purpose. A great proportion of small shopkeepers, for example, are people who have, through the inefficiency that comes from inadequate training and sheer aimlessness, or through improvements in machinery or the drift of trade, been thrown out of employment, and who set up in needless shops as a method of eking out the savings upon which they count. They contrive to make sixty or seventy per cent. of their expenditure, the rest is drawn from the shrinking capital. Essentially their lives are failures, not the sharp and tragic failure of the labourer who gets out of work and starves, but a slow, chronic process of consecutive small losses which may end, if the individual is exceptionally fortunate, in an impoverished deathbed before actual bankruptcy or destitution supervenes. Their chances of ascendant means are less in their shops than in any lottery that was every planned. The secular development of transit and communications has made the organisation of distributing businesses upon large and economical lines inevitable ; except in the chaotic confusions of newly opened countries, the day when a man might earn an independent living by unskilled, or practically unskilled, retailing has gone for ever. Yet every year sees the melancholy procession towards petty bankruptcy and imprisonment for debt go on, and there is no statesmanship in us to avert it. Every issue of every trade journal has its four or five columns of abridged bankruptcy proceedings, nearly every item in which means the final collapse of another struggling family upon the resources of the community, and continually a fresh supply of superfluous artisans and shopassistants, coming out of employment with savings or " help " from relations, of widows with a husband's insurance money, of the ill-trained sons of parsimonious fathers, replaces the fallen in the ill-equipped, jerry-built shops that everywhere abound. . . ."

I quote these fragments from a gifted if unpleasant contemporary for what they are worth. I feel this has to come in here as the broad aspect of this History. I come back to Mr. Polly, sitting upon his gate and swearing in the east wind, and so returning I have a sense of floating across unbridged abysses between the general and the particular. There, on the one hand, is the man of understanding seeing clearly— I suppose he sees clearly—the big process that dooms millions of lives to thwarting and discomfort and unhappy circumstances, and giving us no help, no hint, by which we may get that better " collective will and intelligence " which would dam that stream of human failure ; and on the other hand, Mr. Polly, sitting on his gate, untrained, unwarned, confused, distressed, angry, seeing nothing except that he is, as it were, netted in greyness and discomfort—with life dancing all

about him ; Mr. Polly with a capacity for joy and beauty at
least as keen and subtle as yours or mine.

§ 4

I have hinted that our Mother England had equipped
Mr. Polly for the management of his internal concerns no
whit better than she had for the direction of his external
affairs. With a careless generosity she affords her children
a variety of foods unparalleled in the world's history, including many condiments and preserved preparations novel
to the human economy. And Miriam did the cooking. Mr.
Polly's system, like a confused and ill-governed democracy,
had been brought to a state of perpetual clamour and disorder,
demanding now evil and unsuitable internal satisfactions such
as pickles and vinegar and the crackling on pork, and now
vindictive external expressions, such as war and bloodshed
throughout the world. So that Mr. Polly had been led into
hatred and a series of disagreeable quarrels with his landlord,
his wholesalers, and most of his neighbours.

Rumbold, the china-dealer next door, seemed hostile from
the first for no apparent reason, and always unpacked his
crates with a full back to his new neighbour, and from the
first Mr. Polly resented and hated that uncivil breadth of
expressionless humanity, wanted to prod it, kick it, satirise.
But you cannot satirise a back, if you have no friend to nudge
while you do it.

At last Mr. Polly could stand it no longer. He approached
and prodded Rumbold.

" 'Ello ! " said Rumbold, suddenly erect and turned about.

" Can't we have some other point of view ? " said Mr. Polly.
" I'm tired of the end elevation."

" Eh ? " said Mr. Rumbold, frankly puzzled.

" Of all the vertebracious animals man alone raises his
face to the sky, O' Man. Well, why avert it ? "

Rumbold shook his head with a helpless expression.

" Don't like so much Arreary Pensy."

Rumbold, distressed, in utter obscurity.

" In fact, I'm sick of your turning your back on me, see ? "

A great light shone on Rumbold. " *That's* what you're
talking about ! " he said.

" That's it," said Polly.

Rumbold scratched his ear with the three strawy jampots
he held in his hand. " Way the wind blows, I expect," he
said. " But what's the fuss ? "

" No fuss ! " said Mr. Polly. " Passing remark. I don't
like it, O' Man, that's all."

" Can't help it, if the wind blows my stror," said Mr. Rumbold, still far from clear about it.

" It isn't ordinary civility," said Mr. Polly.

" Got to unpack 'ow it suits me. Can't unpack with the stror blowing into one's eyes."

" Needn't unpack like a pig rooting for truffles, need you ? "

" Truffles ? "

" Needn't unpack like a pig."

Mr. Rumbold apprehended something.

" Pig ! " he said, impressed. " You calling me a pig ? "

" It's the side I seem to get of you."

" 'Ere," said Mr. Rumbold, suddenly fierce, and shouting, and making his points with gesticulated jampots, " you go indoors. I don't want no row with you, and I don't want you to row with me. I don't know what you're after, but I'm a peaceful man—teetotaller, too, and a good thing if *you* was. See ? You go indoors ! "

" You mean to say—— I'm asking you civilly to stop unpacking—with your back to me."

" Pig ain't civil and you ain't sober. You go indoors and lemme go on unpacking. You—you're excited."

" D'you mean—— ! " Mr. Polly was foiled.

He perceived an immense solidity about Rumbold.

" Get back to your shop and lemme get on with my business," said Mr. Rumbold. " Stop calling me pigs. See ? Sweep your pavement."

" I came here to make a civil request."

" You came 'ere to make a row. I don't want no truck with you. See ? I don't like the looks of you. See ? And I can't stand 'ere all day arguing. See ? "

Pause of mutual inspection.

It occurred to Mr. Polly that probably he was to some extent in the wrong.

Mr. Rumbold, blowing heavily, walked past him, deposited the jampots in his shop with an immense affectation that there was no Mr. Polly in the world, returned, turned a scornful back on Mr. Polly, and dived to the interior of the crate. Mr. Polly stood baffled. Should he kick this solid mass before him ? Should he administer a resounding kick ?

No !

He plunged his hands deeply into his trousers pockets, began to whistle, and returned to his own doorstep with an air of profound unconcern. There, for a time, to the tune of " Men of Harlech," he contemplated the receding possibility of kicking Mr. Rumbold hard. It would be splendid—and for the moment satisfying. But he decided not to do it. For indefinable reasons he could not do it. He went indoors and straightened up his dress ties very slowly and thoughtfully. Presently he went to the window and regarded Mr. Rumbold obliquely. Mr. Rumbold was still unpacking. . . .

Mr. Polly had no human intercourse thereafter with Rumbold for fifteen years. He kept up a Hate.

There was a time when it seemed as if Rumbold might go,

but he had a meeting of his creditors and then went on unpacking as before, obtusely as ever.

§ 5

Hinks, the saddler, two shops farther down the street, was
a different case. Hinks was the aggressor—practically.

Hinks was a sporting man in his way, with that taste for
checks in costume and tight trousers which is, under Providence, so mysteriously and invariably associated with equestrian proclivities. At first Mr. Polly took to him as a character,
became frequent in the God's Providence Inn under his
guidance, stood and was stood drinks, and concealed a great
ignorance of horses until Hinks became urgent for him to
play billiards or bet.

Then Mr. Polly took to evading him, and Hinks ceased
to conceal his opinion that Mr. Polly was in reality a softish
sort of flat.

He did not, however, discontinue conversation with Mr.
Polly. He would come along to him whenever he appeared
at his door and converse about sport and women and fisticuffs
and the pride of life with an air of extreme initiation, until
Mr. Polly felt himself the faintest underdeveloped simulacrum
of man that had ever hovered on the verge of non-existence.

So he invented phrases for Hinks' clothes, and took Rusper,
the ironmonger, into his confidence upon the weaknesses of
Hinks. He called him the " chequered Careerist," and spoke
of his patterned legs as " shivery shakys." Good things of
this sort are apt to get round to people.

He was standing at his door one day, feeling bored, when
Hinks appeared down the street, stood still, and regarded
him with a strange, malignant expression for a space.

Mr. Polly waved a hand in a rather belated salutation.

Mr. Hinks spat on the pavement and appeared to reflect.
Then he came towards Mr. Polly portentously and paused,
and spoke between his teeth in an earnest, confidential tone.

" You been flapping your mouth about me, I'm told," he said.

Mr. Polly felt suddenly spiritless. " Not that I know of,"
he answered.

" Not that you know of, be blowed ! You been flapping
your mouth."

" Don't see it," said Mr. Polly.

" Don't see it, be blowed ! You go flapping your silly mouth
about me, and I'll give you a poke in the eye. See ? "

Mr. Hinks regarded the effect of this coldly but firmly,
and spat again.

" Understand me ? " he inquired.

" Don't recollect," began Mr. Polly.

" Don't recollect, be blowed ! You flap your mouth a damn
sight too much. This place gets more of your mouth than
it wants. . . . Seen this ? "

And Mr. Hinks, having displayed a freckled fist of extra-ordinary size and pugginess in an ostentatiously familiar manner to Mr. Polly's close inspection by sight or smell, turned it about this way and that, shaking it gently for a moment or so, replaced it carefully in his pocket as if for future use, receded slowly and watchfully for a pace, and then turned away as if to other matters, and ceased to be, even in outward seeming, a friend. . . .

§ 6

Mr. Polly's intercourse with all his fellow-tradesmen was tarnished sooner or later by some such adverse incident, until not a friend remained to him, and loneliness made even the shop door terrible. Shops bankrupted all about him, and fresh people came, and new acquaintances sprang up, but sooner or later a discord was inevitable—the tension under which these badly-fed, poorly-housed, bored and bothered neighbours lived made it inevitable. The mere fact that Mr. Polly had to see them every day, that there was no getting away from them, was in itself sufficient to make them almost unendurable to his frettingly active mind.

Among other shopkeepers in the High Street there was Chuffles, the grocer, a small, hairy, silently intent polygamist, who was given rough music by the youth of the neighbourhood because of a scandal about his wife's sister, and who was nevertheless totally uninteresting, and Tonks, the second grocer, an old man with an older, very enfeebled wife, both submerged by piety. Tonks went bankrupt, and was succeeded by a branch of the National Provision Company, with a young manager exactly like a fox, except that he barked. The toy and sweetstuff shop was kept by an old woman of repellent manners, and so was the little fish shop at the end of the street. The Berlinwool shop, having gone bankrupt, became a newspaper shop, then fell to a haberdasher in consumption, and finally to a stationer ; the three shops at the end of the street wallowed in and out of insolvency in the hands of a bicycle repairer and dealer, a gramophone dealer, a tobacconist, a six-penny-half-penny bazaar keeper, a shoemaker, a greengrocer, and the exploiter of a cinematograph peep-show—but none of them supplied friendship to Mr. Polly.

These adventurers in commerce were all more or less distraught souls, driving without intelligible comment before the gale of fate. The two milkmen of Fishbourne were brothers who had quarrelled about their father's will and started in opposition to each other. One was stone deaf and no use to Mr. Polly, and the other was a sporting man with a natural dread of epithet, who sided with Hinks. So it was all about him ; on every hand, it seemed, were uncongenial people, uninteresting people, or people who conceived the deepest distrust and hostility towards him—a magic circle of suspicious, preoccupied, and dehumanised humanity. So the poison in his system poisoned the world without.

But Boomer, the wine merchant, and Tashingford, the chemist, be it noted, were fraught with pride, and held themselves to be a cut above Mr. Polly. They never quarrelled with him, preferring to bear themselves from the outset as though they had already done so.

As his internal malady grew upon Mr. Polly, and he became more and more a battle-ground of fermenting foods and warring juices, he came to hate the very sight, as people say, of every one of these neighbours. There they were, every day and all the days, just the same, echoing his own stagnation. They pained him all round the top and back of his head ; they made his legs and arms weary and spiritless. The air was tasteless by reason of them. He lost his human kindliness.

In the afternoons he would hover in the shop, bored to death with his business and his home and Miriam, and yet afraid to go out because of his inflamed and magnified dislike and dread of these neighbours. He could not bring himself to go out and run the gauntlet of the observant windows and the cold and estranged eyes.

One of his last friendships was with Rusper, the ironmonger. Rusper took over Worthington's shop about three years after Mr. Polly opened. He was a tall, lean, nervous, convulsive man, with an upturned, back-thrown, oval head, who read newspapers and the *Review of Reviews* assiduously, had belonged to a Literary Society somewhere once, and had some defect of the palate that at first gave his lightest word a charm and interest for Mr. Polly. It caused a peculiar clinking sound, as though he had something between a giggle and a gas-meter at work in his neck.

His literary admirations were not precisely Mr. Polly's literary admirations ; he thought books were written to enshrine Great Thoughts, and that art was pedagogy in fancy dress ; he had no sense of phrase or epithet or richness of texture, but still he knew there were books. He did know there were books, and he was full of large, windy ideas of the sort he called " Modern (kik) Thought," and seemed needlessly and helplessly concerned about " (kik) the Welfare of the Race."

Mr. Polly would dream about that (kik) at nights.

It seemed to that undesirable mind of his that Rusper's head was the most egg-shaped head he had ever seen ; the similarity weighed upon him, and when he found an argument growing warm with Rusper he would say, " Boil it some more, O' Man ; boil it harder ! " or " Six minutes at least," allusions Rusper could never make head or tail of, and got at last to disregard as a part of Mr. Polly's general eccentricity. For a long time that little tendency threw no shadow over their intercourse, but it contained within it the seeds of an ultimate disruption.

Often during the days of this friendship Mr. Polly would leave his shop and walk over to Mr. Rusper's establishment and stand in his doorway and enquire, " Well, O' Man, how's the Mind of the Age working ? " and get quite an hour of it ; and sometimes Mr. Rusper would come into the outfitter's shop with " Heard the (kik) latest ? " and spend the rest of the morning.

Then Mr. Rusper married ; and he married, very inconsiderately, a woman who was totally uninteresting to Mr. Polly. A coolness grew between them from the first intimation of her advent. Mr. Polly couldn't help thinking when he saw her that she drew her hair back from her forehead a great deal too tightly, and that her elbows were angular. His desire not to mention these things in the apt terms that welled up so richly in his mind made him awkward in her presence, and that gave her an impression that he was hiding some guilty secret from her. She decided he must have a bad influence upon her husband, and she made it a point to appear whenever she heard him talking to Rusper.

One day they became a little heated about the German peril.

" I lay (kik) they'll invade us," said Rusper.

" Not a bit of it. William's not the Xerxiacious sort."

" You'll see, O' Man."

" Just what I shan't do."

" Before (kik) five years are out."

" Not it."

" Yes."

" No."

" Yes."

" Oh, boil it hard ! " said Mr. Polly.

Then he looked up and saw Mrs. Rusper standing behind the counter, half hidden by a trophy of spades and garden shears and a knife-cleaning machine, and by her expression he knew instantly that she understood.

The conversation paled, and presently Mr. Polly withdrew.

After that estrangement increased steadily.

Mr. Rusper ceased altogether to come over to the outfitter's, and Mr. Polly called upon the ironmonger only with the completest air of casualty. And everything they said to each other led now to flat contradiction and raised voices. Rusper had been warned in vague and alarming terms that Mr. Polly insulted and made game of him, he couldn't discover exactly where ; and so it appeared to him now that every word of Mr. Polly's might be an insult meriting his resentment, meriting it none the less because it was masked and cloaked.

Soon Mr. Polly's calls upon Mr. Rusper ceased also ; and then Mr. Rusper, pursuing incomprehensible lines of thought, became afflicted with a specialised shortsightedness that applied only to Mr. Polly. He would look in other directions when Mr. Polly appeared, and his large, oval face assumed an expression of conscious serenity and deliberate happy un-awareness that would have maddened a far less irritable person than Mr. Polly. It evoked a strong desire to mock and ape, and produced in his throat a cough of singular scornfulness, more particularly when Mr. Rusper also assisted with an assumed unconsciousness that was all his own.

Then one day Mr. Polly had a bicycle accident.

His bicycle was now very old, and it is one of the con-comitants of a bicycle's senility that its free-wheel should one day obstinately cease to be free. It corresponds to that epoch in human decay when an old gentleman loses an incisor tooth. It happened just as Mr. Polly was approaching Mr. Rusper's shop, and the untoward chance of a motor-car trying to pass a wagon on the wrong side gave Mr. Polly no choice but to get on to the pavement and dismount. He was always accustomed to take his time and step off his left pedal at its lowest point, but the jamming of the free-wheel gear made that lowest moment a transitory one, and the pedal was lifting his foot for another revolution before he realised what had happened. Before he could dismount according to his habit the pedal had to make a revolution, and before it could make a revolution Mr. Polly found himself among the various sonorous things with which Mr. Rusper adorned the front of his shop—zinc dustbins, household pails, lawn mowers, rakes, spades, and all manner of clattering things. Before he got among them he had one of those agonis-ing moments of helpless wrath and suspense that seem to last ages, in which one seems to perceive everything and think of nothing but words that are better forgotten. He sent a column of pails thundering across the doorway, and dismounted with one foot in a sanitary dustbin, amidst an enormous uproar of falling ironmongery.

" Put all over the place ! " he cried, and found Mr. Rusper emerging from his shop with the large tranquillities of his countenance puckered to anger, like the frowns in the brow of a reefing sail. He gesticulated speechlessly for a moment.

" (kik) Jer doing ? " he said at last.

" Tin mantraps ! " said Mr. Polly.

" Jer (kik) doing ? "

" Dressing all over the pavement as though the blessed town belonged to you ! Ugh ! "

And Mr. Polly, in attempting a dignified movement, realised his entanglement with the dustbin for the first time. With a low, embittering expression, he kicked his foot about in it for a moment very noisily, and finally sent it thundering to the kerb. On its way it struck a pail or so. Then Mr. Polly picked up his bicycle and proposed to resume his homeward way. But the hand of Mr. Rusper arrested him.

" Put it (kik) all (kik) back (kik)."

" Put it (kik) back yourself."

" You got (kik) put it back."

" Get out of the (kik) way."

Mr. Rusper laid one hand on the bicycle handle, and the other gripped Mr. Polly's collar urgently. Whereupon Mr. Polly said " Leggo ! " and again, " D'you *hear* ? Leggo ! " and then drove his elbow with considerable force into the region of Mr. Rusper's midriff. Whereupon Mr. Rusper, with a loud, impassioned cry resembling " Woo kik " more than any other combination of letters, released the bicycle handle, seized Mr. Polly by the cap and hair, and bore his head and shoulders downwards. Thereat Mr. Polly, emitting such words as every one knows and nobody prints, butted his utmost into the concavity of Mr. Rusper, entwined a leg about him, and, after terrific moments of swaying instability, fell headlong beneath him amidst the bicycle and pails. There on the pavement these inexpert children of a pacific age, untrained in arms and uninured to violence, abandoned themselves to amateurish and absurd efforts to hurt and injure one another—of which the most palpable consequences were dusty backs, ruffled hair, and torn and twisted collars. Mr. Polly by accident got his finger into Mr. Rusper's mouth, and strove earnestly for some time to prolong that aperture in the direction of Mr. Rusper's ear before it occurred to Mr. Rusper to bite him (and even then he didn't bite very hard), while Mr. Rusper concentrated his mind almost entirely on an effort to rub Mr. Polly's face on the pavement. (And their positions bristled with chances of the deadliest sort !) They didn't, from first to last, draw blood.

Then it seemed to each of them that the other had become endowed with many hands and several voices and great accessions of strength. They submitted to fate and ceased to struggle. They found themselves torn apart and held up by outwardly scandalised and inwardly delighted neighbours, and invited to explain what it was all about.

" Got to (kik) puttem all back," panted Mr. Rusper, in the expert grasp of Hinks. " Merely asked him to (kik) puttem all back."

Mr. Polly was under restraint of little Clamp of the toyshop, who was holding his hands in a complex and uncomfortable manner that he afterwards explained to Wintershed was a combination of something romantic called " Jiu-jitsu " and something else still more romantic called the " Police Grip."

" Pails," explained Mr. Polly, in breathless fragments. " All over the road. Pails. Bungs up the street with his pails. Look at them ! "

" Deliber (kik) lib (kik) liberately rode into my goods (kik). Constantly (kik) annoying me (kik) ! " said Mr. Rusper.

They were both tremendously earnest and reasonable in

their manner. They wished every one to regard them as responsible and intellectual men acting for the love of right and the enduring good of the world. They felt they must treat this business as a profound and publicly significant affair. They wanted to explain and orate and show the entire necessity of everything they had done. Mr. Polly was convinced he had never been so absolutely correct in all his life as when he planted his foot in the sanitary dustbin, and Mr. Rusper considered his clutch at Mr. Polly's hair as the one faultless impulse in an otherwise undistinguished career. But it was clear in their minds they might easily become ridiculous if they were not careful, if for a second they stepped over the edge of the high spirit and pitiless dignity they had hitherto maintained. At any cost they perceived they must not become ridiculous.

Mr. Chuffles, the scandalous grocer, joined the throng about the principal combatants, mutely, as became an outcast, and with a sad, distressed, helpful expression picked up Mr. Polly's bicycle. Gambell's summer errand-boy, moved by example, restored the dustbin and pails to their self-respect.

" '*E* ought—'*E* ought (kik) pick them up," protested Mr. Rusper.

" What's it all about ? " said Mr. Hinks for the third time, shaking Mr. Rusper gently. " 'As 'e been calling you names ? "

" Simply ran into his pails—as any one might," said Mr. Polly, " and out he comes and scrags me."

" (kik) Assault ! " said Mr. Rusper.

" He assaulted *me*," said Mr. Polly.

" Jumped (kik) into my dustbin," said Mr. Rusper. " That assault ? Or isn't it ? "

" You better drop it," said Mr. Hinks.

" Great pity they can't behave better, both of 'em," said Mr. Chuffles, glad for once to find himself morally unassailable.

" Any one see it begin ? " said Mr. Wintershed.

" *I* was in the shop," said Mrs. Rusper suddenly, from the doorstep, piercing the little group of men and boys with the sharp horror of a woman's voice. " If a witness is wanted, I suppose I've got a tongue. I suppose I got a voice in seeing my own husband injured. My husband went out and spoke to Mr. Polly, who was jumping off and on his bicycle all among our pails and things, and immediately 'E butted him in the stomach—immediately—most savagely—butted him. Just after his dinner, too, and him far from strong. I could have screamed. But Rusper caught hold of him right away, I will say that for Rusper——"

" I'm going," said Mr. Polly suddenly, releasing himself from the Anglo-Japanese grip and holding out his hands for his bicycle.

" Teach you (kik) to leave things alone," said Mr. Rusper, with an air of one who has given a lesson.

The testimony of Mrs. Rusper continued relentlessly in the background.

" You'll hear of me through a summons," said Mr. Polly, preparing to wheel his bicycle.

" (kik) Me too," said Mr. Rusper.

Some one handed Mr. Polly a collar. " This yours ? "

Mr. Polly investigated his neck. " I suppose it is. Any one seen a tie ? "

A small boy produced a grimy strip of spotted blue silk.

" Human life isn't safe with you," said Mr. Polly as a parting shot.

" (kik) Yours isn't," said Mr. Rusper.

And they got small satisfaction out of the Bench, which refused altogether to perceive the relentless correctitude of the behaviour of either party, and reproved the eagerness of Mrs. Rusper—speaking to her gently, firmly but exasperatingly as " My Good Woman," and telling her to " Answer the Question ! Answer the Question ! "

" Seems a Pity," said the chairman, when binding them over to keep the peace, " you can't behave like Respectable Tradesmen. Seems a Great Pity. Bad Example to the Young and all that. Don't do any Good to the town, don't do any Good to yourselves, don't do any manner of Good, to have all the Tradesmen in the Place scrapping about the Pavement of an Afternoon. Think we're letting you off very easily this time, and hope it will be a Warning to you. Don't expect men of your Position to come up before us. Very Regrettable Affair. Eh ? "

He addressed the latter enquiry to his two colleagues.

" Exactly, exactly," said the colleague to the right.

" Err (kik)," said Mr. Rusper.

§ 7

But the disgust that overshadowed Mr. Polly's being as he sat upon the stile had other and profounder justification than his quarrel with Rusper and the indignity of appearing before the county bench. He was, for the first time in his business career, short with his rent for the approaching quarter day ; and, so far as he could trust his own handling of figures, he was sixty or seventy pounds on the wrong side of solvency. And that was the outcome of fifteen years of passive endurance of dullness throughout the best years of his life. What would Miriam say when she learned this, and was invited to face the prospect of exile—Heaven knows what sort of exile—from their present home ? She would grumble and scold and become limply unhelpful, he knew, and none the less so because he could not help things. She would say he ought to have worked harder, and a hundred such exasperating, pointless things. Such thoughts as these require no aid from undigested cold pork and cold potatoes and pickles to darken the soul, and with these aids his soul was black indeed.

" May as well have a bit of a walk," said Mr. Polly at last, after nearly intolerable meditations, and sat round and put a leg over the stile.

He remained still for some time before he brought over the other leg.

" Kill myself," he murmured at last.

It was an idea that came back to his mind nowadays with a continually increasing attractiveness, more particularly after meals. Life, he felt, had no further happiness for him. He hated Miriam, and there was no getting away from her, whatever might betide. And for the rest, there was toil and struggle, toil and struggle with a failing heart and dwindling courage, to sustain that dreary duologue. " Life's insured," said Mr. Polly ; " place is insured. I don't see it does any harm to her or any one."

He stuck his hands in his pockets. " Needn't hurt much," he said. He began to elaborate a plan.

He found it was quite interesting elaborating his plan. His countenance became less miserable and his pace quickened.

There is nothing so good in all the world for melancholia as walking, and the exercise of the imagination in planning something presently to be done, and soon the wrathful wretchedness had vanished from Mr. Polly's face. He would have to do the thing secretly and elaborately, because otherwise there might be difficulties about the life insurance. He began to scheme how he could circumvent that difficulty. . . .

He took a long walk, for, after all, what is the good of hurrying back to shop when you are not only insolvent but very soon to die ? His dinner and the east wind lost their sinister hold upon his soul, and when at last he came back along the Fishbourne High Street his face was unusually bright and the craving hunger of the dyspeptic was returning. So he went into the grocer's and bought a ruddily decorated tin of a brightly pink fish-like substance known as " Deep Sea Salmon." This he was resolved to consume, regardless of cost, with vinegar and salt and pepper as a relish to his supper.

He did, and since he and Miriam rarely talked, and Miriam thought honour and his recent behaviour demanded a hostile silence, he ate fast and copiously and soon gloomily. He ate alone, for she refrained, to mark her sense of his extravagance. Then he prowled into the High Street for a time, thought it an infernal place, tried his pipe and found it foul and bitter, and retired wearily to bed.

He slept for an hour or so, and then woke up to the contemplation of Miriam's hunched back and the riddle of life, and this bright and attractive idea of ending for ever and ever and ever all the things that were locking him in, this bright idea that shone like a baleful star above all the reek and darkness of his misery. . . .

CHAPTER EIGHT

MAKING AN END TO THINGS

§ 1

MR. POLLY designed his suicide with considerable care and a quite remarkable altruism.

His passionate hatred for Miriam vanished directly the idea of getting away from her for ever became clear in his mind. He found himself full of solicitude then for her welfare. He did not want to buy his release at her expense. He had not the remotest intention of leaving her unprotected, with a painfully dead husband and a bankrupt shop on her hands. It seemed to him that he could contrive to secure for her the full benefit of both his life insurance and his fire insurance if he managed things in a tactful manner. He felt happier than he had done for years scheming out this undertaking, albeit it was, perhaps, a larger and somberer kind of happiness than had fallen to his lot before. It amazed him to think he had endured his monotony of misery and failure for so long.

But there were some queer doubts and questions in the dim, half-lit background of his mind that he had very resolutely to ignore.

" Sick of it," he had to repeat to himself aloud to keep his determination clear and firm. His life was a failure ; there was nothing more to hope for but unhappiness. Why shouldn't he ?

His project was to begin the fire with the stairs that led from the ground floor to the underground kitchen and scullery. This he would soak with paraffin, and assist with firewood and paper and a brisk fire in the coal cellar underneath. He would smash a hole or so in the stairs to ventilate the blaze, and have a good pile of boxes and paper, and a convenient chair or so, in the shop above. He would have the paraffin can upset, and the shop lamp, as if awaiting refilling, at convenient distances in the scullery ready to catch. Then he would smash the house lamp on the staircase—a fall with that in his hand was to be the ostensible cause of the blaze—and he would cut his throat at the top of the kitchen stairs, which would then become his funeral pyre. He would do all this on Sunday evening while Miriam was at church, and it would appear that he had fallen downstairs with the lamp and been burned to death. There was really no flaw whatever that he could see in the scheme. He was quite sure he knew how to cut his throat, deep at the side and not to saw at the windpipe, and he was reasonably sure it wouldn't hurt him very much. And then everything would be at an end.

There was no particular hurry to get the thing done, of course, and meanwhile he occupied his mind with possible variations of the scheme. . . .

It needed a particularly dry and dusty east wind, a Sunday dinner of exceptional virulence, a conclusive letter from Konk, Maybrick, Ghool, and Gabbitas, his principal and most urgent creditors, and a conversation with Miriam, arising out of arrears of rent and leading on to mutual character sketching, before Mr. Polly could be brought to the necessary pitch of despair to carry out his plans. He went for an embittering walk, and came back to find Miriam in a bad temper over the tea things, with the brewings of three-quarters of an hour in the pot and hot buttered muffins gone leathery. He sat eating in silence with his resolution made.

" Coming to church ? " said Miriam after she had cleared away.

" Rather. I got a lot to be grateful for," said Mr. Polly.

" You got what you deserve," said Miriam.

" Suppose I have," said Mr. Polly, and went and stared out of the back window at a despondent horse in the hotel yard.

He was still standing there when Miriam came downstairs dressed for church. Something in his immobility struck home to her. " You'd better come to church than mope," she said.

" I shan't mope," he answered.

She remained still. Her presence irritated him. He felt that in another moment he should say something absurd to her, make some last appeal for that understanding she had never been able to give. " Oh ! *go* to church," he said.

In another moment the outer door slammed upon her. " Good riddance ! " said Mr. Polly.

He turned about. " I've had my whack," he said.

He reflected. " I don't see she'll have any cause to holler," he said. " Beastly Home ! Beastly Life ! "

For a space he remained thoughtful. " Here goes ! " he said at last.

§ 2

For twenty minutes Mr. Polly busied himself about the house, making his preparations very neatly and methodically.

He opened the attic windows, in order to make sure of a good draught through the house, and drew down the blinds at the back and shut the kitchen door to conceal his arrangements from casual observation. At the end he would open the door on the yard and so make a clean, clear draught right through the house. He hacked at, and wedged off, the tread of a stair. He cleared out the coals from under the staircase, and built a neat fire of firewood and paper there ; he splashed about paraffin and arranged the lamps and can even as he had designed, and made a fine, inflammable pile of things in the little parlour behind the shop. " Looks pretty arsonical," he said, as he surveyed it all. " Wouldn't do to have a caller now. Now for the stairs ! "

" Plenty of time," he assured himself, and took the lamp

which was to explain the whole affair, and went to the head of
the staircase between the scullery and the parlour. He sat
down in the twilight, with the unlit lamp beside him, and
surveyed things. He must light the fire in the coal cellar under
the stairs, open the back door, then come up them very quickly
and light the paraffin puddles on each step, then sit down here
again and cut his throat. He drew his razor from his pocket
and felt the edge. It wouldn't hurt much, and in ten minutes
he would be indistinguishable ashes in the blaze.

And this was the end of life for him!

The end! And it seemed to him now that life had never
begun for him, never! It was as if his soul had been cramped
and his eyes bandaged from the hour of his birth. Why had
he lived such a life? Why had he submitted to things,
blundered into things? Why had he never insisted on the
things he thought beautiful and the things he desired, never
sought them, fought for them, taken any risk for them, died
rather than abandon them? They were the things that mattered. Safety did not matter. A living did not matter unless
there were things to live for. . . .

He had been a fool, a coward and a fool; he had been fooled,
too, for no one had ever warned him to take a firm hold upon
life, no one had ever told him of the littleness of fear or pain or
death. But what was the good of going through it now again.
It was over and done with.

The clock in the back parlour pinged the half-hour.

" Time ! " said Mr. Polly, and stood up.

For an instant he battled with an impulse to put it all
back, hastily, guiltily, and abandon this desperate plan of
suicide for ever.

But Miriam would smell the paraffin!

" No way out this time, O' Man," said Mr. Polly, and went
slowly downstairs, matchbox in hand.

He paused for five seconds, perhaps, to listen to noises
in the yard of the Royal Fishbourne Hotel before he struck
his match. It trembled a little in his hand. The paper blackened,
and an edge of blue flame ran outward and spread. The fire
burned up readily, and in an instant the wood was crackling
cheerfully.

Some one might hear. He must hurry.

He lit a pool of paraffin on the scullery floor, and instantly
a nest of wavering blue flame became agog for prey. He
went up the stairs three steps at a time, with one eager blue
flicker in pursuit of him. He seized the lamp at the top.
" Now ! " he said, and flung it smashing. The chimney broke,
but the glass receiver stood the shock, and rolled to the bottom,
a potential bomb. Old Rumbold would hear that and wonder
what it was. . . . He'd know soon enough !

Then Mr. Polly stood hesitating, razor in hand, and then
sat down. He was trembling violently, but quite unafraid.

He drew the blade lightly under one ear. "Lord!" but it stung like a nettle!

Then he perceived a little blue thread of flame running up his leg. It arrested his attention, and for a moment he sat, razor in hand, staring at it. It must be paraffin! On his trousers that had caught fire on the stairs. Of course his legs were wet with paraffin! He smacked the flicker with his hand to put it out, and felt his leg burn as he did so. But his trousers still charred and glowed. It seemed to him necessary that he must put this out before he cut his throat. He put down the razor beside him to smack with both hands very eagerly. And as he did so a thin, tall, red flame came up through the hole in the stairs he had made and stood still, quite still, as it seemed, and looked at him. It was a strange-looking flame, a flattish, salmon colour, redly streaked. It was so queer and quiet-mannered that the sight of it held Mr. Polly agape.

"Whuff!" went the can of paraffin below, and boiled over with stinking white fire. At the outbreak, the salmon-coloured flames shivered and ducked and then doubled and vanished, and instantly all the staircase was noisily ablaze.

Mr. Polly sprang up and backwards, as though the up-rushing tongues of fire were a pack of eager wolves.

"Good Lord!" he cried, like a man who wakes up from a dream.

He swore sharply, and slapped again at a recrudescent flame upon his leg.

"What the Deuce shall I do? I'm soaked with the confounded stuff!"

He had nerved himself for throat-cutting, but this was fire! He wanted to delay things, to put the fire out for a moment while he did his business. The idea of arresting all this hurry with water occurred to him.

There was no water in the little parlour and none in the shop. He hesitated for a moment whether he should not run upstairs to the bedroom and get a ewer of water to throw on the flames. At this rate Rumbold's would be ablaze in five minutes. Things were going all too fast for Mr. Polly. He ran towards the staircase door, and its hot breath pulled him up sharply. Then he dashed out through the shop. The catch of the front door was sometimes obstinate; it was now, and instantly he became frantic. He rattled and stormed and felt the parlour already ablaze behind him. In another moment he was in the High Street with the door wide open. The staircase behind him was crackling now like horsewhips and pistol-shots.

He had a vague sense that he wasn't doing as he had proposed, but the chief thing was his sense of that uncontrolled fire within. What was he going to do? There was the fire-brigade station next door but one.

The Fishbourne High Street had never seemed so empty.

Far off, at the corner by the God's Providence Inn, a group of three stiff hobbledehoys in their black neat clothes conversed intermittently with Taplow, the policeman.

" Hi ! " bawled Mr. Polly to them. " Fire ! Fire ! " and, struck by a horrible thought, he thought of Rumbold's deaf mother-in-law upstairs, began to bang and kick and rattle with the utmost fury at Rumbold's shop door.

" Hi ! " he repeated, " Fire ! "

§ 3

That was the beginning of the great Fishbourne fire, which burned its way sideways into Mr. Rusper's piles of crates and straw, and backwards to the petrol and stabling of the Royal Fishbourne Hotel, and spread from that basis until it seemed half Fishbourne would be ablaze. The east wind, which had been gathering in strength all that day, fanned the flames ; everything was dry and ready, and the little shed beyond Rumbold's, in which the local fire brigade kept its manual, was alight before the Fishbourne fire-hose could be saved from disaster. In a marvellously short time a great column of black smoke, shot with red streamers, rose out of the middle of the High Street, and all Fishbourne was alive with excitement.

Much of the more respectable elements of Fishbourne society was in church or chapel ; many, however, had been tempted by the blue sky and the hard freshness of spring to take walks inland, and there had been the usual disappearance of loungers and conversationalists from the beach and the back streets when, at the hour of six, the shooting of bolts and the turning of keys had ended the British Ramadan, that weekly interlude of drought our law imposes. The youth of the place were scattered on the beach or playing in backyards, under threat if their clothes were dirtied ; and the adolescent were disposed in pairs among the more secluded corners to be found upon the outskirts of the place. Several godless youths, seasick, but fishing steadily, were tossing upon the sea in old Tarbold the infidel's boat, and the Clamps were entertaining cousins from Port Burdock. Such few visitors as Fishbourne could boast in the spring were at church or on the beach. To all these that column of smoke did in a manner address itself. " Look here ! " it said, " this, within limits, is your affair ; what are you going to do ? "

The three hobbledehoys, had it been a week-day and they in working clothes, might have felt free to act, but the stiffness of black was upon them, and they simply moved to the corner by Rusper's to take a better view of Mr. Polly beating at his door. The policeman was a young, inexpert constable with far too lively a sense of the public-house. He put his head inside the Private Bar, to the horror of every one there. But there was no breach of the law, thank Heaven ! " Polly's and Rumbold's on fire ! " he said, and vanished again. A window opened in the top-story over Boomer's shop, and Boomer, captain of the fire brigade, appeared, staring out with a blank expression. Still staring, he began to fumble with his collar and tie ; manifestly he had to put on his uniform. Hinks' dog, which had been lying on the pavement outside Wintershed's, woke up, and having regarded Mr. Polly suspiciously for some time, growled nervously and went round the corner into Granville Alley. Mr. Polly continued to beat and kick at Rumbold's door.

Then the public-houses began to vomit forth the less desirable elements of Fishbourne society ; boys and men were moved to run and shout, and more windows went up as the stir increased. Tashingford, the chemist, appeared at his door, in shirt sleeves and an apron, with his photographic plate-holders in his hand. And then, like a vision of purpose, came Mr. Gambell, the greengrocer, running out of Gayford's alley and buttoning on his jacket as he ran. His great brass fireman's helmet was on his head, hiding it all but the sharp nose, the firm mouth, the intrepid chin. He ran straight to the fire station and tried the door, and turned about and met the eye of Boomer still at his upper window. " The key ! " cried Mr. Gambell, " the key ! "

Mr. Boomer made some inaudible explanation about his trousers and half a minute.

" Seen old Rumbold ? " cried Mr. Polly, approaching Mr. Gambell.

" Gone over Downford for a walk," said Mr. Gambell. " He told me ! But look 'ere ! We 'aven't got the key ! "

" Lord ! " said Mr. Polly, and regarded the china shop with open eyes. He knew the old woman must be there alone. He went back to the shop front, and stood surveying it in infinite perplexity. The other activities in the street did not interest him. A deaf old lady somewhere upstairs there ! Precious moments passing ! Suddenly he was struck by an idea, and vanished from public vision into the open door of the Royal Fishbourne Tap.

And now the street was getting crowded, and people were laying their hands to this and that.

Mr. Rusper had been at home reading a number of tracts upon Tariff Reform, during the quiet of the wife's absence in church, and trying to work out the application of the whole question to ironmongery. He heard a clattering in the street, and for a time disregarded it, until a cry of " Fire ! " drew him to the window. He pencil marked the tract of Chiozza Money's that he was reading side by side with one by Mr. Holt Schooling, made a hasty note, " Bal of Trade say 12,000,000," and went to look out. Instantly he opened the window and ceased to believe the Fiscal Question the most urgent of human affairs.

" Good (kik) Gud ! " said Mr. Rusper.

For now the rapidly spreading blaze had forced the partition into Mr. Rumbold's premises, swept across his cellar, clambered his garden wall by means of his well-tarred mushroom shed, and assailed the engine-house. It stayed not to consume, but ran as a thing that seeks a quarry. Polly's shop and upper parts were already a furnace, and black smoke was coming out of Rumbold's cellar gratings. The fire in the engine-house showed only as a sudden rush of smoke from the back, like something suddenly blown up. The fire brigade, still much under strength, were now hard at work in front of the latter building. They had got the door open all too late ; they had rescued the fire-escape and some buckets, and were now lugging out their manual, with the hose already a dripping mass of molten, flaring, stinking rubber. Boomer was dancing about and swearing and shouting ; this direct attack upon his apparatus outraged his sense of chivalry. His subordinates hovered in a disheartened state about the rescued fire-escape, and tried to piece Boomer's comments into some tangible instructions.

" Hi ! " said Rusper from the window. " (kik) What's up ? "

Gambell answered him out of his helmet. " Hose ! " he cried. " Hose gone ! "

" I (kik) got hose," cried Rusper.

He had. He had a stock of several thousand feet of garden hose of various qualities and calibres, and now, he felt, was the time to use it. In another moment his shop door was open, and he was hurling pails, garden syringes, and rolls of garden hose out upon the pavement. " (kik) Undo it ! " he cried to the gathering crowd in the roadway.

They did. Presently a hundred ready hands were unrolling and spreading and tangling up and twisting and hopelessly involving Mr. Rusper's stock of hose, sustained by an unquenchable assurance that presently it would in some manner contain and convey water ; and Mr. Rusper on his knees, kiking violently, became incredibly busy with wire and brass junctions and all sorts of mysteries.

" Fix it to the (kik) bathroom tap ! " said Mr. Rusper.

Next door to the fire station was Mantell and Throbsons', the little Fishbourne branch of that celebrated firm, and Mr. Boomer, seeking in a teeming mind for a plan of action, had determined to save this building. " Some one telephone to the Port Burdock and Hampstead-on-Sea fire brigades," he cried to the crowd, and then to his fellows : " Cut away the woodwork of the fire station ! " and so led the way into the blaze with a whirling hatchet that effected wonders of ventilation in no time.

But it was not, after all, such a bad idea of his. Mantell

and Throbsons' was separated from the fire station in front by a covered glass passage, and at the back the roof of a big outhouse sloped down to the fire station leads. The sturdy longshoremen, who made up the bulk of the fire brigade, assailed the glass roof of the passage with extraordinary gusto, and made a smashing of glass that drowned for a time the rising uproar of the flames.

A number of willing volunteers started off to the new telephone office in obedience to Mr. Boomer's request, only to be told, with cold official politeness, by the young lady at the exchange, that all that had been done on her own initiative ten minutes ago. She parleyed with these heated enthusiasts for a space, and then returned to the window.

And, indeed, the spectacle was well worth looking at. The dusk was falling, and the flames were showing brilliantly at half a dozen points. The Royal Fishbourne Hotel Tap, which adjoined Mr. Polly to the west, was being kept wet by the enthusiastic efforts of a string of volunteers with buckets of water, and above, at a bathroom window, the little German waiter was busy with the garden hose. But Mr. Polly's establishment looked more like a house afire than most houses on fire contrive to look from start to finish. Every window showed eager, flickering flames, and flames like serpents' tongues were licking out of three large holes in the roof, which was already beginning to fall in. Behind, larger and abundantly spark-shot gusts of fire rose from the fodder that was now getting alight in the Royal Fishbourne Hotel stables. Next door to Mr. Polly, Mr. Rumbold's house was disgorging black smoke from the gratings that protected its underground windows, and smoke and occasional shivers of flame were also coming out of its first-floor windows. The fire station was better alight at the back than in front, and its woodwork burned pretty briskly with peculiar greenish flickerings, and a pungent flavour. In the street an inaggressively disorderly crowd clambered over the rescued fire-escape, and resisted the attempts of the three local constables to get it away from the danger of Mr. Polly's tottering façade ; a cluster of busy forms danced and shouted and advised on the noisy and smashing attempt to cut off Mantell and Throbsons' from the fire station that was still in effectual progress. Further, a number of people appeared to be destroying interminable red and grey snakes under the heated direction of Mr. Rusper —it was as if the High Street had a plague of worms ; and beyond again, the more timid and less active crowded in front of an accumulation of arrested traffic. Most of the men were in Sabbatical black, and this, and the white and starched quality of the women and children in their best clothes, gave a note of ceremony to the whole affair.

For a moment the attention of the telephone clerk was held by the activities of Mr. Tashingford, the chemist, who, regardless of every one else, was rushing across the road hurling fire grenades into the fire station and running back for more, and then her eyes lifted to the slanting outhouse roof that went up to a ridge behind the parapet of Mantell and Throbsons'. An expression of incredulity came into the telephone operator's eyes, and gave place to hard activity. She flung up the window and screamed out, " Two people on the roof up there ! Two people on the roof ! "

§ 4

Her eyes had not deceived her. Two figures, which had emerged from the upper staircase window of Mr. Rumbold's and had got, after a perilous paddle in his cistern, on to the fire station, were now slowly but resolutely clambering up the outhouse roof towards the back of the main premises of Messrs. Mantell and Throbsons'. They clambered slowly, and one urged and helped the other, slipping and pausing ever and again amidst a constant trickle of fragments of broken tile.

One was Mr. Polly, with his hair wildly disordered, his face covered with black smudges and streaked with perspiration, and his trouser legs scorched and blackened ; the other was an elderly lady, quietly but becomingly dressed in black with small white frills at her neck and wrists, and a Sunday cap of écru lace enlivened with a black velvet bow. Her hair was brushed back from her wrinkled brow and plastered down tightly, meeting in a small knob behind ; her wrinkled mouth bore that expression of supreme resolution common with the toothless aged. She was shaky, not with fear, but with the vibrations natural to her years, and she spoke with a slow, quavering firmness.

" I don't mind scrambling," she said with piping inflexibility, " but I can't jump, and I won't jump."

" Scramble, old lady, then, scramble ! " said Mr. Polly, pulling her arm. " It's one up and two down on these blessed tiles."

" It's not what I'm used to," she said.

" Stick to it," said Mr. Polly. " Live and learn," and got to the ridge and grasped at her arm to pull her after him.

" I can't jump, mind ye," she repeated, pressing her lips together. " And old ladies like me mustn't be hurried."

" Well, let's get as high as possible, anyhow," said Mr. Polly, urging her gently upwards. " Shinning up a waterspout in your line ? Near as you'll get to Heaven."

" I *can't* jump," she said, " I can do anything but jump."

" Hold on," said Mr. Polly, " while I give you a boost. That's—wonderful."

" So long as it isn't jumping. . . ."

The old lady grasped the parapet above, and there was a moment of intense struggle.

" Urup ! " said Mr. Polly. " Hold on ! Gollys ! where's she
gone to ? . . ."

Then an ill-mended, wavering, yet very reassuring spring-
side boot appeared for an instant.

" Thought perhaps there wasn't any roof there ! " he
explained, scrambling up over the parapet beside her.

" I've never been out on a roof before," said the old lady.
" I'm all disconnected. It's very bumpy. Especially that last
bit. Can't we sit here for a bit and rest ? I'm not the girl I
used to be."

" You sit here ten minutes," shouted Mr. Polly, " and you'll
pop like a roast chestnut. Don't understand me ? *Roast
Chestnut !* ROAST CHESTNUT ! POP ! There ought to be
a limit to deafness. Come on round to the front and see if we
can find an attic window. Look at this smoke ! "

" Nasty ! " said the old lady, her eyes following his gesture,
puckering her face into an expression of great distaste.

" Come on ! "

" Can't hear a word you say."

He pulled her arm. " Come on ! "

She paused for a moment to relieve herself of a series of
entirely unexpected chuckles. " Sich goings on ! " she said.
" I never did ! Where's he going now ? " and came along
behind the parapet to the front of the drapery establishment.

Below, the street was now fully alive to their presence, and
encouraged the appearance of their heads by shouts and cheers.
A sort of free fight was going on round the fire-escape, order
represented by Mr. Boomer and the very young policeman,
and disorder by some partially intoxicated volunteers with
views of their own about the manipulation of the apparatus.
Two or three lengths of Mr. Rusper's garden hose appeared
to have twined themselves round the ladder. Mr. Polly watched
the struggle with a certain impatience, and glanced ever and
again over his shoulder at the increasing volume of smoke and
steam that was pouring up from the burning fire station. He
decided to break an attic window and get in, and so try and
get down through the shop. He found himself in a little bedroom, and returned to fetch his charge. For some time he
could not make her understand his purpose.

" Got to come at once ! " he shouted.

" I hain't 'ad sich a time for years ! " said the old lady.

" We'll have to get down through the house ! "

" Can't do no jumping," said the old lady. " No ! "

She yielded reluctantly to his grasp.

She stared over the parapet. " Runnin' and scurrying about
like black beetles in a kitchen," she said.

" We've got to hurry."

" Mr. Rumbold 'E's a very Quiet man. 'E likes everything
Quiet. He'll be surprised to see me 'ere ! Why ! there 'E
is ! " She fumbled in her garments mysteriously, and at last

produced a wrinkled pocket-handkerchief and began to wave it.

" Oh, come *ON* ! " cried Mr. Polly, and seized her.

He got her into the attic, but the staircase, he found, was full of suffocating smoke, and he dared not venture below the next floor. He took her into a long dormitory, shut the door on those pungent and pervasive fumes, and opened the window, to discover the fire-escape was now against the house, and all Fishbourne boiling with excitement as an immensely helmeted and active and resolute little figure ascended. In another moment the rescuer stared over the window-sill, heroic but just a trifle self-conscious and grotesque.

" Lawks-a-mussy ! " said the old lady. " Wonders and Wonders ! Why ! it's Mr. Gambell ! 'Iding 'is 'ead in that thing ! I *never* did ! "

" Can we get her out ? " said Mr. Gambell. " There's not much time."

" He might git stuck in it."

" *You'll* get stuck in it," said Mr. Polly ; " come along ! "

" Not for jumpin' I don't," said the old lady, understanding his gestures rather than his words. " Not a bit of it. I bain't no good at jumping, and I *wun't.*"

They urged her gently but firmly towards the window.

" You lemme do it my own way," said the old lady at the sill. . . .

" I could do it better if 'e'd take it off."

" Oh ! *carm* on ! "

" It's wuss than Carter's stile," she said, " before they mended it—with a cow looking at you."

Mr. Gambell hovered protectingly below. Mr. Polly steered her aged limbs from above. An anxious crowd below babbled advice and did its best to upset the fire-escape. Within, streamers of black smoke were pouring up through the cracks in the floor. For some seconds the world waited while the old lady gave herself up to reckless mirth again. " Sich times ! " she said. " Poor Rumbold ! "

Slowly they descended, and Mr. Polly remained at the post of danger, steadying the long ladder, until the old lady was in safety below and sheltered by Mr. Rumbold (who was in tears) and the young policeman from the urgent congratulations of the crowd. The crowd was full of an impotent passion to participate. Those nearest wanted to shake her hand, those remoter cheered.

" The fust fire I was ever in, and likely to be my last. It's a scurryin', 'urryin' business, but I'm real glad I haven't missed it," said the old lady, as she was borne rather than led towards the refuge of the Temperance Hotel.

Also she was heard to remark : " 'E was saying something about 'ot chestnuts. *I* haven't 'ad no 'ot chestnuts."

Then the crowd became aware of Mr. Polly awkwardly negotiating the top rungs of the fire-escape. " 'Ere 'e comes ! "

proclaimed a voice ; and Mr. Polly descended into the world
again out of the conflagration he had lit to be his funeral-pyre,
moist, excited, and tremendously alive, amidst a tempest of
applause. As he got lower and lower, the crowd howled like a
pack of dogs at him. Impatient men, unable to wait for him,
seized and shook his descending boots, and so brought him to
earth with a run. He was rescued with difficulty from an
enthusiast who wished to slake at his own expense and to his
own accompaniment a thirst altogether heroic. He was hauled
into the Temperance Hotel and flung like a sack, breathless
and helpless, into the tear-wet embrace of Miriam.

§5

With the dusk and the arrival of some county constabulary,
and first one and presently two other fire-engines from Port
Burdock and Hampstead-on-Sea, the local talent of Fishbourne found itself forced back into a secondary, less responsible, and more observant rôle. I will not pursue the story of
the fire to its ashes, nor will I do more than glance at the
unfortunate Mr. Rusper, a modern Laocoon, vainly trying to
retrieve his scattered hose amidst the tramplings and rushings
of the Port Burdock experts.

In a small sitting-room of the Fishbourne Temperance
Hotel a little group of Fishbourne tradesmen sat and conversed
in fragments, and anon went to the window and looked out
upon the smoking desolation of their houses across the way,
and anon sat down again. They and their families were the
guests of old Lady Bargrave, who had displayed the utmost
sympathy and interest in their misfortunes. She had taken
several people into her own house at Everdean, had engaged
the Temperance Hotel as a temporary refuge, and personally
superintended the housing of Mantell and Throbsons' homeless
assistants. The Temperance Hotel became and remained
extremely noisy and congested with people sitting about
anywhere, conversing in fragments, and totally unable to get
themselves to bed. The manager was an old soldier, and,
following the best traditions of the service, saw that every one
had hot cocoa. Hot cocoa seemed to be about everywhere,
and it was no doubt very heartening and sustaining to every
one. When the manager detected any one disposed to be
drooping or pensive, he exhorted that person at once to drink
further hot cocoa and maintain a stout heart.

The hero of the occasion, the centre of interest, was Mr.
Polly. For he had not only caused the fire by upsetting a
lighted lamp, scorching his trousers and narrowly escaping
death, as indeed he had now explained in detail about twenty
times, but he had further thought at once of that amiable
but helpless old lady next door, had shown the utmost decision
in making his way to her over the yard wall of the Royal
Fishbourne Hotel, and had rescued her with persistence and

vigour, in spite of the levity natural to her years. Every one thought well of him and was anxious to show it, more especially by shaking his hand painfully and repeatedly. Mr. Rumbold, breaking a silence of nearly fifteen years, thanked him profusely, said that he had never understood him properly, and declared he ought to have a medal. There seemed to be a widely diffused idea that Mr. Polly ought to have a medal. Hinks thought so. He declared, moreover, and with the utmost emphasis, that Mr. Polly had a crowded and richly decorated interior—or words to that effect. There was something apologetic in this persistence ; it was as if he regretted past intimations that Mr. Polly was internally defective and hollow. He also said that Mr. Polly was a " white man," albeit, as he developed it, with a liver of the deepest chromatic satisfactions.

Mr. Polly wandered centrally through it all, with his face washed and his hair carefully brushed and parted, looking modest and more than a little absent-minded, and wearing a pair of black dress trousers belonging to the manager of the Temperance Hotel—a larger man than himself in every way.

He drifted upstairs to his fellow-tradesmen, and stood for a time staring into the littered street, with its pools of water and extinguished gas lamps. His companions in misfortune resumed a fragmentary, disconnected conversation. They touched now on one aspect of the disaster and now on another, and there were intervals of silence. More or less empty cocoa cups were distributed over the table, mantelshelf, and piano, and in the middle of the table was a tin of biscuits, into which Mr. Rumbold, sitting round-shouldered, dipped ever and again in an absent-minded way, and munched like a distant shooting of coals. It added to the solemnity of the affair that nearly all of them were in their black Sunday clothes ; little Clamp was particularly impressive and dignified in a wide open frock-coat, a Gladstone-shaped paper collar, and a large white-and-blue tie. They felt that they were in the presence of a great disaster, the sort of disaster that gets into the papers, and is even illustrated by blurred photographs of the crumbling ruins. In the presence of that sort of disaster all honourable men are lugubrious and sententious.

And yet it is impossible to deny a certain element of elation. Not one of those excellent men but was already realising that a great door had opened, as it were, in the opaque fabric of destiny, that they were to get their money again that had seemed sunken for ever beyond any hope in the deeps of retail trade. Life was already in their imagination rising like a Phœnix from the flames.

" I suppose there'll be a public subscription," said Mr. Clamp.

" Not for those who're insured," said Mr. Wintershed.

" I was thinking of them assistants from Mantell and Throbsons'. They must have lost nearly everything."

" They'll be looked after all right," said Mr. Rumbold.
" Never fear."

Pause.

" *I'm* insured," said Mr. Clamp with unconcealed satisfaction. " Royal Salamander."

" Same here," said Mr. Wintershed.

" Mine's the Glasgow Sun," Mr. Hinks remarked.

" Very good company."

" You insured, Mr. Polly ? "

" He deserves to be," said Rumbold.

" Ra—ther," said Hinks. " Blowed if he don't. Hard lines
it *would* be—if there wasn't something for him."

" Commercial and General," answered Mr. Polly over his
shoulder, still staring out of the window. " Oh ! I'm all right."

The topic dropped for a time, though manifestly it continued to exercise their minds.

" It's cleared me out of a lot of old stock," said Mr. Wintershed ; " that's one good thing."

The remark was felt to be in rather questionable taste, and
still more so was his next comment.

" Rusper's a bit sick it didn't reach '*im*."

Every one looked uncomfortable, and no one was willing to
point the reason why Rusper should be a bit sick.

" Rusper's been playing a game of his own," said Hinks.
" Wonder what he thought he was up to ! Sittin' in the
middle of the road with a pair of tweezers he was, and about
a yard of wire—mending somethin'. Wonder he warn't run
over by the Port Burdock engine."

Presently a little chat sprang up upon the causes of fires, and
Mr. Polly was moved to tell for the one-and-twentieth time how
it had happened. His story had now become as circumstantial
and exact as the evidence of a police witness. " Upset the
lamp," he said. " I'd just lighted it. I was going upstairs,
and my foot slipped against where one of the treads was a bit
rotten, and down I went. Thing was aflare in a moment ! . . ."

He yawned at the end of the discussion, and moved doorward.

" So long," said Mr. Polly.

" Good night," said Mr. Rumbold. " You played a brave
man's part ! If you don't get a medal——"

He left an eloquent pause.

" 'Ear, 'ear ! " said Mr. Wintershed and Mr. Clamp.

" Goo'-night, O' Man," said Mr. Hinks.

" Goo'-night, All," said Mr. Polly. . . .

He went slowly upstairs. The vague perplexity common to
popular heroes pervaded his mind. He entered the bedroom
and turned up the electric light. It was quite a pleasant room,
one of the best in the Temperance Hotel, with a nice clean
flowered wallpaper, and a very large looking-glass. Miriam
appeared to be asleep, and her shoulders were humped up under

the clothes in a shapeless, forbidding lump that Mr. Polly had found utterly loathsome for fifteen years. He went softly over to the dressing-table and surveyed himself thoughtfully. Presently he hitched up the trousers. " Miles too big for me," he remarked. " Funny not to have a pair of breeches of one's own. . . . Like being born again. Naked came I into the world."

Miriam stirred and rolled over, and stared at him.

" Hallo ! " she said.

" Hallo."

" Come to bed ? "

" It's three."

Pause while Mr. Polly disrobed slowly.

" I been thinking," said Miriam. " It isn't going to be so bad after all. We shall get your insurance. We can easy begin all over again."

" H'm," said Mr. Polly.

She turned her face away from him and reflected.

" Get a better house," said Miriam, regarding the wallpaper pattern. " I've always 'ated them stairs."

Mr. Polly removed a boot.

" Choose a better position where there's more doing," murmured Miriam. . . .

" Not half so bad," she whispered. . . .

" You *wanted* stirring up," she said, half asleep. . . .

It dawned upon Mr. Polly for the first time that he had forgotten something.

He ought to have cut his throat !

The fact struck him as remarkable, but as now no longer of any particular urgency. It seemed a thing far off in the past, and he wondered why he had not thought of it before. Odd thing life is ! If he had done it he would never have seen this clean and agreeable apartment with the electric light. . . . His thoughts wandered into a question of detail. Where could he have put down the razor ? Somewhere in the little room behind the shop, he supposed, but he could not think where more precisely. Anyhow, it didn't matter now.

He undressed himself calmly, got into bed, and fell asleep almost immediately.

CHAPTER NINE

THE POTWELL INN

§ 1¾

BUT when a man has once broken through the paper walls of everyday circumstance, those unsubstantial walls that hold so many of us securely prisoned from the cradle to the grave, he has made a discovery. If the world does not please you, *you can change it*. Determine to alter it at any price, and you can change it altogether. You may change it to something sinister and angry, to something appalling, but it may be you will change it to something brighter, something more agreeable, and at the worst something much more interesting. There is only one sort of man who is absolutely to blame for his own misery, and that is the man who finds life dull and dreary. There are no circumstances in the world that determined action cannot alter, unless, perhaps, they are the walls of a prison cell, and even those will dissolve and change, I am told, into the infirmary compartment, at any rate, for the man who can fast with resolution. I give these things as facts and information, and with no moral intimations. And Mr. Polly, lying awake at nights, with a renewed indigestion, with Miriam sleeping sonorously beside him, and a general air of inevitableness about his situation, saw through it, understood there was no inevitable any more, and escaped his former despair.

He could, for example, " clear out."

It became a wonderful and alluring phrase to him—" Clear out ! "

Why had he never thought of clearing out before ?

He was amazed and a little shocked at the unimaginative and superfluous criminality in him that had turned old, cramped and stagnant Fishbourne into a blaze and new beginnings. (I wish from the bottom of my heart I could add that he was properly sorry.) But something constricting and restrained seemed to have been destroyed by that flare. *Fishbourne wasn't the world*. That was the new, the essential fact of which he had lived so lamentably in ignorance. Fishbourne, as he had known it and hated it, so that he wanted to kill himself to get out of it, *wasn't the world*.

The insurance money he was to receive made everything humane and kindly and practicable. He would " clear out " with justice and humanity. He would take exactly twenty-one pounds, and all the rest he would leave to Miriam. That seemed to him absolutely fair. Without him, she could do all sorts of things—all the sorts of things she was constantly urging him to do. . . .

And he would go off along the white road that led to Garchester, and on to Crogate and so to Tunbridge Wells, where there was a Toad Rock he had heard of but never seen. (It seemed to him this must needs be a marvel.) And so to other towns and cities. He would walk and loiter by the way, and sleep in inns at night, and get an odd job here and there, and talk to strange people.

Perhaps he would get quite a lot of work, and prosper ; and if he did not do so he would lie down in front of a train, or wait for a warm night and then fall into some smooth, broad river. Not so bad as sitting down to a dentist—not nearly so bad. And he would never open a shop any more.

So the possibilities of the future presented themselves to Mr. Polly as he lay awake at night.

It was springtime, and in the woods, so soon as one got out of reach of the sea wind, there would be anemones and primroses.

§ 2

A month later a leisurely and dusty tramp, plump equatorially and slightly bald, with his hands in his pockets and his lips puckered to a contemplative whistle, strolled along the river bank between Uppingdon and Potwell. It was a profusely budding spring day, and greens such as God had never permitted in the world before in human memory (though, indeed, they come every year and we forget) were mirrored vividly in a mirror of equally unprecedented brown. For a time the wanderer stopped and stood still, and even the thin whistle died away from his lips as he watched a water-vole run to and fro upon a little headland across the stream. The vole plopped into the water, and swam and dived, and only when the last ring of its disturbance had vanished did Mr. Polly resume his thoughtful course to nowhere in particular.

For the first time in many years he had been leading a healthy human life, living constantly in the open air, walking every day for eight or nine hours, eating sparingly, accepting every conversational opportunity, not even disdaining the discussion of possible work. And beyond mending a hole in his coat, that he had made while negotiating barbed wire, with a borrowed needle and thread in a lodging-house, he had done no real work at all. Neither had he worried about business nor about times and seasons. And for the first time in his life he had seen the Aurora Borealis.

So far, the holiday had cost him very little. He had arranged it on a plan that was entirely his own. He had started with four five-pound notes and a pound divided into silver, and he had gone by train from Fishbourne to Ashington. At Ashington he had gone to the post office, obtained a registered letter envelope, and sent his four five-pound notes with a short, brotherly note addressed to himself at Gilhampton Post Office. He sent this letter to Gilhampton for no other reason in the world than that he liked the name of Gilhampton and the rural suggestion of its containing county, which was Sussex ; and having so despatched it, he set himself to discover, mark down, and walk to Gilhampton, and so recover his resources. And having got to Gilhampton at last, he changed a five-pound note, bought four pound postal orders, and repeated his manœuvre with nineteen pounds.

After a lapse of fifteen years he rediscovered this interesting world, about which so many people go incredibly blind and bored. He went along country roads while all the birds were piping and chirruping and cheeping and singing, and looked at fresh new things, and felt as happy and irresponsible as a boy with an unexpected half-holiday. And if ever the thought of Miriam returned to him, he controlled his mind. He came to country inns and sat for unmeasured hours talking of this and that to those sage carters who rest for ever in the taps of country inns, while the big, sleek, brass-jingling horses wait patiently outside with their wagons. He got a job with some van people who were wandering about the country with swings and a steam roundabout, and remained with them three days, until one of their dogs took a violent dislike to him, and made his duties unpleasant. He talked to tramps and wayside labourers. He snoozed under hedges by day, and in outhouses and hayricks at night, and once, but only once, he slept in a casual ward. He felt as the etiolated grass and daisies must do when you move the garden roller away to a new place.

He gathered a quantity of strange and interesting memories.

He crossed some misty meadows by moonlight and the mist lay low on the grass, so low that it scarcely reached above his waist, and houses and clumps of trees stood out like islands in a milky sea, so sharply defined was the upper surface of the mist-bank. He came nearer and nearer to a strange thing that floated like a boat upon this magic lake, and behold, something moved at the stern, and a rope was whisked at the prow, and it had changed into a pensive cow, drowsy-eyed, regarding him. . . .

He saw a remarkable sunset in a new valley near Maidstone, a very red and clear sunset, a wide redness under a pale, cloudless heaven, and with the hills all round the edge of the sky a deep purple blue and clear and flat, looking exactly as he had seen mountains painted in pictures. He seemed transported to some strange country, and would have felt no surprise if the old labourer he came upon leaning silently over a gate had addressed him in an unfamiliar tongue. . . .

Then one night, just towards dawn, his sleep upon a pile of brushwood was broken by the distant rattle of a racing motor-car breaking all the speed regulations, and as he could not sleep again, he got up and walked into Maidstone as the day came. He had never been abroad in a town at four o'clock in his life before, and the stillness of everything in the bright sunrise impressed him profoundly. At one corner was a startling policeman, standing up in a doorway quite motionless like a waxen image. Mr. Polly wished him " good-morning " unanswered, and went down to the bridge over the Medway, and sat on the parapet, very still and thoughtful, watching the town awaken, and wondering what he should do if it didn't, if the world of men never woke again. . . .

One day he found himself going along a road, with a wide space of sprouting bracken and occasional trees on either side, and suddenly this road became strangely and perplexingly familiar. " Lord ! " he said, and turned about and stood. " It can't be."

He was incredulous, then left the road and walked along a scarcely perceptible track to the left, and came in half a minute to an old lichenous stone wall. It seemed exactly the bit of wall he had known so well. It might have been but yesterday he was in that place ; there remained even a little pile of wood. It became absurdly the same wood. The bracken, perhaps, was not so high, and most of its fronds were still coiled up, that was all. Here he had stood, it seemed, and there she had sat and looked down upon him. Where was she now, and what had become of her ? He counted the years back, and marvelled that beauty should have called to him with so imperious a voice—and signified nothing.

He hoisted himself with some little difficulty to the top of the wall, and saw far off under the beech trees two schoolgirls —small, insignificant, pigtailed creatures, with heads of blond and black, with their arms twined about each other's necks, no doubt telling each other the silliest secrets.

But that girl with the red hair—was she a countess ? was she a queen ? Children, perhaps ? Had sorrow dared to touch her ?

Had she forgotten altogether ? . . .

A tramp sat by the roadside, thinking, and it seemed to the man in the passing motor-car he must needs be plotting for another pot of beer. But, as a matter of fact, what the tramp was saying to himself over and over again, was a variant upon a well-known Hebrew word.

" Itchabod," the tramp was saying in the voice of one who reasons on the side of the inevitable. " It's Fair Itchabod, O' Man. There's no going back to things like that."

§ 3

It was about two o'clock in the afternoon, one hot day in May, when Mr. Polly, unhurrying and serene, came upon that broad bend of the river to which the little lawn and garden of the Potwell Inn run down. He stopped at the sight of the place and surveyed its deep tiled roof, nestling under big trees—you never get a decently big, decently shaped tree by the seaside—its sign towards the roadway, its sun-blistered green bench and tables, its shapely white windows and its row of upshooting hollyhock plants in the garden. A hedge separated the premises from a buttercup-yellow meadow, and beyond stood three poplars in a group against the sky, three exceptionally tall, graceful, and harmonious poplars. It is hard to say what there was about them that made them so beautiful to Mr. Polly, but they seemed to him to touch a pleasant scene with a distinction almost divine. He stood admiring them quietly for a long time.

At last the need for coarser æsthetic satisfactions arose in him.

"Provider," he whispered, drawing near to the inn. "Cold sirloin, for choice. And nutbrown brew and wheaten bread."

The nearer he came to the place the more he liked it. The windows on the ground floor were long and low, and they had pleasing red blinds. The green tables outside were agreeably ringed with memories of former drinks, and an extensive grape vine spread level branches across the whole front of the place. Against the wall was a broken oar, two boat-hooks, and the stained and faded red cushions of a pleasure-boat. One went up three steps to the glass-panelled door and peeped into a broad, low room with a bar and a beer-engine, behind which were many bright and helpful-looking bottles against mirrors, and great and little pewter measures, and bottles fastened in brass wire upside down, with their corks replaced by taps, and a white china cask labelled "Shrub," and cigar boxes, and boxes of cigarettes, and a couple of Toby jugs and a beautifully coloured hunting scene framed and glazed, showing the most elegant people taking Piper's Cherry Brandy, and cards such as the law requires about the dilution of spirits and the illegality of bringing children into bars, and satirical verses about swearing and asking for credit, and three very bright, red-cheeked wax apples, and a round-shaped clock.

But these were the mere background to the really pleasant thing in the spectacle, which was quite the plumpest woman Mr. Polly had ever seen, seated in an arm-chair in the midst of all these bottles and glasses and glittering things, peacefully and tranquilly, and without the slightest loss of dignity, asleep. Many people would have called her a fat woman, but Mr. Polly's innate sense of epithet told him from the outset that plump was the word. She had shapely brows and a straight, well-shaped nose, kind lines and contentment about her mouth, and beneath it the jolly chins clustered like chubby little cherubim about the feet of an Assumptioning Madonna. Her plumpness was firm and pink and wholesome, and her hands, dimpled at every joint, were clasped in front of her ; she seemed, as it were, to embrace herself with infinite confidence and kindliness, as one who knew herself good in substance, good in essence, and would show her gratitude to God by that ready acceptance of all that He had given her. Her head was a little on one side, not much, but just enough to speak of trustfulness, and rob her of the stiff effect of self-reliance. And she slept.

"My sort," said Mr. Polly, and opened the door very softly, divided between the desire to enter and come nearer, and an instinctive indisposition to break slumbers so manifestly sweet and satisfying.

She awoke with a start, and it amazed Mr. Polly to see

swift terror flash into her eyes. Instantly it had gone again.

" Law ! " she said, her face softening with relief. " I thought you was Jim."

" I'm never Jim," said Mr. Polly.

" You've got his sort of hat."

" Ah ! " said Mr. Polly, and leaned over the bar.

" It just came into my head you was Jim," said the plump lady, dismissed the topic and stood up. " I believe I was having forty winks," she said, " if all the truth was told. What can I do for you ? "

" Cold meat ? " said Mr. Polly.

" There *is* cold meat," the plump woman admitted.

" And room for it."

The plump woman came and leaned over the bar and regarded him judicially but kindly. " There's some cold boiled beef," she said, and added, " A bit of crisp lettuce ? "

" New mustard," said Mr. Polly.

" And a tankard ! "

" A tankard."

They understood each other perfectly.

" Looking for work ? " asked the plump woman.

" In a way," said Mr. Polly.

They smiled like old friends.

Whatever the truth may be about love, there is certainly such a thing as friendship at first sight. They liked each other's voices, they liked each other's way of smiling and speaking.

" It's such beautiful weather this spring," said Mr. Polly, explaining everything.

" What sort of work do you want ? " she asked.

" I've never properly thought that out," said Mr. Polly. " I've been looking round—for ideas."

" Will you have your beef in the tap or outside ? That's the tap."

Mr. Polly had a glimpse of an oaken settle. " In the tap will be handier for you," he said.

" Hear that ? " said the plump lady.

" Hear what ? "

" Listen."

Presently the silence was broken by a distant howl— " Oooooover ! " " Eh ? " she said.

He nodded.

" That's the ferry. And there isn't a ferryman."

" Could I ? "

" Can you punt ? "

" Never tried."

" Well—pull the pole out before you reach the end of the punt, that's all. Try."

Mr. Polly went out again into the sunshine.

At times one can tell so much so briefly. Here are the

facts then—bare. He found a punt and a pole, got across to
the steps on the opposite side, picked up an elderly gentleman
in an alpaca jacket and a pitch helmet, cruised with him
vaguely for twenty minutes, conveyed him tortuously into
the midst of a thicket of forget-me-not spangled sedges,
splashed some waterweed over him, hit him twice with the
punt pole, and finally landed him, alarmed but abusive,
in treacherous soil at the edge of a hay meadow about forty
yards down-stream, where he immediately got into difficulties
with a noisy, aggressive little white dog that was guarding
a jacket.

Mr. Polly returned in a complicated manner, but with
perfect dignity, to his moorings.

He found the plump woman rather flushed and tearful,
and seated at one of the green tables outside.

" I been laughing at you," she said.

" What for ? " asked Mr. Polly.

" I ain't 'ad such a laugh since Jim come 'ome. When you
'it 'is 'ead, it 'urt my side."

" It didn't hurt his head—not particularly."

" Did you charge him anything ? "

" Gratis," said Mr. Polly. " I never thought of it."

The plump woman pressed her hands to her sides and
laughed silently for a space. " You ought to 'ave charged 'im
Sumpthing," she said. " You better come and have your
cold meat before you do any more puntin'. You and me'll
get on together."

Presently she came and stood watching him eat. " You
eat better than you punt," she said ; and then, " I dessay
you could learn to punt."

" Wax to receive and marble to retain," said Mr. Polly.
" This beef is a Bit of All Right, Ma'm. I could have done
differently if I hadn't been punting on an empty stomach.
There's a leer feeling as the pole goes in——"

" I've never held with fasting," said the plump woman.

" You want a ferryman ? "

" I want an odd man about the place."

" I'm odd all right. What's the wages ? "

" Not much, but you get tips and pickings. I've a sort of
feeling it would suit you."

" I've a sort of feeling it would. What's the duties ? Fetch
and carry ? Ferry ? Garden ? Wash bottles ? *Ceteris paribus?*"

" That's about it," said the fat woman.

" Give me a trial."

" I've more than half a mind. Or I wouldn't have said
anything about it. I suppose you're all right. You've got a
sort of half-respectable look about you. I suppose you 'aven't
done anything ? "

" Bit of Arson," said Mr. Polly, as if he jested.

" So long as you haven't the habit," said the plump woman.

" My first time, Ma'm," said Mr. Polly, munching his way through an excellent big leaf of lettuce. " And my last."

" It's all right if you haven't been to Prison," said the plump woman. " It isn't what a man's happened to do makes 'im bad. We all happen to do things at times. It's bringing it home to him and spoiling his self-respect does the mischief. You don't *look* a wrong 'un. 'Ave you been to prison ? "

" Never."

" Nor a Reformatory ? Nor any Institution ? "

" Not me. Do I *look* reformed ? "

" Can you paint and carpenter a bit ? "

" Ripe for it."

" Have a bit of cheese ? "

" If I might."

And the way she brought the cheese showed Mr. Polly that the business was settled in her mind.

He spent the afternoon exploring the premises of the Potwell Inn and learning the duties that might be expected of him, such as Stockholm tarring fences, digging potatoes, swabbing out boats, helping people land, embarking, landing, and time-keeping for the hirers of two rowing boats and one Canadian canoe, bailing out the said vessels and concealing their leaks and defects from prospective hirers, persuading inexperienced hirers to start down-stream rather than up, repairing row-locks and taking inventories of returning boats with a view to supplementary charges, cleaning boots, sweeping chimneys, house painting, cleaning windows, sweeping out and sanding the Tap and Bar, cleaning pewter, washing glasses, turpentining woodwork, whitewashing generally, plumbing and engineering, repairing locks and clocks, waiting and tapster's work generally, beating carpets and mats, cleaning bottles and saving corks, taking into the cellar, moving, tapping, and connecting beer-casks with their engines, blocking and destroying wasps' nests, doing forestry with several trees, drowning superfluous kittens, dog-fancying as required, assisting in the rearing of ducklings and the care of various poultry, bee-keeping, stabling, baiting and grooming horses and asses, cleaning and " garing " motor-cars and bicycles, inflating tyres and repairing punctures, recovering the bodies of drowned persons from the river as required, and assisting people in trouble in the water, first-aid and sympathy, improvising and superintending a bathing station for visitors, attending inquests and funerals in the interests of the establishment, scrubbing floors and all the ordinary duties of a scullion, the Ferry, chasing hens and goats from the adjacent cottages out of the garden, making up paths and superintending drainage, gardening generally, de-livering bottled beer and soda-water siphons in the neighbour-hood, running miscellaneous errands, removing drunken and offensive persons from the premises by tact or muscle, as occasion required, keeping in with the local policeman, de-

fending the premises in general and the orchard in particular
from nocturnal depredators. . . .

"Can but try it," said Mr. Polly towards tea-time. "When
there's nothing else on hand I suppose I might do a bit of
fishing."

§ 4

Mr. Polly was particularly charmed by the ducklings.

They were piping about among the vegetables in the company of their foster mother, and as he and the plump woman
came down the garden path the little creatures mobbed them,
and ran over their boots and in between Mr. Polly's legs, and
did their best to be trodden upon and killed after the manner
of ducklings all the world over. Mr. Polly had never been near
young ducklings before, and their extreme blondness and the
delicate completeness of their feet and beaks filled him with
admiration. It is open to question whether there is anything
more friendly in the world than a very young duckling. It
was with the utmost difficulty that he tore himself away to
practise punting, with the plump woman coaching from the
bank. Punting, he found, was difficult but not impossible, and
towards four o'clock he succeeded in conveying a second passen-
ger across the sundering flood from the inn to the unknown.

As he returned, slowly indeed, but now one might almost say
surely, to the peg to which the punt was moored, he became
aware of a singularly delightful human being awaiting him
on the bank. She stood with her legs very wide apart, her
hands behind her back, and her head a little on one side, watching his gestures with an expression of disdainful interest. She
had black hair and brown legs and a buff short frock and very
intelligent eyes. And when he had reached a sufficient
proximity she remarked, " Hallo ! "

" Hallo," said Mr. Polly, and saved himself in the nick of
time from disaster.

" Silly," said the young lady, and Mr. Polly lunged nearer.

" What are you called ? "

" Polly."

" Liar ! "

" Why ? "

" I'm Polly."

" Then I'm Alfred. But I meant to be Polly."

" I was first."

" All right. I'm going to be the ferryman."

" I see. You'll have to punt better."

" You should have seen me early in the afternoon."

" I can imagine it . . . I've seen the others."

" What others ? " Mr. Polly had landed now and was
fastening up the punt.

" What Uncle Jim has scooted."

" Scooted ? "

" He comes and scoots them. He'll scoot you, too, I expect."

A mysterious shadow seemed to fall athwart the sunshine and pleasantness of the Potwell Inn.

" I'm not a scooter," said Mr. Polly.

" Uncle Jim is."

She whistled a little flatly for a moment, and threw small stones at a clump of meadowsweet that sprang from the bank. Then she remarked—

" When Uncle Jim comes back he'll cut your insides out. . . . . P'r'aps, very likely, he'll let me see."

There was a pause.

" *Who's* Uncle Jim ? " Mr. Polly asked in a faded voice.

" Don't know who Uncle Jim is ! He'll show you. He's a scorcher, is Uncle Jim. He only came back just a little time ago, and he's scooted three men. He don't like strangers about, don't Uncle Jim. He *can* swear. He's going to teach me, soon as I can whissle properly."

" Teach you to swear ! " cried Mr. Polly, horrified.

" *And* spit," said the little girl proudly. " He says I'm the gamest little beast he ever came across—ever."

For the first time in his life it seemed to Mr. Polly that he had come across something sheerly dreadful. He stared at the pretty thing of flesh and spirit in front of him, lightly balanced on its stout little legs and looking at him with eyes that had still to learn the expression of either disgust or fear.

" I say," said Mr. Polly. " How old are you ? "

" Nine," said the little girl.

She turned away and reflected. Truth compelled her to add one other statement.

" He's not what I should call handsome, not Uncle Jim," she said. " But he's a Scorcher and no Mistake. . . . Gramma don't like him."

§ 5

Mr. Polly found the plump woman in the big bricked kitchen lighting a fire for tea. He went to the root of the matter at once.

" I say," he asked, " who's Uncle Jim ? "

The plump woman blanched and stood still for a moment. A stick fell out of the bundle in her hand unheeded. " That little granddaughter of mine been saying things ? " she asked faintly.

" Bits of things," said Mr. Polly.

" Well, I suppose I must tell you sooner or later. He's—It's Jim. He's the Drorback to this place, that's what he is. The Drorback. I hoped you mightn't hear so soon. . . . Very likely he's gone."

" *She* don't seem to think so."

" 'E 'asn't been near the place these two weeks and more," said the plump woman.

" But who is he ? "

" I suppose I got to tell you," said the plump woman.

" She says he scoots people," Mr. Polly remarked after a pause.

" He's my own sister's son." The plump woman watched the crackling fire for a space. " I suppose I got to tell you," she repeated.

She softened towards tears. " I try not to think of it, and night and day he's haunting me. I try not to think of it. I've been for easy-going all my life. But I'm that worried and afraid, with death and ruin threatened and evil all about me ! I don't know what to do ! My own sister's son, and me a widow woman and 'elpless against his doin's ! "

She put down the sticks she held upon the fender, and felt for her handkerchief. She began to sob and talk quickly.

" I wouldn't mind nothing else half so much if he'd leave that child alone. But he goes talking to her—if I leave her a moment he's talking to her, teaching her Words, and giving her ideas ! "

" That's a Bit Thick," said Mr. Polly.

" Thick ! " cried the plump woman ; " it's 'orrible ! And what am I to do ? He's been here three times now, six days, and a week, and a part of a week, and I pray to God night and day he may never come again. Praying ! Back he's come, sure as fate. He takes my money and he takes my things. He won't let no man stay here to protect me or do the boats or work the ferry. The ferry's getting a scandal. They stand and shout and scream and use language. . . . If I complain they'll say I'm helpless to manage here, they'll take away my licence, out I shall go—and it's all the living I can get—and he knows it, and he plays on it, and he don't care. And here I am. I'd send the child away, but I got nowhere to send the child. I buys him off when it comes to that, and back he comes, worse than ever, prowling round and doing evil. And not a soul to help me. Not a soul ! I just hoped there might be a day or so. Before he comes back again. I was just hoping—— I'm the sort that hopes."

Mr. Polly was reflecting on the flaws and drawbacks that seem to be inseparable from all the more agreeable things of life.

" Biggish sort of man, I expect ? " asked Mr. Polly, trying to get the situation in all its bearings.

But the plump woman did not heed him. She was going on with her fire-making, and retailing in disconnected fragments the fearfulness of Uncle Jim.

" There was always something a bit wrong with him," she said ; " but nothing you mightn't have hoped for, not till they took him, and carried him off, and reformed him. . . .

" He was cruel to the hens and chickings, it's true, and stuck a knife into another boy ; but then I've seen him that nice to a cat, nobody could have been kinder. I'm sure he didn't do no 'arm to that cat whatever any one tries to make out of it. I'd never listen to that. . . . It was that Reformatory ruined him. They put him along of a lot of London boys full of ideas of wickedness, and because he didn't mind pain—and he don't, I *will* admit, try as I would—they made him think himself a hero. Them boys laughed at the teachers they set over them, laughed and mocked at them—and I don't suppose they *was* the best teachers in the world ; I don't suppose, and I don't suppose any one sensible does suppose that every one who goes to be a teacher or a chaplain or a warder in a Reformatory Home goes and changes right away into an Angel of Grace from Heaven——and, oh Lord ! Where was I ? "

" What did they send him to the Reformatory for ? "

" Playing truant and stealing. He stole right enough—stole the money from an old woman, and what was I to do when it came to the trial, but say what I knew. And him like a viper alooking at me—more like a viper than a human boy. He leans on the bar and looks at me. ' All right, Aunt Flo,' he says ; just that, and nothing more. Time after time I've dreamt of it, and now he's come. ' They've Reformed me,' he says, ' and made me a devil, and devil I mean to be to you. So out with it,' he says."

" What did you give him last time ? " asked Mr. Polly.

" Three golden pounds," said the plump woman. " ' That won't last very long,' he says. ' But there ain't no hurry. I'll be back in a week about.' If I wasn't one of the hoping sort——"

She left the sentence unfinished.

Mr. Polly reflected. " What sort of a size is he ? " he asked. " I'm not one of your Herculaceous sort, if you mean that. Nothing very wonderful bicepitally."

" You'll scoot," said the plump woman, with conviction rather than bitterness. " You'd better scoot now, and I'll try and find some money for him to go away again when he comes. It ain't reasonable to expect you to do anything but scoot. But I suppose it's the way of a woman in trouble to try and get help from a man, and hope and hope."

" How long's he been about ? " asked Mr. Polly, ignoring his own outlook.

" Three months it is come the seventh since he come in by that very back door—and I hadn't set eyes on him for seven long years. He stood in the door watchin' me, and suddenly he let off a yelp—like a dog, and there he was grinning at the fright he'd given me. ' Good old Aunty Flo,' he says, ' ain't you dee-lighted to see me ? " he says, ' now I'm Reformed.' "

The plump lady went to the sink and filled the kettle.

" I never did like 'im," she said, standing at the sink. " And seeing him there, with his teeth all black and broken——P'r'aps I didn't give him much of a welcome at first. Not what would have been kind to him. 'Lord!' I said, 'it's Jim.'"

" ' It's Jim,' he said. ' Like a bad shillin'—like a damned bad shilling. Jim and trouble. You all of you wanted me Reformed, and now you got me Reformed. I'm a Reformatory Reformed Character, warranted all right, and turned out as such. Ain't you going to ask me in, Aunty dear ? ' "

" ' Come in,' I said. ' I won't have it said I wasn't ready to be kind to you ! ' "

" He comes in and shuts the door. Down he sits in that chair. ' I come to torment you,' he says, ' you old Sumpthing ! ' and begins at me. . . . No 'uman being could ever have been called such things before. It made me cry out. ' And now,' he says, ' just to show I ain't afraid of 'urting you,' he says, and ups and twists my wrist."

Mr. Polly gasped.

"I could stand even his vi'lence," said the plump woman, " if it wasn't for the child."

Mr. Polly went to the kitchen window and surveyed his namesake, who was away up the garden path, with her hands behind her back, and wisps of black hair in disorder about her little face, thinking, thinking profoundly, about ducklings.

" You two oughtn't to be left," he said.

The plump woman stared at his back with hard hope in her eyes.

" I don't see that it's *my* affair," said Mr. Polly.

The plump woman resumed her business with the kettle.

" I'd like to have a look at him before I go," said Mr. Polly, thinking aloud, and added, " somehow. Not my business, of course."

"Lord ! " he cried, with a start, at a noise in the bar, " who's that ? "

" Only a customer," said the plump woman.

§ 6

Mr. Polly made no rash promises, and thought a great deal.

" It seems a sort of Crib," he said, and added, " for a chap who's looking for Trouble."

But he stayed on, and did various things out of the list I have already given, and worked the ferry, and it was four days before he saw anything of Uncle Jim. And so resistant is the human mind to things not yet experienced, that he could easily have believed in that time that there was no such person in the world as Uncle Jim. The plump woman, after her one outbreak of confidences, ignored the subject, and little Polly seemed to have exhausted her impressions in her first communication, and engaged her mind, now with a simple directness, in the study and subjugation of the new human being Heaven had sent into her world. The first unfavourable impression of his punting was soon effaced ; he could nickname ducklings very amusingly, create boats out of wooden splinters, and stalk and fly from imaginary tigers in the orchard, with a convincing earnestness that was surely beyond the power of any other human being. She conceded at last that he should be called Mr. Polly, in honour of her, Miss Polly, even as he desired.

Uncle Jim turned up in the twilight.

Uncle Jim appeared with none of the disruptive violence Mr. Polly had dreaded. He came quite softly. Mr. Polly was going down the lane behind the church, that led to the Potwell Inn, after posting a letter to the lime-juice people at the post office. He was walking slowly, after his habit, and thinking discursively. With a sudden tightening of the muscles he became aware of a figure walking noiselessly beside him.

His first impression was of a face singularly broad above, and with a wide, empty grin as its chief feature below, of a slouching body and dragging feet.

" 'Arf a mo'," said the figure, as if in response to his start, and speaking in a hoarse whisper. " 'Arf a mo', mister. You the noo bloke at the Potwell Inn ? "

Mr. Polly felt evasive. " S'pose I am," he replied hoarsely, and quickened his pace.

" 'Arf a mo'," said Uncle Jim, taking his arm. " We ain't doing a (sanguinary) Marathon. It ain't a (decorated) cinder track. I want a word with you, mister. See ? "

Mr. Polly wriggled his arm free and stopped. " Whad is it ? " he asked, and faced the terror.

" I jest want a (decorated) word wiv you. See ?—just a friendly word or two. Just to clear up any blooming errors. That's all I want. No need to be so (richly decorated) proud, if you *are* the noo bloke at Potwell Inn. Not a bit of it. See ? "

Uncle Jim was certainly not a handsome person. He was short, shorter than Mr. Polly, with long arms and lean, big hands ; a thin and wiry neck stuck out of his grey flannel shirt, and supported a big head that had something of the snake in the convergent lines of its broad, knobby brow, meanly proportioned face, and pointed chin. His almost toothless mouth seemed a cavern in the twilight. Some accident had left him with one small and active, and one large and expressionless reddish eye, and wisps of straight hair strayed from under the blue cricket cap he had pulled down obliquely over the latter. He spat between his teeth, and wiped his mouth untidily with the soft side of his fist.

" You got to blurry well shift," he said. " See ? "

" Shift ! " said Mr. Polly. " How ? "

" 'Cos the Potwell Inn's *my* beat. See ? "

Mr. Polly had never felt less witty. " How's it your beat ? " he asked.

Uncle Jim thrust his face forward and shook his open hand, bent like a claw, under Mr. Polly's nose. " Not your blooming business," he said. " You got to shift."

" S'pose I don't," said Mr. Polly.

" You got to shift."

The tone of Uncle Jim's voice became urgent and confidential.

" You don't know who you're up against," he said. " It's a kindness I'm doing to warn you. See ? I'm just one of those blokes who don't stick at things, see ? I don't stick at nuffin."

Mr. Polly's manner became detached and confidential—as though the matter and the speaker interested him greatly, but didn't concern him over much.

" What do you think you'll do ? " he asked.

" If you don't clear out ? "

" Yes."

" *Gaw !* " said Uncle Jim. " You'd better ! *'Ere !* "

He gripped Mr. Polly's wrist with a grip of steel, and in an instant Mr. Polly understood the relative quality of their muscles. He breathed, an uninspiring breath, into Mr. Polly's face.

" What *won't* I do," he said, " once I start in on you ? "

He paused, and the night about them seemed to be listening. " I'll make a mess of you," he said, in his hoarse whisper. " I'll do you—injuries. I'll 'urt you. I'll kick you ugly, see ? I'll 'urt you in 'orrible ways—'orrible ugly ways. . . ."

He scrutinised Mr. Polly's face.

" You'll cry," he said, " to see yourself. See ? Cry, you will."

" You got no right," began Mr. Polly.

" Right ! " His note was fierce. " Ain't the old woman me aunt ? "

He spoke still closelier. " I'll make a gory mess of you. I'll cut bits orf you——"

He receded a little. " I got no quarrel with *you*," he said.

" It's too late to go to-night," said Mr. Polly.

" I'll be round to-morrer—'bout eleven. See ? And if I finds you——"

He produced a blood-curdling oath.

" H'm," said Mr. Polly, trying to keep things light. " We'll consider your suggestions."

" You better," said Uncle Jim, and suddenly, noiselessly, was going.

His whispering voice sank until Mr. Polly could hear only the dim fragments of sentences. " 'Orrible things to you— 'Orrible things. . . . Kick yer Ugly. . . . Cut yer—liver out. . . . spread it all about, I will. . . . See ? I don't care a dead rat one way or the uvver."

And with a curious twisting gesture of the arm, Uncle Jim receded until his face was a still, dim thing that watched, and the black shadows of the hedge seemed to have swallowed up his body altogether.

§ 7

Next morning about half-past ten Mr. Polly found himself seated under a clump of fir-trees by the roadside, and about three miles and a half from the Potwell Inn. He was by no means sure whether he was taking a walk to clear his mind, or leaving that threat-marred Paradise for good and all. His reason pointed a lean, unhesitating finger along the latter course.

For, after all, the thing was not *his* quarrel.

That agreeable, plump woman—agreeable, motherly, comfortable as she might be—wasn't his affair ; that child with the mop of black hair, who combined so magically the charm of mouse and butterfly and flitting bird, who was daintier than a flower and softer than a peach, was no concern of his. Good Heavens ! What were they to him ? Nothing ! . . .

Uncle Jim, of course, *had* a claim, a sort of claim.

If it came to duty and chucking up this attractive, indolent, observant, humorous, tramping life, there were those who had a right to him, a legitimate right, a prior claim on his protection and chivalry.

Why not listen to the call of duty and go back to Miriam now ? . . .

He had had a very agreeable holiday. . . .

And while Mr. Polly sat thinking these things as well as he could, he knew that if only he dared to look up, the Heavens had opened, and the clear judgment on his case was written across the sky.

He knew—he knew now as much as a man can know of life. He knew he had to fight or perish.

Life had never been so clear to him before. It had always been a confused, entertaining spectacle. He had responded to this impulse and that, seeking agreeable and entertaining things, evading difficult and painful things. Such is the way of those who grow up to a life that has neither danger nor honour in its texture. He had been muddled and wrapped about and entangled, like a creature born in the jungle who has never seen sea or sky. Now he had come out of it suddenly into a great exposed place. It was as if God and Heaven waited over him, and all the earth was expectation.

" Not my business," said Mr. Polly, speaking aloud. " Where the devil do I come in ? "

And again, with something between a whine and a snarl in his voice, " Not my blasted business ! "

His mind seemed to have divided itself into several compartments, each with its own particular discussion busily in progress, and quite regardless of the others. One was busy with the detailed interpretation of the phrase, " Kick you ugly." There's a sort of French wrestling in which you use and guard against feet. Watch the man's eye, and as his

foot comes up, grip, and over he goes—at your mercy, if you
use the advantage rightly. But how do you use the advantage
rightly ?

When he thought of Uncle Jim the inside feeling of his
body faded away rapidly to a blank discomfort. . . .

" Old cadger ! She hadn't no business to drag me into her
quarrels. Ought to go to the police and ask for help ! Dragging
me into a quarrel that don't concern me.

" Wish I'd never set eyes on the rotten inn ! "

The reality of the case arched over him like the vault of
the sky, as plain as the sweet blue heaven above and the
wide spread of hill and valley about him. Man comes into
life to seek and find his sufficient beauty, to serve it, to win
and increase it, to fight for it, to face anything and dare anything for it, counting death as nothing so long as the dying
eyes still turn to it. And fear and dullness and indolence and
appetite, which, indeed, are no more than fear's three crippled
brothers, who make ambushes and creep by night, are against
him, to delay him, to hold him off, to hamper and beguile
and kill him in that quest. He had but to lift his eyes to see
all that, as much a part of his world as the driving clouds and
the bending grass ; but he kept himself downcast, a grumbling,
inglorious, dirty, fattish little tramp, full of dreams and
quivering excuses.

" Why the hell was I ever born ? " he said, with the truth
almost winning him.

What do you do when a dirty man, who smells, gets you
down and under, in the dirt and dust, with a knee below your
diaphragm, and a large hairy hand squeezing your windpipe
tighter and tighter in a quarrel that isn't, properly speaking,
yours ?

" If I had a chance against him——" protested Mr. Polly.

" It's no Good, you see," said Mr. Polly.

He stood up as though his decision was made, and was for
an instant struck still by doubt.

There lay the road before him, going this way to the east,
and that to the west.

Westward, one hour away now, was the Potwell Inn. Already
things might be happening there. . . .

Eastward was the wise man's course, a road dipping between
hedges to a hop garden and a wood, and presently, no doubt,
reaching an inn, a picturesque church, perhaps, a village, and
fresh company. The wise man's course. Mr. Polly saw himself
going along it, and tried to see himself going along it with all
the self-applause a wise man feels. But somehow it wouldn't
come like that. The wise man fell short of happiness for all
his wisdom. The wise man had a paunch, and round shoulders,
and red ears, and excuses. It was a pleasant road, and why
the wise man should not go along it merry and singing, full of
summer happiness, was a miracle to Mr. Polly's mind. But,

confound it! the fact remained: the figure went slinking —slinking was the only word for it—and would not go otherwise than slinking. He turned his eyes westward as if for an explanation, and if the figure was no longer ignoble, the prospect was appalling.

"One kick in the stummick would settle a chap like me," said Mr. Polly.

"Oh, God!" cried Mr. Polly, and lifted his eyes to heaven, and said for the last time in that struggle, "It isn't my affair!"

And so saying, he turned his face towards the Potwell Inn.

He went back, neither halting nor hastening in his pace after this last decision, but with a mind feverishly busy.

"If I get killed I get killed, and if he gets killed I get hung. Don't seem just somehow.

"Don't suppose I shall *frighten* him off."

§ 8

The private war between Mr. Polly and Uncle Jim for the possession of the Potwell Inn fell naturally into three chief campaigns. There was, first of all, the great campaign which ended in the triumphant eviction of Uncle Jim from the inn premises; there came next, after a brief interval, the futile invasions of the premises by Uncle Jim that culminated in the Battle of the Dead Eel; and, after some months of involuntary truce, there was the last supreme conflict of the Night Surprise. Each of these campaigns merits a section to itself.

Mr. Polly re-entered the inn discreetly.

He found the plump woman seated in her bar, her eyes astare, her face white and wet with tears. "O God!" she was saying over and over again—"O God!" The air was full of a spirituous reek, and on the sanded boards in front of the bar were the fragments of a broken bottle, and an overturned glass.

She turned her despair at the sound of his entry, and despair gave place to astonishment.

"You come back!" she said.

"Ra-ther," said Mr. Polly.

"He's—he's mad drunk and looking for her."

"Where is she?"

"Locked upstairs."

"Haven't you sent to the police?"

"No one to send."

"I'll see to it," said Mr. Polly. "Out this way?"

She nodded.

He went to the crinkly paned window and peered out. Uncle Jim was coming down the garden path towards the house, his hands in his pockets, and singing hoarsely. Mr. Polly remembered afterwards, with pride and amazement, that he felt neither faint nor rigid. He glanced round him, seized a

bottle of beer by the neck as an improvised club, and went
out by the garden door. Uncle Jim stopped, amazed. His
brain did not instantly rise to the new posture of things.
" You ! " he cried, and stopped for a moment. " You—*scoot !* "

" *Your* job," said Mr. Polly, and advanced some paces.

Uncle Jim stood swaying with wrathful astonishment, and
then darted forward with clutching hands. Mr. Polly felt
that if his antagonist closed, he was lost, and smote with all
his force at the ugly head before him. Smash went the bottle,
and Uncle Jim staggered, half stunned by the blow, and
blinded with beer.

The lapses and leaps of the human mind are for ever
mysterious. Mr. Polly had never expected that bottle to
break. In an instant he felt disarmed and helpless. Before
him was Uncle Jim, infuriated and evidently still coming on,
and for defence was nothing but the neck of a bottle.

For a time our Mr. Polly has figured heroic. Now comes
the fall again ; he sounded abject terror ; he dropped that
ineffectual scrap of glass and turned and fled round the corner
of the house.

" Bolls ! " came the thick voice of the enemy behind him,
as one who accepts a challenge, and bleeding but indomitable,
Uncle Jim entered the house.

" Bolls ! " he said, surveying the bar. " Fightin' with bolls !
I'll showim fightin' with bolls ! "

Uncle Jim had learned all about fighting with bottles in
the Reformatory Home. Regardless of his terror-stricken
aunt, he ranged among the bottled beer and succeeded, after
one or two failures, in preparing two bottles to his satisfaction
by knocking off the bottom, and gripping them dagger-wise
by the necks. So prepared, he went forth again to destroy
Mr. Polly.

Mr. Polly, freed from the sense of urgent pursuit, had halted
beyond the raspberry canes, and rallied his courage. The sense
of Uncle Jim victorious in the house restored his manhood.
He went round by the outhouses to the riverside, seeking a
weapon, and found an old paddle boat-hook. With this he
smote Uncle Jim as he emerged by the door of the tap. Uncle
Jim, blaspheming dreadfully, and with dire stabbing intimations in either hand, came through the splintering paddle
like a circus rider through a paper hoop, and once more Mr.
Polly dropped his weapon and fled.

A careless observer, watching him sprint round and round
the inn in front of the lumbering and reproachful pursuit of
Uncle Jim, might have formed an altogether erroneous estimate
of the issue of the campaign. Certain compensating qualities
of the very greatest military value were appearing in Mr.
Polly, even as he ran ; if Uncle Jim had strength and brute
courage, and the rich toughening experience a Reformatory
Home affords, Mr. Polly was nevertheless sober, more mobile

and with a mind now stimulated to an almost incredible nimbleness. So that he not only gained on Uncle Jim, but thought what use he might make of this advantage. The word "strategious" flamed red across the tumult of his mind. As he came round the house for the third time, he darted suddenly into the yard, swung the door to behind himself, and bolted it, seized the zinc pig's pail that stood by the entrance to the kitchen, and had it neatly and resonantly over Uncle Jim's head, as he came belatedly in round the outhouse on the other side. One of the splintered bottles jabbed Mr. Polly's ear—at the time it seemed of no importance—and then Uncle Jim was down and writhing dangerously and noisily upon the yard tiles, with his head still in the pig pail, and his bottle gone to splinters, and Mr. Polly was fastening the kitchen door against him.

"Can't go on like this for ever," said Mr. Polly, whooping for breath, and selecting a weapon from among the brooms that stood behind the kitchen door.

Uncle Jim was losing his head. He was up and kicking the door, and bellowing unamiable proposals and invitations, so that a strategist emerging silently by the tap door could locate him without difficulty, steal upon him unawares, and—— !

But before that felling blow could be delivered, Uncle Jim's ear had caught a footfall, and he turned. Mr. Polly quailed, and lowered his broom—a fatal hesitation.

"*Now* I got you!" cried Uncle Jim, dancing forward in a disconcerting zigzag.

He rushed to close, and Mr. Polly stopped him featly, as it were a miracle, with the head of the broom across his chest. Uncle Jim seized the broom with both hands. "Lea go," he said, and tugged. Mr. Polly shook his head, tugged, and showed pale, compressed lips. Both tugged. Then Uncle Jim tried to get round the end of the broom ; Mr. Polly circled away. They began to circle about one another, both lugging hard, both intensely watchful of the slightest initiative on the part of the other. Mr. Polly wished brooms were longer—twelve or thirteen feet, for example ; Uncle Jim was clearly for shortness in brooms. He wasted breath in saying what was to happen shortly—sanguinary, oriental, soul-blenching things —when the broom no longer separated them. Mr. Polly thought he had never seen an uglier person. Suddenly Uncle Jim flashed into violent activity, but alcohol slows movement, and Mr. Polly was equal to him. Then Uncle Jim tried jerks, and, for a terrible instant, seemed to have the broom out of Mr. Polly's hands. But Mr. Polly recovered it with the clutch of a drowning man. Then Uncle Jim drove suddenly at Mr. Polly's midriff ; but again Mr. Polly was ready, and swept him round in a circle. Then suddenly a wild hope filled Mr. Polly. He saw the river was very near, the post to which the punt was tied not three yards away. With a wild yell he sent the broom home under his antagonist's ribs. " Wooosh ! " he cried, as the resistance gave.

" Oh ! *Gaw !* " said Uncle Jim, going backward helplessly, and Mr. Polly thrust hard, and abandoned the broom to the enemy's despairing clutch.

Splash ! Uncle Jim was in the water, and Mr. Polly had leaped like a cat aboard the ferry punt, and grasped the pole.

Up came Uncle Jim spluttering and dripping. " You (unprofitable matter, and printing it might lead to a Censorship of Novels)—You know I got a weak chess ! "

The pole took him in the throat and drove him backwards and downwards.

" Lea go ! " cried Uncle Jim, staggering, and with real terror in his once awful eyes.

Splash ! Down he fell backwards into a frothing mass of water, with Mr. Polly jabbing at him. Under water he turned round, and came up again, as if in flight towards the middle of the river. Directly his head reappeared, Mr. Polly had him between his shoulders and under again, bubbling thickly. A hand clutched and disappeared.

It was stupendous ! Mr. Polly had discovered the heel of Achilles. Uncle Jim had no stomach for cold water. The broom floated away, pitching gently on the swell. Mr. Polly, infuriated by victory, thrust Uncle Jim under again, and drove the punt round on its chain, in such a manner, that when Uncle Jim came up for the fourth time—and now he was nearly out of his depth, too buoyed up to walk, and apparently nearly helpless—Mr. Polly, fortunately for them both, could not reach him.

Uncle Jim made the clumsy gestures of those who struggle insecurely in the water. " Keep out," said Mr. Polly. Uncle Jim, with a great effort, got a footing, emerged until his armpits were out of water, until his waistcoat buttons showed, one by one, till scarcely two remained, and made for the camp-sheeting.

" Keep out ! " cried Mr. Polly, and leaped off the punt and followed the movements of his victim along the shore.

" I tell you I got a weak chess," said Uncle Jim moistly. " I ate worter. This ain't fair fightin'."

" Keep out ! " said Mr. Polly.

" This ain't fair fightin'," said Uncle Jim, almost weeping, and all his terrors had gone.

" Keep out ! " said Mr. Polly, with an accurately poised pole.

" I tell you I got to land, you Fool," said Uncle Jim, with a sort of despairing wrathfulness, and began moving downstream.

" You keep out," said Mr. Polly in parallel movement. " Don't you ever land on this place again ! . . . "

Slowly, argumentatively, and reluctantly, Uncle Jim waded down-stream. He tried threats, he tried persuasion, he even tried a belated note of pathos ; Mr. Polly remained inexorable, if in secret a little perplexed as to the outcome of the situation. " This cold's getting to my marrer ! " said Uncle Jim.

" You want cooling. You keep out in it," said Mr. Polly.

They came round the bend into sight of Nicholson's ait, where the backwater runs down to the Potwell Mill. And there, after much parley and several feints, Uncle Jim made a desperate effort, and struggled into clutch of the overhanging osiers on the island, and so got out of the water, with the mill-stream between them. He emerged dripping and muddy and vindictive. " By *Gaw* ! " he said. " I'll skin you for this ! "

" You keep off, or I'll do worse to you," said Mr. Polly.

The spirit was out of Uncle Jim for the time, and he turned away to struggle through the osiers towards the mill, leaving a shining trail of water among the green-grey stems.

Mr. Polly returned slowly and thoughtfully to the inn, and suddenly his mind began to bubble with phrases. The plump woman stood at the top of the steps that led up to the inn door, to greet him.

" Law ! " she cried, as he drew near, " asn't 'e killed you ? "

" Do I look it ? " said Mr. Polly.

" But where's Jim ? "

" Gone off."

" 'E was mad drunk and dangerous ! "

" I put him in the river," said Mr. Polly. " That toned down his alcolaceous frenzy ! I gave him a bit of a doing altogether."

" Hain't he 'urt you ? "

" Not a bit of it ! "

" Then what's all that blood beside your ear ? "

Mr. Polly felt. " Quite a cut ! Funny how one overlooks things ! Heated moments ! He must have done that when he jabbed about with those bottles. Hallo, Kiddy ! You venturing downstairs again ? "

" Ain't he killed you ? " asked the little girl.

" Well ! "

" I wish I'd seen more of the fighting."

" Didn't you ? "

" All I saw was you running round the house, and Uncle Jim after you."

There was a little pause. " I was leading him on," said Mr. Polly.

" Some one's shouting at the ferry," she said.

" Right-o. But you won't see any more of Uncle Jim for a bit. We've been having a conversazione about that."

" I believe it *is* Uncle Jim," said the little girl.

" Then he can wait," said Mr. Polly shortly.

He turned round and listened for the words that drifted

across from the little figure on the opposite bank. So far as
he could judge, Uncle Jim was making an appointment for the
morrow. Mr. Polly replied with a defiant movement of the
punt pole. The little figure was convulsed for a moment, and
then went on its way upstream—fiercely.

So it was the first campaign ended in an insecure victory.

§ 9

The next day was Wednesday, and a slack day for the Potwell
Inn. It was a hot, close day, full of the murmuring of bees.
One or two people crossed by the ferry ; an elaborately-
equipped fisherman stopped for cold meat and dry ginger ale
in the bar parlour ; some haymakers came and drank beer for
an hour, and afterwards sent jars and jugs by a boy to be
replenished ; that was all. Mr. Polly had risen early, and was
busy about the place meditating upon the probable tactics
of Uncle Jim. He was no longer strung up to the desperate
pitch of the first encounter. He was grave and anxious. Uncle
Jim had shrunken, as all antagonists that are boldly faced
shrink, after the first battle, to the negotiable, the vulnerable.
Formidable he was, no doubt, but not invincible. He had,
under Providence, been defeated once, and he might be
defeated altogether.

Mr. Polly went about the place considering the militant
possibilities of pacific things—pokers, copper-sticks, garden
implements, kitchen knives, garden nets, barbed wire, oars,
clothes'-lines, blankets, pewter pots, stockings, and broken
bottles. He prepared a club with a stocking and a bottle
inside, upon the best East End model. He swung it round his
head once, broke an outhouse window with a flying fragment
of glass, and ruined the stocking beyond all darning. He
developed a subtle scheme, with the cellar flap as a sort of
pitfall ; but he rejected it finally because (a) it might entrap
the plump woman, and (b) he had no use whatever for Uncle
Jim in the cellar. He determined to wire the garden that
evening, burglar fashion, against the possibilities of a night
attack.

Towards two o'clock in the afternoon three young men
arrived in a capacious boat from the direction of Lammam,
and asked permission to camp in the paddock. It was given
all the more readily by Mr. Polly because he perceived in their
proximity a possible check upon the self-expression of Uncle
Jim. But he did not foresee, and no one could have foreseen,
that Uncle Jim, stealing craftily upon the Potwell Inn in the
late afternoon, armed with a large rough-hewn stake, would
have mistaken the bending form of one of those campers—
who was pulling a few onions by permission in the garden—for
Mr. Polly's, and crept upon it swiftly and silently, and smitten
its wide invitation unforgettably and unforgivably. It was
an error impossible to explain ; the resounding whack went

up to Heaven, the cry of amazement, and Mr. Polly emerged from the inn, armed with the frying-pan he was cleaning, to take this reckless assailant in the rear. Uncle Jim, realising his error, fled blaspheming into the arms of the other two campers, who were returning from the village with butcher's meat and groceries. They caught him, they smacked his face with steak and punched him with a bursting parcel of lump sugar, they held him though he bit them, and their idea of punishment was to duck him. They were hilarious, strong young stock-brokers' clerks, Territorials, and seasoned boating men ; they ducked him as though it was romping and all that Mr. Polly had to do was to pick up lumps of sugar for them and wipe them on his sleeve and put them on a plate, and explain that Uncle Jim was a notorious bad character, and not quite right in his head.

" Got a regular Obsession the Missis is his Aunt," said Mr. Polly, expanding it. " Perfect noosance he is."

But he caught a glance of Uncle Jim's eye as he receded before the campers' urgency that boded ill for him, and in the night he had a disagreeable idea that perhaps his luck might not hold for the third occasion.

That came soon enough. So soon, indeed, as the campers had gone.

Thursday was the early closing day at Lammam, and, next to Sunday, the busiest part of the week at the Potwell Inn. Sometimes as many as six boats all at once would be moored against the ferry punt and hiring row-boats. People could either have a complete tea, a complete tea with jam, cake, and eggs, a kettle of boiling water and find the rest, or Refreshments *à la carte* as they chose. They sat about, but usually the boiling water-ers had a delicacy about using the tables, and grouped themselves humbly on the ground. The complete tea-ers with jam and eggs got the best tablecloth, on the table nearest the steps that led up to the glass-panelled door.

The groups about the lawn were very satisfying to Mr. Polly's sense of amenity. To the right were the complete tea-ers, with everything heart could desire ; then a small group of three young men in remarkable green and violet and pale blue shirts, and two girls in mauve and yellow blouses, with common teas and gooseberry jam, at the green clothless table ; then, on the grass down by the pollard willow, a small family of hot-water-ers with a hamper, a little troubled by wasps in their jam from the nest in the tree, and all in mourning, but happy otherwise ; and on the lawn to the right a ginger beer lot of 'prentices without their collars, and very jocular and happy. The young people in the rainbow shirts and blouses formed the centre of interest ; they were under the leadership of a gold-spectacled senior with a fluting voice and an air of mystery ; he ordered everything, and showed a peculiar knowledge of the qualities of the Potwell jams, preferring gooseberry with

much insistence. Mr. Polly watched him, christened him the
" benifluous influence," glanced at the 'prentices, and went
inside and down into the cellar in order to replenish the stock
of stone ginger beer, which the plump woman had allowed to
run low during the preoccupations of the campaign. It was in
the cellar that he first became aware of the return of Uncle
Jim. He became aware of him as a voice, a voice not only
hoarse but thick, as voices thicken under the influence of
alcohol.

"Where's that muddy-faced mongrel ? " cried Uncle Jim.
" Let 'im come out to me ! Where's that blighted whisp with
the punt pole—I got a word to say to 'im. Come out of it, you
pot-bellied chunk of dirtiness, you ! Come out and 'ave your
ugly face wiped. I got a Thing for you. . . . *Ear* me ?

" 'E's 'iding, that's what 'E's doing," said the voice of
Uncle Jim, dropping for a moment to sorrow, and then with a
great increment of wrathfulness : " Come out of my nest, you
blinking cuckoo, you, or I'll cut your silly insides out ! Come
out of it, you pock-marked Rat ! Stealing another man's
'ome away from 'im ! Come out and look me in the face, you
squinting son of a Skunk ! . . ."

Mr. Polly took the ginger beer and went thoughtfully
upstairs to the bar.

" 'E's back," said the plump woman as he appeared. " I
knew 'e'd come back."

" I heard him," said Mr. Polly, and looked about. " Just
gimme the old poker handle that's under the beer-engine."

The door opened softly, and Mr. Polly turned quickly.
But it was only the pointed nose and intelligent face of the
young man with the gilt spectacles and the discreet manner.
He coughed, and the spectacles fixed Mr. Polly.

" I say," he said with quiet earnestness, " there's a chap out
here seems to *want* some one."

" Why don't he come in ? " said Mr. Polly.

" He seems to want you out there."

" What's he want ? "

" I *think*," said the spectacled young man, after a thoughtful
moment, " he appears to have brought you a present of fish."

" Isn't he shouting ? "

" He *is* a little boisterous."

" He'd better come in."

The manner of the spectacled young man intensified. " I
wish you'd come out and persuade him to go away," he said.
" His language—isn't quite the thing—ladies."

" It never was," said the plump woman, her voice charged
with sorrow.

Mr. Polly moved towards the door and stood with his hand
on the handle. The gold-spectacled face disappeared.

" Now, my man," came his voice from outside, " be careful
what you're saying——"

" OO in all the World and Hereafter are you to call me me man ? " cried Uncle Jim, in the voice of one astonished and pained beyond endurance, and added scornfully, " You gold-eyed Geezer, you ! "

" Tut, tut ! " said the gentleman in gilt glasses. " Restrain yourself ! "

Mr. Polly emerged, poker in hand, just in time to see what followed. Uncle Jim in his shirt-sleeves, and a state of ferocious decolletage, was holding something—yes !—a dead eel by means of a piece of newspaper about its tail, holding it down and back and a little sideways in such a way as to smite with it upward and hard. It struck the spectacled gentleman under the jaw with a peculiar dead thud, and a cry of horror came from the two seated parties at the sight. One of the girls shrieked piercingly, " Horace ! " and every one sprang up. The sense of helping numbers came to Mr. Polly's aid.

" Drop it ! " he cried, and came down the steps waving his poker and thrusting the spectacled gentleman before him, as heretofore great heroes were wont to wield the ox-hide shield.

Uncle Jim gave ground suddenly, and trod upon the foot of a young man in a blue shirt, who immediately thrust at him violently with both hands.

" Lea go ! " howled Uncle Jim. " That's the Chap I'm looking for ! " and pressing the head of the spectacled gentleman aside, smote hard at Mr. Polly.

But at the sight of this indignity inflicted upon the spectacled gentleman a woman's heart was stirred, a pink parasol drove hard and true at Uncle Jim's wiry neck, and at the same moment the young man in the blue shirt sought to collar him, and lost his grip again.

" Suffragettes ! " gasped Uncle Jim, with the ferrule at his throat. " Everywhere ! " and aimed a second more successful blow at Mr. Polly.

" Wup ! " said Mr. Polly.

But now the jam and egg party was joining in the fray. A stout, yet still fairly able-bodied gentleman in white and black checks inquired : " What's the fellow up to ? Ain't there no police here ? " And it was evident that once more public opinion was rallying to the support of Mr. Polly.

" Oh, come on then, all the LOT of you ! " cried Uncle Jim, and backing dexterously, whirled the eel round in a destructive circle. The pink sunshade was torn from the hand that gripped it, and whirled athwart the complete but un-adorned tea-things on the green table.

" Collar him ! Some one get hold of his collar ! " cried the gold-spectacled gentleman, retreating up the steps to the inn door as if to rally his forces.

" Stand clear, you blessed mantel ornaments ! " cried Uncle Jim. " Stand clear ! " and retired backing, staving off attack by means of the whirling eel.

Mr. Polly, undeterred by a sense of grave damage done to his nose, pressed the attack in front, the two young men in violet and blue skirmished on Uncle Jim's flanks, the man in white and black checks sought still further outflanking possibilities, and two of the apprentice boys ran for oars. The gold-spectacled gentleman, as if inspired, came down the wooden steps again, seized the tablecloth of the jam and egg party, lugged it from under the crockery with inadequate precautions against breakage, and advanced with compressed lips, curious lateral crouching movements, swift flashings of his glasses, and a general suggestion of bull-fighting in his pose and gestures. Uncle Jim was kept busy, and unable to plan his retreat with any strategic soundness. He was, moreover, manifestly a little nervous about the river in his rear. He gave ground in a curve, and so came right across the rapidly abandoned camp of the family in mourning, crunching teacups under his heel, oversetting the teapot, and finally tripping backwards over the hamper. The eel flew out at a tangent from his hand, and became a mere looping relic on the sward.

" Hold him ! " cried the gentleman in spectacles. " Collar him ! " and, moving forward with extraordinary promptitude, wrapped the best tablecloth about Uncle Jim's arms and head. Mr. Polly grasped his purpose instantly, the man in checks was scarcely slower, and in another moment Uncle Jim was no more than a bundle of smothered blasphemy, and a pair of wildly active legs.

" Duck him ! " panted Mr. Polly, holding on to the earthquake. " Bes' thing—duck him."

The bundle was convulsed by paroxysms of anger and protest. One boot got the hamper and sent it ten yards.

" Go in the house for a clothes'-line, some one," said the gentleman in gold spectacles. " He'll get out of this in a moment."

One of the apprentices ran.

" Bird-nets in the garden," shouted Mr. Polly. " In the garden."

The apprentice was divided in his purpose.

And then suddenly Uncle Jim collapsed, and became a limp, dead-seeming thing under their hands. His arms were drawn inward, his legs bent up under his person, and so he lay.

" Fainted ! " said the man in checks, relaxing his grip.

" A fit, perhaps," said the man in spectacles.

" Keep hold ! " said Mr. Polly, too late.

For suddenly Uncle Jim's arms and legs flew out like springs released. Mr. Polly was tumbled backwards, and fell over the broken teapot, and into the arms of the father in mourning. Something struck his head—dazingly. In another second Uncle Jim was on his feet, and the tablecloth enshrouded the head of the man in checks. Uncle Jim manifestly considered he had done all that honour required of him ; and against

overwhelming numbers, and the possibility of reiterated duck-
ings, flight is no disgrace.

Uncle Jim fled.

Mr. Polly sat up, after an interval of indeterminate length,
among the ruins of an idyllic afternoon. Quite a lot of things
seemed scattered and broken, but it was difficult to grasp it
all at once. He stared between the legs of people. He became
aware of a voice speaking slowly and complainingly.

"Some one ought to pay for those tea-things," said the
father in mourning. "We didn't bring them 'ere to be danced
on, not by no manner of means."

§ 10

There followed an anxious peace for three days, and then a
rough man in a blue jersey, in the intervals of trying to choke
himself with bread and cheese and pickled onions, broke
abruptly into information.

"Jim's lagged again, Missus," he said.

"What!" said the landlady. "Our Jim?"

"Your Jim," said the man; and after an absolutely necessary pause for swallowing, added, "Stealing a 'atchet."

He did not speak for some moments, and then he replied
to Mr. Polly's inquiries: "Yes, a 'atchet. Down Lammam
way—night before last."

"What'd 'e steal a 'atchet for?" asked the plump woman.

"'E said 'e wanted a 'atchet."

"I wonder what he wanted a hatchet for," said Mr. Polly
thoughtfully.

"I dessay 'e 'ad a use for it," said the gentleman in the
blue jersey, and he took a mouthful that amounted to conversational suicide. There was a prolonged pause in the little
bar, and Mr. Polly did some rapid thinking.

He went to the window and whistled. "I shall stick it,"
he whispered at last. "'Atchets or no 'atchets."

He turned to the man with the blue jersey, when he thought
him clear for speech again. "How much did you say they'd
given him?" he asked.

"Three munce," said the man in the blue jersey, and re-
filled anxiously, as if alarmed at the momentary clearness of
his voice.

§ 11

Those three months passed all too quickly—months of
sunshine and warmth, of varied novel exertion in the open
air, of congenial experiences, of interest and wholesome food
and successful digestion; months that browned Mr. Polly
and hardened him, and saw the beginnings of his beard;
months marred only by one anxiety, an anxiety Mr. Polly
did his utmost to suppress. The day of reckoning was never

mentioned, it is true, by either the plump woman or himself, but the name of Uncle Jim was written in letters of glaring silence across their intercourse. As the term of that respite drew to an end, his anxiety increased, until at last it trenched upon his well-earned sleep. He had some idea of buying a revolver. He compromised upon a small, and very foul and dirty rook rifle, which he purchased in Lammam under a pretext of bird scaring, and loaded carefully and concealed under his bed from the plump woman's eye.

September passed away, October came.

And at last came that night in October whose happenings it is so difficult for a sympathetic historian to drag out of their proper nocturnal indistinctness into the clear, hard light of positive statement. A novelist should present characters, not vivisect them publicly. . . .

The best, the kindliest, if not the justest course, is surely to leave untold such things as Mr. Polly would manifestly have preferred untold.

Mr. Polly has declared that when the cyclist discovered him he was seeking a weapon that should make a conclusive end to Uncle Jim. That declaration is placed before the reader without comment.

The gun was certainly in the possession of Uncle Jim at that time, and no human being but Mr. Polly knows how he got hold of it.

The cyclist was a literary man named Warspite, who suffered from insomnia ; he had risen and come out of his house near Lammam just before the dawn, and he discovered Mr. Polly partially concealed in the ditch by the Potwell churchyard wall. It is an ordinary dry ditch full of nettles, and overgrown with elder and dog-rose, and in no way suggestive of an arsenal. It is the last place in which a sensible man would look for a gun. And he says that when he dismounted to see why Mr. Polly was allowing only the latter part of his person to show (and that, it would seem, by inadvertency), Mr. Polly merely raised his head and advised him to " Look out ! " and added, " He's let fly at me twice already."

He came out under persuasion, and with gestures of extreme caution. He was wearing a white cotton nightgown of the type that has now been so extensively superseded by pyjama sleeping suits, and his legs and feet were bare, and much scratched and torn, and very muddy.

Mr. Warspite takes that exceptionally lively interest in his fellow-creatures which constitutes so much of the distinctive and complex charm of your novelist all the world over, and he at once involved himself generously in the case. The two men returned at Mr. Polly's initiative across the churchyard to the Potwell Inn, and came upon the burst and damaged rook rifle near the new monument to Sir Samuel Harpon at the corner by the yew.

" That must have been his third go," said Mr. Polly. " It sounded a bit funny."

The sight inspirited him greatly, and he explained further that he had fled to the churchyard on account of the cover afforded by tombstones from the flight of small shot. He expressed anxiety for the fate of the landlady of the Potwell Inn and her grandchild, and led the way with enhanced alacrity along the lane to that establishment.

They found the doors of the house standing open, the bar in some disorder—several bottles of whisky were afterwards found to be missing—and Blake, the village policeman, rapping patiently at the open door. He entered with them. The glass in the bar had suffered severely, and one of the mirrors was starred from a blow from a pewter pot. The till had been forced and ransacked, and so had the bureau in the minute room behind the bar.

An upper window was opened, and the voice of the landlady became audible making inquiries. They went out and parleyed with her. She had locked herself upstairs with the little girl, she said, and refused to descend until she was assured that neither Uncle Jim nor Mr. Polly's gun was anywhere on the premises. Mr. Blake and Mr. Warspite proceeded to satisfy themselves with regard to the former condition, and Mr. Polly went to his room in search of garments more suited to the brightening dawn. He returned immediately with a request that Blake and Mr. Warspite would " just come and look." They found the apartment in a state of extraordinary confusion, the bed-clothes in a ball in the corner, the drawers all open and ransacked, the chair broken, the lock of the door forced and broken, one door panel slightly scorched and perforated by shot, and the window wide open. None of Mr. Polly's clothes were to be seen, but some garments which had apparently once formed part of a stoker's workaday outfit, two brownish-yellow halves of a shirt, and an unsound pair of boots, were scattered on the floor. A faint smell of gunpowder still hung in the air, and two or three books Mr. Polly had recently acquired had been shied with some violence under the bed. Mr. Warspite looked at Mr. Blake, and then both men looked at Mr. Polly. " That's *his* boots," said Mr. Polly.

Blake turned his eyes to the window. " Some of these tiles 'ave just got broken," he observed.

" I got out of the window and slid down the scullery tiles," Mr. Polly answered, omitting much, they both felt, from his explanation. . . .

" Well, we better find 'im and 'ave a word with 'im," said Blake. " That's about my business now."

§ 12

But Uncle Jim had gone altogether. . . .

He did not return for some days. That, perhaps, was not very wonderful. But the days lengthened to weeks, and the weeks to months, and still Uncle Jim did not recur. A year passed, and the anxiety of him became less acute; a second healing year followed the first. One afternoon about thirty months after the Night Surprise the plump woman spoke of him.

" I wonder what's become of Jim," she said.

" *I* wonder sometimes," said Mr. Polly.

CHAPTER TEN

MIRIAM REVISITED

§ 1

ONE summer afternoon, about five years after his first coming to the Potwell Inn, Mr. Polly found himself sitting under the pollard willow, fishing for dace. It was a plumper, browner, and healthier Mr. Polly altogether than the miserable bankrupt with whose dyspeptic portrait our novel opened. He was fat, but with a fatness more generally diffused, and the lower part of his face was touched to gravity by a small, square beard. Also he was balder.

It was the first time he had found leisure to fish, though from the very outset of his Potwell career he had promised himself abundant indulgence in the pleasures of fishing. Fishing, as the golden page of English literature testifies, is a meditative and retrospective pursuit, and the varied page of memory, disregarded so long for sake of the teeming duties I have already enumerated, began to unfold itself to Mr. Polly's consideration. Speculation about Uncle Jim died for want of material, and gave place to a reckoning of the years and months that had passed since his coming to Potwell, and that to a philosophical review of his life. He began to think about Miriam, remotely and impersonally. He remembered many things that had been neglected by his conscience during the busier times, as, for example, that he had committed arson and deserted a wife. For the first time he looked these long-neglected facts in the face.

It is disagreeable to think one has committed arson, because it is an action that leads to jail. Otherwise I do not think there was a grain of regret for that in Mr. Polly's composition. But deserting Miriam was in a different category. Deserting Miriam was mean.

This is a history, and not a glorification of Mr. Polly, and

I tell of things as they were with him. Apart from the disagreeable twinge arising from the thought of what might happen if he was found out, he had not the slightest remorse about that fire. Arson, after all, is an artificial crime. Some crimes are crimes in themselves, would be crimes without any law, the cruelties, mockery, the breaches of faith that astonish and wound, but the burning of things is in itself neither good nor bad. A large number of houses deserve to be burned, most modern furniture, an overwhelming majority of pictures and books—one might go on for some time with the list. If our community was collectively anything more than a feeble idiot, it would burn most of London and Chicago, for example, and build sane and beautiful cities in the place of these pestilential heaps of rotten private property. I have failed in presenting Mr. Polly altogether if I have not made you see that he was in many respects an artless child of Nature, far more untrained, undisciplined, and spontaneous than an ordinary savage. And he was really glad, for all that little drawback of fear, that he had had the courage to set fire to his house, and fly, and come to the Potwell Inn.

But he was not glad he had left Miriam. He had seen Miriam cry once or twice in his life, and it had always reduced him to abject commiseration. He now imagined her crying. He perceived in a perplexed way that he had made himself responsible for her life. He forgot how she had spoiled his own. He had hitherto rested in the faith that she had over a hundred pounds of insurance money, but now, with his eye meditatively upon his float, he realised a hundred pounds does not last for ever. His conviction of her incompetence was unflinching ; she was bound to have fooled it away somehow by this time. And then !

He saw her humping her shoulders, and sniffing in a manner he had always regarded as detestable at close quarters, but which now became harrowingly pitiful.

" Damn ! " said Mr. Polly, and down went his float, and he flicked a victim to destruction, and took it off the hook.

He compared his own comfort and health with Miriam's imagined distress.

" Ought to have done something for herself," said Mr. Polly, re-baiting his hook. " She was always talking of doing things. Why couldn't she ? "

He watched the float oscillating gently towards quiescence.

" Silly to begin thinking about her," he said. " Damn silly ! "

But once he had begun thinking about her, he had to go on.

" Oh, blow ! " cried Mr. Polly presently, and pulled up his hook, to find another fish had just snatched at it in the last instant. His handling must have made the poor thing feel itself unwelcome.

He gathered his things together and turned towards the house.

All the Potwell Inn betrayed his influence now, for here, indeed, he had found his place in the world. It looked brighter, so bright, indeed, as to be almost skittish, with the white and green paint he had lavished upon it. Even the garden pailings were striped white and green, and so were the boats; for Mr. Polly was one of those who find a positive sensuous pleasure in the laying on of paint. Left and right were two large boards, which had done much to enhance the inn's popularity with the lighter-minded variety of pleasure-seekers.   Both marked innovations. One bore in large letters the single word " Museum," the other was as plain and laconic with " Omlets." The spelling of the latter word was Mr. Polly's own ; but when he had seen a whole boatload of men, intent on Lammam for lunch, stop open-mouthed, and stare, and grin, and come in and ask in a marked sarcastic manner for " omlets," he perceived that his inaccuracy had done more for the place than his utmost cunning could have contrived. In a year or so the inn was known both up and down the river by its new name of " Omlets," and Mr. Polly, after some secret irritation, smiled, and was content. And the fat woman's omelettes were things to remember.

(You will note I have changed her epithet.   Time works upon us all.)

She stood upon the steps as he came towards the house, and smiled at him richly.

" Caught many ? " she asked.

" Got an idea," said Mr. Polly.   " Would it put you out very much if I went off for a day or two for a bit of a holiday ? There won't be much doing now until Thursday."

§ 2

Feeling recklessly secure behind his beard, Mr. Polly surveyed the Fishbourne High Street once again. The north side was much as he had known it, except that the name of Rusper had vanished. A row of new shops replaced the destruction of the great fire. Mantell and Throbsons' had risen again upon a more flamboyant pattern, and the new fire station was in the Swiss Teutonic style, with much red paint ; next door, in the place of Rumbold's, was a branch of the Colonial Tea Company, and then a Salmon and Gluckstein Tobacco Shop, and then a little shop that displayed sweets, and professed a " Tea Room Upstairs."   He considered this as a possible place in which to prosecute inquiries about his lost wife, wavering a little between it and the God's Providence Inn down the street.   Then his eye caught the name over the window, " Polly," he read, " & Larkins ! Well, I'm—astonished ! "

A momentary faintness came upon him. He walked past, and down the street, returned, and surveyed the shop again.

He saw a middle-aged, rather untidy woman standing behind the counter, who for an instant he thought might be Miriam terribly changed, and then recognised as his sister-in-law Annie, filled out, and no longer hilarious. She stared at him without a sign of recognition as he entered the shop.

" Can I have tea ? " said Mr. Polly.

" Well," said Annie, " you *can*. But our Tea Room's up-stairs. . . . My sister's been cleaning it out—and it's a bit upset."

" It *would* be," said Mr. Polly softly.

" I beg your pardon ? " said Annie.

" I said *I* didn't mind. Up here ? "

" I dare say there'll be a table," said Annie, and followed him up to a room whose conscientious disorder was intensely reminiscent of Miriam.

" Nothing like turning everything upside down when you're cleaning," said Mr. Polly cheerfully.

" It's my sister's way," said Annie impartially. " She's gone out for a bit of air, but I dare say she'll be back soon to finish. It's a nice light room when it's tidy. Can I put you a table over there ? "

" Let *me*," said Mr. Polly, and assisted.

He sat down by the open window and drummed on the table and meditated on his next step, while Annie vanished to get his tea. After all, things didn't seem so bad with Miriam. He tried over several gambits in imagination.

" Unusual name," he said, as Annie laid a cloth before him.

Annie looked interrogation.

" Polly. Polly and Larkins. Real, I suppose ? "

" Polly's my sister's name. She married a Mr. Polly."

" Widow, I presume ? " said Mr. Polly.

" Yes. This five years—come October."

" Lord ! " said Mr. Polly, in unfeigned surprise.

" Found drowned he was. There was a lot of talk in the place."

" Never heard of it," said Mr. Polly. " I'm a stranger—rather."

" In the Medway near Maidstone it was. He must have been in the water for days. Wouldn't have known him, my sister wouldn't, if it hadn't been for the name sewn in his clothes. All whitey and eat away he was."

" Bless my heart ! Must have been rather a shock for her."

" It *was* a shock," said Annie, and added darkly, " But sometimes a shock's better than a long agony."

" No doubt," said Mr. Polly.

He gazed with a rapt expression at the preparations before him. " So I'm drowned," something was saying inside him. " Life insured ? " he asked.

" We started the tea-rooms with it," said Annie.

Why, if things were like this, had remorse and anxiety for Miriam been implanted in his soul ? No shadow of an answer appeared.

" Marriage is a lottery," said Mr. Polly.

" *She* found it so," said Annie. " Would you like some jam ? "

" I'd like an egg," said Mr. Polly. " I'll have two. I've got a sort of feeling— As though I wanted keeping up. . . Wasn't particularly good sort, this Mr. Polly ? "

" He was a *wearing* husband," said Annie. " I've often pitied my sister. He was one of that sort——"

" Dissolute ? " suggested Mr. Polly faintly.

" No," said Annie judiciously, " not exactly dissolute. Feeble's more the word. Weak, 'E was. Weak as water. 'Ow long do you like your eggs boiled ? "

" Four minutes exactly," said Mr. Polly.

" One gets talking," said Annie.

" One does," said Mr. Polly, and she left him to his thoughts.

What perplexed him was his recent remorse and tenderness for Miriam. Now he was back in her atmosphere, all that had vanished, and the old feeling of helpless antagonism returned. He surveyed the piled furniture, the economically managed carpet, the unpleasant pictures on the wall. Why had he felt remorse ? Why had he entertained this illusion of a helpless woman crying aloud in the pitiless darkness for him ? He peered into the unfathomable mysteries of the heart, and ducked back to a smaller issue. *Was* he feeble ? Hang it ! He'd known feebler people by far.

The eggs came up. Nothing in Annie's manner invited a resumption of the discussion.

" Business brisk ? " he ventured to ask.

Annie reflected. " It is," she said, " and it isn't. It's like that."

" Ah ! " said Mr. Polly, and squared himself to his egg. " Was there an inquest on that chap ? "

" What chap ? "

" What was his name ?—Polly ! "

" Of course."

" You're sure it was him ? "

" What you mean ? "

Annie looked at him hard, and suddenly his soul was black with terror.

" Who else could it have been—in the very clo'es 'E wore ? "

" Of course," said Mr. Polly, and began his egg. He was so agitated that he only realised its condition when he was half-way through it, and Annie safely downstairs.

" Lord ! " he said, reaching out hastily for the pepper. " One of Miriam's ! Management ! I haven't tasted such an egg for five years. . . . Wonder where she gets them ! Picks them out, I suppose."

He abandoned it for its fellow.

Except for a slight mustiness, the second egg was very palatable indeed. He was getting to the bottom of it as Miriam came in. He looked up. " Nice afternoon," he said, at her stare, and perceived she knew him at once by the gesture and the voice. She went white, and shut the door behind her. She looked as though she was going to faint. Mr. Polly sprang up quickly, and handed her a chair. " My God ! " she whispered, and crumpled up, rather than sat down.

" It's *you*," she said.

" No," said Mr. Polly very earnestly, " it isn't. It just looks like me. That's all."

" I *knew* that man wasn't you—all along. I tried to think it was. I tried to think perhaps the water had altered your wrists and feet, and the colour of your hair."

" Ah ! "

" I'd always feared you'd come back."

Mr. Polly sat down by his egg. " I haven't come back," he said very earnestly. " Don't you think it."

" 'Ow we'll pay back the Insurance now, I *don't* know."

She was weeping. She produced a handkerchief, and covered her face.

" Look here, Miriam," said Mr. Polly. " I haven't come back, and I'm not coming back. I'm—I'm a Visitant from Another World. You shut up about me, and I'll shut up about myself. I came back because I thought you might be hard up, or in trouble, or some silly thing like that. Now I see you again—I'm satisfied. I'm satisfied completely. See ? I'm going to absquatulate, see ? Hey Presto, right away."

He turned to his tea for a moment, finished his cup noisily, stood up.

" Don't you think you're going to see me again," he said, " for you ain't."

He moved to the door.

" That *was* a tasty egg," he said, hovered for a second, and vanished. . . .

Annie was in the shop.

" The missus has had a bit of a shock," he remarked. " Got some sort of fancy about a ghost. Can't make it out quite. So long ! "

And he had gone.

§ 3

Mr. Polly sat beside the fat woman at one of the little green tables at the back of the Potwell Inn, and struggled with the mystery of life. It was one of those evenings serenely luminous, amply and atmospherically still, when the river bend was at its best. A swan floated against the dark green masses of the further bank, the stream flowed broad and shining to its destiny, with scarce a ripple—except where the reeds came out from the headland, and the three poplars rose clear and harmonious against the sky of green and yellow. It was as if everything lay securely within a great, warm, friendly globe of crystal sky. It was as safe and enclosed and fearless as a child that has still to be born. It was an evening full of quality of tranquil, unqualified assurance. Mr. Polly's mind was filled with the persuasion that indeed all things whatsoever must needs be satisfying and complete. It was incredible that life had ever done more than seemed to jar, that there could be any shadow in life save such velvet softnesses as made the setting for that silent swan, or any murmur but the ripple of the water as it swirled round the chained and gently swaying punt. And the mind of Mr. Polly, exalted and made tender by this atmosphere, sought gently, but sought, to draw together the varied memories that came drifting, half submerged, across the circle of his mind.

He spoke in words that seemed like a bent and broken stick thrust suddenly into water, destroying the mirror of the shapes they sought. " Jim's not coming back again ever," he said. " He got drowned five years ago."

" Where ? " asked the fat woman, surprised.

" Miles from here. In the Medway. Away in Kent."

" Lor ! " said the fat woman.

" It's right enough," said Mr. Polly.

" How d'you know ? "

" I went to my home."

" Where ? "

" Don't matter. I went and found out. He'd been in the water some days. He'd got my clothes, and they'd said it was me."

" They ? "

" It don't matter. I'm not going back to them."

The fat woman regarded him silently for some time. Her expression of scrutiny gave way to a quiet satisfaction. Then her brown eyes went to the river.

" Poor Jim," she said. " 'E 'adn't much Tact—ever."

She added mildly, " I can't 'ardly say I'm sorry."

" Nor me," said Mr. Polly, and got a step nearer the thought in him. " But it don't seem much good his having been alive, does it ? "

" 'E wasn't much good," the fat woman admitted. " Ever."

" I suppose there were things that were good to him," Mr. Polly speculated. " They weren't *our* things."

His hold slipped again. " I often wonder about life," he said weakly.

He tried again. " One seems to start in life," he said, " expecting something. And it doesn't happen. And it doesn't matter. One starts with ideas that things are good and things are bad—and it hasn't much relation to what *is* good and what *is* bad. I've always been the skeptaceous sort, and it's always seemed rot to me to pretend men know good from evil. It's just what I've *never* done. No Adam's apple stuck in *my* throat, Ma'am. I don't own to it."

He reflected.

" I set fire to a house—once."

The fat woman started.

" I don't feel sorry for it. I don't believe it was a bad thing to do—any more than burning a toy, like I did once when I was a baby. I nearly killed myself with a razor. Who hasn't ? —anyhow gone as far as thinking of it ? Most of my time I've been half dreaming. I married like a dream almost. I've never really planned my life, or set out to live. I happened ; things happened to me. It's so with every one. Jim couldn't help himself. I shot at him, and tried to kill him. I dropped the gun and he got it. He very nearly had me. I wasn't a second too soon—ducking. . . . Awkward—that night was. . . . Ma'am. . . . But I don't blame him—come to that. Only I don't see what it's all up to. . . .

" Like children playing about in a nursery. Hurt themselves at times. . . .

" There's something that doesn't mind us," he resumed presently. " It isn't what we try to get that we get, it isn't the good we think we do is good. What makes us happy isn't our trying, what makes others happy isn't our trying. There's a sort of character people like, and stand up for, and a sort they won't. You got to work it out, and take the consequences. . . . Miriam was always trying."

" Who was Miriam ? " asked the fat woman.

" No one you know. But she used to go about with her brows knit, trying not to do whatever she wanted to do—if ever she did want to do anything——"

He lost himself.

" You can't help being fat," said the fat woman, after a pause, trying to get up to his thoughts.

" *You* can't," said Mr. Polly.

" It helps, and it hinders."

" Like my upside down way of talking."

" The magistrates wouldn't 'ave kept on the licence to me if I 'adn't been fat. . . . "

" Then what have we done," said Mr. Polly, " to get an evening like this ? Lord ! Look at it ! " He sent his arm round the great curve of the sky.

" If I was a nigger or an Italian I should come out here and sing. I whistle sometimes, but, bless you, it's singing I've got in my mind. Sometimes I think I live for sunsets."

" I don't see that it does you any good always looking at sunsets, like you do," said the fat woman.

" Nor me. But I do. Sunsets and things I was made to like."

" They don't help you," said the fat woman thoughtfully.

" Who cares ? " said Mr. Polly.

A deeper strain had come to the fat woman. " You got to die some day," she said.

" Some things I can't believe," said Mr. Polly suddenly, " and one is your being a skeleton. . . . " He pointed his hand towards the neighbour's hedge. " Look at 'em—against the yellow—and they're just stingin' nettles. Nasty weeds— if you count things by their uses. And no help in the life hereafter. But just look at the look of them ! "

" It isn't only looks," said the fat woman.

" Whenever there's signs of a good sunset, and I'm not too busy," said Mr. Polly, " I'll come and sit out here."

The fat woman looked at him with eyes in which content- ment struggled with some obscure reluctant protest, and at last turned them slowly to the black nettle pagodas against the golden sky."

" I wish we could," she said.

" I will."

The fat woman's voice sank nearly to the inaudible.

" Not always," she said.

Mr. Polly was some time before he replied. " Come here always, when I'm a ghost," he replied.

" Spoil the place for others," said the fat woman, abandon- ing her moral solicitudes for a more congenial point of view.

" Not my sort of ghost wouldn't," said Mr. Polly, emerging from another long pause. " I'd be a sort of diaphalous feeling —just mellowish and warmish like. . . . "

They said no more, but sat on in the warm twilight, until at last they could scarcely distinguish each other's faces. They were not so much thinking, as lost in a smooth, still quiet of the mind. A bat flitted by.

" Time we was going in, O' Party," said Mr. Polly, standing up. " Supper to get. It's as you say, we can't sit here for ever."

THE WAR
IN THE AIR

CONTENTS

PREFACE

A SHORT preface to *The War in the Air* has become necessary if the reader is to do justice to that book. It is one of a series of stories I have written at different times; *The World Set Free* is another, and *When the Sleeper Wakes* a third; which are usually spoken of as "scientific romances" or "futurist romances," but which it would be far better to call "fantasias of possibility." They take some developing possibility in human affairs and work it out so as to develop the broad consequences of that possibility. This *War in the Air* was written, the reader should note, in 1907, and it began to appear as a serial story in the *Pall Mall Magazine* in January, 1908. This was before the days of the flying machine; Blériot did not cross the Channel until July, 1909; and the Zeppelin airship was still in its infancy. The reader will find it amusing now to compare the guesses and notions of the author with the achieved realities of to-day.

But the book, I venture to think, has not been altogether superseded. The main idea is not that men will fly, or to show how they will fly; the main idea is a thesis that the experiences of the intervening years strengthen rather than supersede. The thesis is this: that with the flying machine war alters in its character; it ceases to be an affair of "fronts" and becomes an affair of "areas"; neither side, victor or loser, remains immune from the gravest injuries, and while there is a vast increase in the destructiveness of war, there is also an increased indecisiveness. Consequently "War in the Air" means social destruction instead of victory as the end of war. It not only alters the methods of war but the consequences of war. After all that has happened since this fantasia of possibility was written, I do not think that there is much wrong with that thesis. And after a recent journey to Russia, of which I have given an account in *Russia in the Shadows*, I am inclined to think very well of myself as I re-read the entirely imaginary account of the collapse of civilisation under the strain of modern war which forms the Epilogue of this story. In 1907 this chapter was read with hearty laughter as the production of an "imaginative novelist's" distempered brain. Is it quite so wildly funny to-day?

And I ask the reader to remember that date of 1907 also when he reads of Prince Karl Albert and the Graf von Winterfeld. Seven years before the Great War, its shadow stood out upon our sunny world as plainly as all that, for the "imaginative novelist"—or any one else with ordinary common sense—to see. The great catastrophe marched upon us in the daylight. But everybody thought that somebody else would

167

stop it before it really arrived. Behind that great catastrophe march others to-day. The steady deterioration of currency, the shrinkage of production, the ebb of educational energy in Europe, work out to consequences that are obvious to every clear-headed man. National and imperialist rivalries march whole nations at the quickstep towards social collapse. The process goes on as plainly as the militarist process was going on in the years when *The War in the Air* was written.

Do we still trust to somebody else ?

H. G. WELLS.

Easton Glebe, 1921.

CHAPTER I

OF PROGRESS AND THE SMALLWAYS FAMILY

§ 1

"THIS here Progress," said Mr. Tom Smallways, "it keeps on.

"You'd hardly think it *could* keep on," said Mr. Tom Smallways.

It was long before the War in the Air began that Mr. Smallways made this remark. He was sitting on the fence at the end of his garden and surveying the great Bun Hill gas-works with an eye that neither praised nor blamed. Above the clustering gasometers three unfamiliar shapes appeared, thin, wallowing bladders that flapped and rolled about, and grew bigger and bigger and rounder and rounder—balloons in course of inflation for the South of England Aero Club's Saturday-afternoon ascent.

"They goes up every Saturday," said his neighbour, Mr. Stringer, the milkman. "It's only yestiday, so to speak, when all London turned out to see a balloon go over, and now every little place in the country has its weekly outings—uppings, rather. It's been the salvation of them gas companies."

"Larst Satiday I got three barrer-loads of gravel off my petaters," said Mr. Tom Smallways. "Three barrer-loads! What they dropped as ballase. Some of the plants was broke, and some was buried."

"Ladies, they say, goes up!"

"I suppose we got to call 'em ladies," said Mr. Tom Smallways. "Still, it ain't hardly my idea of a lady—flying about in the air, and throwing gravel at people. It ain't what I been accustomed to consider ladylike, whether or no."

Mr. Stringer nodded his head approvingly, and for a time they continued to regard the swelling bulks with expressions that had changed from indifference to disapproval.

Mr. Tom Smallways was a greengrocer by trade and a gardener by disposition; his little wife, Jessica, saw to the shop, and Heaven had planned him for a peaceful world. Unfortunately Heaven had not planned a peaceful world for him. He lived in a world of obstinate and incessant change, and in parts where its operations were unsparingly conspicuous. Vicissitude was in the very soil he tilled; even his garden was upon a yearly tenancy, and overshadowed by a huge board that proclaimed it not so much a garden as an eligible building site. He was horticulture under notice to quit, the last patch of country in a district flooded by new and urban things. He did his best to console himself, to imagine matters near the turn of the tide.

" You'd hardly think it could keep on," he said.

Mr. Smallways' aged father could remember Bun Hill as an idyllic Kentish village. He had driven Sir Peter Bone until he was fifty, and then he took to drink a little and driving the station bus, which lasted him until he was seventy-eight. Then he retired. He sat by the fireside, a shrivelled, very, very old coachman, full charged with reminiscences and ready for any careless stranger. He could tell you of the vanished estate of Sir Peter Bone, long since put up for building, and how that magnate ruled the country-side when it was country-side, of shooting and hunting and of coaches along the high road, of how " where the gas-works is " was a cricket-field, and of the coming of the Crystal Palace. The Crystal Palace was six miles away from Bun Hill, a great façade that glittered in the morning and was a clear blue outline against the sky in the afternoon, and at night a source of gratuitous fireworks for all the population of Bun Hill. And then had come the railway, and then villas and villas, and then the gas-works and the water-works and a great ugly sea of workmen's houses, and then drainage, and the water vanished out of the Otter-bourne and left it a dreadful ditch, and then a second railway station, Bun Hill South, and more houses and more, more shops, more competition, plate-glass shops, a board-school, rates, omnibuses, tramcars—going right away into London itself—bicycles, motor-cars, and then more motor-cars, a Carnegie library.

" You'd hardly think it could keep on," said Mr. Tom Smallways, growing up among these marvels.

But it kept on. Even from the first the greengrocer's shop which he had set up in one of the smallest of the old surviving village houses in the tail of the High Street had a submerged air, an air of hiding from something that was looking for it. When they had made up the pavement of the High Street, they levelled that up so that one had to go down three steps into the shop. Tom did his best to sell only his own excellent but limited range of produce ; but Progress came shoving things into his window, French artichokes and aubergines, foreign apples—apples from the State of New York, apples from California, apples from Canada, apples from New Zealand, "pretty lookin' fruit, but not what I should call English apples," said Tom—bananas, unfamiliar nuts, grape fruits, mangoes.

The motor-cars that went by northward and southward grew more and more powerful and efficient, whizzed faster and smelt worse ; there appeared great, clangorous petrol trolleys delivering coal and parcels in the place of vanishing horse-vans ; motor-omnibuses ousted the horse-omnibuses, even the Kentish strawberries going Londonward in the night took to machinery and clattered instead of creaking, and became affected in flavour by progress and petrol.

And then young Bert Smallways got a motor-bicycle.

§ 2

Bert, it is necessary to explain, was a progressive Smallways.

Nothing speaks more eloquently of the pitiless insistence of progress and expansion in our time than that it should get into the Smallways blood. But there was something advanced and enterprising about young Smallways before he was out of short frocks. He was lost for a whole day when he was five, and nearly drowned in the reservoir of the new water-works before he was seven. He had a real pistol taken away from him by a real policeman when he was ten. And he learnt to smoke, not with pipes and brown paper and cane as Tom had done, but with a penny packet of Boys of England American cigarettes. His language shocked his father before he was twelve, and by that age, what with touting for parcels at the station and selling the Bun Hill *Weekly Express*, he was making three shillings a week or more, and spending it on *Chips*, *Comic Cuts*, *Ally Sloper's Half-Holiday*, cigarettes, and all the concomitants of a life of pleasure and enlightenment. All of this without hindrance to his literary studies, which carried him up to the seventh standard at an exceptionally early age. I mention these things so that you may have no doubt at all concerning the sort of stuff Bert had in him.

He was six years younger than Tom, and for a time there was an attempt to utilise him in the greengrocer's shop when Tom at twenty-one married Jessica—who was thirty, and had saved a little money in service. But it was not Bert's *forte* to be utilised. He hated digging, and when he was given a basket of stuff to deliver, a nomadic instinct arose irresistibly, it became his pack, and he did not seem to care how heavy it was nor where he took it, so long as he did not take it to its destination. Glamour filled the world, and he strayed after it, basket and all. So Tom took his goods out himself, and sought employers for Bert who did not know of this strain of poetry in his nature. Bert touched the fringe of a number of trades in succession—draper's porter, chemist's boy, doctor's page, junior assistant gas-fitter, envelope addresser, milk-cart assistant, golf-caddie, and at last help in a bicycle shop. Here, apparently, he found the progressive quality his nature had craved. His employer was a pirate-souled young man named Grubb, with a black-smeared face by day and a music-hall side in the evening, who dreamt of a patent lever chain ; and it seemed to Bert that he was the perfect model of a gentleman of spirit. He hired out quite the dirtiest and unsafest bicycles in the whole south of England, and conducted the subsequent discussions with astonishing verve. Bert and he settled down very well together. Bert lived in, became almost a trick rider—he could ride bicycles for miles that would have come to pieces instantly under you or me—took to washing his face after business and sometimes even his neck, and spent his surplus money upon remarkable ties and collars, cigarettes, and shorthand classes at the Bun Hill Institute.

He would go round to Tom at times, and look and talk so brilliantly that Tom and Jessica, who both had a natural tendency to be respectful to anybody or anything, looked up to him immensely.

" He's a go-ahead chap, is Bert," said Tom. " He knows a thing or two."

" Let's hope he don't know too much," said Jessica, who had a fine sense of limitations.

" It's go-ahead Times," said Tom. " Noo petaters, and English at that ; we'll be having 'em in March if things go on as they do go. I never see such Times. See his tie last night ? "

" It wasn't suited to him, Tom. It was a gentleman's tie. He wasn't up to it — not the rest of him. It wasn't becoming. . . . "

Then presently Bert got a cyclist's suit, cap, badge and all ; and to see him and Grubb going down to Brighton (and back)—heads down, handlebars down, backbones curved— was a revelation in the possibilities of the Smallways blood.

Go-ahead Times !

Old Smallways would sit over the fire mumbling of the greatness of other days, of old Sir Peter, who drove his coach to Brighton and back in eight-and-twenty hours, of old Sir Peter's white top-hats, of Lady Bone, who never set foot to ground except to walk in the garden, of the great prize-fights at Crawley. He talked of pink and pig-skin breeches, of foxes at Ring's Bottom where now the County Council pauper lunatics were enclosed, of Lady Bone's chintzes and crino- lines. Nobody heeded him. The world had thrown up a new type of gentleman altogether—a gentleman of most ungentle- manly energy, a gentleman in dusty oilskins and motor goggles and a wonderful cap, a stink-making gentleman, a swift, high- class badger, who fled perpetually along high roads from the dust and stink he perpetually made. And his lady, as they were able to see her at Bun Hill, was a weather-bitten goddess as free from refinement as a gipsy—not so much dressed as packed for transit at a high velocity.

So Bert grew up, filled with ideals of speed and enterprise, and became, so far as he became anything, a kind of bicycle engineer of the let's-'ave-a-look-at-it and enamel chipping variety. Even a road-racer, geared to a hundred and twenty, failed to satisfy him, and for a time he pined in vain at twenty miles an hour along roads that were continually more dusty and more crowded with mechanical traffic. But at last his savings accumulated, and his chance came. The hire-purchase system bridged a financial gap, and one bright and memorable Sunday morning he wheeled his new possession through the shop into the road, got on to it with the advice and assistance of Grubb, and teuf-teuffed off into the haze of the traffic-tortured high road to add himself as one more voluntary public danger to the amenities of the south of England.

" Orf to Brighton ! " said old Smallways, regarding his youngest son from the sitting-room window over the green-grocer's shop with something between pride and reprobation. " When I was 'is age, I'd never been to London, never bin south of Crawley—never bin anywhere on my own where I couldn't walk. And nobody didn't go. Not unless they was gentry. Now everybody's orf everywhere ; the whole dratted country sims flying to pieces. Wonder they all get back. Orf to Brighton, indeed ! Anybody want to buy 'orses ? "

" You can't say *I* bin to Brighton, father," said Tom.

" Nor don't want to go," said Jessica, sharply ; " creering about and spendin' your money."

§ 3

For a time the possibilities of the motor-bicycle so occupied Bert's mind that he remained regardless of the new direction in which the striving soul of man was finding exercise and refreshment. He failed to observe that the type of motor-car, like the type of bicycle, was settling down and losing its adventurous quality. Indeed, it is as true as it is remarkable that Tom was the first to observe the new development. But his gardening made him attentive to the heavens, and the proximity of the Bun Hill gas-works and the Crystal Palace, from which ascents were continually being made, and presently the descent of ballast upon his potatoes conspired to bear in upon his unwilling mind the fact that the Goddess of Change was turning her disturbing attention to the sky. The first great boom in aeronautics was beginning.

Grubb and Bert heard of it in a music-hall, then it was driven home to their minds by the cinematograph, then Bert's imagination was stimulated by a sixpenny edition of that aeronautic classic, Mr. George Griffith's *The Outlaws of the Air*, and so the thing really got hold of them.

At first the most obvious aspect was the multiplication of balloons. The sky of Bun Hill began to be infested by balloons ! On Wednesday and Saturday afternoons particularly you could scarcely look skyward for a quarter of an hour without dis-covering a balloon somewhere. And then one bright day Bert, motoring towards Croydon, was arrested by the insur-gence of a huge, bolster-shaped monster from the Crystal Palace grounds, and obliged to dismount and watch it. It was like a bolster with a broken nose, and below it, and com-paratively small, was a stiff framework bearing a man and an engine with a screw that whizzed round in front and a sort of canvas rudder behind. The framework had an air of dragging the reluctant gas-cylinder after it like a brisk little terrier towing a shy, gas-distended elephant into society. The combined monster certainly travelled and steered. It went overhead perhaps a thousand feet up (Bert heard the engine), sailed away southward, vanished over the hills, reappeared a little blue outline far off in the east, going now very fast before a gentle south-west gale, returned above the Crystal Palace towers, circled round them, chose a position for descent, and sank down out of sight.

Bert sighed deeply, and turned to his motor-bicycle again.

And that was only the beginning of a succession of strange phenomena in the heavens—cylinders, cones, pear-shaped monsters, even at last a thing of aluminium that glittered wonderfully, and that Grubb, through some confusion of ideas about armour plates, was inclined to consider a war machine.

There followed actual flight.

This, however, was not an affair that was visible from Bun Hill; it was something that occurred in private grounds or other enclosed places and under favourable conditions, and it was brought home to Grubb and Bert Smallways only by means of the magazine page of the halfpenny newspapers or by cinematograph records. But it was brought home very insistently, and in those days if ever one heard a man saying in a public place in a loud, reassuring confident tone, "It's bound to come," the chances were ten to one he was talking of flying. And Bert got a box lid and wrote out in correct window-ticket style, and Grubb put in the window this inscription, "Aeroplanes made and repaired." It quite upset Tom—it seemed taking one's shop so lightly ; but most of the neighbours, and all the sporting ones, approved of it as being very good indeed.

Everybody talked of flying, everybody repeated over and over again, "Bound to come," and then you know it didn't come. There was a hitch. They flew—that was all right ; they flew in machines heavier than air. But they smashed. Sometimes they smashed the engine, sometimes they smashed the aeronaut, usually they smashed both. Machines that made flights of three or four miles and came down safely, went up the next time to headlong disaster. There seemed no possible trusting to them. The breeze upset them, the eddies near the ground upset them, a passing thought in the mind of the aeronaut upset them. Also they upset—simply.

"It's this 'stability' does 'em," said Grubb, repeating his newspaper. "They pitch and they pitch, till they pitch themselves to pieces."

Experiments fell away after two expectant years of this sort of success, the public and then the newspapers tired of the expensive photographic reproductions, the optimistic reports, the perpetual sequence of triumph and disaster and silence. Flying slumped, even ballooning fell away to some extent, though it remained a fairly popular sport, and continued to lift gravel from the wharf of the Bun Hill gas-works and drop it upon deserving people's lawns and gardens. There were half a dozen reassuring years for Tom—at least so far as flying was concerned. But that was the great time of mono-rail development, and his anxiety was only diverted from the high heavens by the most urgent threats and symptoms of change in the lower sky.

There had been talk of mono-rails for several years. But the real mischief began when Brennan sprang his gyroscopic mono-rail car upon the Royal Society. It was the leading sensation of the 1907 soirées ; that celebrated demonstration-room was all too small for its exhibition. Brave soldiers, leading Zionists, deserving novelists, noble ladies, congested the narrow passage, and thrust distinguished elbows into ribs the world would not willingly let break, deeming themselves fortunate if they could see " just a little bit of the rail." Inaudible but convincing, the great inventor expounded his discovery, and sent his obedient little model of the trains of the future up gradients, round curves and across a sagging wire. It ran along on its single rail, on its single wheels, simple and sufficient ; it stopped, reversed, stood still, balancing perfectly. It maintained its astounding equilibrium amidst a thunder of applause. The audience dispersed at last, discussing how far they would enjoy crossing an abyss on a wire cable. " Suppose the gyroscope stopped ! " Few of them anticipated a tithe of what the Brennan mono-rail would do for their railway securities and the face of the world.

In a few years they realised better. In a little while no one thought anything of crossing an abyss on a wire, and the mono-rail was superseding the tram-lines, railways, and indeed every form of track for mechanical locomotion. Where land was cheap the rail ran along the ground, where it was dear the rail lifted up on iron standards and passed overhead ; its swift, convenient cars went everywhere and did everything that had once been done along made tracks upon the ground.

When old Smallways died, Tom could think of nothing more striking to say of him than that, " When he was a boy, there wasn't nothing higher than your chimbleys—there wasn't a wire nor a cable in the sky ! "

Old Smallways went to his grave under an intricate network of wires and cables, for Bun Hill became not only a sort of minor centre of power distribution—the Home Counties Power Distribution Company set up transformers and a generating station close beside the old gas-works—but also a junction on the suburban mono-rail system. Moreover, every tradesman in the place, and indeed nearly every house, had its own telephone.

The mono-rail cable standards became a striking fact in urban landscape, for the most part stout iron erections rather like tapering trestles, and painted a bright bluish green. One, it happened, bestrode Tom's house, which looked still more retiring and apologetic beneath its immensity ; and another giant stood just inside the corner of his garden, which was still not built upon and unchanged except for a couple of advertisement boards, one recommending a two-and-sixpenny watch, and one a nerve restorer. These, by the bye, were placed almost horizontally to catch the eye of the passing mono-rail passengers above, and so served admirably to roof over a tool-shed and a mushroom-shed for Tom. All day and all night the fast cars from Brighton and Hastings went murmuring by overhead—long, broad, comfortable-looking cars, that were brightly lit after dusk. As they flew by at night, transient flares of light and a rumbling sound of passage, they kept up a perpetual summer lightning and thunder-storm in the street below.

Presently the English Channel was bridged—a series of great iron Eiffel Tower pillars carrying mono-rail cables at a height of a hundred and fifty feet above the water, except near the middle, where they rose higher to allow the passage of the London and Antwerp shipping and the Hamburg-America liners.

Then heavy motor-cars began to run about on only a couple of wheels, one behind the other, which for some reason upset Tom dreadfully, and made him gloomy for days after the first one passed the shop. . . . `

All this gyroscopic and mono-rail development naturally absorbed a vast amount of public attention, and there was also a huge excitement consequent upon the amazing gold discoveries off the coast of Anglesea made by a submarine prospector, Miss Patricia Giddy. She had taken her degree in geology and mineralogy in the University of London, and while working upon the auriferous rocks of North Wales after a brief holiday spent in agitating for women's suffrage, she had been struck by the possibility of these reefs cropping up again under the water. She had set herself to verify this supposition by the use of the submarine crawler invented by Doctor Alberto Cassini. By a happy mingling of reasoning and intuition peculiar to her sex she found gold at her first descent, and emerged after three hours' submersion with about two hundredweight of ore containing gold in the unparalleled quantity of seventeen ounces to the ton. But the whole story of her submarine mining, intensely interesting as it is, must be told at some other time ; suffice it now to remark simply that it was during the consequent great rise of prices, confidence, and enterprise that the revival of interest in flying occurred.

§ 4

It is curious how the final boom of flying began. It was like the coming of a breeze on a quiet day ; nothing started it, it came. People began to talk of flying with an air of never having for one moment dropped the subject. Pictures of flying and flying machines returned to the newspapers ; articles and allusions increased and multiplied in the serious magazines. People asked in mono-rail trains, " When are we going to fly ? " A new crop of inventors sprang up in a night or so like fungi. The Aero Club announced the project of a great Flying Exhibition in a large area of ground that the removal of slums in Whitechapel had rendered available.

The advancing wave soon produced a sympathetic ripple in the Bun Hill establishment. Grubb routed out his flying machine model again, tried it in the yard behind the shop, got a kind of flight out of it, and broke seventeen panes of glass and nine flower-pots in the greenhouse that occupied the next yard but one.

And then, springing from nowhere, sustained one knew not how, came a persistent, disturbing rumour that the problem had been solved, that the secret was known. Bert met it one early-closing afternoon as he refreshed himself in an inn near Nutfield, whither his motor-bicycle had brought him. There smoked and meditated a person in khaki, an engineer, who presently took an interest in Bert's machine. It was a sturdy piece of apparatus, and it had acquired a kind of documentary value in these quick-changing times ; it was now nearly eight years old. Its points discussed, the soldier broke into a new topic with, " My next's going to be an aeroplane, so far as I can see. I've had enough of roads and ways."

" They *tork*," said Bert.

" They talk — and they do," said the soldier. " The thing's coming."

" It keeps *on* coming," said Bert ; " I shall believe when I see it."

" That won't be long," said the soldier.

The conversation seemed degenerating into an amiable wrangle of contradiction.

" I tell you they *are* flying," the soldier insisted. " I see it myself."

" We've all seen it," said Bert.

" I don't mean flap up and smash up ; I mean real, safe, steady, controlled flying, against the wind, good and right."

" You ain't seen that ! "

" I 'ave ! Aldershot. They try to keep it a secret. They got it right enough. You bet—our War Office isn't going to be caught napping this time."

Bert's incredulity was shaken. He asked questions, and the soldier expanded.

" I tell you they got nearly a square mile fenced in—a sort of valley. Fences of barbed wire ten feet high, and inside that they do things. Chaps about the camp—now and then we get a peep. It isn't only us neither. There's the Japanese ; you bet they got it too—and the Germans ! And I never knowed anything of this sort yet that the Frencheys didn't get ahead with—after their manner ! They started ironclads, they started submarines, they started navigables, and you bet they won't be far be'ind at this.''

The soldier stood with his legs very wide apart, and filled his pipe thoughtfully. Bert sat on the low wall against which his motor-bicycle was leaning.

" Funny thing fighting'll be,'' he said.

" Flying's going to break out,'' said the soldier. " When it *does* come, when the curtain does go up, I tell you you'll find every one on the stage—busy. . . . Such fighting, too! . . . I suppose you don't read the papers about this sort of thing ? ''

" I read 'em a bit,'' said Bert.

" Well, have you noticed what one might call the remarkable case of the disappearing inventor—the inventor who turns up in a blaze of publicity, fires off a few successful experiments, and vanishes ? ''

" Can't say I 'ave,'' said Bert.

" Well, I 'ave, anyhow. You get anybody come along who does anything striking in this line, and, you bet, he vanishes. Just goes off quietly out of sight. After a bit, you don't hear anything more of 'em at all. See ? They disappear. Gone— no address. First—oh ! it's an old story now—there was those Wright Brothers out in America. They glided—they glided miles and miles. Finally they glided off stage. Why, it must be nineteen hundred and four, or five, *they* vanished ! Then there was those people in Ireland—no, I forget their names. Everybody said they could fly. *They* went. They ain't dead that I've heard tell ; but you can't say they're alive. Not a feather of 'em can you see. Then that chap who flew round Paris and upset in the Seine. De Booley, was it ? I forget. That was a grand fly, in spite of the accident ; but where's he got to ? The accident didn't hurt him. Eh ? '*E's* gone to cover.''

The soldier prepared to light his pipe.

" Looks like a secret society got hold of them,'' said Bert.

" Secret society ! *Naw !* ''

The soldier lit his match, and drew. " Secret society,'' he repeated in response to these words, with his pipe between his teeth and the match flaring. " War Departments ; that's more like it.'' He threw his match aside, and walked to his machine. " I tell you, sir,'' he said, " there isn't a big Power in Europe, *or* Asia, *or* America, *or* Africa, that hasn't got at least one or two flying machines hidden up its sleeve at the present time. Not one. Real, workable, flying machines. And the spying ! The spying and manœuvring to find out what the others have got. I tell you, sir, a foreigner, or, for the matter of that, an unaccredited native, can't get within four miles of Lydd nowadays—not to mention our little circus at Aldershot, and the experimental camp in Galway. No ! "

" Well," said Bert, " I'd like to see one of them, anyhow. Jest to help believing. I'll believe when I see, that I'll promise you."

" You'll see 'em fast enough," said the soldier, and led his machine out into the road.

He left Bert on his wall, grave and pensive, with his cap on the back of his head, and a cigarette smouldering in the corner of his mouth.

" If what he says is true," said Bert, " me and Grubb, we been wasting our blessed old time. Besides incurring expense with thet green'ouse."

§ 5

It was while this mysterious talk with the soldier still stirred in Bert Smallways' imagination that the most astounding incident in the whole of that dramatic chapter of human history, the coming of flying, occurred. People talked glibly enough of epoch-making events ; this *was* an epoch-making event. It was the unanticipated and entirely successful flight of Mr. Alfred Butteridge from the Crystal Palace to Glasgow and back in a small business-like-looking machine heavier than air—an entirely manageable and controllable machine that could fly as well as a pigeon.

It wasn't, one felt, a fresh step forward in the matter so much as a giant stride, a leap. Mr. Butteridge remained in the air altogether for about nine hours, and during that time he flew with the ease and assurance of a bird. His machine was, however, neither bird-like nor butterfly-like, nor had it the wide, lateral expansion of the ordinary aeroplane. The effect upon the observer was rather something in the nature of a bee or wasp. Parts of the apparatus were spinning very rapidly, and gave one a hazy effect of transparent wings ; but parts, including two peculiarly curved " wing-cases "—if one may borrow a figure from the flying beetles—remained expanded stiffly. In the middle was a long, rounded body like the body of a moth, and on this Mr. Butteridge could be seen sitting astride, much as a man bestrides a horse. The wasp-like resemblance was increased by the fact that the apparatus flew with a deep, booming hum, exactly the sound made by a wasp at a window-pane.

Mr. Butteridge took the world by surprise. He was one of those gentlemen from nowhere Fate still succeeds in producing for the stimulation of mankind. He came, it was variously said, from Australia and America and the South of France. He was also described quite incorrectly as the son of a man who had amassed a comfortable fortune in the manufacture of gold nibs and the Butteridge fountain pens. But this was an entirely different strain of Butteridges. For some years, in spite of a loud voice, a large presence, an aggressive swagger, and an implacable manner, he had been an undistinguished member of most of the existing aeronautical associations. Then one day he wrote to all the London papers to announce that he had made arrangements for an ascent from the Crystal Palace of a machine that would demonstrate satisfactorily that the outstanding difficulties in the way of flying were finally solved. Few of the papers printed his letter, still fewer were the people who believed in his claim. No one was excited even when a fracas on the steps of a leading hotel in Piccadilly, in which he tried to horsewhip a prominent German musician upon some personal account, delayed his promised ascent. The quarrel was inadequately reported, and his name spelt variously Betteridge and Betridge. Until his flight, indeed, he did not and could not contrive to exist in the public mind. There were scarcely thirty people on the look out for him, in spite of all his clamour, when about six o'clock one summer morning the doors of the big shed in which he had been putting together his apparatus opened—it was near the big model of a megatherium in the Crystal Palace grounds—and his giant insect came droning out into a negligent and incredulous world.

But before he had made his second circuit of the Crystal Palace towers, Fame was lifting her trumpet, she drew a deep breath as the startled tramps who sleep on the seats of Trafalgar Square were roused by his buzz and awoke to discover him circling the Nelson column, and by the time he had got to Birmingham, which place he crossed about half-past ten, her deafening blast was echoing throughout the country. The despaired-of thing was done. A man was flying securely and well.

Scotland was agape for his coming. Glasgow he reached by one o'clock, and it is related that scarcely a shipyard or factory in that busy hive of industry resumed work before half-past two. The public mind was just sufficiently educated in the impossibility of flying to appreciate Mr. Butteridge at his proper value. He circled the University buildings, and dropped to within shouting distance of the crowds in West End Park and on the slope of Gilmorehill. The thing flew quite steadily at a pace of about three miles an hour, in a wide circle, making a deep hum that would have drowned his full, rich voice completely had he not provided himself with a megaphone. He avoided churches, buildings, and mono-rail cables with consummate ease as he conversed.

"Me name's Butteridge," he shouted; "B-U-T-T-E-R-I-D-G-E. Got it? Me mother was Scotch."

And having assured himself that he had been understood,

he rose amidst cheers and shouting and patriotic cries, and then flew up very swiftly and easily into the south-eastern sky, rising and falling with long, easy undulations in an extraordinary wasp-like manner.

His return to London—he visited and hovered over Manchester and Liverpool and Oxford on his way, and spelt his name out to each place—was an occasion of unparalleled excitement. Every one was staring heavenward. More people were run over in the streets upon that one day than in the previous three months, and a County Council steamboat, the *Isaac Walton*, collided with a pier of Westminster Bridge, and narrowly escaped disaster by running ashore—it was low water—on the mud on the south side. He returned to the Crystal Palace grounds, that classic starting-point of aeronautical adventure, about sunset, re-entered his shed without disaster, and had the doors locked immediately upon the photographers and journalists who had been waiting his return.

"Look here, you chaps," he said, as his assistant did so, "I'm tired to death, and saddle sore. I can't give you a word of talk. I'm too—done. My name's Butteridge. B-U-T-T-E-R-I-D-G-E. Get that right. I'm an imperial Englishman. I'll talk to you all to-morrow."

Foggy snapshots still survive to record that incident. His assistant struggles in a sea of aggressive young men carrying notebooks or upholding cameras and wearing bowler hats and enterprising ties. He himself towers up in the doorway, a big figure with a mouth—an eloquent cavity beneath a vast black moustache—distorted by his shout to those relentless agents of publicity. He towers there, the most famous man in the country. Almost symbolically he holds and gesticulates with a megaphone in his left hand.

§ 6

Tom and Bert Smallways both saw that return. They watched from the crest of Bun Hill, from which they had so often surveyed the pyrotechnics of the Crystal Palace. Bert was excited, Tom kept calm and lumpish, but neither of them realised how their own lives were to be invaded by the fruits of that beginning. "P'raps old Grubb'll mind the shop a bit now," he said, "and put his blessed model in the fire. Not that that can save us, if we don't tide over with Steinhart's account."

Bert knew enough of things and the problem of aeronautics to realise that this gigantic imitation of a bee would, to use his own idiom, "give the newspapers fits." The next day it was clear the fits had been given even as he said, their magazine pages were black with hasty photographs, their prose was convulsive, they foamed at the headline. The next day they were worse. Before the week was out they were not so much published as carried screaming into the street.

The dominant fact in the uproar was the exceptional personality of Mr. Butteridge, and the extraordinary terms he demanded for the secret of his machine.

For it was a secret, and he kept it secret in the most elaborate fashion. He built his apparatus himself, in the safe privacy of the great Crystal Palace sheds, with the assistance of inattentive workmen, and the day next following his flight he took it to pieces single handed, packed certain portions, and then secured unintelligent assistance in packing and dispersing the rest. Sealed packing-cases went north and east and west to various pantechnicons, and the engines were boxed with peculiar care. It became evident these precautions were not inadvisable, in view of the violent demand for any sort of photograph or impressions of his machine. But Mr. Butteridge, having once made his demonstration, intended to keep his secret safe from any further risk of leakage. He faced the British public now with the question whether they wanted his secret or not; he was, he said perpetually, an " Imperial Englishman," and his first wish and his last was to see his invention the privilege and monopoly of the Empire. Only——

It was there the difficulty began.

Mr. Butteridge, it became evident, was a man singularly free from any false modesty—indeed, from any modesty of any kind—singularly willing to see interviewers, answer questions upon any topic except aeronautics, volunteer opinions, criticism and autobiography, supply portraits and photographs of himself, and generally spread his personality across the terrestrial sky. The published portraits insisted primarily upon an immense black moustache, and secondarily upon a fierceness behind the moustache. The general impression upon the public was that Butteridge was a small man. No one big, it was felt, could have so virulently aggressive an expression, though, as a matter of fact, Butteridge had a height of six feet two inches, and a weight altogether proportionate to that. Moreover, he had a love affair of large and unusual dimensions and irregular circumstances, and the still largely decorous British public learnt with reluctance and alarm that a sympathetic treatment of this affair was inseparable from the exclusive acquisition of the priceless secret of aerial stability by the British Empire. The exact particulars of the irregularity never came to light, but apparently the lady had, in a fit of high-minded inadvertence, gone through the ceremony of marriage with—one quotes the unpublished discourse of Mr. Butteridge—" a white-livered skunk," and this zoological aberration did in some legal and vexatious manner mar her social happiness. He wanted to talk about the business, to show the splendour of her nature in the light of its complications. It was really most embarrassing to a press that has always possessed a considerable turn for reticence, that wanted things personal, indeed, in the modern fashion, but not too personal. It was embarrassing, I say, to be inexorably confronted with Mr. Butteridge's great heart, to see it laid open in relentless self-vivisection, and its pulsating dissepiments adorned with emphatic flag labels.

Confronted they were, and there was no getting away from it. He would make this appalling viscus beat and throb before the shrinking journalists—no uncle with a big watch and a little baby ever harped upon it so relentlessly ; whatever evasion they attempted he set aside. He " gloried in his love," he said, and compelled them to write it down.

" That's, of course, a private affair, Mr. Butteridge," they would object.

" The injustice, sorr, is public. I do not care whether I am up against institutions or individuals. I do not care if I am up against the Universal All. I am pleading the cause of a woman, a woman I lurve, sorr—a noble woman—misunderstood. I intend to vindicate her, sorr, to the four winds of heaven !

" I lurve England," he used to say—" I lurve England, but Puritanism, sorr, I abhor. It fills me with loathing. It raises my gorge. Take my own case. . . . "

He insisted relentlessly upon his heart and upon seeing proofs of the interview. If they had not done justice to his erotic bellowings and gesticulations, he stuck in, in a large inky scrawl, all and more than they had omitted.

It was a strangely embarrassing thing for British journalism. Never was there a more obvious or uninteresting affair ; never had the world heard the story of erratic affection with less appetite or sympathy. On the other hand, it was extremely curious about Mr. Butteridge's invention. But when Mr. Butteridge could be deflected for a moment from the cause of the lady he championed, then he talked chiefly, and usually with tears of tenderness in his voice, about his mother and his childhood—his mother who crowned a complete encyclopædia of maternal virtue by being " largely Scotch." She was not quite neat, but nearly so. " I owe everything in me to me mother," he asserted—" everything. Eh ! " and—" ask any man who's done anything. You'll hear the same story. All we have we owe to women. They are the species, sorr. Man is but a dream. He comes and goes. The woman's soul leadeth us upward and on ! "

He was always going on like that.

What in particular he wanted from the Government for his secret did not appear, nor what beyond a money payment could be expected from a modern state in such an affair. The general effect upon judicious observers, indeed, was not that he was treating for anything, but that he was using an unexampled opportunity to bellow and show off to an attentive world. Rumours of his real identity spread abroad. It was said that he had been the landlord of an ambiguous hotel in Cape Town, and had there given shelter to, and witnessed the experiments, and finally stolen the papers and plans of an extremely shy and friendless young inventor named Palliser, who had come to South Africa from England in an advanced stage of consumption, and died there. This, at any rate, was the allegation of the more outspoken American press. But the proof or disproof of that never reached the public.

Mr. Butteridge also involved himself passionately in a tangle of disputes for the possession of a great number of valuable money prizes. Some of these had been offered so long ago as 1906 for successful mechanical flight. By the time of Mr. Butteridge's success a really very considerable number of newspapers, tempted by the impunity of the pioneers in this direction, had pledged themselves to pay in some cases quite overwhelming sums to the first person to fly from Manchester to Glasgow, from London to Manchester, one hundred miles, two hundred miles in England and the like. Most had hedged a little with ambiguous conditions, and now offered resistance ; one or two paid at once, and vehemently called attention to the fact ; and Mr. Butteridge plunged into litigation with the more recalcitrant, while at the same time sustaining a vigorous agitation and canvass to induce the Government to purchase his invention.

One fact, however, remained permanent throughout all the developments of this affair behind Butteridge's preposterous love interest, his politics and personality and all his shouting and boasting, and that was that, so far as the mass of people knew, he was in sole possession of the secret of the practicable aeroplane in which, for all one could tell to the contrary, the key of the future empire of the world resided. And presently, to the great consternation of innumerable people, including among others Mr. Bert Smallways, it became apparent that whatever negotiations were in progress for the acquisition of this precious secret by the British Government were in danger of falling through. The London *Daily Requiem* first voiced the universal alarm, and published an interview under the terrific caption of, " Mr. Butteridge speaks his Mind."

Therein the inventor—if he was an inventor—poured out his heart.

" I came from the end of the earth," he said, which rather seemed to confirm the Cape Town story, " bringing me Motherland the secret that would give her the empire of the world. And what do I get ? " He paused. " I am sniffed at by elderly mandarins ! . . . And the woman I love is treated like a leper !

" I am an Imperial Englishman," he went on in a splendid outburst, subsequently written into the interview by his own hand ; " but there are limits to the human heart ! There are

younger nations—living nations ! Nations that do not snore
and gurgle helplessly in paroxysms of plethora upon beds of
formality and red tape ! There are nations that will not fling
away the empire of earth in order to slight an unknown man
and insult a noble woman whose boots they are not fitted to
unlatch. There are nations not blinded to science, not given
over hand and foot to effete snobocracies and Degenerate
Decadents. In short, mark my words—*there are other nations* ! . . ."

This speech it was that particularly impressed Bert Smallways. " If them Germans or them Americans get hold of this,"
he said impressively to his brother, " the British Empire's
done. It's U.P. The Union Jack, so to speak, won't be worth
the paper it's written on, Tom."

" I suppose you couldn't lend us a hand this morning," said
Jessica, in his impressive pause. " Everybody in Bun Hill
seems wanting early potatoes at once. Tom can't carry half
of them."

" We're living on a volcano," said Bert, disregarding the
suggestion. " At any moment war may come—such a war ! "

He shook his head portentously.

" You'd better take this lot first, Tom," said Jessica. She
turned briskly on Bert. " Can you spare us a morning ? " she
asked.

" I dessay I can," said Bert. " The shop's very quiet
s'morning. Though all this danger to the Empire worries me
something frightful."

" Work'll take it off your mind," said Jessica.

And presently he, too, was going out into a world of change
and wonder, bowed beneath a load of potatoes and patriotic
insecurity, that merged at last into a very definite irritation
at the weight and want of style of the potatoes and a very
clear conception of the entire detestableness of Jessica.

CHAPTER TWO

HOW BERT SMALLWAYS GOT INTO DIFFICULTIES

§ 1

IT did not occur to either Tom or Bert Smallways that this
remarkable aerial performance of Mr. Butteridge was likely
to affect either of their lives in any special manner, that it
would in any way single them out from the millions about
them ; and when they had witnessed it from the crest of Bun
Hill, and seen the fly-like mechanism, its rotating planes a
golden haze in the sunset, sink humming to the harbour of
its shed again, they turned back towards the sunken green-
grocery beneath the great iron standard of the London to
Brighton mono-rail, and their minds reverted to the discussion

that had engaged them before Mr. Butteridge's triumph had come in sight out of the London haze.

It was a difficult and unsuccessful discussion. They had to carry it on in shouts because of the moaning and roaring of the gyroscopic motor-cars that traversed the High Street, and in its nature it was contentious and private. The Grubb business was in difficulties, and Grubb in a moment of financial eloquence had given half a share in it to Bert, whose relations with his employer had been for some time unsalaried and pallish and informal.

Bert was trying to impress Tom with the idea that the reconstructed Grubb and Smallways offered unprecedented and unparalleled opportunities to the judicious small investor. It was coming home to Bert, as though it were an entirely new fact, that Tom was entirely impervious to ideas. In the end he put the financial issues on one side and, making the thing entirely a matter of fraternal affection, succeeded in borrowing a sovereign on the security of his word of honour.

The firm of Grubb and Smallways, formerly Grubb had indeed been persistently unlucky in the last year or so. For many years the business had struggled along with a flavour of romantic insecurity in a small, dissolute-looking shop in the High Street, adorned with brilliantly coloured advertisements of cycles, a display of bells, trouser-clips, oil-cans, pump-clips, frame-cases, wallets, and other accessories, and the announcement of " Bicycles on Hire," " Repairs," " Free Inflation," " Petrol," and similar attractions. They were agents for several obscure makes of bicycle, two samples constituted the stock and occasionally they effected a sale, they also repaired punctures and did their best—though luck was not always on their side—with any other repairing that was brought to them. They handled a line of cheap gramophones, and did a little with musical boxes. The staple of their business was, however, the letting of bicycles on hire. It was a singular trade, obeying no known commercial or economic principles— indeed, no principles. There was a stock of ladies' and gentlemen's bicycles in a state of disrepair that passes description, the hiring stock, and these were let to unexacting and reckless people, inexpert in the things of this world, at a nominal rate of one shilling for the first hour and sixpence per hour afterwards. But really there were no fixed prices, and insistent boys could get bicycles and the thrill of danger for an hour for so low a sum as threepence, provided they could convince Grubb that that was all they had. The saddle and handle-bar were then sketchily adjusted by Grubb, a deposit exacted, except in the case of familiar boys, the machine lubricated, and the adventurer started upon his career. Usually he or she came back, but at times, when the accident was serious, Bert or Grubb had to go out and fetch the machine home. Hire was always charged up to the hour of return to the shop and deducted from the deposit. It was rare that a bicycle started out from their hands in a state of pedantic efficiency. Romantic possibilities of accident lurked in the worn thread of the screw that adjusted the saddle, in the precarious pedals, in the loose-knit chain, in the handle-bars, above all in the brakes and tyres. Tappings and clankings and strange rhythmic creakings awoke as the intrepid hirer pedalled out into the country. Then perhaps the bell would jam or a brake fail to act on a hill ; or the seat pillar would get loose, and the saddle drop three or four inches with a disconcerting bump ; or the loose and rattling chain would jump the cogs of the chain-wheel as the machine ran downhill, and so bring the mechanism to an abrupt and disastrous stop without at the same time arresting the forward momentum of the rider ; or a tyre would bang, or sigh quietly, and give up the struggle and scrabble in the dust.

When the hirer returned, a heated pedestrian, Grubb would ignore all verbal complaints, and examine the machine gravely.

" This ain't 'ad fair usage," he used to begin.

He became a mild embodiment of the spirit of reason. " You can't expect a bicycle to take you up in its arms and carry you," he used to say. " You got to show intelligence. After all—it's machinery.''

Sometimes the process of liquidating the consequent claims bordered on violence. It was always a very rhetorical and often trying affair, but in these progressive times you have to make a noise to get a living. It was often hard work, but nevertheless this hiring was a fairly steady source of profit, until one day all the panes in the window and door were broken and the stock on sale in the window greatly damaged and disordered by two over-critical hirers with no sense of rhetorical irrelevance. They were big, coarse stokers from Gravesend—one was annoyed because his left pedal had come off, and the other because his tyre had become deflated, small and indeed negligible accidents by Bun Hill standards, due entirely to the ungentle handling of the delicate machines entrusted to them, and they failed to see clearly how they put themselves in the wrong by this method of argument. It is a poor way of convincing a man that he has let you a defective machine to throw his foot-pump about his shop, and take his stock of gongs outside in order to return them through the window-panes. It carried no real conviction to the minds of either Grubb or Bert ; it only irritated and vexed them. One quarrel makes many, and this unpleasantness led to a violent dispute between Grubb and the landlord upon the moral aspects of and legal responsibility for the consequent re-glazing. Matters came to a climax upon the even of the Whitsuntide Holidays.

In the end Grubb and Smallways were put to the expense of a strategic nocturnal removal to another position.

It was a position they had long considered. It was a small

shed-like shop with a plate-glass window and one room behind, just at the sharp bend in the road at the bottom of Bun Hill, and here they struggled along bravely in spite of persistent annoyance from their former landlord, hoping for certain eventualities the peculiar situation of the shop seemed to promise. Here, too, they were doomed to disappointment.

The High Road from London to Brighton that ran through Bun Hill was like the British Empire or the British Constitution—a thing that had grown to its present importance. Unlike any other roads in Europe the British high roads have never been subjected to any organised attempts to grade or straighten them out, and to that, no doubt, their peculiar picturesqueness is to be ascribed. The old Bun Hill High Street drops at its end for perhaps eighty or a hundred feet of descent at an angle of one in five, turns at right angles to the left, runs in a curve for about thirty yards to a brick bridge over the dry ditch that had once been the Otterbourne, and then bends sharply to the right again round a dense clump of trees and goes on, a simple, straightforward, peaceful high road. There had been one or two horse and van and bicycle accidents in the place before the shop Bert and Grubb took was built, and, to be frank, it was the probability of others that attracted them to it.

Its possibilities had come to them first with a humorous flavour.

" Here's one of the places where a chap might get a living by keeping hens," said Grubb.

" You can't get a living by keeping hens," said Bert.

" You'd keep the hen and have it spatch-cocked," said Grubb. " The motor chaps would pay for it."

When they really came to take the place they remembered this conversation. Hens, however, were out of the question ; there was no place for a run unless they had it in the shop. It would have been obviously out of place there. The shop was much more modern than their former one, and had a plate-glass front. " Sooner or later," said Bert, " we shall get a motor-car through this."

" That's all right," said Grubb. " Compensation. I don't mind *when* that motor-car comes along. I don't mind even if it gives me a shock to the system."

" And meanwhile," said Bert, with great artfulness, " *I'm* going to buy myself a dog."

He did. He bought three in succession. He surprised the people at the Dog's Home in Battersea by demanding a deaf retriever, and rejecting every candidate that pricked up its ears. " I want a good, deaf, slow-moving dog," he said. " A dog that doesn't put himself out for things."

They displayed inconvenient curiosity ; they declared a great scarcity of deaf dogs.

" You see," they said, " dogs aren't deaf."

" Mine's got to be," said Bert. " I've *had* dogs that aren't deaf. All I want. It's like this, you see—I sell gramophones. Naturally I got to make 'em talk and tootle a bit to show 'em orf. Well, a dog that isn't deaf doesn't like it—gets excited, smells round, barks, growls. That upsets the customer. See ? Then a dog that has his hearing fancies things. Makes burglars out of passing tramps. Wants to fight every motor that makes a whiz. All very well if you want livening up, but our place is lively enough. I don't want a dog of that sort. I want a quiet dog."

In the end he got three in succession, but none of them turned out well. The first strayed off into the infinite, heeding no appeals ; the second was killed in the night by a fruit motor-wagon which fled before Grubb could get down ; the third got itself entangled in the front wheel of a passing cyclist, who came through the plate glass, and proved to be an actor out of work and an undischarged bankrupt. He demanded compensation for some fancied injury, would hear nothing of the valuable dog he had killed or the window he had broken, obliged Grubb by sheer physical obduracy to straighten his buckled front wheel, and pestered the struggling firm with a series of inhumanly worded solicitor's letters. Grubb answered them—stingingly, and put himself, Bert thought, in the wrong.

Affairs got more and more exasperating and strained under these pressures. The window was boarded up, and an unpleasant altercation about their delay in repairing it with the new landlord, a Bun Hill butcher—and a loud, bellowing, unreasonable person at that—served to remind them of their unsettled troubles with the old. Things were at this pitch when Bert bethought himself of creating a sort of debenture capital in the business for the benefit of Tom. But, as I have said, Tom had no enterprise in his composition. His idea of investment was the stocking ; he bribed his brother not to keep the offer open.

And then ill luck made its last lunge at their crumbling business and brought it to the ground.

§ 2

It is a poor heart that never rejoices, and Whitsuntide had an air of coming as an agreeable break in the business complications of Grubb and Smallways. Encouraged by the practical outcome of Bert's negotiations with his brother, and by the fact that half the hiring stock was out from Saturday to Monday, they decided to ignore the residuum of hiring-trade on Sunday and devote that day to much-needed relaxation and refreshment—to have, in fact, an unstinted good time, a beano on Whit Sunday, and return invigorated to grapple with their difficulties and the Bank Holiday repairs on the Monday. No good thing was ever done by exhausted and dispirited men. It happened that they had made the acquaint-

ance of two young ladies in employment in Clapham, Miss
Flossie Bright and Miss Edna Bunthorne, and it was resolved,
therefore, to make a cheerful little cyclist party of four into
the heart of Kent, and to picnic and spend an indolent
afternoon and evening among the trees and bracken between
Ashford and Maidstone.

Miss Bright could ride a bicycle, and a machine was found
for her, not among the hiring stock, but specially in the sample
held for sale. Miss Bunthorne, whom Bert particularly affected,
could not ride, and so with some difficulty he hired a basket-
work trailer from the big business of Wray's in the Clapham
Road. To see our young men, brightly dressed and cigarettes
alight, wheeling off to the rendezvous, Grubb guiding the
lady's machine beside him with one skilful hand, and Bert
teuf-teuffing steadily, was to realise how pluck may triumph
even over insolvency. Their landlord, the butcher, said " Gurr!"
as they passed, and shouted " Go it!" in a loud, savage tone to
their receding backs.

Much they cared!

The weather was fine, and though they were on their way
southward before nine o'clock, there was already a great
multitude of holiday people abroad upon the roads. There
were quantities of young men and women on bicycles and
motor-bicycles, and a majority of gyroscopic motor-cars running bicycle-fashion on two wheels, mingled with old-fashioned
four-wheeled traffic. Bank Holiday times always bring out
old stored-away vehicles and odd people ; one saw tricars and
electric broughams and dilapidated old racing motors with
huge pneumatic tyres. Once our holiday-makers saw a horse
and cart, and once a youth riding a black horse amidst the
badinage of the passers-by. And there were several navigable
gas airships, not to mention balloons, in the air. It was all
immensely interesting and refreshing after the dark anxieties
of the shop. Edna wore a brown straw hat with poppies, that
suited her admirably, and sat in the trailer like a queen, and
the eight-year-old motor-bicycle ran like a thing of yesterday.

Little it seemed to matter to Mr. Bert Smallways that a
newspaper placard proclaimed :—

GERMANY DENOUNCES THE MONROE
DOCTRINE

AMBIGUOUS ATTITUDE OF JAPAN

WHAT WILL BRITAIN DO ?

IS IT WAR ?

This sort of thing was always going on, and on holidays
one disregarded it as a matter of course. Week-days, in the

slack time after the midday meal, then perhaps one might worry about the Empire and international politics ; but not on a sunny Sunday, with a pretty girl trailing behind one, and envious cyclists trying to race you. Nor did our young people attach any great importance to the flitting suggestions of military activity they glimpsed ever and again. Near Maidstone they came on a string of eleven motor-guns of peculiar construction halted by the roadside, with a number of business-like engineers grouped about them watching through field-glasses some sort of entrenchment that was going on near the crest of the downs. It signified nothing to Bert.

" What's up ? " said Edna.

" Oh !—manœuvres," said Bert.

" Oh ! I thought they did them at Easter," said Edna, and troubled no more.

The last great British war, the Boer War, was over and forgotten, and the public had lost the fashion of expert military criticism.

Our four young people picnicked cheerfully, and were happy in the manner of a happiness that was an ancient mode in Nineveh. Eyes were bright, Grubb was funny and almost witty, and Bert achieved epigrams ; the hedges were full of honeysuckle and dog-roses ; in the woods the distant toot-toot-toot of the traffic on the dust-hazy high road might have been no more than the horns of elf-land. They laughed and gossiped and picked flowers and made love and talked, and the girls smoked cigarettes. Also they scuffled playfully. Among other things they talked aeronautics, and how they would come for a picnic together in Bert's flying-machine before ten years were out. The world seemed full of amusing possibilities that afternoon. They wondered what their great grandparents would have thought of aeronautics. In the evening about seven, the party turned homeward, expecting no disaster, and it was only on the crest of the downs, between Wrotham and Kingsdown, that disaster came.

They had come up the hill in the twilight, Bert was anxious to get as far as possible before he lit—or attempted to light, for the issue was a doubtful one—his lamps, and they had scorched past a number of cyclists, and by a four-wheeled motor-car of the old style lamed by a deflated tyre. Some dust had penetrated Bert's horn, and the result was a curious, amusing, wheezing sound had got into his " honk, honk." For the sake of merriment and glory he was making this sound as much as possible, and Edna was in fits of laughter in the trailer. They made a sort of rushing cheerfulness along the road that affected their fellow travellers variously according to their temperaments. She did notice a good lot of blueish, evil-smelling smoke coming from about the bearings between his feet, but she thought this was one of the natural con-comitants of motor-traction, and troubled no more about it, until abruptly it burst into a little yellow-tipped flame.

" Bert ! " she screamed.

But Bert had put on the brakes with such suddenness that she found herself involved with his leg as he dismounted. She got to the side of the road and hastily readjusted her hat, which had suffered.

" Gaw ! " said Bert.

He stood for some fatal seconds watching the petrol drip and catch, and the flame, which was now beginning to smell of enamel as well as oil, spread and grew. His chief idea was the sorrowful one that he had not sold the machine second-hand a year ago, and that he ought to have done so—a good idea in its way, but not immediately helpful. He turned upon Edna sharply. " Get a lot of wet sand," he said. Then he wheeled the machine a little towards the side of the roadway and laid it down and looked about for a supply of wet sand. The flames received this as a helpful attention, and made the most of it. They seemed to brighten and the twilight to deepen about them. The road was a flinty road in the chalk country, and ill provided with sand.

Edna accosted a short, fat cyclist. " We want wet sand," she said, and added, " our motor's on fire." The short fat cyclist stared blankly for a moment, then with a helpful cry began to scrabble in the road grit. Whereupon Bert and Edna also scrabbled in the road grit. Other cyclists arrived, dismounted and stood about, and their flame-lit faces expressed satisfaction, interest, curiosity. " Wet sand," said the short, fat man scrabbling terribly—" wet sand." One joined him. They threw hard-earned handfuls of road grit upon the flames, which accepted them with enthusiasm.

Grubb arrived, riding hard. He was shouting something. He sprang off and threw his bicycle into the hedge. " Don't throw water on it ! " he said—" don't throw water on it ! " He displayed commanding presence of mind. He became captain of the occasion. Others were glad to repeat the things he said and imitate his actions. " Don't throw water on it ! " they cried. Also there was no water.

" Beat it out, you fools ! " he said.

He seized a rug from the trailer (it was an Austrian blanket, and Bert's winter coverlet) and began to beat at the burning petrol. For a wonderful minute he seemed to succeed. But he scattered burning pools of petrol on the road, and others, fired by his enthusiasm, imitated his action. Bert caught up a trailer-cushion and began to beat ; there was another cushion and a table-cloth, and these also were seized. A young hero pulled off his jacket and joined the beating. For a moment there was less talking than hard breathing, and a tremendous flapping. Flossie, arriving on the outskirts of the crowd, cried, " Oh, my God ! " and burst loudly into tears. " Help ! " she said, and " Fire ! "

The lame motor-car arrived, and stopped in consternation. A tall, goggled, gray-haired man who was driving inquired with an Oxford intonation and a clear, careful enunciation, " Can *we* help at all ? "

It became manifest that the rug, the table-cloth, the cushions, the jacket were getting smeared with petrol and burning. The soul seemed to go out of the cushion Bert was swaying, and the air was full of feathers, like a snowstorm in the still twilight.

Bert had got very dusty and sweaty and strenuous. It seemed to him his weapon had been wrested from him at the moment of victory. The fire lay like a dying thing, close to the ground and wicked, it gave a leap of anguish at every whack of the beaters. But now Grubb had gone off to stamp out the burning blanket ; the others were slacking just at the moment of victory. One was running to the motor-car. " *'Ere !* " cried Bert ; " keep on ! "

He flung the deflated burning rags of cushion aside, whipped off his jacket and sprang at the flames with a shout. He stamped into the ruin until the flames ran up his boots. Edna saw him, a red-lit hero, and thought it was good to be a man.

A bystander was hit by a hot halfpenny flying out of the air. Then Bert thought of the papers in his pockets, and staggered back, trying to extinguish his burning jacket— checked, repulsed, dismayed.

Edna was struck by the benevolent appearance of an elderly spectator in a silk hat and Sabbatical garments. " Oh ! " she cried to him. " Help this young man ! How can you stand and see it ? "

A cry of " The tarpauling ! " arose.

An earnest-looking man in a very light gray cycling-suit had suddenly appeared at the side of the lame motor-car and addressed the owner. " Have you a tarpauling ? " he said.

" Yes," said the gentlemanly man. " Yes. We've got a tarpauling."

" That's it," said the earnest-looking man suddenly shouting. " Let's have it, quick ! "

The gentlemanly man, with feeble and deprecatory gestures, and in the manner of a hypnotised person, produced an excellent large tarpauling.

" Here ! " cried the earnest-looking man to Grubb. " Ketch holt ! "

Then everybody realised that a new method was to be tried. A number of willing hands seized upon the Oxford gentleman's tarpauling. The others stood away with approving noises. The tarpauling was held over the burning bicycle like a canopy, and then smothered down upon it.

" We ought to have done this before," panted Grubb.

There was a moment of triumph. The flames vanished. Everyone who could contrive to do so touched the edge of the tarpauling. Bert held down a corner with two hands and a foot. The tarpauling, bulged up in the centre, seemed to be suppressing triumphant exaltation. Then its self-approval became too much for it; it burst into a bright red smile in the centre. It was exactly like the opening of a mouth. It laughed with a gust of flames. They were reflected redly in the observant goggles of the gentleman who owned the tarpauling. Everybody recoiled.

" Save the trailer ! " cried some one, and that was the last round in the battle. But the trailer could not be detached ; its wicker work had caught, and it was the last thing to burn. A sort of hush fell upon the gathering. The petrol burnt low the wicker-work trailer banged and crackled. The crowd divided itself into an outer circle of critics, advisers, and secondary characters, who had played undistinguished parts or no parts at all in the affair, and a central group of heated and distressed principals. A young man with an inquiring mind and a considerable knowledge of motor-bicycles fixed on to Grubb and wanted to argue that the thing could not have happened. Grubb was short and inattentive with him, and the young man withdrew to the back of the crowd, and there told the benevolent old gentleman in the silk hat that people who went out with machines they didn't understand had only themselves to blame if things went wrong.

The old gentleman let him talk for some time, and then remarked in a tone of rapturous enjoyment : " Stone deaf," and added, " Nasty things."

A rosy-faced man in a straw hat claimed attention. " I *did* save the front wheel," he said, " you'd have had that tyre catch, too, if I hadn't kept turning it round." It became manifest that this was so. The front wheel had retained its tyre, was intact, was still rotating slowly among the blackened and twisted ruins of the rest of the machine. It had something of that air of conscious virtue, of unimpeachable respectability, that distinguishes a rent collector in a low neighbourhood. " That wheel's worth a pound," said the rosy-faced man, making a song of it. " I kep' turning it round."

New-comers kept arriving from the south with the question, " What's up ? " until it got on Grubb's nerves. Londonward the crowd was constantly losing people ; they would mount their various wheels with the satisfied manner of spectators who have had the best. Their voices would recede into the twilight ; one would hear a laugh at the memory of this particularly salient incident or that.

" I'm afraid," said the gentleman of the motor-car, " my tarpauling's a bit done for."

Grubb admitted that the owner was the best judge of that.

" Nothing else I can do for you ? " said the gentleman of the motor-car, it may be, with a suspicion of irony.

Bert was roused to action. " Look here," he said. " There's

my young lady. If she ain't 'ome by ten they lock her out. See ? Well, all my money was in my jacket pocket, and it's all mixed up with the burnt stuff, and that's too 'ot to touch. *Is* Clapham out of your way ? "

" All in the day's work," said the gentleman with the motor-car, and turned to Edna. " Very pleased indeed," he said, " if you'll come with us. We're late for dinner as it is, so it won't make much difference for us to go home by way of Clapham. We've got to get to Surbiton, anyhow. I'm afraid you'll find us a little slow."

" But what's Bert going to do ? " said Edna.

" I don't know that we can accommodate Bert," said the motor-car gentleman, " though we're tremendously anxious to oblige."

" You couldn't take the whole lot ? " said Bert, waving his hand at the deboshed and blackened ruins on the ground.

" I'm awfully afraid I can't," said the Oxford man. " Awfully sorry, you know."

" Then I'll have to stick 'ere for a bit," said Bert. " I got to see the thing through. You go on, Edna."

" Don't like leavin' you, Bert."

" You can't 'elp it, Edna." . . .

The last Edna saw of Bert was his figure, in charred and blackened shirt-sleeves, standing in the dusk. He was musing deeply by the mixed ironwork and ashes of his vanished motor-bicycle, a melancholy figure. His retinue of spectators had shrunk now to half a dozen figures. Flossie and Grubb were preparing to follow her desertion.

" Cheer up, old Bert," cried Edna, with artificial cheerfulness. " So long."

" So long, Edna," said Bert.

" See you to-morrer."

" See you to-morrer," said Bert, though he was destined, as a matter of fact, to see much of the habitable globe before he saw her again.

Bert began to light matches from a borrowed boxful, and searched for a half-crown that still eluded him among the charred remains. His face was grave and melancholy.

" I *wish* that 'adn't 'appened," said Flossie, riding on with Grubb. . . .

And at last Bert was left almost alone, a sad, blackened Promethean figure, cursed by the gift of fire. He had entertained vague ideas of hiring a cart, of achieving miraculous repairs, of still snatching some residual value from his one chief possession. Now, in the darkening night he perceived the vanity of such intentions. Truth came to him bleakly and laid her chill conviction upon him. He took hold of the handlebar, stood the thing up, tried to push it forward. The tyreless hind-wheel was jammed hopelessly, even as he feared. For a minute or so he stood upholding his machine, a motionless despair. Then with a great effort he thrust the ruins from him into the ditch, kicked at it once, regarded it for a moment, and turned his face resolutely Londonward.

He did not once look back.

" That's the end of *that* game," said Bert. " No more teuf-teuf-teuf for Bert Smallways for a year or two. Good-bye 'Olidays! . . . Oh! I ought to 'ave sold the blasted thing when I had a chance three years ago."

§ 3

The next morning found the firm of Grubb and Smallways was in a state of profound despondency. It seemed a small matter to them that the newspaper and cigarette shop opposite displayed such placards as this :—

REPORTED AMERICAN ULTIMATUM

BRITAIN MUST FIGHT

OUR INFATUATED WAR OFFICE STILL
REFUSES TO LISTEN TO MR. BUTTERIDGE

GREAT MONO-RAIL DISASTER AT TIMBUCTOO

or this :—

WAR A QUESTION OF HOURS

NEW YORK CALM

EXCITEMENT IN BERLIN

or again :—

WASHINGTON STILL SILENT

WHAT WILL PARIS DO ?

THE PANIC ON THE BOURSE

THE KING'S GARDEN PARTY TO THE
MASKED TWAREGS

MR. BUTTERIDGE MAKES AN OFFER

LATEST BETTING FROM TEHERAN

or this :—

WILL AMERICA FIGHT ?

ANTI-GERMAN RIOT IN BAGDAD

THE MUNICIPAL SCANDALS AT DAMASCUS

MR. BUTTERIDGE'S INVENTION
FOR AMERICA

Bert stared at these over the card of pump-clips in the pane in the door with unseeing eyes. He wore a blackened flannel shirt, and the jacketless ruins of the holiday suit of yesterday. The boarded-up shop was dark and depressing beyond words, the few scandalous hiring machines had never looked so hopelessly disreputable. He thought of their fellows who were " out," and of the approaching disputations of the afternoon. He thought of their new landlord and of their old landlord, and of bills and claims. Life presented itself for the first time as a hopeless fight against fate. . . .

" Grubb, O' man," he said, distilling the quintessence, " I'm fair sick of this shop."

" So'm I," said Grubb.

" I'm out of conceit with it. I don't seem to care ever to speak to a customer again."

" There's that trailer," said Grubb, after a pause.

" Blow the trailer ! " said Bert. " Anyhow, I didn't leave a deposit on it. I didn't do that. Still——"

He turned round on his friend. " Look 'ere," he said, " we aren't gettin' on here. We been losing money hand over fist. We got things tied up in fifty knots."

" What can we do ? " said Grubb.

" Clear out. Sell what we can for what it will fetch, and quit. See ? It's no good 'anging on to a losing concern. No sort of good. Jest foolishness."

" That's all right," said Grubb—" that's all right ; but it ain't your capital been sunk in it."

" No need for us to sink after our capital," said Bert, ignoring the point.

" I'm not going to be held responsible for that trailer, anyhow. That ain't my affair."

" Nobody arst you to make it your affair. If you like to stick on here, well and good. I'm quitting. I'll see Bank Holiday through, and then I'm O.R.P.H. See ? "

" Leavin' me ? "

" Leavin' you. If you must be left."

Grubb looked round the shop. It certainly had become distasteful. Once upon a' time it had been bright with hope and

new beginnings and stock and the prospect of credit. Now—
now it was failure and dust. Very likely the landlord would be
round presently to go on with the row about the window. . . .
"Where d'you think of going, Bert?" Grubb asked.

Bert turned round and regarded him. "I thought it out
as I was walking 'ome, and in bed. I couldn't sleep a wink."

"What did you think out?"

"Plans."

"What plans?"

"Oh! You're for sticking here."

"Not if anything better was to offer."

"It's only an ideer," said Bert.

"Let's 'ear it."

"You made the girls laugh yestiday, that song you sang."

"Seems a long time ago now," said Grubb.

"And old Edna nearly cried—over that bit of mine."

"She'd got a fly in her eye," said Grubb; "I saw it. But
what's this got to do with your plan?"

"No end," said Bert.

"'Ow?"

"Don't you see?"

"Not singing in the streets?"

"Streets! No fear! But 'ow about the Tour of the Waterin'
Places of England, Grubb? Singing! Young men of family
doing it for a lark? You ain't got a bad voice, you know, and
mine's all right. I never see a chap singing on the beach yet
that I couldn't 'ave sung into a cocked hat. And we both
know how to put on the toff a bit. Eh? Well, that's my
ideer. Me and you, Grubb, with a refined song and a breakdown. Like we was doing for foolery yestiday. That was what
put it into my 'ead. Easy make up a programme—easy. Six
choice items, and one or two for encores and patter. I'm all
right in the patter—anyhow."

Grubb remained regarding his darkened and disheartening
shop; he thought of his former landlord and his present
landlord, and of the general disgustingness of business in an
age which re-echoes to The Bitter Cry of the Middle Class;
and then it seemed to him that afar off he heard the twankle,
twankle of a banjo, and the voice of a stranded siren singing.
He had a sense of hot sunshine upon sand, of the children of
at least transiently opulent holiday-makers in a circle round
about him, of the whisper, "They are really gentlemen," and
then dollop, dollop came the coppers in the hat. Sometimes
even silver. It was all income; no outgoings, no bills. "I'm
on, Bert," he said. "Right-o!" said Bert, and, "Now we
shan't be long."

"We needn't start without capital neither," said Grubb.
"If we take the best of these machines up to the Bicycle Mart
in Finsbury we'd raise six or seven pounds on 'em. We could
easy do that to-morrow before anybody much was about. . . .

" Nice to think of old Suet-and-Bones coming round to make his usual row with us, and finding a card up, ' Closed for Repairs.' "

" We'll do that," said Grubb with zest—" we'll do that. And we'll put up another notice, and jest arst all inquirers to go round to 'im and inquire. See ? Then they'll know all about us."

Before the day was out the whole enterprise was planned. They decided at first that they would call themselves the Naval Mr. O's, a plagiarism, and not perhaps a very good one, from the title of the well-known troupe of " Scarlet Mr. E's," and Bert rather clung to the idea of a uniform of bright blue serge, with a lot of gold lace and cord and ornamentation, rather like a naval officer's, but more so. But that had to be abandoned as impracticable, it would have taken too much time and money to prepare. They perceived they must wear some cheaper and more readily prepared costume, and Grubb fell back on white dominoes. They entertained the notion for a time of selecting the two worst machines from the hiring-stock, painting them over with crimson enamel paint, replacing the bells by the loudest sort of motor-horn, and doing a ride about to begin and end the entertainment. They doubted the advisability of this step.

" There's people in the world," said Bert, " who wouldn't recognise us, who'd know them bicycles again like a shot, and we don't want to go on with no old stories. We want a fresh start."

" I do," said Grubb, " badly."

" We want to forget things—and cut all these rotten old worries. They ain't doin' us good."

Nevertheless, they decided to take the risk of these bicycles, and they decided their costumes should be brown stockings and sandals, and cheap unbleached sheets with a hole cut in the middle, and wigs and beards of tow. The rest their normal selves ! " The Desert Dervishes," they would call themselves, and their chief songs would be those popular ditties, " In my Trailer," and " What Price Hairpins Now ? "

They decided to begin with small seaside places, and gradually, as they gained confidence, attack larger centres. To begin with they selected Littlestone in Kent, chiefly because of its unassuming name.

So they planned, and it seemed a small and unimportant thing to them that as they chattered the Governments of half the world and more were drifting into war. About midday they became aware of the first of the evening-paper placards shouting to them across the street :—

THE WAR-CLOUD DARKENS

Nothing else but that.

"Always rottin' about war now," said Bert. "They'll get it in the neck in real earnest one of these days, if they ain't precious careful."

§ 4

So you will understand the sudden apparition that surprised rather than delighted the quiet informality of Dymchurch sands. Dymchurch was one of the last places on the coast of England to be reached by the mono-rail, and so its spacious sands were still, at the time of this story, the secret and delight of quite a limited number of people. They went there to flee vulgarity and extravagances, and to bathe and sit and talk and play with the children in peace, and the Desert Dervishes did not please them at all.

The two white figures on scarlet wheels came upon them out of the infinite along the sands from Littlestone, grew nearer and larger and more audible, honk-honking and emitting weird cries, and generally threatening liveliness of the most aggressive type. "Good Heavens!" said Dymchurch, "what's this?"

Then our young men, according to a preconcerted plan, wheeled round from file to line, dismounted and stood at attention. "Ladies and gentlemen," they said, "we beg to present ourselves — the Desert Dervishes." They bowed profoundly.

The few scattered groups upon the beach regarded them with horror for the most part, but some of the children and young people were interested and drew nearer. "There ain't a bob on the beach," said Grubb in an undertone, and the Desert Dervishes piled their bicycles with comic "business," that got a laugh from one very unsophisticated little boy. Then they took a deep breath and struck into the cheerful strain of "What Price Hairpins Now?" Grubb sang the song, Bert did his best to make the chorus a rousing one, and at the end of each verse they danced certain steps, skirts in hand, that they had carefully rehearsed.

> Ting-a-ling-a-ting-a-ling-a-ting-a-ling-a-tang.
> What Price Hairpins Now?

So they chanted and danced their steps in the sunshine on Dymchurch beach, and the children drew near these foolish young men, marvelling that they should behave in this way, and the older people looked cold and unfriendly.

All round the coasts of Europe that morning banjos were ringing, voices were bawling and singing, children were playing in the sun, pleasure boats went to and fro ; the common, abundant life of the time, unsuspicious of all the dangers that gathered darkly against it, flowed on its cheerful, aimless way.

In the cities men fussed about their businesses and engagements. The newspaper placards that had cried " wolf ! " so often, cried " wolf ! " now in vain.

§ 5

Now as Bert and Grubb bawled their chorus for the third time, they became aware of a very big, golden-brown balloon low in the sky to the north-west, and coming rapidly towards them. " Jest as we're gettin' hold of 'em," muttered Grubb, " up comes a counter-attraction. Go it, Bert ! "

> Ting-a-ling-a-ting-a-ling-a-ting-a-ling-a-tang.
> What Price Hairpins Now ?

The balloon rose and fell, went out of sight — " landed, thank goodness," said Grubb — reappeared with a leap. " *Eng !* " said Grubb. " Step it, Bert, or they'll see it ! "

They finished their dance, and then stood frankly staring.

" There's something wrong with that balloon," said Bert.

Everybody now was looking at the balloon drawing rapidly nearer before a brisk north-westerly breeze. The song and dance were a " dead frost." Nobody thought any more about it. Even Bert and Grubb forgot it, and ignored the next item on the programme altogether. The balloon was bumping as though its occupants were trying to land ; it would approach, sinking slowly, touch the ground, and instantly jump fifty feet or so in the air and immediately begin to fall again. Its car touched a clump of trees, and the black figure that had been struggling in the ropes fell back, or jumped back, into the car. In another moment it was quite close. It seemed a huge affair, as big as a house, and it floated down swiftly towards the sands ; a long rope trailed behind it, and enormous shouts came from the man in the car. He seemed to be taking off his clothes, then his head came over the side of the car. " Catch hold of the rope ! " they heard quite plain.

" Salvage, Bert ! " cried Grubb, and started to head off the rope.

Bert followed him, and collided, without upsetting, with a fisherman bent upon a similar errand. A woman carrying a baby in her arms, two small boys with toy spades, and a stout gentleman in flannels all got to the trailing rope at about the same time, and began to dance over it in their attempts to secure it. Bert came up to this wriggling, elusive serpent and got his foot on it, went down on all fours and achieved a grip. In half a dozen seconds the whole diffused population of the beach had, as it were, crystallised on the rope, and was pulling against the balloon under the vehement and stimulating directions of the man in the car. " Pull, I tell you," said the man in the car—" Pull ! "

For a second or so the balloon obeyed its momentum and

the wind and tugged its human anchor seaward. It dropped, touched the water, and made a flat, silvery splash, and recoiled as one's finger recoils when one touches anything hot. " Pull her in," said the man in the car. " *She's fainted !* "

He occupied himself with some unseen object while the people on the rope pulled him in. Bert was nearest the balloon, and much excited and interested. He kept stumbling over the tail of the Dervish costume in his zeal. He had never imagined before what a big, light, wallowing thing a balloon was. The car was of brown, coarse wicker-work, and comparatively small. The rope he tugged at was fastened to a stout-looking ring, four or five feet above the car. At each tug he drew in a yard or so of rope, and the waggling wicker-work was drawn so much nearer. Out of the car came wrathful bellowings : " Fainted, she has ! " and then : " It's her heart—broken with all she's had to go through."

The balloon ceased to struggle, and sank downward. Bert dropped the rope, and ran forward to catch it in a new place. In another moment he had his hand on the car. " Lay hold of it," said the man in the car, and his face appeared close to Bert's—a strangely familiar face, fierce eyebrows, a flattish nose, a huge black moustache. He had discarded coat and waistcoat—perhaps with some idea of presently having to swim for his life—and his black hair was extraordinarily disordered. " Will all you people get hold round the car," he said. " There's a lady here fainted—or got failure of the heart. Heaven alone knows which ! My name is Butteridge. Butteridge, my name is—in a balloon. Now, please, all on to the edge. This is the last time I trust myself to one of these paleolithic contrivances. The ripping-cord failed, and the valve wouldn't act. If ever I meet the scoundrel who ought to have seen—— "

He stuck his head out between the ropes abruptly, and said, in a note of earnest expostulation : " Get some brandy ! —some neat brandy ! " Some one went up the beach for it.

In the car, sprawling upon a sort of bed-bench, in an attitude of elaborate self-abandonment, was a large, blonde lady, wearing a fur coat and a big floriferous hat. Her head lolled back against the padded corner of the car, and her eyes were shut and her mouth open. " Me dear ! " said Mr. Butteridge, in a common loud voice, " we're safe ! "

She gave no sign.

" Me dear ! " said Mr. Butteridge, in a greatly intensified loud voice, " we're safe ! "

She was still quite impassive.

Then Mr. Butteridge showed the fiery core of his soul. " If she is dead," he said, slowly lifting a fist towards the balloon above him, and speaking in an immense tremulous bellow— " if she is dead, I will r-r-rend the heavens like a garment ! I must get her out," he cried, his nostrils dilated with emotion

—" I must get her out. I cannot have her die in a wicker-work basket nine feet square—she who was made for kings' palaces ! Keep holt of this car ! Is there a strong man among ye to take her if I hand her out ? "

He swept the lady together by a powerful movement of his arms, and lifted her. " Keep the car from jumping," he said to those who clustered about him. " Keep your weight on it. She is no light woman, and when she is out of it—it will be relieved."

Bert leapt lightly into a sitting position on the edge of the car. The others took a firmer grip upon the ropes and ring.

" Are you ready ? " said Mr. Butteridge.

He stood upon the bed-bench and lifted the lady carefully. Then he sat down on the wicker edge opposite to Bert, and put one leg over to dangle outside. A rope or so seemed to incommode him. " Will some one assist me ? " he said. " If they would take this lady ? "

It was just at this moment, with Mr. Butteridge and the lady balanced finely on the basket brim, that she came-to. She came-to suddenly and violently with a loud, heart-rending cry of " Alfred ! Save me !" And she waved her arms searchingly, and then clasped Mr. Butteridge about.

It seemed to Bert that the car swayed for a moment and then buck-jumped and kicked him. Also he saw the boots of the lady and the right leg of the gentleman describing arcs through the air, preparatory to vanishing over the side of the car. His impressions were complex, but they also comprehended the fact that he had lost his balance, and was going to stand on his head inside this creaking basket. He spread out clutching arms. He did stand on his head, more or less, his tow-beard came off and got in his mouth, and his cheek slid along against padding. His nose buried itself in a bag of sand. The car gave a violent lurch, and became still.

" Confound it ! " he said.

He had an impression he must be stunned, because of a surging in his ears, and because all the voices of the people about him had become small and remote. They were shouting like elves inside a hill.

He found it a little difficult to get on his feet. His limbs were mixed up with the garments Mr. Butteridge had discarded when that gentleman had thought he must needs plunge into the sea. Bert bawled out half angry, half rueful, " You might have said you were going to tip the basket." Then he stood up and clutched the ropes of the car convulsively.

Below him, far below him, shining blue, were the waters of the English Channel. Far off, a little thing in the sunshine, and rushing down as if some one was bending it hollow, was the beach and the irregular cluster of houses that constituted

Dymchurch. He could see the little crowd of people he had so abruptly left. Grubb, in the white wrapper of a Desert Dervish, was running along the edge of the sea. Mr. Butteridge was knee-deep in the water, bawling immensely. The lady was sitting up with her floriferous hat in her lap, shockingly neglected. The beach, east and west, was dotted with little people—they seemed all heads and feet—looking up. And the balloon, released from the twenty-five stone or so of Mr. Butteridge and his lady, was rushing up into the sky at the pace of a racing motor-car. " My crikey ! " said Bert ; " here's a go ! "

He looked down with a pinched face at the receding beach, and reflected that he wasn't giddy ; then he made a superficial survey of the cords and ropes about him with a vague idea of " doing something." " I'm not going to mess about with the thing," he said at last, and sat down upon the mattress. " I'm not going to touch it. . . . I wonder what one ought to do ? "

Soon he got up again and stared for a long time at the sinking world below, at white cliffs to the east and flattening marsh to the left, at a minute wide prospect of weald and downland, at dim towns and harbours, and rivers and ribbon-like roads, at ships and ships, decks and fore-shortened funnels upon the ever-widening sea, and at the great mono-rail bridge that straddled the Channel from Folkestone to Boulogne, until at length, first little wisps and then a veil of filmy cloud hid the prospect from his eyes. He wasn't at all giddy nor very much frightened, only in a state of enormous consternation.

CHAPTER THREE

THE BALLOON

§ 1

BERT SMALLWAYS was a vulgar little creature, the sort of pert, limited soul that the old civilisation of the early twentieth century produced by the million in every country of the world. He had lived all his life in narrow streets, and between mean houses he could not look over, and in a narrow circle of ideas from which there was no escape. He thought the whole duty of man was to be smarter than his fellows, get his hands, as he put it, " on the dibs," and have a good time. He was, in fact, the sort of man who had made England and America what they were. The luck had been against him so far, but that was by the way. He was a mere aggressive and acquisitive individual with no sense of the State, no habitual loyalty, no devotion, no code of honour, no code even of courage. Now by a curious accident he found himself lifted out of his marvellous modern world for a time, out of all the

rush and confused appeals of it, and floating like a thing dead
and disembodied between sea and sky. It was as if Heaven
was experimenting with him, had picked him out as a sample
from the English millions to look at him more nearly and to
see what was happening to the soul of man. But what Heaven
made of him in that case I cannot profess to imagine, for I
have long since abandoned all theories about the ideals and
satisfactions of Heaven.

To be alone in a balloon at a height of fourteen or fifteen
thousand feet—and to that height Bert Smallways presently
rose—is like nothing else in human experience. It is one of
the supreme things possible to man. No flying-machine can
ever better it. It is to pass extraordinarily out of human things.
It is to be still and alone to an unprecedented degree. It is
solitude without the suggestion of intervention ; it is calm
without a single irrelevant murmur. It is to see the sky.

No sound reaches one of all the roar and jar of humanity,
the air is clear and sweet beyond the thought of defilement.
No bird, no insect comes so high. No wind blows ever in a
balloon, no breeze rustles, for it moves with the wind and is
itself a part of the atmosphere. Once started it does not rock
or sway ; you cannot feel whether it rises or falls. Bert felt
acutely cold, but he wasn't mountain-sick ; he put on the
coat and overcoat and gloves Butteridge had discarded—put
them over the " Desert Dervish " sheet that covered his cheap
best suit—and sat very still for a long time, overawed by the
new-found quiet of the world. Above him was the light, translucent, billowing globe of shining brown oiled silk and the
blazing sunlight and the great deep blue dome of the sky.
Below, far below, was a torn floor of sunlit cloud, slashed by
enormous rents, through which he saw the sea.

If you had been watching him from below you would have
seen his head, a motionless little black knob, sticking out
from the car first of all for a long time on one side, and then
vanishing to reappear after a time at some other point.

He wasn't in the least degree uncomfortable nor afraid. He
did think that as this uncontrollable thing had thus rushed
up the sky with him it might presently rush down again, but
this consideration did not trouble him very much. Essentially
his state was wonder. There is no fear nor trouble in balloons
—until they descend.

" Gollys ! " he said at last, feeling a need for talking ; " It's
better than a motor-bike.

" It's all right !

" I suppose they're telegraphing about, about me. . . . "

The second hour found him examining the equipment of the
car with great particularity. Above him was the throat of
the balloon bunched and tied together, but with an open lumen
through which Bert could peer up into a vast, empty, quiet
interior, and out of which descended two fine cords of unknown

import, one white, one crimson, to pockets below the ring. The netting about the balloon ended in cords attached to the ring, a big steel-bound hoop to which the car was slung by ropes. From it depended the trail rope and grapnel, and over the sides of the car were a number of canvas bags that Bert decided must be ballast to " chuck down " if the balloon fell. (" Not much falling just yet," said Bert.)

There were an aneroid and another box-shaped instrument hanging from the ring. The latter had an ivory plate bearing " statoscope " and other words in French, and a little indicator quivered and waggled between *Montée* and *Descente*. " That's all right," said Bert. " That tells if you're going up or down." On the crimson padded seat of the balloon there lay a couple of rugs and a Kodak, and in opposite corners of the bottom of the car were an empty champagne bottle and a glass. " Refreshments," said Bert meditatively, tilting the empty bottle. Then he had a brilliant idea. The two padded bed-like seats, each with blankets and mattress, he perceived, were boxes, and within he found Mr. Butteridge's conception of an adequate equipment for a balloon ascent ; a hamper which included a game pie, a Roman pie, a cold fowl, tomatoes, lettuce, ham sandwiches, shrimp sandwiches, a large cake, knives and forks and paper plates, self-heating tins of coffee and cocoa, bread, butter, and marmalade, several carefully packed bottles of champagne, bottles of Perrier water, and a big jar of water for washing, a portfolio, maps, and a compass, a rücksack containing a number of conveniences, including curling-tongs and hairpins, a cap with ear-flaps, and so forth.

" A 'ome from 'ome," said Bert, surveying this provision as he tied the ear-flaps under his chin.

He looked over the side of the car. Far below were the shining clouds. They had thickened so that the whole world was hidden. Southward they were piled in great snowy masses ; he was half disposed to think them mountains ; northward and eastward they were in wavelike levels, and blindingly sunlit.

" Wonder how long a balloon keeps up," he said.

He imagined he was not moving, so insensibly did the monster drift with the air about it. " No good coming down till we shift a bit," he said.

He consulted the statoscope.

" Still Monty," he said.

" Wonder what would happen if you pulled a cord ?

" No," he decided. " I ain't going to mess it about."

Afterwards he did pull both the ripping- and the valve-cords, but, as Mr. Butteridge had already discovered, they had fouled a fold of silk in the throat. Nothing happened. But for that little hitch the ripping-cord would have torn the balloon open as though it had been slashed by a sword, and hurled Mr. Smallways to eternity at the rate of some thousand feet a second. " No go ! " he said, giving it a final tug. Then he lunched.

He opened a bottle of champagne, which, as soon as he cut the wire, blew its cork out with incredible violence, and for the most part followed it into space. Bert, however, got about a tumblerful. " Atmospheric pressure," said Bert, finding an application at last for the elementary physiography of his seventh-standard days. " I'll have to be more careful next time. No good wastin' drink."

Then he routed about for matches to utilise Mr. Butteridge's cigars ; but here again luck was on his side, and he couldn't find any wherewith to set light to the gas above him. Or else he would have dropped in a flare, a splendid but transitory pyrotechnic display. 'Eng old Grubb ! " said Bert, slapping unproductive pockets. " 'E didn't ought to 'ave kep' my box. 'E's always sneaking matches."

He reposed for a time. Then he got up, paddled about, rearranged the ballast bags on the floor, watched the clouds for a time, and turned over the maps on the locker. Bert liked maps, and he spent some time in trying to find one of France or the Channel ; but they were all British ordnance maps of English counties. That set him thinking about languages and trying to recall his seventh-standard French. " Je suis Anglais. C'est une méprise. Je suis arrivé par accident ici," he decided upon as convenient phrases. Then it occurred to him that he would entertain himself by reading Mr. Butteridge's letters and examining his pocket-book, and in this manner he whiled away the afternoon.

§ 2

He sat upon the padded locker, wrapped about very carefully, for the air, though calm, was exhilaratingly cold and clear. He was wearing first a modest suit of blue serge and all the unpretending underwear of a suburban young man of fashion, with sandal-like cycling shoes and brown stockings drawn over his trouser ends ; then the perforated sheet proper to a Desert Dervish ; then the coat and waistcoat and big fur-trimmed overcoat of Mr. Butteridge ; then a lady's large fur cloak, and round his knees a blanket. Over his head was a tow wig, surmounted by a large cap of Mr. Butteridge's with the flaps down over his ears. And some fur sleeping-boots of Mr. Butteridge's warmed his feet. The car of the balloon was small and neat, some bags of ballast the untidiest of its contents, and he had found a light folding-table and put it at his elbow, and on that was a glass with champagne. And about him, above and below, was space—such a clear emptiness and silence of space as only the aeronaut can experience.

He did not know where he might be drifting, or what might happen next. He accepted this state of affairs with a serenity creditable to the Smallways' courage, which one might reasonably have expected to be of a more degenerate and contemptible quality altogether. His impression was that he was bound to come down somewhere, and that then, if he wasn't smashed, some one, some "society," perhaps, would probably pack him and the balloon back to England. If not, he would ask very firmly for the British Consul. " Le Consuelo Britannique," he decided this would be. " Apportez-moi à le consuelo Britannique, s'il vous plait," he would say, for he was by no means ignorant of French. In the meanwhile he found the intimate aspects of Mr. Butteridge an interesting study.

There were letters of an entirely private character addressed to Mr. Butteridge, and among others several love-letters of a devouring sort in a large feminine hand. These are no business of ours, and one remarks with regret that Bert read them.

When he had read them he remarked, " Gollys ! " in an awestricken tone, and then, after a long interval, " I wonder if that was her ? "

" Lord ! "

He mused for a time.

He resumed his exploration of the Butteridge interior. It included a number of press cuttings of interviews and also several letters in German, then some in the same German handwriting, but in English. " Hal-*lo* ! " said Bert.

One of the latter, the first he took, began with an apology to Butteridge for not writing to him in English before, and for the inconvenience and delay that had been caused him by that, and went on to matter that Bert found exciting in the highest degree. " We can understand entirely the difficulties of your position, and that you shall possibly be watched at the present juncture. But, sir, we do not believe that any serious obstacles will be put in your way if you wished to endeavour to leave the country and come to us with your plans by the customary routes—either via Dover, Ostend, Boulogne, or Dieppe. We find it difficult to think you are right in supposing yourself to be in danger of murder for your invaluable invention."

" Funny ! " said Bert, and meditated.

Then he went through the other letters.

" They seem to want him to come," said Bert ; " but they don't seem hurting themselves to get 'im. Or else they're shamming don't care to get his prices down.

" They don't quite seem to be the gov'ment," he reflected, after an interval. " It's more like some firm's paper. All this printed stuff at the top. *Drachenflieger. Drachenballons. Ballonstoffe. Kugelballons.* Greek to me.

" But he was trying to sell his blessed secret abroad. That's all right. No Greek about that ! Gollys ! Here *is* the secret ! "

He tumbled off the seat, opened the locker, and had the portfolio open before him on the folding-table. It was full of drawings done in the peculiar flat style and conventional colours engineers adopt. And, in addition, there were some rather under-exposed photographs, obviously done by an amateur at close quarters, of the actual machine Butteridge had made, in its shed near the Crystal Palace. Bert found he was trembling. " Lord ! " he said, " here am I and the whole blessed secret of flying—lost up here on the roof of everywhere.

" Let's see ! " He fell studying the drawings and comparing them with the photographs. They puzzled him. Half of them seemed to be missing. He tried to imagine how they fitted together, and found the effort too great for his mind.

" It's tryin'," said Bert. " I wish I'd been brought up to the engineering. If I could only make it out ! "

He went to the side of the car and remained for a time staring with unseeing eyes at a huge cluster of great clouds —a cluster of slowly dissolving Monte Rosas, sunlit below. His attention was arrested by a strange black spot that moved over them. It alarmed him. It was a black spot moving slowly with him far below, following him down there, indefatigably over the cloud mountains. Why should such a thing follow him ? What could it be ? . . .

He had an inspiration. " Uv course ! " he said. It was the shadow of the balloon. But he still watched it dubiously for a time.

He returned to the plans on the table.

He spent a long afternoon between his struggles to understand them and fits of meditation. He evolved a remarkable new sentence in French. " Voici Mossoo !—Je suis un inventeur Anglais. Mon nom est Butteridge. Beh. oo. teh. teh. eh. arr. E. deh. ghe. eh. J'avais ici pour vendre le secret de le *flying-machine*. Comprenez ? Vendre pour l'argent tout suite, l'argent en main. Comprenez ? C'est le machine à jouer dans l'air. Comprenez ? C'est le machine à faire l'oiseau. Comprenez ? Balancer ? Oui exactement ! Battir l'oiseau en fait, à son propre jeu. Je désire de vendre ceci à votre gouvernement national. Voulez-vous me directer là ? "

" Bit rummy, I expect, from the point of view of grammar," said Bert, " but they ought to get the hang of it all right."

" But then, if they arst me to explain the blessed thing ? "

He returned in a worried way to the plans. " I don't believe it's all here ! " he said. . . .

He got more and more perplexed up there among the clouds as to what he should do with this wonderful find of his. At any moment, so far as he could tell, he might descend among he knew not what foreign people.

" It's the chance of my life ! " he said.

It became more and more manifest to him that it wasn't. " Directly I come down they'll telegraph—put it in the papers. Butteridge'll know of it and come along—on my track."

Butteridge would be a terrible person to be on any one's track. Bert thought of the great black moustaches, the tri-

angular nose, the searching bellow and the glare. His afternoon's dream of a marvellous seizure and sale of the great
Butteridge secret crumpled up in his mind, dissolved, and
vanished. He awoke to sanity again.

"Wouldn't do. What's the good of thinking of it ? " He
proceeded slowly and reluctantly to replace the Butteridge
papers in pockets and portfolio as he had found them. He
became aware of a splendid golden light upon the balloon
above him, and of a new warmth in the blue dome of the sky.
He stood up and beheld the sun, a great ball of blinding gold,
setting upon a tumbled sea of gold-edged crimson and purple
clouds, strange and wonderful beyond imagining. Eastward
cloudland stretched for ever, darkling blue, and it seemed to
Bert the whole round hemisphere of the world was under his
eyes.

Then far away over the blue he caught sight of three long,
dark shapes like hurrying fish that drove one after the other,
as porpoises follow one another in the water. They were very
fish-like indeed—with tails. It was an unconvincing impression
in that light. He blinked his eyes, stared again, and they had
vanished. For a long time he scrutinised those remote blue
levels and saw no more. . . .

"Wonder if I ever saw anything," he said, and then :
"There ain't such things. . . . "

Down went the sun and down and down, not diving steeply, but passing northward as it sank, and then suddenly daylight and the
expansive warmth of daylight had gone altogether, and the
index of the statoscope quivered over to *Descente*.

§ 3

"*Now* what's going to 'appen ? " said Bert.

He found the cold, gray cloud wilderness rising towards
him with a wide, slow steadiness. As he sank down among
them the clouds ceased to seem the snowclad mountain-slopes
they had resembled heretofore, became unsubstantial, confessed an immense silent drift and eddy in their substance.
For a moment, when he was nearly among their twilight
masses, his descent was checked. Then abruptly the sky was
hidden, the last vestiges of daylight gone, and he was falling
rapidly in an evening twilight through a whirl of fine snowflakes that streamed past him towards the zenith, that drifted
in upon the things about him and melted, that touched his
face with ghostly fingers. He shivered. His breath came
smoking from his lips, and everything was instantly bedewed
and wet.

He had an impression of a snowstorm pouring with unexampled and increasing fury *upward* ; then he realised that
he was falling faster and faster.

Imperceptibly a sound grew upon his ears. The great
silence of the world was at an end.

" What was this confused sound ?

He craned his head over the side, concerned, perplexed.

First he seemed to see, and then not to see. Then he saw clearly little edges of foam pursuing each other, and a wide waste of weltering waters below him. Far away was a pilot boat with a big sail bearing dim black letters, and a little pinkish-yellow light, and it was rolling and pitching—rolling and pitching in a gale, while he could feel no wind at all. Soon the sound of waters was loud and near. He was dropping, dropping—into the sea !

He became convulsively active.

" Ballast ! " he cried, and seized a little sack from the floor, and heaved it overboard. He did not wait for the effect of that, but sent another after it. He looked over in time to see a minute white splash in the dim waters below him, and then he was back in the snow and clouds again.

He sent out quite needlessly a third sack of ballast and a fourth, and presently had the immense satisfaction of soaring up out of the damp and chill into the clear, cold, upper air in which the day still lingered. " Thang-God ! " he said, with all his heart.

A few stars now had pierced the blue, and in the east there shone brightly a prolate moon.

§ 4

That first downward plunge filled Bert with a haunting sense of boundless waters below. It was a summer's night, but it seemed to him, nevertheless, extraordinarily long. He had a feeling of insecurity that he fancied quite irrationally the sunrise would dispel. Also he was hungry. He felt in the dark in the locker, put his fingers in the Roman pie, and got some sandwiches, and he also opened rather successfully a half-bottle of champagne. That warmed and restored him, he grumbled at Grubb about the matches, wrapped himself up warmly on the locker and dozed for a time. He got up once or twice to make sure that he was still securely high above the sea. The first time the moonlit clouds were white and dense, and the shadow of the balloon ran athwart them like a dog that followed ; afterwards they seemed thinner. As he lay still, staring up at the huge dark balloon above, he made a discovery. His—or rather Mr. Butteridge's—waistcoat rustled as he breathed. It was lined with papers. But Bert could not see to get them out or examine them, much as he wished to do so.

He was awakened by the crowing of cocks, the barking of dogs, and a clamour of birds. He was driving slowly at a low level over a broad land lit golden by sunrise under a clear sky. He stared out upon hedgeless, well-cultivated fields intersected by roads, each lined with cable-bearing red poles. He had just passed over a compact, whitewashed village with a straight church tower and steep red-tiled roofs. A number of peasants, men and women, in shiny blouses and lumpish footwear, stood regarding him, arrested on their way to work. He was so low that the end of his rope was trailing.

He stared out at these people. " I wonder how you land," he thought.

" S'pose I *ought* to land ? "

He found himself drifting down towards a mono-rail line, and hastily flung out two or three handfuls of ballast to clear it.

" Lemme see ! One might say just ' Prenez ! ' Wish I knew the French for ' take hold of the rope , ! . . . I suppose they are French.

He surveyed the country again. " Might be Holland. Or Luxembourg. Or Lorraine's far as *I* know. Wonder what those big affairs over there are. Some sort of kiln ? Prosperous-looking country. . . ."

The respectability of the country's appearance awakened answering chords in his nature.

" Make myself a bit ship-shape first," he said.

He resolved to rise a little and get rid of his wig (which now felt hot on his head), and so forth. He threw out a bag of ballast, and was astonished to find himself careering up through the air very rapidly.

" Blow ! " said Mr. Smallways. " I've overdone the ballast trick. . . . Wonder when I shall get down again ? . . . Brekfus' on board, anyhow."

He removed his cap and wig, for the air was warm, and an improvident impulse made him cast the latter object overboard. The statoscope responded with a vigorous swing to " Montée."

" The blessed thing goes up if you only *look* overboard," he remarked, and assailed the locker. He found among other items several tins of liquid cocoa containing explicit directions for opening that he followed with minute care. He pierced the bottom with the key provided in the holes indicated, and forthwith the can grew from cold to hotter and hotter, until at last he could scarcely touch it, and then he opened the can at the other end, and there was his cocoa smoking, without the use of match or flame of any sort. It was an old invention, but new to Bert. There was also ham and marmalade and bread, so that he had a really very tolerable breakfast indeed.

Then he took off his overcoat, for the sunshine was now inclined to be hot, and that reminded him of the rustling he had heard in the night. He took off the waistcoat and examined it. " Old Butteridge won't like me unpicking this." He hesitated, and finally proceeded to unpick it. He found the missing drawings of the lateral rotating planes, on which the whole stability of the flying-machine depended.

An observant angel would have seen Bert sitting for a long time after this discovery in a state of intense meditation. Then at last he rose with an air of inspiration, took Mr. Butteridge's ripped, demolished, and ransacked waistcoat, and hurled it from the balloon—whence it fluttered down slowly and eddyingly until at last it came to rest with a contented flop upon the face of a German tourist sleeping peacefully beside the Höhenweg, near Wildbad. Also this sent the balloon higher, and so into a position still more convenient for observation by our imaginary angel, who would next have seen Mr. Smallways tear open his own jacket and waistcoat, remove his collar, open his shirt, thrust his hand into his bosom, and tear his heart out—or at least, if not his heart, some large, bright scarlet object. If the observer, overcoming a thrill of celestial horror, had scrutinised this scarlet object more narrowly, one of Bert's most cherished secrets, one of his essential weaknesses, would have been laid bare. It was a red-flannel chest protector, one of those large, quasi-hygienic objects that with pills and medicines take the place of beneficial relics and images among the Protestant peoples of Christendom. Always Bert wore this thing; it was his cherished delusion, based on the advice of a shilling fortune-teller at Margate, that he was weak in the lungs.

He now proceeded to unbutton his fetish, to attack it with a penknife, and to thrust the new-found plans between the two layers of imitation Saxony flannel of which it was made. Then with the help of Mr. Butteridge's small shaving-mirror and his folding canvas basin he readjusted his costume with the gravity of a man who has taken an irrevocable step in life, buttoned up his jacket, cast the white sheet of the Desert Dervish on one side, washed temperately, shaved, resumed the big cap and the fur overcoat, and, much refreshed by these exercises, surveyed the country below him.

It was indeed a spectacle of incredible magnificence. If, perhaps, it was not so strange and magnificent as the sunlit cloudland of the previous day, it was at any rate infinitely more interesting. The air was at its utmost clearness, and, except to the south and south-west, there was not a cloud in the sky. The country was hilly, with occasional fir plantations and bleak upland spaces, but also with numerous farms, and the hills were deeply intersected by the gorges of several winding rivers interrupted at intervals by the banked-up ponds and weirs of electric generating wheels. It was dotted with bright-looking, steep-roofed villages, and each showed a distinctive and interesting church beside its wireless telegraph steeple ; here and there were large châteaux and parks and white roads, and paths lined with red and white cable posts were extremely conspicuous in the landscape. There were walled enclosures like gardens and rickyards, and great roofs of barns and many electric dairy centres. The uplands were populous with cattle. At places he would see the track of one of the old rail-roads (converted now to mono-rails) dodging through tunnels and crossing embankments, and a rushing hum would mark the passing of a train. Everything was extraordinarily clear as

well as minute. Once or twice he saw guns and soldiers, and
was reminded of the stir of military preparations he had
witnessed on the Bank Holiday in England ; but there was
nothing to tell him that these military preparations were
abnormal, or to explain an occasional faint irregular firing of
guns that drifted up to him.

"Wish I knew how to get down," said Bert, ten thousand
feet or so above it all, and gave himself up to much futile
tugging at the red and white cords. Afterwards he made a sort
of inventory of the provisions. Life in the high air was giving
him an appalling appetite, and it seemed to him discreet at
this stage to portion out his supply into rations. So far as he
could see, he might pass a week in the air.

At first all the vast panorama below had been as silent as a
painted picture. But as the day wore on, and the gas diffused
slowly from the balloon, it sank earthward again, details
increased, men became more visible, and he began to hear the
whistle and moan of trains and cars, sounds of cattle, bugles
and kettle-drums, and presently even men's voices. And at
last his guide-rope was trailing again, and he found it possible
to attempt a landing. Once or twice, as the rope dragged over
cables, he found his hair erect with electricity, and once he
had a slight shock, and sparks snapped about the car. He took
these things among the chances of the voyage. He had one
idea now very clear in his mind, and that was to drop the iron
grapnel that hung from the ring.

From the first this attempt was unfortunate, perhaps because
the place for descent was ill-chosen. A balloon should come in
an empty open space, and he chose a crowd. He made his
decision suddenly, and without proper reflection. As he trailed,
Bert saw ahead of him one of the most attractive little towns
in the world—a cluster of steep gables surmounted by a high
church tower and diversified with trees, walled, and with a
fine, large gateway opening out upon a tree-lined high road.
All the wires and cables of the country-side converged upon it
like guests to entertainment. It had a most homelike and
comfortable quality, and it was made gayer by abundant flags.
Along the road a quantity of peasant folk, in big pair-wheeled
carts and afoot, were coming and going, beside an occasional
mono-rail car ; and at the car-junction, under the trees outside
the town, was a busy little fair of booths. It seemed a warm,
human, well-rooted, and altogether delightful place to Bert.
He came low over the tree-tops, with his grapnel ready to throw,
and so anchor him—a curious, interested, and interesting guest,
so his imagination figured it, in the very middle of it all.

He thought of himself performing feats with the sign language
and chance linguistics amidst a circle of admiring rustics. . . .

And then the chapter of adverse accidents began.

The rope made itself unpopular long before the crowd had
fully realised his advent over the trees. An elderly and

apparently intoxicated peasant in a shiny black hat, and carrying a large crimson umbrella, caught sight of it first as it trailed past him, and was seized with a discreditable ambition to kill it. He pursued it briskly with unpleasant cries. It crossed the road obliquely, splashed into a pan of milk upon a stall, and slapped its milky tail athwart a motor-car load of factory girls halted outside the town gates. They screamed loudly. People looked up and saw Bert making what he meant to be genial salutations, but what they considered, in view of the feminine outcry, to be insulting gestures. Then the car hit the roof of the gatehouse smartly, snapped a flagstaff, played a tune upon some telegraph wires and sent a broken wire like a whip-lash to do its share in accumulating unpopularity. Bert, by clutching convulsively, just escaped being pitched headlong. Two young soldiers and several peasants shouted things up to him and shook fists at him, and began to run in pursuit as he disappeared over the wall into the town. Admiring rustics, indeed!

The balloon leapt at once, in the manner of balloons when part of their weight is released by touching down, with a sort of flippancy, and in another moment Bert was over a street crowded with peasants and soldiers, that opened into a busy market-square. The wave of unfriendliness pursued him.

" Grapnel," said Bert, and then with an afterthought shouted, " *Têtes*, there, you ! I say ! I say ! *Têtes*. Eng it ! " The grapnel clattered down a steeply sloping roof, followed by an avalanche of broken tiles, jumped the street amidst shrieks and cries, and smashed into a plate-glass window with an immense and sickening impact. The balloon rolled nauseatingly, and the car pitched. But the grapnel had not held. It emerged at once bearing on one fluke, with a ridiculous air of fastidious selection, a small child's chair, and pursued by a maddened shopman. It lifted its catch, swung about with an appearance of painful indecision amidst a roar of wrath, and dropped it at last neatly, and as if by inspiration, over the head of a peasant woman in charge of an assortment of cabbages in the market-place.

Everybody now was aware of the balloon. Everybody was either trying to dodge the grapnel or catch the trail rope. With a pendulum-like swoop through the crowd, that sent people flying right and left, the grapnel came to earth again, tried for and missed a stout gentleman in a blue suit and a straw hat, smacked away a trestle from under a stall of haberdashery, made a cyclist soldier in knickerbockers leap like a chamois, and secured itself uncertainly among the hind-legs of a sheep— which made convulsive, ungracious efforts to free itself, and was dragged into a position of rest against a stone cross in the middle of the place. The balloon pulled up with a jerk. In another moment a score of willing hands were tugging it earthward. At the same instant Bert became aware for the first time of a fresh breeze blowing about him.

For some seconds he stood staggering in the car, which now swayed sickeningly, surveying the exasperated crowd below him and trying to collect his mind. He was extraordinarily astonished at this run of mishaps. Were the people really so annoyed ? Everybody seemed angry with him. No one seemed interested or amused by his arrival. A disproportionate amount of the outcry had the quality of imprecation—had, indeed, a strong flavour of riot. Several greatly uniformed officials in cocked hats struggled in vain to control the crowd. Fists and sticks were shaken. And when Bert saw a man on the outskirts of the crowd run to a haycart and get a brightly-pronged pitch-fork, and a blue-clad soldier unbuckle his belt, his doubt whether this little town was after all such a good place for a landing became a certainty.

He had clung to the fancy that they would make something of a hero of him. Now he knew that he was mistaken.

He was perhaps ten feet above the people when he made his decision. His paralysis ceased. He leapt up on the seat, and, at imminent risk of falling headlong, disengaged the grapnel rope from the toggle that held it, sprang on to the trail rope and released that also. A hoarse shout of disgust greeted the descent of the grapnel-rope and the swift leap of the balloon and something—he fancied afterwards it was a turnip—whizzed by his head. The trail-rope followed its fellow. The crowd seemed to jump away from him. With an immense and horrifying rustle the balloon brushed against a telephone pole, and for a tense instant he anticipated either an electric explosion or a bursting of the oiled silk, or both. But fortune was with him.

In another second he was cowering in the bottom of the car, and, released from the weight of the grapnel and the two ropes, rushing up once more through the air. For a time he remained crouching, and when at last he looked out again, the little town was very small and travelling with the rest of lower Germany in a circular orbit round and round the car—or at least it appeared to be doing that.

When he got used to it he found this rotation of the balloon rather convenient ; it saved moving about in the car.

§ 5

Late in the afternoon of a pleasant summer day in the year 191-, if one may borrow a mode of phrasing that once found favour with the readers of the late G. P. R. James, a solitary balloonist—replacing the solitary horseman of the classic romances—might have been observed wending his way across Franconia in a north-easterly direction, at a height of about eleven thousand feet above the sea and still spinning slowly. His head was craned over the side of the car, and he surveyed the country below with an expression of profound perplexity ; ever and again his lips shaped inaudible words. " Shootin' at a chap," for example, and " I'll come down right enough soon as I find out 'ow." Over the side of the basket the robe of the Desert Dervish was hanging, an appeal for consideration, an ineffectual white flag.

He was now very distinctly aware that the world below him, so far from being the naïve country-side of his earlier imaginings that day, sleepily unconscious of him and capable of being amazed and nearly reverential at his descent, was acutely irritated by his career, and extremely impatient with the course he was taking. But indeed it was not he who took that course, but his masters, the winds of heaven. Mysterious voices spoke to him in his ear, jerking the words up to him by means of megaphones, in a weird and startling manner, in a great variety of languages. Official-looking persons had signalled to him by means of flag-flapping and arm waving. On the whole a guttural variant of English prevailed in the sentences that alighted upon the balloon ; chiefly he was told to " gome down or you will be shot."

" All very well," said Bert, " but 'OW ? "

Then they shot a little wide of the car. Latterly he had been shot at six or seven times, and once the bullet had gone by with a sound so persuasively like the tearing of silk that he had resigned himself to the prospect of a headlong fall. But either they were aiming near him or they had missed, and as yet nothing was torn but the air about him—and his anxious soul.

He was now enjoying a respite from these attentions, but he felt it was at best an interlude, and he was doing what he could to appreciate his position. Incidentally he was having some hot coffee and pie in an untidy, inadvertent manner with an eye fluttering nervously over the side of the car. At first he had ascribed the growing interest in his career to his ill-conceived attempt to land in the bright little upland town, but now he was beginning to realise that the military rather than the civil arm was concerned about him.

He was quite involuntarily playing that weird, mysterious part—the part of an International Spy. He was seeing secret things. He had, in fact, crossed the designs of no less a power than the German Empire, he had blundered into the hot focus of Welt-Politik, he was drifting helplessly towards the great Imperial secret, the immense aeronautic park that had been established at a headlong pace in Franconia to develop silently, swiftly, and on a colossal scale the great discoveries of Hunstedt and Stossel, and so to give Germany before all other nations a fleet of airships, the air power and the Empire of the world.

Later, just before they shot him down altogether, Bert saw that great area of passionate work, warm lit in the evening light, a great area of upland on which the airships lay like a herd of grazing monsters at their feed. It was a vast, busy space, stretching away northward as far as he could see, methodically cut up into numbered sheds, gasometers, squad encampments, storage areas, interlaced with the omnipresent mono-rail lines, and altogether free from overhead wires or cables. Everywhere was the white, black, and yellow of Imperial Germany, everywhere the black eagles spread their wings. Even without these indications, the large, vigorous neatness of everything would have marked it German. Vast multitudes of men went to and fro, many in white and drab fatigue uniforms busy about the balloons, others drilling in sensible drab. Here and there a full uniform glittered.

The airships chiefly engaged his attention, and he knew at once it was three of these he had seen on the previous night, taking advantage of the cloud welkin to manœuvre unobserved.

They were altogether fish-like. For the great airships with which Germany attacked New York in her last gigantic effort for world supremacy—before humanity realised that world supremacy was a dream—were the lineal descendants of the Zeppelin airship that flew over Lake Constance in 1906, and of the Lebaudy navigables that made their memorable excursions over Paris in 1907 and 1908.

These German airships were held together by rib-like skeletons of steel and aluminium and a stout, inelastic canvas outer-skin, within which was an impervious rubber gas-bag, cut up by transverse dissepiments into from fifty to a hundred compartments. These were all absolutely gas tight and filled with hydrogen, and the entire aerostat was kept at any level by means of a long, internal balloonette of oiled and toughened silk canvas, into which air could be forced and from which it could be pumped. So the airship could be made either heavier or lighter than air, and losses of weight through the consumption of fuel, the casting of bombs and so forth, could also be compensated by admitting air to sections of the general gas-bag. Ultimately that made a highly explosive mixture ; but in all these matters risks must be taken and guarded against. There was a steel axis to the whole affair, a central back-bone which terminated in the engine and propeller, and the men and magazines were forward in a series of cabins under the expanded headlike forepart. The engine, which was of the extraordinarily powerful Pforzheim type, that supreme triumph of German invention, was worked by electric controls from this forepart, which was indeed the only really habitable part of the ship. If anything went wrong the engineers went aft along a rope ladder beneath the frame or along a passage through the gas chambers. The tendency of the whole affair to roll was partly corrected by a horizontal lateral fin on either side, and steering was chiefly effected by two vertical fins, which normally lay back like gill-flaps on either side of the head. It was, indeed, a most complete adaptation of the fish form to aerial conditions, the position of swimming-bladder, eyes, and brain being, however, below instead of above. A striking and unfish-like feature was the apparatus for wireless telegraphy that dangled from the forward cabin—that is to say, under the chin of the fish.

These monsters were capable of ninety miles an hour in a calm, so that they could face and make headway against nearly everything except the fiercest tornado. They varied in length from eight hundred to two thousand feet, and they had a carrying power of from seventy to two hundred tons. How many Germany possessed history does not record, but Bert counted nearly eighty great bulks receding in perspective during his brief inspection. Such were the instruments on which she relied to sustain her in her repudiation of the Monroe Doctrine and her bold bid for a share in the empire of the New World. But not altogether did she rely on these ; she had also a one-man bomb-throwing *Drachenflieger* of unknown value among her resources.

But the *Drachenflieger* were away in the second great aero-nautic park east of Hamburg, and Bert Smallways saw nothing of them in the bird's-eye view he took of the Franconian establishment before they shot him down. For they shot him down very neatly. They used the new bullets with steel trailers that Wolffe of Engelberg had invented for aerial warfare. The bullet tore past him and made a sort of pop as its trailer rent his balloon—a pop that was followed by a rustling sigh and a steady downward movement. And when in the confusion of the moment he dropped a bag of ballast, the Germans very politely but firmly overcame his scruples by shooting his balloon again twice.

CHAPTER IV

THE GERMAN AIR-FLEET

§ 1

OF all the productions of the human imagination that made the world in which Mr. Bert Smallways lived confusingly wonderful, there was none quite so strange, so headlong and disturbing, so noisy and persuasive and dangerous, as the modernisations of patriotism produced by imperial and international politics. In the soul of all men is a liking for kind, a pride in one's own atmosphere, a tenderness for one's mother speech and one's familiar land. Before the coming of the Scientific Age this group of gentle and noble emotions had been a fine factor in the equipment of every worthy human being, a fine factor that had its less amiable aspect in a usually harmless hostility to strange people, and a usually harmless detraction of strange lands. But with the wild rush of change in the pace, scope, materials, scale, and possibilities of human life that then occurred, the old boundaries, the old seclusions and separations were violently broken down. All the old settled mental habits and traditions of men found themselves not simply confronted by new conditions, but by constantly renewed and changing new conditions. They had no chance of adapting themselves. They were annihilated or perverted or inflamed beyond recognition.

Bert Smallways' grandfather, in the days when Bun Hill was a village under the sway of Sir Peter Bone's parent, had " known his place " to the uttermost farthing, touched his hat to his betters, despised and condescended to his inferiors, and hadn't changed an idea from the cradle to the grave. He was Kentish and English, and that meant hops, beer, dog-roses, and the sort of sunshine that was best in the world. Newspapers and politics and visits to " Lunnon " weren't for the likes of him. Then came the change. These earlier chapters have given an idea of what happened to Bun Hill, and how the flood of novel things had poured over its devoted rusticity. Bert Smallways was only one of countless millions in Europe and America and Asia who, instead of being born rooted in the soil, were born struggling in a torrent they never clearly understood. All the faiths of their fathers had been taken by surprise, and startled into the strangest forms and reactions. Particularly did the fine old tradition of patriotism get per-verted and distorted in the rush of the new times. Instead of the sturdy establishment in prejudice of Bert's grandfather, to whom the word " Frenchified " was the ultimate term of contempt, there flowed through Bert's brain a squittering succession of thinly violent ideas about German competition, about the Yellow Danger, about the Black Peril, about the White Man's Burthen—that is to say, Bert's preposterous right to muddle further the naturally very muddled politics of the entirely similar little cads to himself (except for a smear of brown) who smoked cigarettes and rode bicycles in Buluwayo, Kingston (Jamaica), or Bombay. These were Bert's " Subject Races," and he was ready to die—by proxy in the person of any one who cared to enlist—to maintain his hold upon that right. It kept him awake at nights to think that he might lose it.

The essential fact of the politics of the age in which Bert Smallways lived—the age that blundered at last into the catastrophe of the War in the Air—was a very simple one, if only people had had the intelligence to be simple about it. The development of Science had altered the scale of human affairs. By means of rapid mechanical traction it had brought men nearer together, so much nearer socially, economically, physically, that the old separations into nations and kingdoms were no longer possible, a newer, wider synthesis was not only needed but imperatively demanded. Just as the once indepen-dent dukedoms of France had to fuse into a nation, so now the nations had to adapt themselves to a wider coalescence, they had to keep what was precious and practicable, and concede what was obsolete and dangerous. A saner world would have perceived this patent need for a reasonable synthesis, would have discussed it temperately, achieved and gone on to organise the great civilisation that was manifestly possible to mankind.

The world of Bert Smallways did nothing of the sort. Its national governments, its national interests, would not hear of anything so obvious ; they were too suspicious of each other, too wanting in generous imagination. They began to behave like ill-bred people in a crowded public car, to squeeze against one another, elbow, thrust, dispute and quarrel. Vain to point out to them that they had only to rearrange themselves to be comfortable. Everywhere, all over the world, the historian of the early twentieth century finds the same thing, the flow and rearrangement of human affairs inextricably entangled by the old areas, the old prejudices and a sort of heated irascible stupidity ; and everywhere congested nations in inconvenient areas, slopping population and produce into each other, annoying each other with tariffs and every possible commercial vexation, and threatening each other with navies and armies that grew every year more portentous.

It is impossible now to estimate how much of the intellectual and physical energy of the world was wasted in military preparation and equipment, but it was an enormous proportion. Great Britain spent upon army and navy money and capacity that, directed into the channels of physical culture and education, would have made the British the aristocracy of the world. Her rulers could have kept the whole population learning and exercising up to the age of eighteen, and made a broad-chested and intelligent man of every Bert Smallways in the islands, had they given the resources they spent in war material to the making of men. Instead of which they waggled flags at him until he was fourteen, incited him to cheer, and then turned him out of school to begin that career of private enterprise we have compactly recorded. France achieved similar imbecilities ; Germany was, if possible, worse ; Russia under the waste and stresses of militarism festered towards bankruptcy and decay. All Europe was producing big guns and countless swarms of little Smallways. The Asiatic peoples had been forced in self-defence into a like diversion of the new powers science had brought them. On the eve of the outbreak of the war there were six great powers in the world and a cluster of smaller ones, each armed to the teeth and straining every nerve to get ahead of the others in deadliness of equipment and military efficiency. The great powers were first the United States, a nation addicted to commerce, but roused to military necessities by the efforts of Germany to expand into South America, and by the natural consequences of her own unwary annexations of land in the very teeth of Japan. She maintained two immense fleets east and west, and internally she was in violent conflict between Federal and State governments upon the question of universal service in a defensive militia. Next came the great alliance of Eastern Asia, a close-knit coalescence of China and Japan, advancing with rapid strides year by year to predominance in the world's affairs.

Then the German alliance still struggled to achieve its dream of imperial expansion, and its imposition of the German language upon a forcibly united Europe. These were the three most spirited and aggressive powers in the world. Far more pacific was the British Empire, perilously scattered over the globe, and distracted now by insurrectionary movements in Ireland and among all its Subject Races. It had given these Subject Races cigarettes, boots, bowler hats, cricket, race meetings, cheap revolvers, petroleum, the factory system of industry, halfpenny newspapers in both English and the vernacular, inexpensive university degrees, motor-bicycles, and electric trams ; it had produced a considerable literature expressing contempt for the Subject Races and rendered it freely accessible to them, and it had been content to believe that nothing would result from these stimulants because somebody once wrote " the immemorial east " ; and also, in the inspired words of Kipling :—

> East is east and west is west,
> And never the twain shall meet.

Instead of which, Egypt, India, and the subject countries generally had produced new generations in a state of passionate indignation and the utmost energy, activity, and modernity. The governing class in Great Britain was slowly adapting itself to a new conception of the Subject Races as waking peoples, and finding its efforts to keep the Empire together under these strains and changing ideas greatly impeded by the entirely sporting spirit with which Bert Smallways at home (by the million) cast his vote, and by the tendency of his more highly coloured equivalents to be disrespectful to irascible officials. Their impertinence was excessive ; it was no mere stone throwing and shouting. They would quote Burns at them and Mill and Darwin, and confute them in arguments.

Even more pacific than the British Empire were France and its allies, the Latin powers, heavily armed states indeed, but reluctant warriors, and in many ways socially and politically leading western civilisation. Russia was a pacific power perforce, divided within itself, torn between revolutionaries and reactionaries who were equally incapable of social reconstruction, and so sinking towards a tragic disorder of chronic political vendetta. Wedged in among these portentous larger bulks, swayed and threatened by them, the smaller states of the world maintained a precarious independence, each keeping itself armed as dangerously as its utmost ability could contrive.

So it came about that in every country a great and growing proportion of its energetic and inventive men was busied either for offensive or defensive ends, in elaborating the apparatus of war, until the accumulating tensions should reach the breaking-point. Each power sought to keep its preparations secret, to hold new weapons in reserve, to anticipate and learn the preparations of its rivals. The feeling of danger from fresh discoveries affected the patriotic imagination of every people in the world. Now it was rumoured the British had an overwhelming gun, now the French an invincible rifle, now the Japanese a new explosive, now the Americans a submarine that would drive every ironclad from the seas. Each time there would be a war panic.

The strength and heart of the nations was given to the thought of war, and yet the mass of their citizens was a teeming democracy as heedless of and unfitted for fighting, mentally, morally, physically, as any population has ever been—or, one ventures to add, could ever be. That was the paradox of the time. It was a period altogether unique in the world's history. The apparatus of warfare, the art and method of fighting, changed absolutely every dozen years in a stupendous progress towards perfection, and people grew less and less warlike, and there was no war.

And then at last it came. It came as a surprise to all the world because its real causes were hidden. Relations were strained between Germany and the United States because of the intense exasperation of a tariff conflict and the ambiguous attitude of the former power towards the Monroe Doctrine, and they were strained between the United States and Japan because of the perennial citizenship question. But in both cases these were standing causes of offence. The real deciding cause, it is now known, was the perfecting of the Pforzheim engine by Germany and the consequent possibility of a rapid and entirely practicable airship. At that time Germany was by far the most efficient power in the world, better organised for swift and secret action, better equipped with the resources of modern science, and with her official and administrative classes at a higher level of education and training. These things she knew, and she exaggerated that knowledge to the pitch of contempt for the secret counsels of her neighbours. It may be that with the habit of self-confidence her spying upon them had grown less thorough. Moreover, she had a tradition of unsentimental and unscrupulous action that vitiated her international outlook profoundly. With the coming of these new weapons her collective intelligence thrilled with the sense that now her moment had come. Once again in the history of progress it seemed she held the decisive weapon. Now she might strike and conquer—before the others had anything but experiments in the air.

Particularly she must strike America swiftly, because there, if anywhere, lay the chance of an aerial rival. It was known that America possessed a flying-machine of considerable practical value, developed out of the Wright model ; but it was not supposed that the Washington War Office had made any wholesale attempts to create an aerial navy. It was necessary to strike before they could do so. France had a fleet of slow navigables, several dating from 1908, that could make no possible headway against the new type. They had been built solely for reconnoitring purposes on the eastern frontier, they were mostly too small to carry more than a couple of dozen men without arms or provisions, and not one could do forty miles an hour. Great Britain, it seemed, in an access of meanness, temporised and wrangled with the imperial-spirited Butteridge and his extraordinary invention. That also was not in play—and could not be for some months at the earliest. From Asia there came no sign. The Germans explained this by saying the yellow peoples were without invention. No other competitor was worth considering. "Now or never," said the Germans—"now or never we may seize the air—as once the British seized the seas ! While all the other powers are still experimenting."

Swift and systematic and secret were their preparations, and their plan most excellent. So far as their knowledge went, America was the only dangerous possibility ; America, which was also now the leading trade rival of Germany and one of the chief barriers to her Imperial expansion. So at once they would strike at America. They would fling a great force across the Atlantic heavens and bear America down unwarned and unprepared.

Altogether it was a well-imagined and most hopeful and spirited enterprise, having regard to the information in the possession of the German government. The chances of it being a successful surprise were very great. The airship and the flying-machine were very different things from ironclads, which take a couple of years to build. Given hands, given plant, they could be made innumerably in a few weeks. Once the needful parks and foundries were organised, airships and *Drachenflieger* could be poured into the sky. Indeed, when the time came, they did pour into the sky like, as a bitter French writer put it, flies roused from filth.

The attack upon America was to be the first move in this tremendous game. But no sooner had it started than instantly the aeronautic parks were to proceed to put together and inflate the second fleet, which was to dominate Europe and manœuvre significantly over London, Paris, Rome, St. Petersburg, or wherever else its moral effect was required. A World Surprise it was to be—no less, a World Conquest ; and it is wonderful how near the calmly adventurous minds that planned it came to succeeding in their colossal design.

Von Sternberg was the Moltke of this War in the Air, but it was the curious hard romanticism of Prince Karl Albert that won over the hesitating Emperor to the scheme. Prince Karl Albert was indeed the central figure of the world drama. He was the darling of the Imperialist spirit in Germany, and the ideal of the new aristocratic feeling—the new Chivalry, as it

was called—that followed the overthrow of Socialism through
its internal divisions and lack of discipline, and the concentration of wealth in the hands of a few great families. He was
compared by obsequious flatterers to the Black Prince, to
Alcibiades, to the young Cæsar. To many he seemed Nietzsche's
Overman revealed. He was big and blond and virile, and
splendidly non-moral. The first great feat that startled Europe,
and almost brought about a new Trojan war, was his abduction
of the Princess Helena of Norway and his blank refusal to
marry her. Then followed his marriage with Gretchen Krass,
a Swiss girl of peerless beauty. Then came the gallant rescue,
which almost cost him his life, of three drowning tailors whose
boat had upset in the sea near Heligoland. For that and his
victory over the American yacht *Defender*, C.C.I., the Emperor
forgave him and placed him in control of the new aeronautic
arm of the German forces. This he developed with marvellous
energy and ability, being resolved, as he said, to give to
Germany land and sea and sky. The national passion for
aggression found in him its supreme exponent, and achieved
through him its realisation in this astounding war. But his
fascination was more than national ; all over the world his
ruthless strength dominated minds as the Napoleonic legend
had dominated minds. Englishmen turned in disgust from the
slow, complex, civilised methods of their national politics to
this uncompromising forceful figure. Frenchmen believed in
him. Poems were written to him in American.

He made the war.

Quite equally with the rest of the world, the general German
population was taken by surprise by the swift vigour of the
Imperial government. A considerable literature of military
forecasts beginning as early as 1906, with Rudolf Martin, the
author not merely of a brilliant book of anticipations, but of a
proverb, " The future of Germany lies in the air," had, however, partially prepared the German imagination for some such
enterprise.

§ 2

Of all these world forces and gigantic designs Bert Smallways
knew nothing until he found himself in the very focus of it all
and gaped down amazed on the spectacle of that giant herd of
airships. Each one seemed as long as the Strand, and as big
about as Trafalgar Square. Some must have been a third of a
mile in length. He had never before seen anything so vast and
disciplined as this tremendous park. For the first time in his
life he really had an intimation of the extraordinary and quite
important things of which a contemporary may go in ignorance.
He had always clung to the illusion that Germans were fat,
absurd men, who smoked china pipes and were addicted to
knowledge and horseflesh and sauerkraut and indigestible things
generally.

His bird's-eye view was quite transitory. He ducked at the first shot ; and directly his balloon began to drop, his mind ran confusedly upon how he might explain himself, and whether he should pretend to be Butteridge or not. " O Lord ! " he groaned, in an agony of indecision. Then his eye caught his sandals, and he felt a spasm of self-disgust. " They'll think I'm a bloomin' idiot," he said, and then it was he rose up desperately and threw over the sand-bag and provoked the second and third shots.

It flashed into his head, as he cowered in the bottom of the car, that he might avoid all sorts of disagreeable and complicated explanations by pretending to be mad.

That was his last idea before the airships seemed to rush up about him as if to look at him, and his car hit the ground and bounded and pitched him out on his head. . . .

He awoke to find himself famous, and to hear a voice crying, " Booteraidge ! Ja ! Ja ! Herr Booteraidge ! Selbst ! "

He was lying on a little patch of grass beside one of the main avenues of the aeronautic park. The airships receded down a great vista, an immense perspective, and the blunt prow of each was adorned with a black eagle of a hundred feet or so spread. Down the other side of the avenue ran a series of gas generators, and big hose-pipes trailed everywhere across the intervening space. Close at hand was his now nearly deflated balloon and the car on its side looking minutely small, a mere broken toy, a shrivelled bubble, in contrast with the gigantic bulk of the nearer airship. This he saw almost end-on, rising like a cliff and sloping forward towards its fellow on the other side so as to overshadow the alley between them. There was a crowd of excited people about him, mostly big men in tight uniforms. Everybody was talking, and several were shouting, in German ; he knew that, because they splashed and aspirated sounds like startled kittens. Only one phrase, repeated again and again, could he recognise—the name of " Herr Booteraidge."

" Gollys ! " said Bert. " They've spotted it."

" Besser," said some one, and some rapid German followed.

He perceived that close at hand was a field telephone, and that a tall officer in blue was talking thereat about him. Another stood close beside him with the portfolio of drawings and photographs in his hand. They looked round at him.

" Do you spik Cherman, Herr Booteraidge ? "

Bert decided that he had better be dazed. He did his best to seem thoroughly dazed. " Where *am* I ? " he asked.

Volubility prevailed. " Der Prinz " was mentioned. A bugle sounded far away, and its call was taken up by one nearer, and then by one close at hand. This seemed to increase the excitement greatly. A mono-rail car bumbled past. The telephone bell rang passionately, and the tall officer seemed to engage in a heated altercation. Then he approached the group about Bert, calling out something about " mitbringen."

An earnest-faced, emaciated man with a white moustache appealed to Bert. " Herr Booteraidge, sir, we are chust to start ! "

" Where am I ? " Bert repeated.

Some one shook him by the other shoulder. " Are you Herr Booteraidge ? " he asked.

" Herr Booteraidge, we are chust to start ! " repeated the white moustache, and then helplessly, " What is de goot ? What can we do ? "

The officer from the telephone repeated his sentence about " Der Prinz " and " mitbringen." The man with the moustache stared for a moment, grasped an idea, and became violently energetic, stood up and bawled directions at unseen people. Questions were asked, and the doctor at Bert's side answered, " Ja ! Ja ! " several times, also something about " Kopf." With a certain urgency he got Bert rather unwillingly to his feet. Two huge soldiers in gray advanced upon Bert and seized hold of him. " 'Ullo ! " said Bert, startled. " What's up ? "

" It is all right," the doctor explained ; " they are to carry you."

" Where ? " asked Bert, unanswered.

" Put your arms round their —hals—round them ! "

" Yes ! but where ? "

" Hold tight ! "

Before Bert could decide to say anything more he was whisked up by the two soldiers. They joined hands to seat him, and his arms were put about their necks. " Vorwärts ! " Some one ran before him with the portfolio, and he was borne rapidly along the broad avenue between the gas generators and the airships, rapidly and on the whole smoothly, except that once or twice his bearers stumbled over hose-pipes and nearly let him down.

He was wearing Mr. Butteridge's Alpine cap, and his little shoulders were in Mr. Butteridge's fur-lined overcoat, and he had responded to Mr. Butteridge's name. The sandals dangled helplessly. Gaw ! Everybody seemed in a devil of a hurry. Why ? He was carried joggling and gaping through the twilight, marvelling beyond measure.

The systematic arrangement of wide convenient spaces, the quantities of businesslike soldiers everywhere, the occasional neat piles of material, the ubiquitous mono-rail lines, and the towering ship-like hulls about him, reminded him a little of impressions he had got as a boy on a visit to Woolwich Dockyard. The whole camp reflected the colossal power of modern science that had created it. A peculiar strangeness was produced by the lowness of the electric light, which lay upon the ground, casting all shadows upwards, and making a grotesque shadow figure of himself and his bearers on the airship sides, fusing all three of them into a monstrous animal with attenuated legs and an immense fan-like humped body. The lights were on the ground because as far as possible all poles and standards had been dispensed with to prevent complications when the airships rose.

It was deep twilight now, a tranquil blue-skyed evening ; everything rose out from the splashes of light upon the ground into dim, translucent, tall masses ; within the cavities of the airships small inspecting lamps glowed like cloud-veiled stars, and made them seem marvellously unsubstantial. Each airship had its name in black letters on white on either flank, and forward the Imperial eagle sprawled an overwhelming bird in the dimness. Bugles sounded, mono-rail cars of quiet soldiers slithered burbling by. The cabins under the heads of the air-ships were being lit up ; doors opened in them, and revealed padded passages. Now and then a voice gave directions to workers indistinctly seen.

There was a matter of sentinels, gangways, and a long narrow passage, a scramble over a disorder of baggage, and then Bert found himself lowered to the ground and standing in the door-way of a spacious cabin—it was perhaps ten feet square and eight high, furnished with crimson padding and aluminium. A tall, bird-like young man with a small head, a long nose, and very pale hair, with his hands full of things like shaving-strops, boot-trees, hair-brushes, and toilet tidies, was saying things about Gott and thunder and Dummer Booteraidge as Bert entered. He was apparently an evicted occupant. Then he vanished, and Bert was lying back on a locker in the corner with a pillow under his head and the door of the cabin shut upon him. He was alone. Everybody had hurried out again astonishingly.

" Gollys ! " said Bert. " What next ? "

He stared about him at the room.

" Butteridge ! Shall I try to keep it up, or shan't I ? "

The room he was in puzzled him. " 'Tisn't a prison and 'tisn't a norfis ? " Then the old trouble came uppermost. " I wish to 'eaven I 'adn't these silly sandals on," he cried querulously to the universe. " They give the whole blessed show away."

§ 3

His door was flung open, and a compact young man in uni-form appeared, carrying Mr. Butteridge's portfolio, rücksac, and shaving-glass. " I say ! " he said, in faultless English, as he entered. He had a beaming face, and a sort of pinkish blond hair. " Fancy you being Butteridge ! "

He slapped Bert's meagre luggage down.

" We'd have started," he said, " in another half-hour ! You didn't give yourself much time ! "

He surveyed Bert curiously. His gaze rested for a fraction of a moment on the sandals. " You ought to have come on your flying machine, Mr. Butteridge."

He didn't wait for an answer. " The Prince says I've got

to look after you. Naturally he can't see you now, but he thinks your coming's providential. Last grace of Heaven. Like a sign. Hallo ! "

He stood still and listened.

Outside there was a going to and fro of feet, a sound of distant bugles suddenly taken up and echoed close at hand, men called out in loud tones short, sharp, seemingly vital things, and were answered distantly. A bell jangled, and feet went down the corridor. Then came a stillness more distracting than sound, and then a great gurgling and rushing and splashing of water. The young man's eyebrows lifted. He hesitated, and dashed out of the room. Presently came a stupendous bang to vary the noises without, then a distant cheering. The young man reappeared.

" They're running the water out of the balloonette already."

" What water ? " asked Bert.

" The water that anchored us. Artful dodge. Eh ? "

Bert tried to take it in.

" Of course ! " said the compact young man. " You don't understand."

A gentle quivering crept upon Bert's senses.

" That's the engine," said the compact young man approvingly. " Now we shan't be long."

Another long listening interval.

The cabin swayed. " By Jove ! we're starting already," he cried. " We're starting ! "

" Starting ! " cried Bert, sitting up. " Where ? "

But the young man was out of the room again. There were noises of German in the passage, and other nerve-shaking sounds.

The swaying increased. The young man reappeared. " We're off, right enough ! "

" I say ! " said Bert, " where are we starting ? I wish you'd explain. What's this place ? I don't understand."

" What ! " cried the young man, " you don't understand ? "

" No. I'm all dazed-like from that crack on the nob I got. Where *are* we ? *Where* are we starting ? "

" Don't you know where you are—what this is ? "

" Not a bit of it ! What's all the swaying and the row ? "

" What a lark ! " cried the young man. " I say ! What a thundering lark ! Don't you know ? We're off to America, and you haven't realised. You've just caught us by a neck. You're on the blessed old flagship with the Prince. You won't miss anything. Whatever's on, you bet the *Vaterland* will be there."

" Us !—off to America ? "

" Ra-ther ! "

" In an airship ? "

" What do *you* think ? "

" Me ! going to America on an airship ! After that balloon !

'Ere ! I say—I don't want to go ! I want to walk about on my legs. Let me get out ! I didn't understand."

He made a dive for the door.

The young man arrested Bert with a gesture, took hold of a strap, lifted up a panel in the padded wall, and a window appeared. "Look ! " he said. Side by side they looked out.

"Gaw ! " said Bert. "We're going up ! "

"We are ! " said the young man, cheerfully ; "fast ! "

They were rising in the air smoothly and quietly, and moving slowly to the throb of the engine athwart the aeronautic park. Down below it stretched, dimly geometrical in the darkness, picked out at regular intervals by glow-worm spangles of light. One black gap in the long line of gray, round-backed airships marked the position from which the *Vaterland* had come. Beside it a second monster now rose softly, released from its bonds and cables, into the air. Then, taking a beautifully exact distance, a third ascended, and then a fourth.

"Too late, Mr. Butteridge ! " the young man remarked. "We're off ! I dare say it *is* a bit of a shock to you, but there you are ! The Prince said you'd have to come."

"Look 'ere," said Bert. "I really *am* dazed. What's this thing ? Where are we going ? "

"This, Mr. Butteridge," said the young man, taking pains to be explicit, "is an airship. It's the flagship of Prince Karl Albert. This is the German air-fleet, and it is going over to America, to give that spirited people 'what for.' The only thing we were at all uneasy about was your invention. And here you are ! "

"But !—you a German ? " asked Bert.

"Lieutenant Kurt. Luft-lieutenant Kurt, at your service."

"But you speak English ! "

"Mother was English—went to school in England. Afterwards, Rhodes scholar. German none the less for that. Detailed for the present, Mr. Butteridge, to look after you. You're shaken by your fall. It's all right, really. They're going to buy your machine and everything. You sit down, and take it quite calmly. You'll soon get the hang of the position."

§ 4

Bert sat down on the locker collecting his mind, and the young man talked to him about the airship.

He was really a very tactful young man indeed, in a natural sort of way. "Dare say all this is new to you," he said ; "not your sort of machine. These cabins aren't half bad."

He got up and walked round the little apartment, showing its points.

"Here is the bed," he said, whipping down a couch from the wall and throwing it back again with a click. "Here are toilet things," and he opened a neatly arranged cupboard. "Not much washing. No water we've got ; no water at all except for drinking. No baths or anything until we get to America and land. Rub over with loofah. One pint of hot for shaving. That's all. In the locker below you are rugs and blankets ; you will need them presently. They say it gets cold. I don't know. Never been up before. Except a little work with gliders—which is mostly going down. Three-quarters of the chaps in the fleet haven't. Here's a folding-chair and table behind the door. Compact, eh ? "

He took the chair and balanced it on his little finger. " Pretty light, eh ? Aluminium and magnesium alloy and a vacuum inside. All these cushions stuffed with hydrogen. Foxy ! The whole ship's like that. And not a man in the fleet, except the Prince and one or two others, over eleven stone. Couldn't sweat the Prince, you know. We'll go all over the thing to-morrow. I'm frightfully keen on it."

He beamed at Bert. " You *do* look young," he remarked. " I always thought you'd be an old man with a beard—a sort of philosopher. I don't know why one should expect clever people always to be old. I do."

Bert parried that compliment a little awkwardly, and then the lieutenant was struck with the riddle why Herr Butteridge had not come in his own flying-machine.

" It's a long story," said Bert. " Look here ! " he said abruptly, " I wish you'd lend me a pair of slippers, or something. I'm regular sick of these sandals. They're rotten things. I've been trying them for a friend."

" Right-o ! "

The ex-Rhodes scholar whisked out of the room and reappeared with a considerable choice of footwear, pumps, cloth bath-slippers, and a purple pair adorned with golden sun-flowers.

But these he repented of at the last moment. " I don't even wear them myself," he said. " Only brought 'em in the zeal of the moment." He laughed confidentially. " Had 'em worked for me—in Oxford. By a friend. Take 'em everywhere."

So Bert chose the pumps.

The lieutenant broke into a cheerful snigger. " Here we are trying on slippers," he said, " and the world going by like a panorama below. Rather a lark, eh ? Look ! "

Bert peeped with him out of the window, looking from the bright prettiness of the red-and-silver cabin into a dark immensity. The land below, except for a lake, was black and featureless, and the other airships were hidden. " See more outside," said the lieutenant. " Let's go ! There's a sort of little gallery."

He led the way into the long passage, which was lit by one small electric light, past some notices in German, to an open balcony and a light ladder and gallery of metal lattice over-hanging empty space. Bert followed his leader down to the gallery slowly and cautiously. From it he was able to watch the wonderful spectacle of the first air-fleet flying through the night. They flew in a wedge-shaped formation, the *Vaterland* highest and leading, the tail receding into the corners of the sky. They flew in long, regular undulations, great dark, fish-like shapes, showing hardly any light at all, the engines making a throb-throb-throbbing sound that was very audible out on the gallery. They were going at a level of five or six thousand feet, and rising steadily. Below the country lay silent, a clear darkness dotted and lined out with clusters of furnaces, and the lit streets of a group of big towns. The world seemed to lie in a bowl ; the overhanging bulk of the airship above hid all but the lowest levels of the sky.

They watched the landscape for a space.

" Jolly it must be to invent things," said the lieutenant suddenly. " How did you come to think of your machine first ? "

" Worked it out," said Bert, after a pause. " Jest ground away at it."

" Our people are frightfully keen on you. They thought the British had got you. Weren't the British keen ? "

" In a way," said Bert. " Still—it's a long story."

" I think it's an immense thing—to invent. I couldn't invent a thing to save my life."

They both fell silent, watching the darkened world and following their thoughts until a bugle summoned them to a belated dinner. Bert was suddenly alarmed. " Don't you 'ave to dress and things ? " he said. " I've always been too hard at Science and things to go into Society and all that."

" No fear," said Kurt. " Nobody's got more than the clothes they wear. We're travelling light. You might, perhaps, take your overcoat off. They've an electric radiator each end of the room."

And so presently Bert found himself sitting to eat in the presence of the " German Alexander "—that great and puissant Prince, Prince Karl Albert, the War Lord, the hero of two hemispheres. He was a handsome blond man, with deep-set eyes, a snub nose, upturned moustache, and long white hands. He sat higher than the others, under a black eagle with widespread wings and the German Imperial flags ; he was, as it were, enthroned, and it struck Bert greatly that as he ate he did not look at people, but over their heads like one who sees visions. Twenty officers of various ranks stood about the table—and Bert. They all seemed extremely curious to see the famous Butteridge, and their astonishment at his appearance was ill-controlled. The Prince gave him a dignified salutation, to which, by an inspiration he bowed. Standing next the Prince was a brown-faced, wrinkled man with silver spectacles and fluffy, dingy-gray side-whiskers, who regarded Bert with a peculiar and disconcerting attention. The company sat after ceremonies Bert could not understand. At the other end of the table was the bird-faced officer Bert had dispossessed. still looking hostile and whispering about Bert to his neighbour, Two soldiers waited. The dinner was a plain one—a soup, some fresh mutton, and cheese—and there was very little talk.

A curious solemnity, indeed, brooded over every one. Partly this was reaction after the intense toil and restrained excitement of starting ; partly it was the overwhelming sense of strange new experiences, of portentous adventure. The Prince was lost in thought. He roused himself to drink to the Emperor in champagne, and the company cried " Hoch ! " like men repeating responses in church.

No smoking was permitted, but some of the officers went down to the little open gallery to chew tobacco. No lights whatever were safe amidst that bundle of inflammable things. Bert suddenly fell yawning and shivering. He was overwhelmed by a sense of his own insignificance amidst these great rushing monsters of the air. He felt life was too big for him—too much for him altogether.

He said something to Kurt about his head, went up the steep ladder from the swaying little gallery into the airship again, and so, as if it were a refuge, to bed.

§ 5

Bert slept for a time, and then his sleep was broken by dreams. Mostly he was fleeing from formless terrors down an interminable passage in an airship—a passage paved at first with ravenous trapdoors, and then with openwork canvas of the most careless description.

" Gaw ! " said Bert, turning over after his seventh fall through infinite space that night.

He sat up in the darkness and nursed his knees. The progress of the airship was not nearly so smooth as a balloon ; he could feel a regular swaying up, up, up and then down, down, down, and the throbbing and tremulous quiver of the engines.

His mind began to teem with memories—more memories and more.

Through them, like a struggling swimmer in broken water, came the perplexing question, what am I to do to-morrow ? To-morrow, Kurt had told him, the Prince's secretary, the Graf von Winterfeld, would come to him and discuss his flyingmachine, and then he would see the Prince. He would have to stick it out now that he was Butteridge, and sell his invention. And then, if they found him out ! He had a vision of infuriated Butteridges. . . . Suppose after all he owned up ? Pretended it was their misunderstanding ? He began to scheme devices for selling the secret and circumventing Butteridge.

What should he ask for the thing ? Somehow twenty thousand pounds struck him as about the sum indicated.

He fell into that despondency that lies in wait in the small hours. He had got too big a job on—too big a job. . . .

Memories swamped his scheming.

" Where was I this time last night ? "

He recapitulated his evenings tediously and lengthily. Last night he had been up above the clouds in Butteridge's balloon. He thought of the moment when he dropped through them and saw the cold twilight sea close below. He still remembered that disagreeable incident with a nightmare vividness. And the night before he and Grubb had been looking for cheap lodgings at Littlestone in Kent. How remote that seemed now. It might be years ago. For the first time he thought of his fellow Desert Dervish, left with the two red-painted bicycles on Dymchurch sands. " 'E won't make much of a show of it, not without me. Any'ow 'e did 'ave the treasury—such as it was in his pocket ! " . . . The night before that was Bank Holiday night, and they had sat discussing their minstrel enterprise, drawing up a programme and rehearsing steps. And the night before was Whit Sunday.

" Lord ! " cried Bert, " what a doing that motor-bicycle give me ! " He recalled the empty flapping of the eviscerated cushion, the feeling of impotence as the flames rose again.

From among the confused memories of that tragic flare one little figure emerged very bright and poignantly sweet, Edna, crying back reluctantly from the departing motor-car, " See you to-morrer, Bert ? "

Other memories of Edna clustered round that impression. They led Bert's mind step by step to an agreeable state that found expression in, " I'll marry 'er if she don't look out." And then in a flash it followed in his mind that if he sold the Butteridge secret he could ! Suppose after all he did get twenty thousand pounds ; such sums have been paid ! With that he could buy house and garden, buy new clothes beyond dreaming, buy a motor, travel, have every delight of the civilised life as he knew it, for himself and Edna. Of course, risks were involved. " I'll 'ave old Butteridge on my track, I expect ! "

He meditated upon that. He declined again to despondency. As yet he was only in the beginning of the adventure. He had still to deliver the goods and draw the cash. And before that——
Just now he was by no means on his way home. He was flying off to America to fight there. " Not much fighting," he considered ; " all our own way." Still, if a shell did happen to hit the *Vaterland* on the underside ! . . .

" S'pose I ought to make my will."

He lay back for some time composing wills—chiefly in favour of Edna. He had settled now it was to be twenty thousand pounds. He left a number of minor legacies. The wills became more and more meandering and extravagant. . . .

He woke from the eighth repetition of his nightmare fall through space. " This flying gets on one's nerves," he said.

He could feel the airship diving down, down, down, then slowly swinging to up, up, up. Throb, throb, throb, throb, quivered the engine.

He got up presently and wrapped himself about with Mr. Butteridge's overcoat and all the blankets, for the air was very keen. Then he peeped out of the window to see a gray dawn breaking over clouds, then turned up his light and bolted his door, sat down to the table, and produced his chest-protector.

He smoothed the crumpled plans with his hand, and contemplated them. Then he referred to the other drawings in the portfolio. Twenty thousand pounds. If he worked it right ! It was worth trying, anyhow.

Presently he opened the drawer in which Kurt had put paper and writing materials.

Bert Smallways was by no means a stupid person, and up to a certain limit he had not been badly educated. His board-school had taught him to draw up to certain limits, taught him to calculate and understand a specification. If at that point his country had tired of its efforts, and handed him over unfinished to scramble for a living in an atmosphere of advertisements and individual enterprise, that was really not his fault. He was as his State had made him, and the reader must not imagine because he was a little Cockney cad, that he was absolutely incapable of grasping the idea of the Butteridge flying-machine. But he found it stiff and perplexing. His motor-bicycle and Grubb's experiments and the " mechanical drawing " he had done in standard seven all helped him out ; and, moreover, the maker of these drawings, whoever he was, had been anxious to make his intentions plain. Bert copied sketches, he made notes, he made a quite tolerable and intelligent copy of the essential drawings and sketches of the others. Then he fell into a meditation upon them.

At last he rose with a sigh, folded up the originals that had formerly been in his chest-protector and put them into the breast-pocket of his jacket, and then very carefully deposited the copies he had made in the place of the originals. He had no very clear plan in his mind in doing this, except that he hated the idea of altogether parting with the secret. For a long time he meditated profoundly—nodding. Then he turned out his light and went to bed again and schemed himself to sleep.

§ 6

The hochgeborene Graf von Winterfeld was also a light sleeper that night, but then he was one of those people who sleep little and play chess problems in their heads to while away the time—and that night he had a particularly difficult problem to solve.

He came in upon Bert while he was still in bed in the glow of the sunlight reflected from the North Sea below, consuming the rolls and coffee a soldier had brought him. He had a portfolio under his arm, and in the clear, early morning light his dingy gray hair and heavy, silver-rimmed spectacles made him look almost benevolent. He spoke English fluently, but with a strong German flavour. He was particularly bad with his " b's," and his " th's " softened towards weak " z'ds." He called Bert explosively, " Pooterage." He began with some indistinct civilities, bowed, took a folding-table and chair from behind the door, put the former between himself and Bert, sat down on the latter, coughed dryly, and opened his portfolio. Then he put his elbows on the table, pinched his lower lip with his two forefingers, and regarded Bert disconcertingly with magnified eyes. " You came to us, Herr Pooterage, against your will," he said at last.

" 'Ow d'you make that out ? " asked Bert, after a pause of astonishment.

" I chuge by ze maps in your car. They were all English. And your provisions. They were all picnic. Also your cords were entangled. You haf been tugging—but no good. You could not manage ze balloon, and anuzzer power than yours prought you to us. Is it not so ? "

Bert thought.

" Also—where is ze laty ? "

" 'Ere !—what lady ? "

" You started with a laty. That is evident. You shtarted for an afternoon excursion—a picnic. A man of your temperament—he would take a laty. She was not wiz you in your balloon when you came down at Dornhof. No ! Only her chacket ! It is your affair. Still, I am curious."

Bert reflected. " 'Ow d'you know that ? "

" I chuge by ze nature of your farious provisions. I cannot account, Mr. Pooterage, for ze laty, what you haf done with her. Nor can I tell why you should wear nature-sandals, nor why you should wear such cheap plue clothes. These are outside my instructions. Trifles, perhaps. Officially they are to be ignored. Laties come and go—I am a man of ze worldt. I haf known wise men wear sandals and efen practise vegetarian habits. I haf known men—or at any rate I haf known chemists—who did not schmoke. You haf, no doubt, put ze laty down somewhere. Well. Let us get to business. A higher power "—his voice changed its emotional quality, his magnified eyes seemed to dilate—" has prought you and your secret straight to us. So ! "—he bowed his head—" so pe it. It is ze Destiny of Germany and my Prince. I can undershtandt you always carry zat secret. You are afraidt of roppers and spies. So it comes wiz you—to us. Mr. Pooterage, Chermany will puy it."

" Will she ? "

" She will," said the secretary, looking hard at Bert's abandoned sandals in the corner of the locker. He roused himself, consulted a paper of notes for a moment, and Bert eyed his brown and wrinkled face with expectation and terror. "Chermany, I am instructed to say," said the secretary, with his eyes on the table and his notes spread out, " has always been willing to puy your secret. We haf indeed peen eager to acquire it—fery eager ; and it was only ze fear that you might be, on patriotic groundts, acting in collusion with your Pritish War office zat has made us discreet in offering for your marvellous invention through intermediaries. We haf no hesitation whatefer now, I am instructed, in agreeing to your proposal of a hundert tousand poundts."

" Crikey ! " said Bert, overwhelmed.

" I peg your pardon ? "

" Jest a twinge," said Bert, raising his hand to his bandaged head.

" Ah ! Also I am instructed to say that as for that noble, unrightly accused laty you haf championed so brafely against Pritish hypocrisy and coldness, all ze chivalry of Chermany is on her site."

" Lady ? " said Bert faintly, and then recalled the great Butteridge love story. Had the old chap also read the letters ? He must think him a scorcher if he had. " Oh ! that's aw-right," he said, " about 'er. I 'adn't any doubts about that. I——"

He stopped. The secretary certainly had a most appalling stare. It seemed ages before he looked down again. " Well, ze laty as you please. She is your affair. I haf performt my instructions. And ze title of Paron, zat also can pe done. It can all pe done, Herr Pooterage." He drummed on the table for a second or so, and resumed. " I haf to tell you, sir, zat you come to us at a crisis in—Welt-Politik. There can be no harm now for me to tell our plans to you. Pefore you leafe this ship again they will be manifest to all ze worldt. War is perhaps already declared. We go—to America. Our fleet will descend out of ze air upon ze United States—it is a country quite unprepared for war eferywhere—eferywhere. Zey have always relied on ze Atlantic. And their navy. We have selected a certain point—it is at present ze secret of our commanders—which we shall seize, and zen we shall establish a depot—a sort of inland Gibraltar. It will be—what will it be ?—an eagle's nest. Zere our airships will gazzer and repair, and thence they will fly to and fro ofer ze United States, terrorising cities, dominating Washington, levying what is necessary, until ze terms we dictate are accepted. You follow me ? "

" Go on ! " said Bert.

" We could haf done all zis wiz such *Luftschiffe* and *Drachen-flieger* as we possess, but ze accession of your machine renders our project complete. It not only gifs us a better *Drachen-flieger*, but it remofes our last uneasiness as to Great Pritain. Wizout you, sir, Great Pritain, ze land you lofed so well and zat has requited you so ill, zat land of Pharisees and reptiles, can do nozzing !—nozzing ! You see, I am perfectly frank wiz you. Well, I am instructed that Chermany recognises all this. We want you to blace yourself at our disposal. We want you to become our Chief Head Flight Engineer. We want you to manufacture, we want to equip a swarm of hornets unter your direction. We want you to direct this force. And it is at our depot in America we want you. So we offer you simply, and without haggling, ze full terms you demanded weeks ago—one hundert tousand poundts in cash, a salary of three tousand poundts a year, a pension of one tousand poundts a year, and ze title of Paron as you desired. These are my instructions."

He resumed his scrutiny of Bert's face.

" That's all right, of course," said Bert, a little short of breath, but otherwise resolute and calm ; and it seemed to him that now was the time to bring his nocturnal scheming to the issue.

The secretary contemplated Bert's collar with sustained attention. Only for one moment did his gaze move to the sandals and back.

" Jes' lemme think a bit," said Bert, finding the stare debilitating. " Look 'ere ! " he said at last, with an air of great explicitness, " I *got* the secret."

" Yes."

" But I don't want the name of Butteridge to appear—see ? I been thinking that over."

" A little delicacy ? "

" Exactly. You buy the secret—leastways, I give it you— from Bearer—see ? "

His voice failed him a little, and the stare continued. " I want to do the thing Enonymously. See ? "

Still staring, Bert drifted on like a swimmer caught by a current. " Fact is, I'm going to edop' the name of Small- ways. I don't want no title of Baron ; I've altered my mind. And I want the money quiet-like. I want the hundred thousand pounds paid into banks—thirty thousand into the London and County Bank Branch at Bun Hill in Kent directly I 'and over the plans ; twenty thousand into the Bank of England ; 'arf the rest into a good French bank, the other 'arf the German National Bank, see ? I want it put there, right away. I don't want it put in the name of Butteridge. I want it put in the name of Albert Peter Smallways ; that's the name I'm going to edop'. That's my condition one."

" Go on ! " said the secretary.

" The nex' condition," said Bert, " is that you don't make any inquiries as to title. I mean what English gentlemen do when they sell or let you land. You don't arst 'ow I got it. See ? 'Ere I am—I deliver you the goods ; that's all right. Some people 'ave the cheek to say this isn't my in-

vention, see ? It is, you know—*that's* all right ; but I don't
want that gone into. I want a fair and square agreement
saying that's all right. See ? "

His " See ? " faded into a profound silence.

The secretary sighed at last, leant back in his chair and
produced a toothpick, and used it to assist his meditation on
Bert's case. " What was that name ? " he asked at last, putting
away the toothpick ; " I must write it down."

" Albert Peter Smallways," said Bert, in a mild tone.

The secretary wrote it down, after a little difficulty about
the spelling because of the different names of the letters of
the alphabet in the two languages.

" And now, Mr. Schmallvays," he said at last, leaning back
and resuming the stare, " tell me : how did you ket hold of
Mister Pooterage's balloon ? "

§ 7

When at last the Graf von Winterfeld left Bert Smallways,
he left him in an extremely deflated condition, with all his
little story told.

He had, as people say, made a clean breast of it. He had
been pursued into details. He had had to explain the blue
suit, the sandals, the Desert Dervishes—everything. For a
time scientific zeal consumed the secretary, and the question
of the plans remained in suspense. He even went into speculation about the previous occupants of the balloon. " I suppose,"
he said, " the laty *was* the laty. Bot that is not our affair.

" It is fery curious and amusing, yes : but I am afraid the
Prince may be annoyt. He acted wiz his usual decision—
always he acts wiz wonderful decision. Like Napoleon. Directly
he was tolt of your descent into the camp at Dornhof, he said,
' Pring him !—pring him ! It is my schtar ! ' His schtar of
Destiny ! You see ? He will be dthwarted. He directed you
to come as Herr Pooterage, and you haf not done so. You
haf triet, of course ; but it has peen a poor try. His chugments
of men are fery just and right, and it is better for men to
act up to them—gompletely. Especially now. Barticularly
now."

He resumed that attitude of his, with his underlip pinched
between his forefingers. He spoke almost confidentially. " It
will be awkward. I triet to suggest some doubt, but I was
overruled. The Prince does not listen. He is impatient in
the high air. Perhaps he will think his schtar has been making
a fool of him. Perhaps he will think *I* haf been making a
fool of him." He wrinkled his forehead, and drew in the
corners of his mouth.

" I got the plans," said Bert.

" Yes. There is that ! Yes. But, you see, the Prince was
interested in Herr Pooterage because of his romantic seit.
Herr Pooterage was so much more—ah !—in the picture.

I am afraid you are not equal to controlling the flying machine
department of our aerial park as he wished you to do. He
hadt promised himself that. . . .

"And der was also the prestige—the worldt prestige of
Pooterage with us. . . . Well, we must see what we can do."
He held out his hand. "Gif me the plans."

A terrible chill ran through the being of Mr. Smallways.
To the end of his life he was never clear in his mind whether
he wept or no, but certainly there was weeping in his voice.
" 'Ere, I say ! " he protested. "Ain't I to 'ave—nothin' for
'em ? "

The secretary regarded him with benevolent eyes. "You
do not deserve anyzing ! " he said.

"I might 'ave tore 'em up."

"Zey are not yours ! "

"They weren't his, very likely."

"No need to pay anyzing."

Bert's being seemed to tighten towards desperate deeds.
"Gaw ! " he said, clutching his coat, " *ain't* there ? "

"Pe galm," said the secretary. "Listen ! You shall haf
five hundert poundts. You shall haf it on my promise. I
will do that for you, and that is all I can do. Take it from
me. Gif me the name of that bank. Write it down. So ! I
tell you the Prince—is no choke. I do not think he approffed
of your appearance last night. No ! I can't answer for him.
He wanted Pooterage, and you haf spoilt it. The Prince—
I do not understandt quite, he is in a strange state. It is the
excitement of the starting and this great soaring in the air.
I cannot account for what he does. But if all goes well I will
see to it—you shall haf five hundert poundts. Will that do ?
Then gif me the plans."

"Old beggar ! " said Bert, as the door clicked. "Gaw !—
what an ole beggar !—*Sharp !* "

He sat down in the folding-chair, and whistled noiselessly
for a time.

"Nice old swindle for 'im if I tore 'em up ! I could 'ave."

He rubbed the bridge of his nose thoughtfully. "I gave
the whole blessed show away. If I'd jes' kep' quiet about
being Enonymous. . . . Gaw ! . . . Too soon, Bert, my
boy—too soon and too rushy. I'd like to kick my silly self.

"I couldn't 'ave kep' it up.

"After all, it ain't so very bad," he said.

"After all, five 'undred pounds. . . . It isn't *my* secret,
anyhow. It's jes' a pick-up on the road. Five 'undred.

"Wonder what the fare is from America back 'ome ? "

§ 8

And later in the day an extremely shattered and disorganised Bert Smallways stood in the presence of the Prince
Karl Albert.

The proceedings were in German. The Prince was in his own cabin, the end room of the airship, a charming apartment furnished in wicker-work with a long window across its entire breadth, looking forward. He was sitting at a folding-table of green baize, with Von Winterfeld and two officers sitting beside him, and littered before them was a number of American maps and Mr. Butteridge's letters and his portfolio and a number of loose papers. Bert was not asked to sit down and remained standing throughout the interview. Von Winterfeld told his story, and every now and then the words Balloon and Pooterage struck on Bert's ears. The Prince's face remained stern and ominous, and the two officers watched it cautiously or glanced at Bert. There was something a little strange in their scrutiny of the Prince—a curiosity, an apprehension. Then presently he was struck by an idea, and they fell discussing the plans. The Prince asked Bert abruptly in English. " Did you ever see this thing go op ? "

Bert jumped. " Saw it from Bun 'Ill, your Royal Highness."

Von Winterfeld made some explanation.

" How fast did it go ? "

" Couldn't say, your Royal Highness. The papers, leastways the *Daily Courier*, said eighty miles an hour."

They talked German over that for a time.

" Couldt it standt still ? Op in the air ? That is what I want to know."

" It could 'ovver, your Royal Highness, like a wasp," said Bert.

" *Viel besser, nicht wahr ?* " said the Prince to Von Winterfeld, and then went on in German for a time.

Presently they came to an end, and the two officers looked at Bert. One rang a bell, and the portfolio was handed to an attendant, who took it away.

Then they reverted to the case of Bert, and it was evident the Prince was inclined to be hard with him. Von Winterfeld protested. Apparently theological considerations came in, for there were several mentions of " Gott ! " Some conclusions emerged, and it was apparent that Von Winterfeld was instructed to convey them to Bert.

" Mr. Schmallvays, you haf obtained a footing in this airship," he said, " by disgraceful and systematic lying."

" 'Ardly systematic," said Bert. " I——"

The Prince silenced him by a gesture.

" And it is within the power of his Highness to dispose of you as a spy."

" 'Ere !—I came to sell——"

" S-sh ! " said one of the officers.

" However, in consideration of the happy chance that mate you the instrument unter Gott of this Pooterage flyingmachine reaching his Highness's hand, you haf been spared. Yes—You were the pearer of goot tidings. You will be allowed to remain on this ship until it is convenient to dispose of you. Do you understand ? "

" We will bring him," said the Prince, and added terribly with a terrible glare, " *als Ballast.*"

" You are to come with us," said Winterfeld, " as—pallast. Do you understandt ? "

Bert opened his mouth to ask about the five hundred pounds, and then a saving gleam of wisdom silenced him. He met Von Winterfeld's eye, and it seemed to him the secretary nodded slightly. " Go ! " said the Prince, with a sweep of the great arm and hand towards the door. Bert went out like a leaf before a gale.

§ 9

But in between the time when the Graf von Winterfeld had talked to him and this alarming conference with the Prince, Bert had explored the *Vaterland* from end to end. He had found it interesting in spite of grave preoccupations. Kurt, like the greater number of the men upon the German air-fleet, had known hardly anything of aeronautics before his appointment to the new flag-ship. But he was extremely keen upon this wonderful new weapon Germany had assumed so suddenly and dramatically. He showed things to Bert with a boyish eagerness and appreciation. It was as if he showed them over again to himself, like a child showing a new toy. " Let's go all over the ship," he said with zest. He pointed out particularly the lightness of everything, the use of exhausted aluminium tubing, of springy cushions inflated with compressed hydrogen ; the partitions were hydrogen bags covered with light imitation leather, the very crockery was a light biscuit glazed in a vacuum, and weighed next to nothing. Where strength was needed there was the new Charlottenburg alloy German steel as it was called, the toughest and most resistent metal in the world.

There was no lack of space. Space did not matter, so long as load did not grow. The habitable part of the ship was two hundred and fifty feet long, and the rooms in two tiers, above these one could go up into remarkable little white-metal turrets with big windows and air-tight double doors that enabled one to inspect the vast cavity of the gas-chambers. This inside view impressed Bert very much. He had never realised before that an airship was not one simple continuous gas-bag containing nothing but gas. Now he saw far above him the backbone of the apparatus and its big ribs, " like the neural and hæmal canals," said Kurt, who had dabbled in biology.

" Rather ! " said Bert appreciatively, though he had not the ghost of an idea what these phrases meant.

Little electric lights could be switched on up there if anything went wrong in the night. There were even ladders across the space. " But you can't go into the gas," protested Bert. " You can't breve it."

The lieutenant opened a cupboard door and displayed a diver's suit, only that it was made of oiled silk, and both its compressed-air knapsack and its helmet were of an alloy of aluminium and some light metal. " We can go all over the inside netting and stick up bullet holes or leaks," he explained. " There's netting inside and out. The whole outer-case is rope ladder, so to speak."

Aft of the habitable part of the airship was the magazine of explosives, coming near the middle of its length. They were all bombs of various types—mostly in glass—none of the German airships carried any guns at all except one small pom-pom (to use the old English nickname dating from the Boer War), which was forward in the gallery upon the shield at the heart of the eagle. From the magazine amid-ships a covered canvas gallery with aluminium treads on its floor and a hand-rope, ran back underneath the gas-chamber to the engine-room at the tail ; but along this Bert did not go, and from first to last he never saw the engines. But he went up a ladder against a gale of ventilation—a ladder that was encased in a kind of gas-tight fire-escape and ran right athwart the great forward air-chamber to the little look-out gallery with a telephone, that gallery that bore the light pom-pom of German steel and its locker of shells. This gallery was all of aluminium-magnesium alloy, the tight front of the airship swelled cliff-like above and below, and the black eagle sprawled overwhelmingly gigantic, its extremities all hidden by the bulge of the gas-bag.

And far down, under the soaring eagles, was England, four thousand feet below, perhaps, and looking very small and defenceless indeed in the morning sunlight.

The realisation that there was England gave Bert sudden and unexpected qualms of patriotic compunction. He was struck by a quite novel idea. After all, he might have torn up those plans and thrown them away. These people could not have done so very much to him. And even if they did, ought not an Englishman to die for his country ? It was an idea that had hitherto been rather smothered up by the cares of a competitive civilisation. He became violently depressed. He ought, he perceived, to have seen it in that light before. Why hadn't he seen it in that light before ?

Indeed, wasn't he a sort of traitor ?

He wondered how the aerial fleet must look from down there. Tremendous, no doubt. and dwarfing all the buildings.

He was passing between Manchester and Liverpool, Kurt told him ; a gleaming band across the prospect was the Ship Canal, and a weltering ditch of shipping far away ahead, the Mersey estuary. Bert was a southerner ; he had never been north of the Midland counties, and the multitude of factories and chimneys—the latter for the most part obsolete and smokeless now, superseded by huge electric generating stations that consumed their own reek—old railway viaducts, monorail networks and goods yards, and the vast areas of dingy homes and narrow streets, spreading aimlessly, struck him as though Camberwell and Rotherhithe had run to seed. Here and there, as if caught in a net, were fields and agricultural fragments. It was a sprawl of undistinguished population. There were, no doubt, museums and town halls and even cathedrals of a sort to mark theoretical centres of municipal and religious organisation in this confusion ; but Bert could not see them, they did not stand out at all in that wide, disorderly vision of congested workers' houses and places to work, and shops and meanly conceived chapels and churches. And across this landscape of an industrial civilisation swept the shadows of the German airships like a hurrying shoal of fishes.

Kurt and he fell talking of aerial tactics, and presently went down to the under-gallery in order that Bert might see the *Drachenflieger* that the airships of the right wing had picked up overnight and were towing behind them ; each airship towing three or four. They looked like big box-kites of an exaggerated form, soaring at the ends of invisible cords. They had long, square heads and flattened tails, with lateral propellers.

" Much skill is required for those !—much skill ! "

" Rather ! "

Pause.

" Your machine is different from that, Mr. Butteridge ? "

" Quite different," said Bert. " More like an insect, and less like a bird. And it buzzes, and don't drive about so. What can those things do ? "

Kurt was not very clear upon that himself, and was still explaining when Bert was called to the conference we have recorded with the Prince.

And after that was over, the last traces of Butteridge fell from Bert like a garment, and he became Smallways to all on board. The soldiers ceased to salute him, and the officers ceased to seem aware of his existence, except Lieutenant Kurt. He was turned out of his nice cabin, and packed in with his belongings to share that of Lieutenant Kurt, whose luck it was to be junior, and the bird-headed officer, still swearing slightly and carrying strops and aluminium boot-trees and weightless hairbrushes and hand-mirrors and pomade in his hands, resumed possession. Bert was put in with Kurt because there was nowhere else for him to lay his bandaged head in that close-packed vessel. He was to mess, he was told, with the men.

Kurt came and stood with his legs wide apart, and surveyed him for a moment as he sat despondent in his new quarters.

" What's your real name, then ? " said Kurt, who was only imperfectly informed of the new state of affairs.

" Smallways."

" I thought you were a bit of a fraud—even when I thought you were Butteridge. You're jolly lucky the Prince took it calmly. He's a pretty tidy blazer when he's roused. He wouldn't stick a moment at pitching a chap of your sort overboard if he thought fit. No ! They've shoved you on to me, but it's my cabin, you know."

" I won't forget," said Bert.

Kurt left him, and when he came to look about him the first thing he saw pasted on the padded wall was a reproduction of the great picture by Siegfried Schmalz of the War God, that terrible, trampling figure with the viking helmet and the scarlet cloak, wading through destruction, sword in hand, which had so strong a resemblance to Karl Albert, the prince it was painted to please.

CHAPTER FIVE

THE BATTLE OF THE NORTH ATLANTIC

§ 1

THE Prince Karl Albert had made a profound impression upon Bert. He was quite the most terrifying person Bert had ever encountered. He filled the Smallways soul with passionate dread and antipathy. For a long time Bert sat alone in Kurt's cabin, doing nothing and not venturing even to open the door lest he should be by so much nearer that appalling presence.

So it came about that he was probably the last person on board to hear the news that wireless telegraphy was bringing to the airship in throbs and fragments of a great naval battle in progress in mid-Atlantic.

He learnt it at last from Kurt.

Kurt came in with a general air of ignoring Bert, but muttering to himself in English nevertheless. " Stupendous ! " Bert heard him say. " Here ! " he said, " get off this locker." And he proceeded to rout out two books and a case of maps. He spread them on the folding-table, and stood regarding them. For a time his Germanic discipline struggled with his English informality and his natural kindliness and talkativeness, and at last lost.

" They're at it, Smallways," he said.

" At what, sir ? " said Bert, broken and respectful.

" Fighting ! The American North Atlantic squadron and pretty nearly the whole of our fleet. Our *Eiserne Kreuz* has had a gruelling and is sinking, and their *Miles Standish*—she's one of their biggest—has sunk with all hands. Torpedoes,

I suppose. She was a bigger ship than the *Karl der Grosse*, but
five or six years older. . . . Gods ! I wish we could see it,
Smallways ; a square fight in blue water, guns or nothing, and
all of 'em steaming ahead ! "

He spread his maps, he had to talk, and so he delivered a
lecture on the naval situation to Bert.

" Here it is," he said, " latitude 30° 50′ N., longitude 30°
50′ W. It's a good day off us anyhow, and they're all going
south-west by south full pelt as hard as they can go. We
shan't see a bit of it, worse luck ! Not a sniff we shan't get ! "

§ 2

The naval situation in the North Atlantic at that time was
a peculiar one. The United States was by far the stronger of
the two powers upon the sea, but the bulk of the American
fleet was still in the Pacific. It was in the direction of Asia
that war had been most feared, for the situation between
Asiatic and white had become unusually violent and dangerous, and the Japanese Government had shown itself quite
unprecedentedly difficult. The German attack found half
the American strength at Manilla, and what was called the
Second Fleet strung out across the Pacific in wireless contact
between the Asiatic station and San Francisco. The North
Atlantic Squadron was the sole American force on her eastern
shore ; it was returning from a friendly visit to France and
Spain, and was pumping oil-fuel from tenders in mid-Atlantic
—for most of its ships were steamships—when the international
situation became acute. It was made up of four battleships
and five armoured cruisers, ranking almost with battleships,
not one of which was of a later date than 1913. The Americans
had, indeed, grown so accustomed to the idea that Great
Britain could be trusted to keep the peace of the Atlantic that
a naval attack on the eastern seaboard found them unprepared
even in their imaginations. But long before the declaration
of war—indeed, on Whit Monday—the whole German fleet
of eighteen battleships, with a flotilla of fuel tenders and converted liners containing stores, to be used in support of the
air-fleet, had passed through the Straits of Dover and headed
boldly for New York. Not only did these German battleships
outnumber the Americans two to one, but they were more
heavily armed and more modern in construction—at least
seven of them having high explosive engines built of Charlottenburg steel, and all carrying Charlottenburg steel guns.

The fleets came into contact on Wednesday before any
actual declaration of war. The Americans had strung out in
the modern fashion at distances of thirty miles or so, and were
steaming to keep themselves between the Germans and either
the eastern states or Panama ; because vital as it was to defend
the seaboard cities, and particularly New York, it was still
more vital to save the canal from any attack that might pre-

vent the return of the main fleet from the Pacific. No doubt, said Kurt, this was now making records across that ocean, " unless the Japanese have had the same idea as the Germans." It was obviously beyond human possibility that the American North Atlantic fleet could hope to meet and defeat the German ; but, on the other hand, with luck it might fight a delaying action and inflict such damage as to weaken greatly the attack upon the coast defences. Its duty, indeed, was not victory but devotion, the severest task in the world. Meanwhile the submarine defences of New York, Panama, and the other more vital points could be put in some sort of order.

This was the naval situation, and until Wednesday in Whit week it was the only situation the American people had realised. It was then they heard for the first time of the real scale of the Dornhof aeronautic park, and the possibility of an attack coming upon them not only by sea but by the air. But it is curious that so discredited were the newspapers of that period, that a large majority of New Yorkers, for example, did not believe the most copious and circumstantial accounts of the German air-fleet until it was actually in sight of New York.

Kurt's talk was half soliloquy. He stood with a map on Mercator's projection before him, swaying to the swaying of the ship and talking of guns and tonnage, of ships, and their build and powers and speed, of strategic points and bases of operation. A certain shyness that reduced him to the status of a listener at the officers' table no longer silenced him.

Bert stood by, saying very little, but watching Kurt's finger on the map. " They've been saying things like this in the papers for a long time," he remarked. " Fancy it coming real ! "

Kurt had a detailed knowledge of the *Miles Standish*. " She used to be a crack ship for gunnery—held the record. I wonder if we beat her shooting or how ? I wish I was in it. I wonder which of our ships beat her. Maybe she got a shell in her engines. It's a running fight ! I wonder what the *Barbarossa* is doing," he went on. " She's my old ship. Not a first-rater, but good stuff. I bet she's got a shot or two home by now if old Schneider's up to form. Just think of it ! There they are whacking away at each other, great guns going, shells exploding, magazines bursting, ironwork flying about like straw in a gale, all we've been dreaming of for years ! I suppose we shall fly right away to New York—just as though it wasn't anything at all. I suppose we shall reckon we aren't wanted down there. It's no more than a covering fight on our side. All those tenders and storeships of ours are going on south-west by west to New York to make a floating depot for us. See ? " He dabbed his forefinger on the map. " Here we are. Our train of stores goes there, our battleships elbow the Americans out of our way there." . . .

When Bert went down to the men's mess-room to get his evening ration, hardly any one took notice of him, except just to point him out for an instant. Every one was talking of the battle, suggesting, contradicting—at times, until the petty officers hushed them, it rose to a great uproar. There was a new bulletin, but what it said he did not gather, except that it concerned the *Barbarossa*. Some of the men stared at him, and he heard the name of " Booteraidge " several times ; but no one molested him, and there was no difficulty about his soup and bread when his turn at the end of the queue came. He had feared there might be no ration for him, and if so he did not know what he would have done.

Afterwards he ventured out upon the little hanging gallery with the solitary sentinel. The weather was still fine, but the wind was rising and the rolling swing of the airship increasing. He clutched the rail tightly and felt rather giddy. They were now out of sight of land, and over blue water rising and falling in great masses. A dingy old brigantine under the British flag rose and plunged amid the broad blue waves—the only ship in sight.

§ 3

In the evening it began to blow and the airship to roll like a porpoise as it swung through the air. Kurt said that several of the men were sea-sick, but the motion did not inconvenience Bert, whose luck it was to be of that mysterious gastric disposition which constitutes a good sailor. He slept well, but in the small hours the light awoke him, and he found Kurt staggering about in search of something. He found it at last in the locker, and held it in his hand unsteadily—a compass. Then he compared his map.

" We've changed our direction," he said, " and come into the wind. I can't make it out. We've turned away from New York to the south. Almost as if we were going to take a hand—— "

He continued talking to himself for some time.

Day came, wet and windy. The window was bedewed externally, and they could see nothing through it. It was also very cold, and Bert decided to keep rolled up in his blankets on the locker until the bugle summoned him to his morning ration. That consumed, he went out on the little gallery ; but he could see nothing but eddying clouds driving headlong by, and the dim outlines of the nearer airships. Only at rare intervals could he get a glimpse of gray sea through the pouring cloud-drift.

Later in the morning the *Vaterland* changed altitude, and soared up suddenly in a high, clear sky, going, Kurt said, to a height of nearly thirteen thousand feet.

Bert was in his cabin, and chanced to see the dew vanish from the window and caught the gleam of sunlight outside.

He looked out, and saw once more that sunlit cloud floor he had seen first from the balloon, and the ships of the German air-fleet rising one by one from the white, as fish might rise and become visible from deep water. He stared for a moment and then ran out to the little gallery to see this wonder better. Below was cloudland and storm, a great drift of tumbled weather going hard away to the north-east, and the air about him was clear and cold and serene save for the faintest chill breeze and a rare drifting snowflake. Throb, throb, throb, throb, went the engines in the stillness. That huge herd of airships rising one after another had an effect of strange, portentous monsters breaking into an altogether unfamiliar world. . . .

Either there was no news of the naval battle that morning, or the Prince kept to himself whatever came until past mid-day. Then the bulletins came with a rush, bulletins that made the lieutenant wild with excitement.

" *Barbarossa* disabled and sinking," he cried. " Gott im Himmel ! *Der alte Barbarossa ! Aber welch ein braver Krieger!*"

He walked about the swinging cabin, and for a time he was wholly German.

Then he became English again. " Think of it, Smallways ! The old ship we kept so clean and tidy ! All smashed about, and the iron flying about in fragments, and the chaps one knew—Gott !—flying about too ! Scalding water squirting, fire, and the smash, smash of the guns ! They smash when you're near ! Like everything bursting to pieces ! Wool won't stop it—nothing ! And me up here—so near and so far ! *Der alte Barbarossa !* "

" Any other ships ? " asked Smallways presently.

" Gott ! Yes ! We've lost the *Karl der Grosse*, our best and biggest. Run down in the night by a British liner that blundered into the fighting—in trying to blunder out. They're fighting in a gale. The liner's afloat with her nose broken, sagging about ! There never was such a battle !—never before ! Good ships and good men on both sides—and a storm and the night and the dawn and all in the open ocean full steam ahead! No stabbing ! No submarines ! Guns and shooting ! Half our ships we don't hear of any more, because their masts are shot away. Latitude, 30° 38′ N.—longitude, 40° 31′ W.—where's that ? "

He routed out his map again, and stared at it with eyes that did not see.

" *Der alte Barbarossa !* I can't get it out of my head—with shells in her engine-room, and the fires flying out of her furnaces, and the stokers and engineers scalded and dead. Men I've messed with, Smallways—men I've talked to close ! And they've had their day at last ! And it wasn't all luck for them !

" Disabled and sinking ! I suppose everybody can't have

all the luck in a battle. Poor old Schneider ! I bet he gave
'em something back ! "

So it was the news of the battle came filtering through to
them all that morning. The Americans had lost a second
ship, name unknown ; the *Hermann* had been damaged in
covering the *Barbarossa*. . . . Kurt fretted like an imprisoned
animal about the airship, now going up to the forward gallery
under the eagle, now down into the swinging gallery, now
poring over his maps. He infected Smallways with a sense of
the immediacy of this battle that was going on just over the
curve of the earth. But when Bert went down to the gallery
the world was empty and still, a clear, inky-blue sky above
and a rippled veil of still, thin sunlit cirrus below, through
which one saw a racing drift of rain-cloud, and never a glimpse
of sea. Throb, throb, throb, throb, went the engines, and the
long, undulating wedge of airships hurried after the flagship
like a flight of swans after their leader. Save for the quiver
of the engines it was as noiseless as a dream. And down there,
somewhere in the wind and rain, guns roared, shells crashed
home, and, after the old manner of warfare, men toiled and
died.

§ 4

As the afternoon wore on the lower weather abated, and
the sea became intermittently visible again. The air-fleet
dropped slowly to the middle air, and towards sunset they had
a glimpse of the disabled *Barbarossa* far away to the east.
Smallways heard men hurrying along the passage, and was
drawn out to the gallery, where he found nearly a dozen
officers collected and scrutinising the helpless ruins of the
battleship through field-glasses. Two other vessels stood by
her, one an exhausted petrol tank, very high out of the water,
and the other a converted liner. Kurt was at the end of the
gallery, a little apart from the others.

" Gott ! " he said at last, lowering his binocular, " it is like
seeing an old friend with his nose cut off — waiting to be
finished. *Der Barbarossa* ! "

With a sudden impulse he handed his glass to Bert, who
had peered beneath his hands, ignored by every one, seeing
the three ships merely as three brown-black lines upon the
sea.

Never had Bert seen the like of that magnified slightly
hazy image before. It was not simply a battered ironclad
that wallowed helpless, it was a mangled ironclad. It seemed
wonderful she still floated. Her powerful engines had been her
ruin. In the long chase of the night, she had got out of line
with her consorts, and nipped in between the *Susquehanna*
and the *Kansas City*. They discovered her proximity, dropped
back until she was nearly broadside on to the former battleship, and signalled up the *Theodore Roosevelt* and the little

Monitor. As the dawn broke she had found herself hostess of a circle. The fight had not lasted five minutes before the appearance of the *Hermann* to the east, and immediately after the *Fürst Bismarck* in the west, forced the Americans to leave her, but in that time they had smashed her iron to rags. They had vented the accumulated tensions of their hard day's retreat upon her. As Bert saw her, she seemed a mere metal-worker's fantasy of frozen metal writhings. He could not tell part from part of her, except by its position.

" Gott ! " murmured Kurt, taking the glasses Bert restored to him—" Gott ! Da waren Albrecht—der gute Albrecht und der alte Zimmermann—und von Rosen ! . . . "

Long after the *Barbarossa* had been swallowed up in the twilight and distance he remained on the gallery peering through his glasses, and when he came back into his cabin he was unusually silent and thoughtful.

" This is a rough game, Smallways," he said at last—" this war is a rough game. Somehow one sees it different after a thing like that. Many men there were worked to make that *Barbarossa*, and there were men in it—one does not meet the like of them every day. Albrecht—there was a man named Albrecht—played the zither and improvised ; I keep on wondering what has happened to him. He and I—we were very close friends, after the German fashion."

§ 5

Smallways woke the next night to discover the cabin in darkness, a draught blowing through it, and Kurt talking to himself in German. He could see him dimly by the window, which he had unscrewed and opened, peering down. That cold, clear, attenuated light which is not so much light as a going of darkness, which casts inky shadows and so often heralds the dawn in the high air, was on his face.

" What's the row ? " said Bert.

" Shut up ! " said the lieutenant. " Can't you hear ? "

Into the stillness came the repeated heavy thud of guns, one, two, a pause, then three in quick succession.

" Gaw ! " said Bert—" guns ! " and was instantly at the lieutenant's side. The airship was still very high and the sea below was masked by a thin veil of clouds. The wind had fallen, and Bert, following Kurt's pointing finger, saw dimly through the colourless veil first a red glow, then a quick red flash and then at a little distance from it another. They were, it seemed for a while, silent flashes, and seconds after, when one had ceased to expect them, came the belated thuds—thud, thud. Kurt spoke in German very quickly.

A bugle rang through the airship.

Kurt sprang to his feet, saying something in an excited tone, still using German, and went to the door.

" I say ! What's up ? " cried Bert. " What's that ? "

The lieutenant stopped for an instant in the doorway, dark against the light passage. " You stay where you are, Smallways. You keep there and do nothing. We're going into action," he explained, and vanished.

Bert's heart began to beat rapidly. He felt himself poised over the fighting vessels far below. In a moment, were they to drop like a hawk striking a bird ? " Gaw ! " he whispered at last, in awestricken tones.

Thud ! . . . thud ! He discovered far away a second ruddy flare flashing back at the first. He perceived some difference on the *Vaterland* for which he could not account, and then he realised that the engines had slowed to an almost inaudible beat. He stuck his head out of the window and saw in the bleak air the other airships slowed down to a scarcely perceptible motion.

A second bugle sounded, was taken up faintly from ship to ship. Out went the lights ; the fleet became dim, dark bulks against an intense blue sky that still retained an occasional star. For a long time they hung, for an interminable time it seemed to him, and then began the sound of air being pumped into the balloonette, and slowly, slowly the *Vaterland* sank down towards the clouds.

He craned his neck, but he could not see if the rest of the fleet was following them ; the overhang of the gas-chambers intervened. There was something that stirred his imagination deeply in that stealthy, noiseless descent.

The obscurity deepened for a time, the last fading star on the horizon vanished, and he felt the cold presence of cloud. Then suddenly the glow beneath assumed distinct outlines, became flames, and the *Vaterland* ceased to descend and hung observant, and it would seem unobserved just beneath a drifting stratum of cloud a thousand feet, perhaps, over the battle below.

In the night the struggling naval battle and retreat had entered upon a new phase. The Americans had drawn together the ends of the flying line skilfully and dexterously, until at last it was a column and well to the south of the lax sweeping pursuit of the Germans. Then in the darkness before the dawn they had come about and steamed northward in close order with the idea of passing through the German battle-line and falling upon the flotilla that was making for New York in support of the German air-fleet. Much had altered since the first contact of the fleets. By this time the American Admiral, O'Connor, was fully informed of the existence of the airships, and he was no longer vitally concerned for Panama, since the submarine flotilla was reported arrived there from Key West, and the *Delaware* and *Abraham Lincoln*, two powerful and entirely modern ships, were already at Rio Grande, on the Pacific side of the canal. His manœuvre was, however, delayed by a boiler explosion on board the *Susque-*

hanna, and dawn found this ship in sight of and indeed so close to the *Bremen* and *Weimar* that they instantly engaged. There was no alternative to her abandonment but a fleet engagement. O'Connor chose the latter course. It was by no means a hopeless fight. The Germans, though much more numerous and powerful than the Americans, were in a dispersed line measuring nearly forty-five miles from end to end, and there were many chances that before they could gather in for the fight the column of seven Americans would have ripped them from end to end.

The day broke dim and overcast, and neither the *Bremen* nor the *Weimar* realised they had to deal with more than the *Susquehanna* until the whole column drew out from behind her at a distance of a mile or less and bore down on them. This was the position of affairs when the *Vaterland* appeared in the sky. The red glow Bert had seen through the column of clouds came from the luckless *Susquehanna* ; she lay almost immediately below, burning fore and aft, but still fighting two of her guns and steaming slowly southward. The *Bremen* and the *Weimar*, both hit in several places, were going west by south and away from her. The American fleet, headed by the *Theodore Roosevelt*, was crossing behind them, pounding them in succession, steaming in between them and the big modern *Fürst Bismarck*, which was coming up from the west. To Bert, however, the names of all these ships were unknown, and for a considerable time, indeed, misled by the direction in which the combatants were moving, he imagined the Germans to be Americans and the Americans Germans. He saw what appeared to him to be a column of six battleships pursuing three others, who were supported by a new-comer, until the fact that the *Bremen* and *Weimar* were firing into the *Susquehanna* upset his calculations. Then for a time he was hopelessly at a loss. The noise of the guns, too, confused him, they no longer seemed to boom ; they went whack, whack, whack, whack, and each faint flash made his heart jump in anticipation of the instant impact. He saw these ironclads, too, not in profile, as he was accustomed to see ironclads in pictures, but in plan and curiously fore-shortened. For the most part they presented empty decks, but here and there little knots of men sheltered behind steel bulwarks. The long, agitated noses of their big guns jetting thin transparent flashes and the broadside activity of the quick-firers, were the chief facts in this bird's-eye view. The Americans, being steam-turbine ships, had from two to four blast funnels each ; the Germans lay lower in the water, having explosive engines which now for some reason made an unwonted muttering roar. Because of their steam propulsion, the American ships were larger and with a more graceful outline. He saw all these fore-shortened ships rolling considerably and fighting their guns over a sea of huge, low waves and under the cold, explicit light of dawn. The whole spectacle waved slowly with the long, rhythmic rising and beat of the airship.

At first only the *Vaterland* of all the flying fleet appeared upon the scene below. She hovered high over the *Theodore Roosevelt*, keeping pace with the full speed of that ship. From that ship she must have been intermittently visible through the drifting clouds. The rest of the German fleet remained above the cloud canopy at a height of six or seven thousand feet, communicating with the flagship by wireless telegraphy, but risking no exposure to the artillery below.

It is doubtful at what particular time the unlucky Americans realised the presence of this new factor in the fight. No account now survives of their experience. We have to imagine as well as we can what it must have been to a battle-strained sailor suddenly glancing upward to discover that huge, long, silent shape overhead, vaster than any battleship, and trailing now from its hinder quarter a big German flag. Presently, as the sky cleared, more of such ships appeared in the blue through the dissolving clouds, and more, all disdainfully free of guns or armour, all flying fast to keep pace with the running fight below.

From first to last no gun whatever was fired at the *Vaterland*, and only a few rifle shots. It was a mere adverse stroke of chance that she had a man killed aboard her. Nor did she take any direct share in the fight until the end. She flew above the doomed American fleet while the Prince by wireless telegraphy directed the movements of her consorts. Meanwhile the *Vogel-stern* and *Preussen*, each with half a dozen drachen-flieger in tow, went full speed ahead and then dropped through the clouds, perhaps five miles ahead of the Americans. The *Theodore Roosevelt* let fly at once with the big guns in her forward barbette, but the shells burst far below the *Vogel-stern*, and forthwith a dozen single-man drachenflieger were swooping down to make their attack.

Bert, craning his neck through the cabin porthole, saw the whole of that incident, that first encounter of aeroplane and ironclad. He saw the queer German drachenflieger, with their wide, flat wings and square, box-shaped heads, their wheeled bodies and their single-man riders, soar down the air like a flight of birds. " Gaw ! " he said. One to the right pitched extravagantly, shot steeply up into the air, burst with a loud report, and flamed down into the sea ; another plunged nose forward into the water and seemed to fly to pieces as it hit the waves. He saw little men on the deck of the *Theodore Roosevelt* below, men foreshortened in plan into mere heads and feet, running out preparing to shoot at the others. Then the fore-most flying-machine was rushing between Bert and the Ameri-can's deck, and then bang ! came the thunder of its bomb flung neatly at the forward barbette, and a thin little crackling of rifle shots in reply. Whack, whack, whack, went the quick-firing guns of the American's battery and smash came an answering shell from the *Fürst Bismarck*. Then a second and third flying-machine passed between Bert and the American ironclad, dropping bombs also, and a fourth, its rider hit by a bullet, reeled down and dashed itself to pieces and exploded between the shot-torn funnels, blowing them apart. Bert had a momentary glimpse of a little black creature jumping from the crumpling frame of the flying-machine, hitting the funnel, and falling limply, to be instantly caught and driven to nothingness by the blaze and rush of the explosion.

Smash! came a vast explosion in the forward part of the flagship, and a huge piece of metal-work seemed to lift out of her and dump itself into the sea, dropping men and leaving a gap into which a prompt drachenflieger planted a flaring bomb. And then for an instant Bert perceived only too clearly in the growing, pitiless light a number of minute, convulsively active animalculae scorched and struggling in the *Theodore Roosevelt's* foaming wake. What were they ? Not men— surely not men ? Those drowning, mangled little creatures tore with their clutching fingers at Bert's soul. " Oh, Gord ! " he cried, " Oh, Gord ! " almost whimpering. He looked again and they had gone, and the black stem of the *Andrew Jackson*, a little disfigured by the sinking *Bremen's* last shot, was parting the water that had swallowed them into two neatly symmetrical waves. For some moments sheer blank horror blinded Bert to the destruction below.

Then with an immense rushing sound, bearing as it were a straggling volley of crashing minor explosions on its back, the *Susquehanna*, three miles and more now to the east, blew up and vanished abruptly in a boiling, steaming welter. For a moment nothing was to be seen but tumbled water, and then there came belching up from below, with immense gulping noises, eructations of steam and air and petrol and fragments of canvas and woodwork and men.

That made a distinct pause in the fight. It seemed a long pause to Bert. He found himself looking for the drachen-flieger. The flattened ruin of one was floating abeam of the *Monitor*, the rest had passed, dropping bombs down the American column ; several were in the water and apparently uninjured, and three or four were still in the air and coming round now in a wide circle to return to their mother airships. The American ironclads were no longer in column formation ; the *Theodore Roosevelt*, badly damaged, had turned to the south-east, and the *Andrew Jackson*, greatly battered but un-injured in any fighting part, was passing between her and the still fresh and vigorous *Fürst Bismarck* to intercept and meet the latter's fire. Away to the west the *Hermann* and the *Germanicus* had appeared and were coming into action.

In the pause after the *Susquehanna's* disaster Bert became aware of a trivial sound like the noise of an ill-greased, ill-hung door that falls ajar—the sound of the men in the *Fürst Bismarck* cheering.

And in that pause in the uproar, too, the sun rose, the dark waters became luminously blue, and a torrent of golden light irradiated the world. It came like a sudden smile in a scene of hate and terror. The cloud veil had vanished as if by magic and the whole immensity of the German air-fleet was revealed in the sky ; the air-fleet stooping now upon its prey.

" Whack-bang, whack-bang," the guns resumed, but ironclads were not built to fight the zenith, and the only hits the Americans scored were a few lucky chances in a generally ineffectual rifle fire. Their column was now badly broken, the *Susquehanna* had gone, the *Theodore Roosevelt* had fallen astern out of the line, with her forward guns disabled, in a heap of wreckage, and the *Monitor* was in some grave trouble. These two had ceased fire altogether, and so had the *Bremen* and *Weimar*, all four ships lying within shot of each other in an involuntary truce and with their respective flags still displayed. Only four American ships now, with the *Andrew Jackson* leading, kept to the south-easterly course. And the *Fürst Bismarck*, the *Hermann*, and the *Germanicus* steamed parallel to them and drew ahead of them, fighting heavily. The *Vaterland* rose slowly in the air in preparation for the concluding act of the drama.

Then falling into place, one behind the other, a string of a dozen airships dropped with unhurrying swiftness down the air in pursuit of the American fleet. They kept at a height of two thousand feet or more until they were over and a little in advance of the rearmost ironclad, and then stooped swiftly down into a fountain of bullets, and going just a little faster than the ship below, pelted her thinly protected decks with bombs until they became sheets of detonating flame. So the airships passed one after the other along the American column as it sought to keep up its fight with the *Fürst Bismarck*, the *Hermann*, and the *Germanicus*, and each airship added to the destruction and confusion its predecessor had made. The American gunfire ceased, except for a few heroic shots, but they still steamed on, obstinately unsubdued, bloody, battered, and wrathfully resistent, spitting bullets at the airships and unmercifully pounded by the German ironclads. But now Bert had but intermittent glimpses of them between the nearer bulks of the airships that assailed them. . . .

It struck Bert suddenly that the whole battle was receding and growing small and less thunderously noisy. The *Vaterland* was rising in the air, steadily and silently, until the impact of the guns no longer smote upon the heart but came to the ear dulled by distance, until the four silenced ships to the eastward were little distant things : but were there four ? Bert now could see only three of those floating, blackened, and smoking rafts of ruin against the sun. But the *Bremen*

had two boats out ; the *Theodore Roosevelt* was also dropping
boats to where the drift of minute objects struggled, rising
and falling on the big, broad Atlantic waves. . . . The *Vaterland*
was no longer following the fight. The whole of that hurrying
tumult drove away to the south-eastward, growing smaller
and less audible as it passed. One of the airships lay on the
water burning, a remote, monstrous fount of flames, and far
in the south-west appeared first one and then three other
German ironclads hurrying in support of their consorts. . . .

§ 6

Steadily the *Vaterland* soared, and the air-fleet soared with
her and came round to head for New York, and the battle
became a little thing far away, an incident before breakfast.
It dwindled to a string of dark shapes and one smoking yellow
flare that presently became a mere indistinct smear upon the
vast horizon and the bright new day, that was at last altogether
lost to sight. . . .

So it was that Bert Smallways saw the first fight of the
airship and the final fight of those strangest things in the
whole history of war ; the ironclad battleships, which began
their career with the floating batteries of the Emperor Napoleon
III. in the Crimean war and lasted, with an enormous expenditure of human energy and resources, for seventy years. In
that space of time the world produced over twelve thousand
five hundred of these strange monsters, in schools, in types,
in series, each larger and heavier and more deadly than its
predecessors. Each in its turn was hailed as the last birth of
time, most in their turn were sold for old iron. Only about
five per cent. of them ever fought in a battle. Some foundered,
some went ashore and broke up, several rammed one another
by accident and sank. The lives of countless men were spent
in their service, the splendid genius and patience of thousands
of engineers and inventors, wealth and material beyond estimating ; to their account we must put stunted and starved
lives on land, millions of children sent to toil unduly, innumerable opportunities of fine living undeveloped and lost.
Money had to be found for them at any cost—that was the
law of a nation's existence during that strange time. Surely
they were the weirdest, most destructive and wasteful mega-
theria in the whole history of mechanical invention.

And then cheap things of gas and basket-work made an end
of them altogether, smiting out of the sky ! . . .

Never before had Bert Smallways seen pure destruction,
never had he realised the mischief and waste of war. His
startled mind rose to the conception, this also is in life. Out
of all this fierce torrent of sensation one impression rose and
became cardinal—the impression of the men of the *Theodore
Roosevelt* who had struggled in the water after the explosion
of the first bomb. " Gaw ! " he said at the memory ; " It

might 'ave been me and Grubb ! . . . I suppose you kick about, and get the water in your mouf. I don't suppose it lasts long."

He became anxious to see how Kurt was affected by these things. Also he perceived he was hungry. He hesitated towards the door of the cabin and peeped out into the passage. Down forward, near the gangway to the men's mess, stood a little group of air sailors looking at something that was hidden from him in a recess. One of them was in the light diver's costume Bert had already seen in the gas chamber turret, and he was moved to walk along and look at this person more closely and examine the helmet he carried under his arm. But he forgot about the helmet when he got to the recess, because there he found lying on the floor the dead body of the boy who had been killed by a bullet from the *Theodore Roosevelt*.

Bert had not observed that any bullets at all had reached the *Vaterland*, or, indeed, imagined himself under fire. He could not understand for a time what had killed the lad and no one explained to him.

The boy lay just as he had fallen and died, with his jacket torn and scorched, his shoulder-blade smashed and burst away from his body and all the left side of his body ripped and rent. There was much blood. The sailors stood listening to the man with the helmet, who made explanations and pointed to the round bullet hole in the floor and the smash in the panel of the passage upon which the still vicious missile had spent the residue of its energy. All the faces were grave and earnest ; they were the faces of sober, blond, blue-eyed men accustomed to obedience and an orderly life, to whom this waste, wet, painful thing that had been a comrade came almost as strangely as it did to Bert.

A peal of wild laughter sounded down the passage in the direction of the little gallery and something spoke—almost shouted—in German, in tones of exultation.

Other voices at a lower, more respectful pitch replied.

" *Der Prinz*," said a voice, and all the men became stiffer and less natural. Down the passage appeared a group of figures, Lieutenant Kurt walking in front carrying a packet of papers.

He stopped point-blank when he saw the thing in the recess, and his ruddy face went white. " So ! " said he in surprise.

The Prince was following him, talking over his shoulder to Von Winterfeld and the Kapitän. " Eh ? " he said to Kurt, stopping in mid-sentence, and followed the gesture of Kurt's hand. He glared at the crumpled object in the recess and seemed to think for a moment.

He made a slight, careless gesture towards the boy's body and turned to the Kapitän.

" Dispose of that," he said in German, and passed on, finishing his sentence to Von Winterfeld in the same cheerful tone in which it had begun.

§ 7

The deep impression of helplessly drowning men that Bert had brought from the actual fight in the Atlantic mixed itself up inextricably with that of the lordly figure of Prince Karl Albert gesturing aside the dead body of the *Vaterland* sailor. Hitherto he had rather liked the idea of war as being a jolly, smashing, exciting affair, something like a Bank Holiday rag on a large scale, and on the whole agreeable and exhilarating. Now he knew it a little better.

The next day there was added to his growing disillusionment a third ugly impression, trivial indeed to describe, a mere necessary everyday incident of a state of war, but very distressing to his urbanised imagination. One writes " urbanised " to express the distinctive gentleness of the period. It was quite peculiar to the crowded townsmen of that time, and different altogether from the normal experience of any preceding age, that they never saw anything killed, never encountered, save through the mitigating media of book or picture, the fact of lethal violence that underlies all life. Three times in his existence, and three times only, had Bert seen a dead human being, and he had never assisted at the killing of anything bigger than a new-born kitten.

The incident that gave him his third shock was the execution of one of the men on the *Adler* for carrying a box of matches. The case was a flagrant one. The man had forgotten he had it upon him when coming aboard. Ample notice had been given to every one of the gravity of this offence, and notices appeared at numerous points all over the airships. The man's defence was that he had grown so used to the notices, and had been so preoccupied with his work, that he hadn't applied them to himself ; he pleaded, in his defence, what is indeed in military affairs another serious crime, inadvertency. He was tried by his captain, and the sentence confirmed by wireless telegraphy by the Prince, and it was decided to make his death an example to the whole fleet. " The Germans," the Prince declared, " hadn't crossed the Atlantic to go wool gathering." And in order that this lesson in discipline and obedience might be visible to every one, it was determined not to electrocute or drown, but hang the offender.

Accordingly, the air-fleet came clustering round the flagship like carp in a pond at feeding-time. The *Adler* hung at the zenith immediately alongside the flagship. The whole crew of the *Vaterland* assembled upon the hanging gallery ; the crews of the other airships manned the air-chambers, that is to say, clambered up the outer netting to the upper sides. The officers appeared upon the machine-gun platforms. Bert thought it an altogether stupendous sight, looking down, as he was, upon the entire fleet. Far off below two steamers on the rippled blue water, one British, and the other flying the American flag, seemed the minutest objects, and marked the scale. They were immensely distant. Bert stood on the gallery, curious to see the execution, but uncomfortable because that terrible blond Prince was within a dozen feet of him, glaring terribly, with his arms folded, and his heels together in military fashion.

They hung the man from the *Adler*. They gave him sixty feet of rope, so that he should hang and dangle in the sight of all evil-doers who might be hiding matches or contemplating any kindred disobedience. Bert saw the man standing, a living, reluctant man, no doubt scared and rebellious enough in his heart, but outwardly erect and obedient, on the lower gallery of the *Adler* about a hundred yards away. Then they had thrust him overboard. . . .

Down he fell, hands and feet extending, until with a jerk he was at the end of the rope. Then he ought to have died and swung edifyingly, but instead a more terrible thing happened ; his head came right off, and down the body went spinning to the sea, feeble, grotesque, fantastic, with the head racing in its fall.

" Ugh ! " said Bert, clutching the rail before him, and a sympathetic grunt came from several of the men beside him.

" So ! " said the Prince, stiffer and sterner, glared for some seconds, then turned to the gangway up into the airship.

For a long time Bert remained clinging to the railing of the gallery. He was almost physically sick with the horror of this trifling incident. He found it far more dreadful than the battle. He was indeed a very degenerate, latter-day, civilised person.

Late that afternoon Kurt came into the cabin and found him curled up on his locker, and looking very white and miserable. Kurt had also lost something of his pristine freshness.

" Sea-sick ? " he asked.

" No ! "

" We ought to reach New York this evening. There's a good breeze coming up under our tails. Then we shall see things."

Bert did not answer.

Kurt opened out folding chair and table, and rustled for a time with his maps. Then he fell thinking darkly. He roused himself presently, and looked at his companion. "What's the matter ? " he said.

" Nothing ! "

Kurt stared threateningly. " What's the matter ? " he repeated.

" I saw them kill that chap. I saw that flying-machine man hit the funnels of the big ironclad. I saw that dead chap in the passage. I seen too much smashing and killing to-day. That's the matter. I don't like it. I didn't know war was this sort of thing. I'm a civilian. I don't like it."

" *I* don't like it," said Kurt. " By Jove, no ! "

" I've read about war, and all that, but when you see it it's different. And I'm gettin' giddy. I'm gettin' giddy. I didn't mind a bit being up in that balloon at first, but all this looking down and floating over things and smashing up people, it's getting on my nerves. See ? "

" It'll have to get off again. . . ."

Kurt thought. " You're not the only one. The men are all getting strung up. The flying—that's just flying. Naturally it makes one a little swimmy in the head at first. As for the killing, we've got to be blooded ; that's all. We're tame, civilised men. And we've got to get blooded. I suppose there's not a dozen men on the ship who've really seen blood-shed. Nice, quiet, law-abiding Germans they've been so far. . . . Here they are—in for it. They're a bit squeamy now, but you wait till they've got their hands in."

He reflected. " Everybody's getting a bit strung up," he said.

He turned again to his maps. Bert sat crumpled up in the corner, apparently heedless of him. For some time both kept silence.

" Whadid the Prince want to go and 'ang that chap for ? " asked Bert suddenly.

" That was all right," said Kurt, " that was all right. *Quite* right. Here were the orders, plain as the nose on your face, and here was that fool going about with matches——"

" Gaw ! I shan't forget that bit in a 'urry," said Bert irrelevantly.

Kurt did not answer him. He was measuring their distance from New York and speculating. " Wonder what the American aeroplanes are like ? " he said. " Something like our drachen-flieger. . . . We shall know by this time to-morrow. . . . I wonder what we shall know ? I wonder. Suppose, after all, they put up a fight. . . . Rum sort of fight ! "

He whistled softly and mused. Presently he fretted out of the cabin, and later Bert found him in the twilight upon the swinging platform, staring ahead, and speculating about the things that might happen on the morrow. Clouds veiled the sea again, and the long, straggling wedge of airships rising and falling as they flew, seemed like a flock of strange new births in a Chaos that had neither earth nor water, but only mist and sky.

CHAPTER SIX

HOW WAR CAME TO NEW YORK

§ I

THE City of New York was in the year of the German attack the largest, richest, in many respects the most splendid, and in some, the wickedest city the world had ever seen. She was the supreme type of the City of the Scientific Commercial Age ; she displayed its greatness, its power, its ruthless anarchic enterprise, and its social disorganisation most strikingly and completely. She had long ousted London from her pride of place as the modern Babylon, she was the centre of the world's finance, the world's trade, and the world's pleasure ; and men likened her to the apocalyptic cities of the ancient prophets. She sat drinking up the wealth of a continent, as Rome once drank the wealth of the Mediterranean, and Babylon the wealth of the east. In her streets one found the extremes of magnificence and misery, of civilisation and disorder. In one quarter, palaces of marble, laced and crowned with light and flame and flowers, towered up into her marvellous twilights beautiful beyond description ; in another a black and sinister polyglot population sweltered in indescribable congestion in warrens and excavations beyond the power and knowledge of government. Her vice, her crime, her law alike were inspired by a fierce and terrible energy, and like the great cities of mediæval Italy, her ways were dark and adventurous with private war.

It was the peculiar shape of Manhattan Island, pressed in by arms of the sea on either side, and incapable of comfortable expansion except along a narrow northward belt, that first gave the New York architects their bias for extreme vertical dimensions. Every need was lavishly supplied them—money, material, labour ; only space was restricted. To begin with, therefore, they built high perforce. But to do so was to discover a whole new world of architectural beauty, of exquisite ascendant lines, and long after the central congestion had been relieved by tunnels under the sea, four colossal bridges over the East River, and a dozen mono-rail cables east and west, the upward growth went on. In many ways New York and her gorgeous plutocracy repeated Venice ; in the magnificence of her architecture, painting, metal work, and sculpture, for example, in the grim intensity of her political method, in her maritime and commercial ascendancy. But she repeated no previous state at all in the lax disorder of her internal administration, a laxity that made vast sections of her area lawless beyond precedent, so that it was possible for whole districts to be impassable while civil war raged between street and street,

and for Alsatias to exist in her midst in which the official
police never set foot. She was an ethnic whirlpool. The flags
of all nations flew in her harbour, and at the climax, the yearly
coming and going overseas numbered together upwards of
two million human beings. To Europe she was America, to
America she was the gateway of the earth. But to tell the
story of New York would be to write a social history of the
world ; saints and martyrs, dreamers and scoundrels, the
traditions of a thousand races and a thousand religions, went
to her making and throbbed and jostled in her streets. And
over all that torrential confusion of men and purposes fluttered
that strange flag, the stars and stripes, that meant at once the
noblest thing in life and the least noble, that is to say Liberty
on the one hand and on the other the base jealousy the individual self-seeker feels towards the common purpose of the
State.

For many generations New York had taken no heed of war,
save as a thing that happened far away, that affected prices
and supplied the newspapers with exciting headlines and
pictures. The New Yorkers felt, perhaps, even more certainly
than the English had done that war in their own land was an
impossible thing. In that they shared the delusion of all North
America. They felt as secure as spectators at a bull-fight ;
they risked their money perhaps on the result, but that was
all. And such ideas of war as the common Americans possessed
were derived from the limited, picturesque, adventurous war
of the past. They saw war as they saw history, through an
iridescent mist, deodorised, scented indeed, with all its essential
cruelties tactfully hidden away. They were inclined to regret
it as something ennobling, to sigh that it could no longer come
into their own private experience. They read with interest,
if not with avidity, of their new guns, of their immense and
still more immense ironclads, of their incredible and still more
incredible explosives, but just what these tremendous engines
of destruction might mean for their personal lives never entered
their heads. They did not, so far as one can judge, from their
contemporary literature, think that they meant anything to
their personal lives at all. They thought America was safe
amidst all this piling up of explosives. They cheered the flag
by habit and tradition, they despised other nations, and whenever there was an international difficulty they were intensely
patriotic, that is to say, they were ardently against any native
politician who did not threaten and do harsh and uncompromising things to the antagonist people. They were spirited to
Asia, spirited to Germany, so spirited to Great Britain that
the international attitude of the mother country to her great
daughter was constantly compared in contemporary caricature
to that between a henpecked husband and a vicious young
wife. For the rest, they all went about their business and
pleasure as if war had died out with the megatherium. . . .

And, then, suddenly, into a world peacefully busied for the most part upon armaments and the perfection of explosives, war came ; came the shock of realising that the guns were going off, that the masses of inflammable material all over the world were at last ablaze.

§ 2

The immediate effect upon New York of the sudden onset of war was merely to intensify her normal vehemence.

The newspapers and magazines that fed the American mind —for books upon this impatient continent had become simply material for the energy of collectors—were instantly a coruscation of war pictures and of headlines that rose like rockets and burst like shells.   To the normal high-strung energy of New York streets was added a touch of war-fever.   Great crowds assembled, more especially in the dinner-hour, in Madison Square about the Farragut monument, to listen to and cheer patriotic speeches, and a veritable epidemic of little flags and buttons swept through these great torrents of swiftly moving young people, who poured into New York of a morning by car and mono-rail and subway and train, to toil and ebb home again between the hours of five and seven.   It was dangerous not to wear a war button.   The splendid music-halls of the time sank every topic in patriotism and evolved scenes of wild enthusiasm, strong men wept at the sight of the national banner sustained by the whole strength of the ballet, and special searchlights and illuminations amazed the watching angels.   The churches re-echoed the national enthusiasm in graver key and slower measure, and the aerial and naval preparations on the East River were greatly incommoded by the multitude of excursion steamers which thronged, helpfully cheering, about them.   The trade in small arms was enormously stimulated, and many overwrought citizens found an immediate relief for their emotions in letting off fireworks of a more or less heroic, dangerous, and national character in the public streets.   Small children's air-balloons of the latest model attached to string became a serious check to the pedestrian in Central Park.   And amidst scenes of indescribable emotion the Albany legislature in permanent session, with a generous suspension of rules and precedents, passed through both Houses the long-disputed Bill for universal military service in New York State.

Critics of the American character are disposed to consider that up to the actual impact of the German attack the people of New York dealt altogether too much with the war as if it were a political demonstration.   Little or no damage, they urge, was done to either the German or Japanese forces by the wearing of buttons, the waving of small flags, the fireworks or the songs.   They forgot that under the conditions of warfare a century of science had brought about, the non-military section of the population could do no serious damage in any form to their enemies, and that there was no reason, therefore, why they should not do as they did. The balance of military efficiency was shifting back from the many to the few, from the common to the specialised. The days when the emotional infantryman decided battles had passed by for ever. War had become a matter of apparatus, of special training and skill of the most intricate kind. It had become undemocratic. And whatever the value of the popular excitement, there can be no denying that the small regular establishment of the United States Government, confronted by this totally unexpected emergency of an armed invasion from Europe, acted with vigour, science, and imagination. They were taken by surprise so far as the diplomatic situation was concerned, and their equipment for building either navigables or aeroplanes was contemptible in comparison with the huge German parks. Still, they set to work at once to prove to the world that the spirit that had created the *Monitor* and the Southern submarines of 1864 was not dead. The chief of the aeronautic establishment near West Point was Cabot Sinclair, and he allowed himself but one single moment of the posturing that was so universal in that democratic time. " We have chosen our epitaphs," he said to a reporter, " and we are going to have, ' They did all they could.' Now run away ! "

The curious thing is that they did all do all they could ; there is no exception known. Their only defect, indeed, was a defect of style.

One of the most striking facts historically about this war, and the one that makes the complete separation that had arisen between the methods of warfare and the necessity of democratic support, is the effectual secrecy of the Washington authorities about their airships. They did not bother to confide a single fact of their preparations to the public. They did not even condescend to talk to Congress. They burked and suppressed every inquiry. The war was fought by the President and the secretaries of State in an entirely autocratic manner. Such publicity as they sought was merely to anticipate and prevent inconvenient agitation to defend particular points. They realised that the chief danger in aerial warfare from an excitable and intelligent public would be a clamour for local airships and aeroplanes to defend local interests. This, with such resources as they possessed, might lead to a fatal division and distribution of the national forces. Particularly they feared that they might be forced into a premature action to defend New York. They realised with prophetic insight that this would be the particular advantage the Germans would seek. So they took great pains to direct the popular mind towards defensive artillery, and to divert it from any thought of aerial battle. Their real preparations they masked beneath ostensible ones. There was at Washington a large reserve of naval guns, and these were distributed rapidly, conspicuously, and with much press attention, among the eastern cities. They were mounted for the most part upon hills and prominent crests round the threatened centres of population. They were mounted upon rough adaptations of the Doan swivel, which at that time gave the maximum vertical range to a heavy gun. Much of this artillery was still unmounted, and nearly all of it was unprotected when the German air-fleet reached New York. And down in the crowded streets when that occurred, the readers of the New York papers were regaling themselves with wonderful and wonderfully illustrated accounts of such matters as :—

THE SECRET OF THE THUNDERBOLT

AGED SCIENTIST PERFECTS ELECTRIC GUN TO ELECTROCUTE AIR-SHIP CREWS BY UPWARD LIGHTNING

WASHINGTON ORDERS FIVE HUNDRED

WAR SECRETARY LODGE DELIGHTED

SAYS THEY WILL SUIT THE GERMANS DOWN ·TO THE GROUND

PRESIDENT PUBLICLY APPLAUDS THIS MERRY QUIP

---

§ 3

The German fleet reached New York in advance of the news of the American naval disaster. It reached New York in the late afternoon and was first seen by watchers at Ocean Grove and Long Branch coming swiftly out of the southward sea and going away to the north-west. The flagship passed almost vertically over the Sandy Hook observation station, rising rapidly as it did so, and in a few minutes all New York was vibrating to the Staten Island guns.

Several of these guns, and especially that at Giffords and the one on Beacon Hill above Matawan, were remarkably well handled. The former, at a distance of five miles, and with an elevation of six thousand feet, sent a shell to burst so close to the *Vaterland* that a pane of the Prince's forward window was smashed by a fragment. This sudden explosion made Bert tuck in his head with the celerity of a startled tortoise. The whole air-fleet immediately went up steeply to a height of about twelve thousand feet, and at that level passed unscathed over the ineffectual guns. The airships lined out as they moved forward into the form of a flattened V, with its apex towards the city, and with the flagship going highest at the apex. The two ends of the V passed over Plumfield and Jamaica Bay respectively, and the Prince directed his course a little to the east of the Narrows, soared over the Upper Bay, and came to rest above Jersey City in a position that dominated lower New York. There the monsters hung, large and wonderful in the evening light, serenely regardless of the occasional rocket explosions and flashing shell-bursts in the lower air.

It was a pause of mutual inspection. For a time naïve humanity swamped the conventions of warfare altogether ; the interest of the millions below and of the thousands above alike was spectacular. The evening was unexpectedly fine— only a few thin level bands of clouds at seven or eight thousand feet broke its luminous clarity. The wind had dropped ; it was an evening infinitely peaceful and still. The heavy con-concussions of the distant guns and those incidental harmless pyrotechnics at the level of the clouds seemed to have as little to do with killing and force, terror and submission, as a salute at a naval review. Below, every point of vantage bristled with spectators, the roofs of the towering buildings, the public squares, the active ferry boats, and every favourable street intersection had its crowds : all the river piers were dense with people, the Battery Park was solid black with east-side popu-lation, black with position of advantage in Central Park and along Riverside Drive had its peculiar and characteristic assembly from the adjacent streets. The footways of the great bridges over the East River were also closely packed and blocked. Everywhere shopkeepers had left their shops, men their work, and women and children their homes, to come out and see the marvel.

" It beat," they declared, " the newspapers."

And from above, many of the occupants of the airships stared with an equal curiosity. No city in the world was ever so finely placed as New York, so magnificently cut up by sea and bluff and river, so admirably disposed to display the tall effects of buildings, the complex immensities of bridges and mono-railways and feats of engineering. London, Paris, Berlin, were shapeless, low agglomerations beside it. Its port reached to its heart like Venice, and, like Venice, it was obvious, dramatic, and proud. Seen from above it was alive with crawling trains and cars, and at a thousand points it was already breaking into quivering light. New York was alto-gether at its best that evening, its splendid best.

" Gaw ! *What* a place ! " said Bert.

It was so great, and in its collective effect so pacifically magnificent, that to make war upon it seemed incongruous beyond measure, like laying siege to the National Gallery or attacking respectable people in an hotel dining-room with battle-axe and mail. It was in its entirety so large, so complex, so delicately immense, that to bring it to the issue of warfare was like driving a crowbar into the mechanism of a clock. And the fish-like shoal of great airships hovering light and sunlit above, filling the sky, seemed equally remote from the ugly forcefulness of war. To Kurt, to Smallways, to I know not how many more of the people in the air-fleet came the distinctest apprehension of these incompatibilities. But in the head of the Prince Karl Albert were the vapours of romance; he was a conqueror, and this was the enemy's city. The greater the city the greater the triumph. No doubt he had a time of tremendous exultation and sensed beyond all precedent the joys of power that night.

There came an end at last to that pause. Some wireless communications had failed of a satisfactory ending and fleet and city remembered they were hostile powers. " Look ! " cried the multitude ; " Look ! "

" What are they doing ? "

" What ? " . . . Down through the twilight sank five attacking airships, one to the Navy Yard on East River, one to City Hall, two over the great business buildings of Wall Street and Lower Broadway, one to the Brooklyn Bridge, dropping from among their fellows through the danger zone from the distant guns smoothly and rapidly to a safe proximity to the city masses. At that descent all the cars in the street stopped with dramatic suddenness, and all the lights that had been coming on in the streets and houses went out again. For the City Hall had awakened and was conferring by telephone with the Federal command and taking measures for defence. The City Hall was asking for airships, refusing to surrender as Washington advised, and developing into a centre of intense emotion, of hectic activity. Everywhere and hastily the police began to clear the assembled crowds. " Go to your homes," they said ; and the word was passed from mouth to mouth, " There's going to be trouble." A chill of apprehension ran through the city, and men hurrying in the unwonted darkness across City Hall Park and Union Square came upon the dim forms of soldiers and guns, and were challenged and sent back. In half an hour New York had passed from serene sunset and gaping admiration to a troubled and threatening twilight.

The first loss of life occurred in the panic rush from Brooklyn Bridge as the airship approached it.

With the cessation of the traffic an unusual stillness came upon New York, and the disturbing concussions of the futile defending guns on the hills about grew more and more audible. At last these ceased also. A pause of further negotiation followed. People sat in darkness, sought counsel from telephones that were dumb. Then into the expectant hush came a great crash and uproar, the breaking down of the Brooklyn Bridge, the rifle fire from the Navy Yard, and the bursting of bombs in Wall Street and the City Hall. New York as a whole could do nothing, could understand nothing. New York in the darkness peered and listened to these distant sounds until presently they died away as suddenly as they had begun. " What could be happening ? " They asked it in vain.

A long, vague period intervened, and people looking out of the windows of upper rooms discovered the dark hulls of German airships, gliding slowly and noiselessly, quite close at hand. Then quietly the electric lights came on again, and an uproar of nocturnal newsvenders began in the streets.

The units of that vast and varied population bought and learnt what had happened ; there had been a fight and New York had hoisted the white flag. . . .

§ 4

The lamentable incidents that followed the surrender of New York seem now in the retrospect to be but the necessary and inevitable consequence of the clash of modern appliances and social conditions produced by the scientific century on the one hand, and the tradition of a crude, romantic patriotism on the other. At first people received the fact with an irresponsible detachment, much as they would have received the slowing down of the train in which they were travelling or the erection of a public monument by the city to which they belonged.

" We have surrendered. Dear me ! *have* we ? " was rather the manner in which the first news was met. They took it in the same spectacular spirit they had displayed at the first apparition of the air-fleet. Only slowly was this realisation of a capitulation suffused with the flush of patriotic passion, only with reflection did they make any personal application. " *We* have surrendered ! " came later ; " in us America is defeated." Then they began to burn and tingle.

The newspapers which were issued about one in the morning contained no particulars of the terms upon which New York had yielded—nor did they give any intimation of the quality of the brief conflict that had preceded the capitulation. The later issues remedied these deficiencies. There came the explicit statement of the agreement to victual the German airships, to supply the complement of explosives to replace those employed in the fight and in the destruction of the North Atlantic fleet, to pay the enormous ransom of forty million dollars, and to surrender the flotilla in the East River. There came, too, longer and longer descriptions of the smashing up of the City Hall and the Navy Yard, and people began to realise faintly what those brief minutes of uproar had meant. They read the tale of men blown to bits, of futile soldiers in that localised battle fighting against hope amidst an indescribable wreckage, of flags hauled down by weeping men. And these strange nocturnal editions contained also the brief cables from Europe of the fleet disaster, the North Atlantic fleet for which New

York had always felt an especial pride and solicitude. Slowly, hour by hour, the collective consciousness woke up, the tide of patriotic astonishment and humiliation came flowing in. America had come upon disaster ; suddenly New York discovered herself, with amazement giving place to wrath unspeakable, a conquered city under the hand of her conqueror.

As that fact shaped itself in the public mind, there sprang up, as flames spring up, an angry repudiation. " No ! " cried New York waking in the dawn. " No ! I am not defeated. This is a dream."

Before day broke the swift American anger was running through all the city, through every soul in those contagious millions. Before it took action, before it took shape, the men in the airships could feel the gigantic insurgence of emotion, as cattle and natural creatures feel, it is said, the coming of an earthquake. The newspapers of the Knype group first gave the things words and a formula. " We do not agree," they said simply. " We have been betrayed ! " Men took that up everywhere, it passed from mouth to mouth, at every street corner under the paling lights of dawn orators stood unchecked, calling upon the spirit of America to arise, making the shame a personal reality to every one who heard. To Bert, listening five hundred feet above, it seemed that the city, which had at first produced only confused noises, was now humming like a hive of bees—of very angry bees.

After the smashing of the City Hall and Post Office, the white flag had been hoisted from a tower of the old Park Row Building, and thither had gone Mayor O'Hagen, urged thither indeed by the terror-stricken property owners of lower New York, to negotiate the capitulation with Von Winterfeld. The *Vaterland* having dropped the secretary by a rope ladder, remained hovering, circling very slowly above the great buildings, old and new, that clustered round City Hall Park while the *Helmholz*, which had done the fighting there, rose overhead to a height of perhaps two thousand feet. So Bert had a near view of all that occurred in that central place. The City Hall and Court House, the Post Office and a mass of buildings on the west side of Broadway, had been badly damaged, and the three former were a heap of blackened ruins. In the case of the first two the loss of life had not been considerable, but a great multitude of workers, including many girls and women, had been caught in the destruction of the Post Office, and a little army of volunteers with white badges entered behind the firemen, bringing out the often still living bodies, for the most part frightly charred, and carrying them into the big Monson building close at hand. Everywhere the busy firemen were directing their bright streams of water upon the smouldering masses : their hose lay about the square, and long cordons of police held back the gathering black masses of people, chiefly from the east side, from these central activities.

In violent and extraordinary contrast with this scene of destruction, close at hand were the huge newspaper establishments of Park Row. They were all alight and working ; they had not been abandoned even while the actual bomb throwing was going on, and now staff and presses were vehemently active, getting out the story, the immense and dreadful story of the night, developing comment and, in most cases, spreading the idea of resistance under the very noses of the airships. For a long time Bert could not imagine what these callously active offices could be, then he detected the noise of the presses and emitted his " Gaw ! "

Beyond these newspaper buildings again, and partially hidden by the arches of the old Elevated Railway of New York (long since converted into a mono-rail), there was another cordon of police and a sort of encampment of ambulances and doctors, busy with the dead and wounded who had been killed early in the night by the panic upon Brooklyn Bridge. All this he saw in the perspectives of a bird's-eye view, as things happening in a big, irregular-shaped pit below him, between cliffs of high building. Northward he looked along the steep cañon of Broadway, down whose length at intervals crowds were assembling about excited speakers ; and when he lifted his eyes he saw the chimneys and cable-stacks and roof spaces of New York, and everywhere now over these the watching, debating people clustered, except where the fires raged and the jets of water flew. Everywhere, too, were flagstaffs devoid of flags ; one white sheet drooped and flapped and drooped again over the Park Row buildings. And upon the lurid lights, the festering movement and intense shadows of this strange scene, there was breaking now the cold, impartial dawn.

For Bert Smallways all this was framed in the frame of the open porthole. It was a pale, dim world outside that dark and tangible rim. All night he had clutched at that rim, jumped and quivered at explosions, and watched phantom events. Now he had been high and now low ; now almost beyond hearing, now flying close to crashings and shouts and outcries. He had seen airships flying low and swift over darkened and groaning streets ; watched great buildings, suddenly red-lit amidst the shadows, crumple at the smashing impact of bombs ; witnessed for the first time in his life the grotesque, swift onset of insatiable conflagrations. From it all he felt detached, disembodied. The *Vaterland* did not even fling a bomb ; she watched and ruled. Then down they had come at last to hover over City Hall Park, and it had crept in upon his mind, chillingly terrifyingly, that these illuminated black masses were great offices afire, and that the going to and fro of minute dim spectres of lantern-lit gray and white was a harvesting of the wounded and the dead. As the light grew clearer he began to understand more and more what these crumpled black things signified. . . .

He had watched hour after hour since first New York had risen out of the blue indistinctness of the landfall. With the daylight he experienced an intolerable fatigue.

He lifted weary eyes to the pink flush in the sky, yawned immensely, and crawled back whispering to himself across the cabin to the locker. He did not so much lie down upon that as fall upon it and instantly become asleep.

There, hours after, sprawling undignified and sleeping profoundly, Kurt found him, a very image of the democratic mind confronted with the problems of a time too complex for its apprehension. His face was pale and indifferent, his mouth wide open, and he snored. He snored disagreeably.

Kurt regarded him for a moment with a mild distaste. Then he kicked his ankle.

" Wake up ! " he said to Smallways' stare, " and lie down decent."

Bert sat up and rubbed his eyes.

" Any more fightin' yet ? " he asked.

" No," said Kurt, and sat down, a tired man.

" Gott ! " he cried presently, rubbing his hands over his face, " but I'd like a cold bath ! I've been looking for stray bullet holes in the air-chambers all night until now." He yawned. " I must sleep. You'd better clear out, Smallways. I can't stand you here this morning. You're so infernally ugly and useless. Have you had your rations ? No ! Well, go in and get 'em, and don't come back. Stick in the gallery." . . .

§ 5

So Bert, slightly refreshed by coffee and sleep, resumed his helpless co-operation in the War in the Air. He went down into the little gallery as the lieutenant had directed, and clung to the rail at the extreme end beyond the lookout man, trying to seem as inconspicuous and harmless a fragment of life as possible.

A wind was rising rather strongly from the south-east. It obliged the *Vaterland* to come about in that direction, and made her roll a great deal as she went to and fro over Manhattan Island. Away in the north-west clouds gathered. The throb, throb of her slow screw working against the breeze was much more perceptible than when she was going full speed ahead ; and the friction of the wind against the underside of the gas-chamber drove a series of shallow ripples along it and made a faint, flapping sound like, but fainter than, the beating of ripples under the stem of a boat. She was stationed over the temporary City Hall in the Park Row building, and every now and then she would descend to resume communication with the mayor and with Washington. But the restlessness of the Prince would not suffer him to remain for long in any one place. Now he would circle over the Hudson and East River ; now he would go up high, as if to peer away into the blue distances ; once he ascended so swiftly and so far that mountain sickness overtook him and the crew and forced him down again ; and Bert shared the dizziness and nausea.

The swaying view varied with these changes of altitude. Now they would be low and close, and he would distinguish in that steep, unusual perspective, windows, doors, street and sky signs, people and the minutest details, and watch the enigmatical behaviour of crowds and clusters upon the roofs and in the streets ; then as they soared, the details would shrink, the sides of streets draw together, the view widen, the people cease to be significant. At the highest the effect was that of a concave relief map ; Bert saw the dark and crowded land everywhere intersected by shining waters, saw the Hudson River like a spear of silver, and Lower Island Sound like a shield. Even to Bert's unphilosophical mind the contrast of city below and fleet above pointed an opposition, the opposition of the adventurous American's tradition and character with German order and discipline. Below, the immense buildings, tremendous and fine as they were, seemed like the giant trees of a jungle fighting for life ; their picturesque magnificence was as planless as the chances of crag and gorge, their casualty enhanced by the smoke and confusion of still unsubdued and spreading conflagrations. In the sky soared the German airships like beings in a different, entirely more orderly world, all oriented to the same angle of the horizon, uniform in build and appearance, moving accurately with one purpose as a pack of wolves will move, distributed with the most precise and effectual co-operation.

It dawned upon Bert that hardly a third of the fleet was visible. The others had gone upon errands he could not imagine, beyond the compass of that great circle of earth and sky. He wondered, but there was no one to ask. As the day wore on, about a dozen reappeared in the east with their stores replenished from the flotilla and towing a number of drachenflieger. Towards afternoon the weather thickened, driving clouds appeared in the south-west and ran together and seemed to engender more clouds, and the wind came round into that quarter and blew stronger. Towards the evening the wind became a gale into which the now tossing airships had to beat.

All that day the Prince was negotiating with Washington, while his detached scouts sought far and wide over the Eastern States for anything resembling an aeronautic park. A squadron of twenty airships detached overnight had dropped out of the air upon Niagara and was holding the town and power works.

Meanwhile the insurrectionary movement in the giant city grew uncontrollable. In spite of five great fires, already involving many acres, and spreading steadily, New York was still not satisfied that she was beaten.

At first the rebellious spirit below found vent only in isolated shouts, street-crowd speeches, and newspaper suggestions ; then it found much more definite expression in the appearance in the morning sunlight of American flags at point after point above the architectural cliffs of the city. It is quite possible that in many cases this spirited display of bunting by a city already surrendered was the outcome of the innocent informality of the American mind, but it is also undeniable that in many it was a deliberate indication that the people " felt wicked."

The German sense of correctitude was deeply shocked by this outbreak. The Graf von Winterfeld immediately communicated with the mayor, and pointed out the irregularity, and the fire look-out stations were instructed in the matter. The New York police was speedily hard at work, and a foolish contest in full swing between impassioned citizens resolved to keep the flag flying, and irritated and worried officers instructed to pull it down.

The trouble became acute at last in the streets above Columbia University. The captain of the airship watching this quarter seems to have stooped to lasso and drag from its staff a flag hoisted upon Morgan Hall. As he did so a volley of rifle and revolver shots was fired from the upper windows of the huge apartment building that stands between the University and Riverside Drive.

Most of these were ineffectual, but two or three perforated gas-chambers, and one smashed the hand and arm of a man upon the forward platform. The sentinel on the lower gallery immediately replied, and the machine gun on the shield of the eagle let fly and promptly stopped any further shots. The airship rose and signalled the flagship and City Hall, police and militiamen were directed at once to the spot, and this particular incident closed.

But hard upon that came the desperate attempt of a party of young clubmen from New York who, inspired by patriotic and adventurous imaginations, slipped off in half a dozen motor-cars to Beacon Hill, and set to work with remarkable vigour to improvise a fort about the Doan swivel gun that had been placed there. They found it still in the hands of the disgusted gunners, who had been ordered to cease fire at the capitulation, and it was easy to infect these men with their own spirit. They declared their gun hadn't had half a chance, and were burning to show what it could do. Directed by the new-comers, they made a trench and bank about the mounting of the piece, and constructed flimsy shelter-pits of corrugated iron.

They were actually loading the gun when they were observed by the airship *Preussen*, and the shell they succeeded in firing

before the bombs of the latter smashed them and their crude
defences to fragments, burst over the middle gas-chambers
of the *Bingen*, and brought her to earth, disabled, upon
Staten Island. She was badly deflated, and dropped among
trees, over which her empty central gas-bags spread in canopies
and festoons. Nothing, however, had caught fire, and her
men were speedily at work upon her repair. They behaved
with a confidence that verged upon indiscretion. While most
of them commenced patching the tears of the membrane,
half a dozen of them started off for the nearest road in search
of a gas main, and presently found themselves prisoners in
the hands of a hostile crowd. Close at hand was a number
of villa residences, whose occupants speedily developed from
an unfriendly curiosity to aggression. At that time the police
control of the large polyglot population of Staten Island had
become very lax, and scarcely a household but had its rifle
or pistols and ammunition. These were presently produced,
and after two or three misses one of the men at work was
hit in the foot. Thereupon the Germans left their sewing
and mending, took cover among the trees, and replied.

The crackling of shots speedily brought the *Preussen* and
Kiel on the scene, and with a few hand grenades they made
short work of every villa within a mile. A number of non-
combatant American men, women, and children were killed
and the actual assailants driven off. For a time the repairs
went on in peace under the immediate protection of these
two airships. Then when they returned to their quarters
an intermittent sniping and fighting round the stranded
Bingen was resumed, and went on all the afternoon, and
merged at last in the general combat of the evening. . . .

About eight the *Bingen* was rushed by an armed mob, and
all its defenders killed after a fierce, disorderly struggle.

The difficulty of the Germans in both these cases came
from the impossibility of landing any efficient force or, indeed,
any force at all from the air-fleet. The airships were quite
unequal to the transport of any adequate landing parties ;
their complement of men was just sufficient to manœuvre
and fight them in the air. From above they could inflict
immense damage ; they could reduce any organised Government to a capitulation in the briefest space, but they could
not disarm, much less could they occupy, the surrendered
areas below. They had to trust to the pressure upon the
authorities below of a threat to renew the bombardment.
It was their sole resource. No doubt, with a highly organised
and undamaged Government and a homogeneous and well-
disciplined people that would have sufficed to keep the peace.
But this was not the American case. Not only was the New
York Government a weak one and insufficiently provided
with police, but the destruction of the City Hall and Post-
Office and other central ganglia had hopelessly disorganised

the co-operation of part with part. The street cars and rail-ways had ceased ; the telephone service was out of gear and only worked intermittently. The Germans had struck at the head, and the head was conquered and stunned—only to release the body from its rule. New York had become a headless monster, no longer capable of collective submission. Everywhere it lifted itself rebelliously ; everywhere authorities and officials, left to their own initiative, were joining in the arming and flag-hoisting and excitement of that afternoon.

§ 6

The disintegrating truce gave place to a definite general breach with the assassination of the *Wetterhorn*—for that is the only possible word for the act—above Union Square, and not a mile away from the exemplary ruins of City Hall. This occurred late in the afternoon, between five and six. By that time the weather had changed very much for the worse, and the operations of the airships were embarrassed by the necessity they were under of keeping head-on to the gusts. A series of squalls, with hail and thunder, followed one another from the south by south-east, and in order to avoid these as much as possible, the air-fleet came low over the houses, diminishing its range of observation and exposing itself to a rifle attack.

Overnight there had been a gun placed in Union Square. It had never been mounted, much less fired, and in the dark-ness after the surrender it was taken with its supplies and put out of the way under the arches of the great Dexter building. Here late in the morning it was remarked by a number of patriotic spirits. They set to work to hoist and mount it inside the upper floors of the place. They made, in fact, a masked battery behind the decorous office blinds, and there lay in wait as simply excited as children, until at last the stem of the luckless *Wetterhorn* appeared, beating and rolling at quarter speed over the recently reconstructed pinnacles of Tiffany's. Promptly that one-gun battery un-masked. The airship's look-out man must have seen the whole of the tenth story of the Dexter building crumble out and smash in the street below to discover the black muzzle looking out from the shadows behind. Then, perhaps, the shell hit him.

The gun fired two shells before the frame of the Dexter building collapsed, and each shell raked the *Wetterhorn* from stem to stern. They smashed her exhaustively. She crumpled up like a can that has been kicked by a heavy boot, her fore-part came down in the square, and the rest of her length, with a great snapping and twisting of shafts and stays, de-scended, collapsing athwart Tammany Hall and the streets towards Second Avenue. Her gas escaped to mix with air, and the air of her rent balloonette poured into her deflating gas-chambers. Then with an immense impact she exploded. . . .

The *Vaterland* at that time was beating up to the south of City Hall from over the ruins of the Brooklyn Bridge, and the reports of the gun, followed by the first crashes of the collapsing Dexter Buildings, brought Kurt and Smallways to the cabin porthole. They were in time to see the flash of the exploding gun, and then they were first flattened against the window and then rolled head over heels across the floor of the cabin by the air wave of the explosion. The *Vaterland* bounded like a football some one has kicked, and when they looked out again Union Square was small and remote and shattered, as though some cosmically vast giant had rolled over it. The buildings to the east of it were ablaze at a dozen points, under the flaming tatters and warping skeleton of the airship, and all the roofs and walls were ridiculously askew and crumbling as one looked. " Gaw ! " said Bert. " What's happened ? Look at the people ! "

But before Kurt could produce an explanation, the shrill bells of the airship were ringing to quarters, and he had to go. Bert hesitated and stepped thoughtfully into the passage, looking back at the window as he did so. He was knocked off his feet at once by the Prince, who was rushing headlong from his cabin to the central magazine.

Bert had a momentary impression of the great figure of the Prince, white with rage, bristling with gigantic anger, his huge fist swinging. " Blut und Eisen ! " cried the Prince, as one who swears. " Oh ! Blut und Eisen ! "

Some one fell over Bert—something in the manner of falling suggested von Winterfeld—and some one else paused and kicked him spitefully and hard. Then he was sitting up in the passage, rubbing a freshly bruised cheek and readjusting the bandage he still wore on his head. " Dem that Prince," said Bert, indignant beyond measure. " 'E 'asn't the menners of a 'og ! "

He stood up, collected his wits for a minute, and then went slowly towards the gangway of the little gallery. As he did so he heard noises suggestive of the return of the Prince. The lot of them were coming back again. He shot into his cabin like a rabbit into its burrow, just in time to escape that shouting terror.

He shut the door, waited until the passage was still, then went across to the window and looked out. A drift of cloud made the prospect of the streets and squares hazy, and the rolling of the airship swung the picture up and down. A few people were running to and fro, but for the most part the aspect of the district was desertion. The streets seemed to broaden out, they became clearer, and the little dots that were people larger as the *Vaterland* came down again. Presently she was swaying along above the lower end of Broadway. The dots below, Bert saw, were not running now, but standing and looking up. Then suddenly they were all running again.

Something had dropped from the aeroplane, something that looked small and flimsy. It hit the pavement near a big archway just underneath Bert. A little man was sprinting along the sidewalk within half a dozen yards, and two or three others and one woman were bolting across the roadway. They were odd little figures, so very small were they about the heads, so very active about the elbows and legs. It was really funny to see their legs going. Fore-shortened humanity has no dignity. The little man on the pavement jumped comically—no doubt with terror—as the bomb fell beside him.

Then blinding flames squirted out in all directions from the point of impact, and the little man who had jumped became, for an instant, a flash of fire and vanished—vanished absolutely. The people running out into the road took preposterous clumsy leaps, then flopped down and lay still, with their torn clothes smouldering into flame. Then pieces of the archway began to drop, and the lower masonry of the building to fall in with the rumbling sound of coals being shot into a cellar. A faint screaming reached Bert, and then a crowd of people ran out into the street, one man limping and gesticulating awkwardly. He halted, and went back towards the building. A falling mass of brickwork hit him and sent him sprawling to lie still and crumpled where he fell. Dust and black smoke came pouring into the street, and were presently shot with red flame. . . .

In this manner the massacre of New York began. She was the first of the great cities of the Scientific Age to suffer by the enormous powers and grotesque limitations of aerial warfare. She was wrecked as in the previous century endless barbaric cities had been bombarded, because she was at once too strong to be occupied, and too undisciplined and proud to surrender in order to escape destruction. Given the circumstances the thing had to be done. It was impossible for the Prince to desist and own himself defeated, and it was impossible to subdue the city except by largely destroying it. The catastrophe was the logical outcome of the situation created by the application of science to warfare. It was unavoidable that great cities should be destroyed. In spite of his intense exasperation with his dilemma, the Prince sought to be moderate even in massacre. He tried to give a memorable lesson with the minimum waste of life and the minimum expenditure of explosives. For that night he proposed only the wrecking of Broadway. He directed the air-fleet to move in column over the route of this thoroughfare, dropping bombs, the *Vaterland* leading. And so our Bert Smallways became a participant in one of the most cold-blooded slaughters in the world's history, in which men who were neither excited nor, except for the remotest chance of a bullet, in any danger, poured death and destruction upon homes and crowds below.

He clung to the frame of the porthole as the airship tossed and swayed, and stared down through the light rain that now drove before the wind, into the twilight streets, watching people running out of the houses, watching buildings collapse and fires begin. As the airships sailed along they smashed up the city as a child will shatter its cities of brick and card. Below, they left ruins and blazing conflagrations and heaped and scattered dead ; men, women, and children mixed together as though they had been no more than Moors, or Zulus, or Chinese. Lower New York was soon a furnace of crimson flames, from which there was no escape. Cars, railways, ferries, all had ceased, and never a light led the way of the distracted fugitives in that dusky confusion but the light of burning. He had glimpses of what it must mean to be down there—glimpses. And it came to him suddenly as an incredible dis-covery, that such disasters were not only possible now in this strange, gigantic, foreign New York, but also in London—in Bun Hill ! that the little island in the silver seas was at the end of its immunity, that nowhere in the world any more was there a place left where a Smallways might lift his head proudly and vote for war and a spirited foreign policy, and go secure from such horrible things.

CHAPTER SEVEN

THE " VATERLAND " IS DISABLED

§ 1

AND then above the flames of Manhattan Island came a battle, the first battle in the air. The Americans had realised the price their waiting game must cost, and struck with all the strength they had, if haply they might still save New York from this mad Prince of Blood and Iron, and from fire and death.

They came down upon the Germans on the wings of a great gale in the twilight, amidst thunder and rain. They came from the yards of Washington and Philadelphia, full tilt in two squadrons, and but for one sentinel airship hard by Tren-ton, the surprise would have been complete.

The Germans, sick and weary with destruction, and half empty of ammunition, were facing up into the weather when the news of this onset reached them. New York they had left behind to the south-eastward, a darkened city with one hideous red scar of flames. All the airships rolled and staggered, bursts of hail-storm bore them down and forced them to fight their way up again ; the air had become bitterly cold. The Prince was on the point of issuing orders to drop earthward and trail copper lightning chains when the news of the aero-plane attack came to him. He faced his fleet in line abreast south, had the drachenflieger manned and held ready to cast loose, and ordered a general ascent into the freezing clearness above the wet and darkness.

The news of what was imminent came slowly to Bert's perceptions. He was standing in the mess-room at the time, and the evening rations were being served out. He had resumed Butteridge's coat and gloves, and, in addition, he had wrapped his blanket about him. He was dipping his bread into his soup and biting off big mouthfuls. His legs were wide apart, and he leant against the partition in order to steady himself amidst the pitching and oscillation of the airship. The men about him looked tired and depressed ; a few talked, but most were sullen and thoughtful, and one or two were air-sick. They all seemed to share the peculiarly outcast feeling that had followed the murders of the evening, a sense of a land beneath them and an outraged humanity grown more hostile than the sea.

Then the news lit them. A red-faced, sturdy man, a man with light eyelashes and a scar, appeared in the doorway and shouted something in German that manifestly startled every one. Bert felt the shock of the altered tone though he could not understand a word that was said. The announcement was followed by a pause, and then a great outcry of questions and suggestions. Even the air-sick men flushed and spoke. For some minutes the mess-room was Bedlam, and then, as if it were a confirmation of the news, came the shrill ringing of the bells that called the men to their posts.

Bert, with pantomime suddenness, found himself alone.

" What's up ? " he said, though he partly guessed.

He stayed only to gulp down the remainder of his soup and then ran along the swaying passage and, clutching tightly, down the ladder to the little gallery. The weather hit him like cold water squirted from a hose. The airship engaged in some new feat of atmospheric Jiu-Jitsu. He drew his blanket closer about him, clutching with one straining hand. He found himself tossing in a wet twilight, with nothing to be seen but mist pouring past him. Above him the airship was warm with lights and busy with the movements of men going to their quarters. Then abruptly the lights went out, and the *Vaterland* with bounds and twists and strange writhings was fighting her way up the air.

He had a glimpse, as the *Vaterland* rolled over, of some large buildings burning close below them, a quivering acanthus of flames, and then he saw indistinctly through the driving weather another airship wallowing along like a porpoise, and also working up. Presently the clouds swallowed her again for a time, and then she came back to sight as a dark and whale-like monster, amidst streaming weather. The air was full of flappings and pipings, of void, gusty shouts and noises ; it buffeted him and confused him ; ever and again his atten-

tion became rigid—a blind and deaf balancing and clutching.
" Wow ! "

Something fell past him out of the vast darknesses above
and vanished into the tumults below, going obliquely downward. It was a German drachenflieger. The thing was going
so fast he had but an instant apprehension of the dark figure
of the aeronaut crouched together clutching at his wheel.
It might be a manœuvre, but it looked like a catastrophe.

" Gaw ! " said Bert.

" Pup-pup-pup," went a gun somewhere in the mirk ahead,
and suddenly and quite horribly the *Vaterland* lurched, and
Bert and the sentinel were clinging to the rail for dear life.
" Bang ! " came a vast impact out of the zenith, followed by
another huge roll, and all about him the tumbled clouds
flashed red and lurid in response to flashes unseen, revealing
immense gulfs. The rail went right overhead, and he was
hanging loose in the air holding on to it.

For a time Bert's whole mind and being was given to clutching. " I'm going into the cabin," he said, as the airship righted
again and brought back the gallery floor to his feet. He began
to make his way cautiously towards the ladder. " Whee-wow ! "
he cried, as the whole gallery reared itself up forward and then
plunged down like a desperate horse.

Crack ! Bang ! Bang ! Bang ! And then hard upon this
little rattle of shots and bombs came, all about him, enveloping
him, engulfing him, immense and overwhelming, a quivering
white blaze of lightning and a thunder-clap that was like the
bursting of a world.

Just for the instant before that explosion, the universe
seemed to be standing still in a shadowless glare.

It was then he saw the American aeroplane. He saw it in
the light of the flash as a thing altogether motionless. Even
its screw appeared still, and its men were rigid dolls. (For
it was so near he could see the men upon it quite distinctly.)
Its stern was tilting down and the whole machine was heeling
over. It was of the Colt-Coburn-Langley pattern, with double
uptilted wings and the screw ahead, and the men were in a
boat-like body netted over. From this very light long body,
magazine guns projected on either side. One thing that was
strikingly odd and wonderful in that moment of revelation
was that the left upper wing was burning *downward* with a
reddish, smoky flame. But this was not the most wonderful
thing about this apparition. The most wonderful thing was
that it and a German airship five hundred yards below were
threaded, as it were, on the lightning flash, which turned out
of its path as if to take them, and that out from the corners
and projecting points of its huge wings everywhere, little
branching thorn-trees of lightning were streaming.

Like a picture Bert saw these things, a picture a little blurred
by a thin veil of wind-torn mist.

The crash of the thunder-clap followed the flash and seemed a part of it, so that it is hard to say whether Bert was the rather deafened or blinded in that instant.

And then darkness, utter darkness, and a heavy report and a thin, small sound of voices that went wailing downward into the abyss below.

§ 2

There followed upon these things a long, deep swaying of the airship, and then Bert began a struggle to get back to his cabin. He was drenched and cold and terrified beyond measure, and now more than a little air-sick. It seemed to him that the strength had gone out of his knees and hands, and that his feet had become icily slippery over the metal they trod upon. But that was because a thin film of ice had frozen upon the gallery.

He never knew how long his ascent of the ladder back into the airship took him, but in his dreams afterwards, when he recalled it, that experience seemed to last for hours. Below, above, around him were gulfs, monstrous gulfs of howling wind and eddies of dark, whirling snowflakes, and he was protected from it all by a little metal grating and a rail, a grating and rail that seemed madly infuriated with him, passionately eager to wrench him off and toss him into the tumult of space.

Once he had a fancy that a bullet tore by his ear, and that the clouds and snowflakes were lit by a flash, but he never even turned his head to see what new assailant whirled past them in the void. He wanted to get into the passage ! He wanted to get into the passage ! He wanted to get into the passage ! Would the arm by which he was clinging hold out, or would it give way and snap ? A handful of hail smacked him in the face, so that for a time he was breathless and nearly insensible. Hold tight, Bert ! He renewed his efforts.

He found himself, with an enormous sense of relief and warmth, in the passage. The passage was behaving like a dice-box, its disposition was evidently to rattle him about and then throw him out again. He hung on with the convulsive clutch of instinct until the passage lurched down ahead. Then he would make a short run cabin-ward, and clutch again as the fore-end rose.

Behold ! He was in the cabin !

He snapped to the door, and for a time he was not a human being, he was a case of air-sickness. He wanted to get somewhere that would fix him, that he needn't clutch. He opened the locker and got inside among the loose articles, and sprawled there helplessly, with his head sometimes bumping one side and sometimes the other. The lid shut upon him with a click. He did not care then what was happening any more. He did not care who fought who, or what bullets were fired or explosions occurred. He did not care if presently he was shot or smashed to pieces. He was full of feeble, inarticulate rage and despair. "Foolery!" he said, his one exhaustive comment on human enterprise, adventure, war, and the chapter of accidents that had entangled him. "Foolery! Ugh!" He included the order of the universe in that comprehensive condemnation. He wished he was dead.

He saw nothing of the stars as presently the *Vaterland* cleared the rush and confusion of the lower weather, nor of the duel she fought with two circling aeroplanes, how they shot her rearmost chambers through, and how she fought them off with explosive bullets, and turned to run as she did so.

The rush and swoop of these wonderful night-birds was all lost upon him; their heroic dash and self-sacrifice. The *Vaterland* was rammed, and for some moments she hung on the verge of destruction, and sinking swiftly, with the American aeroplane entangled with her smashed propeller, and the Americans trying to scramble aboard. It signified nothing to Bert. To him it conveyed itself simply as vehement swaying. Foolery! When the American airship dropped off at last, with most of its crew shot or fallen, Bert in his locker appreciated nothing but that the *Vaterland* had taken a hideous upward leap.

But then came infinite relief, incredibly blissful relief. The rolling, the pitching, the struggle ceased, ceased instantly and absolutely. The *Vaterland* was no longer fighting the gale; her smashed and exploded engines throbbed no more; she was disabled and driving before the wind as smoothly as a balloon, a huge, wind-spread, tattered cloud of aerial wreckage.

To Bert it was no more than the end of a series of disagreeable sensations. He was not curious to know what had happened to the airship, nor what had happened to the battle. For a long time he lay waiting apprehensively for the pitching and tossing and his qualms to return, and so lying, boxed up in the locker, he presently fell asleep.

§ 3

He awoke tranquil but very stuffy, and at the same time very cold, and quite unable to recollect where he could be. His head ached, and his breath was suffocated. He had been dreaming confusedly of Edna, and Desert Dervishes, and of riding bicycles in an extremely perilous manner through the upper air amidst a pyrotechnic display of crackers and Bengal lights—to the great annoyance of a sort of composite person made up of the Prince and Mr. Butteridge. Then for some reason Edna and he had begun to cry pitifully for each other, and he woke up with wet eyelashes into this ill-ventilated darkness of the locker. He would never see Edna any more, never see Edna any more.

He thought he must be back in the bedroom behind the cycle shop at the bottom of Bun Hill, and he was sure the vision he had had of the destruction of a magnificent city, a city quite incredibly great and splendid, by means of bombs, was no more than a particularly vivid dream.

" Grubb ! " he called, anxious to tell him.

The answering silence, and the dull resonance of the locker to his voice, supplementing the stifling quality of the air, set going a new train of ideas. He lifted up his hands and feet, and met an inflexible resistance. He was in a coffin, he thought ! He had been buried alive ! He gave way at once to wild panic. " 'Elp ! " he screamed. " 'Elp ! " and drummed with his feet, and kicked and struggled. " Let me out ! Let me out ! "

For some seconds he struggled with this intolerable horror, and then the side of his imagined coffin gave way, and he was flying out into daylight. Then he was rolling about on what seemed to be a padded floor with Kurt, and being punched and sworn at lustily.

He sat up. His head bandage had become loose and got over one eye, and he whipped the whole thing off. Kurt was also sitting up, a yard away from him, pink as ever, wrapped in blankets, and with an aluminium diver's helmet over his knee, staring at him with a severe expression, and rubbing his downy, unshaven chin. They were both on a slanting floor of crimson padding, and above them was an opening like a long, low cellar flap that Bert by an effort perceived to be the cabin door in a half-inverted condition. The whole cabin had in fact turned on its side.

" What the deuce do you mean by it, Smallways ? " said Kurt, " jumping out of that locker when I was certain you had gone overboard with the rest of them ? Where have you been ? "

" What's up ? " asked Bert.

" This end of the airship is up. Most other things are down."

" Was there a battle ? "

" There was."

" Who won ? "

" I haven't seen the papers, Smallways. We left before the finish. We got disabled and unmanageable, and our colleagues—consorts, I mean—were too busy most of them to trouble about us, and the wind blew us—Heaven knows where the wind *is* blowing us. It blew us right out of action at the rate of eighty miles an hour or so. Gott ! what a wind that was ! What a fight ! And here we are ! "

" Where ? "

" In the air, Smallways—in the air ! When we get down on the earth again we shan't know what to do with our legs."

" But what's below us ? "

"Canada, to the best of my knowledge—and a jolly, bleak, empty, inhospitable country it looks."

"But why ain't we right ways up?"

Kurt made no answer for a space.

"Last I remember was seeing a sort of flying-machine in a lightning flash," said Bert. "Gaw! that was 'orrible. Guns going off! Things explodin'! Clouds and 'ail. Pitching and tossing. I got so scared and desperate—and sick. . . . You don't know how the fight came off?"

"Not a bit of it. I was up with my squad in those divers' dresses, inside the gas-chambers, with sheets of silk for caulking. We couldn't see a thing outside except the lightning flashes. I never saw one of those American aeroplanes. Just saw the shots flicker through the chambers and sent off men for the tears. We caught fire a bit—not much, you know. We were too wet, so the fires spluttered out before we banged. And then one of their infernal things dropped out of the air on us and rammed. Didn't you feel it?"

"I felt everything," said Bert. "I didn't notice any particular smash——"

"They must have been pretty desperate if they meant it. They slashed down on us like a knife; simply ripped the after gas-chambers like gutting herrings; crumpled up the engines and screw. Most of the engines dropped out as they fell off us, or we'd have grounded—but the rest is sort of dangling. We just turned up our nose to the heavens and stayed there. Eleven men rolled off us from various points, and poor old Winterfeld fell through the door of the Prince's cabin into the chart-room and broke his ankle. Also we got our electric gear shot or carried away—no one knows how. That's the position, Smallways. We're driving through the air like a common aerostat, at the mercy of the elements, almost due north—probably to the North Pole. We don't know what aeroplanes the Americans have, or anything at all about it. Very likely we have finished 'em up. One fouled us, one was struck by lightning, some of the men saw a third upset, apparently just for fun. They were going cheap anyhow. Also we've lost most of our drachenflieger. They just skated off into the night. No stability in 'em. That's all. We don't know if we've won or lost. We don't know if we're at war with the British Empire yet or at peace. Consequently we daren't get down. We don't know what we are up to or what we are going to do. Our Napoleon is alone, forward, and I suppose he's rearranging his plans. Whether New York was our Moscow or not remains to be seen. We've had a high old time and murdered no end of people! War! Noble war! I'm sick of it this morning. I like sitting in rooms right way up and not on slippery partitions. I'm a civilised man. I keep thinking of old Albrecht and the *Barbarossa* . . . I feel I want a wash and kind words and a quiet home. When I look at you,

I *know* I want a wash. Gott ! ''—he stifled a vehement yawn—
" What a Cockney tadpole of a ruffian you look ! "

" Can we get any grub ? " asked Bert.

" Heaven knows ! " said Kurt.

He meditated upon Bert for a time. " So far as I can judge,
Smallways," he said, " the Prince will probably want to throw
you overboard—next time he thinks of you. He certainly
will if he sees you. . . . After all, you know, you came *als
Ballast.* . . . And we shall have to lighten ship extensively
pretty soon. Unless I'm mistaken, the Prince will wake up
presently and start doing things with tremendous vigour. . . .
I've taken a fancy to you. It's the English strain in me. You're
a rum little chap. I shan't like seeing you whizz down the air.
. . . You'd better make yourself useful, Smallways. I think
I shall requisition you for my squad. You'll have to work,
you know, and be infernally intelligent, and all that. And
you'll have to hang about upside down a bit. Still, it's the
best chance you have. We shan't carry passengers much
farther this trip, I fancy. Ballast goes overboard—if we don't
want to ground precious soon and be taken prisoners of war.
The Prince won't do that anyhow. He'll be game to the last."

§ 4

By means of a folding chair, which was still in its place
behind the door, they got to the window and looked out in
turn and contemplated a sparsely wooded country below, with
no railways nor roads, and only occasional signs of habitation.
Then a bugle sounded, and Kurt interpreted it as a summons
to food. They got through the door and clambered with some
difficulty up the nearly vertical passage, holding on desperately
with toes and finger-tips to the ventilating perforations in
its floor. The mess stewards had found their fireless heating
arrangements intact, and there was hot cocoa for the officers
and hot soup for the men.

Bert's sense of the queerness of his experience was so keen
that it blotted out any fear he might have felt. Indeed, he
was far more interested now than afraid. He seemed to have
touched down to the bottom of fear and abandonment overnight. He was growing accustomed to the idea that he would
probably be killed presently, that this strange voyage in the
air was in all probability his death journey. No human being
can keep permanently afraid : fear goes at last to the back
of one's mind, accepted, and shelved, and done with. He
squatted over his soup, sopping it up with his bread, and
contemplated his comrades. They were all rather yellow and
dirty with four-day beards, and they grouped themselves in
the tired, unpremeditated manner of men on a wreck. They
talked little. The situation perplexed them beyond any suggestion of ideas. Three had been hurt in the pitching up of the
ship during the fight, and one had a bandaged bullet wound.

It was incredible that this little band of men had committed murder and massacre on a scale beyond precedent. None of them who squatted on the sloping, gas-padded partition, soup mug in hand, seemed really guilty of anything of the sort, seemed really capable of hurting a dog wantonly. They were all so manifestly built for homely chalets on the solid earth and carefully tilled fields and blond wives and cheery merry-making. The red-faced, sturdy man with light eyelashes who had brought the first news of the air battle to the men's mess had finished his soup, and with an expression of maternal solicitude was readjusting the bandages of a youngster whose arm had been sprained.

Bert was crumbling the last of his bread into the last of his soup, eking it out as long as possible, when suddenly he became aware that every one was looking at a pair of feet that were dangling across the down-turned open doorway. Kurt appeared and squatted across the hinge. In some mysterious way he had shaved his face and smoothed down his light golden hair. He looked extraordinarily cherubic. " Der Prinz," he said.

A second pair of boots followed, making wide and magnificent gestures in their attempts to feel the door frame. Kurt guided them to a foothold, and the Prince, shaved and brushed and beeswaxed and clean and big and terrible, slid down into position astride of the door. All the men and Bert also stood up and saluted.

The Prince surveyed them with the gesture of a man who sits a steed. The head of the Kapitän appeared beside him.

Then Bert had a terrible moment. The blue blaze of the Prince's eye fell upon him, the great finger pointed, a question was asked. Kurt intervened with explanations.

" So," said the Prince, and Bert was disposed of.

Then the Prince addressed the men in short, heroic sentences, steadying himself on the hinge with one hand and waving the other in a fine variety of gesture. What he said Bert could not tell, but he perceived that their demeanour changed, their backs stiffened. They began to punctuate the Prince's discourse with cries of approval. At the end their leader burst into song and all the men with him, " Ein feste Burg ist unser Gott," they chanted on deep, strong tones, with an immense moral uplifting. It was glaringly inappropriate in a damaged, half-overturned and sinking airship, which had been disabled and blown out of action after inflicting the cruellest bombardment in the world's history ; but it was immensely stirring nevertheless. Bert was deeply moved. He could not sing any of the words of Luther's great hymn, but he opened his mouth and emitted loud, deep, and partially harmonious notes. . . .

Far below, this deep chanting struck on the ears of a little camp of christianised half-breeds who were lumbering. They

were breakfasting, but they rushed out cheerfully quite prepared for the Second Advent. They stared at the shattered
and twisted *Vaterland*, driving before the gale, amazed beyond
words. In so many respects it was like their idea of the Second
Advent, and then again in so many respects it wasn't. They
stared at its passage, awestricken and perplexed beyond their
power of words. The hymn ceased. Then after a long interval
a voice came out of heaven. " Vat id diss blace here galled
itself ; vat ? "

They made no answer. Indeed, they did not understand,
though the question was repeated.

And at last the monster drove away northward over a crest
of pine woods and was no more seen. They fell into a hot and
long disputation. . . .

The hymn ended. The Prince's legs dangled up the passage
again, and everyone was briskly prepared for heroic exertion
and triumphant acts. " Smallways ! " cried Kurt, " come
here ! "

§ 5

Then Bert, under Kurt's direction, had his first experience
of the work of an air-sailor.

The immediate task before the captain of the *Vaterland*
was a very simple one. He had to keep afloat. The wind,
though it had fallen from its earlier violence, was still blowing
strongly enough to render the grounding of so clumsy a mass
extremely dangerous, even if it had been desirable for the
Prince to land in inhabited country, and so risk capture. It
was necessary to keep the airship up until the wind fell and
then, if possible, to descend in some lonely district of the
Territory where there would be a chance of repair or rescue by
some searching consort. In order to do this weight had to be
dropped, and Kurt was detailed with a dozen men to climb
down among the wreckage of the deflated air-chambers, and
cut the stuff clear, portion by portion, as the airship sank.
So Bert, armed with a sharp cutlass, found himself clambering
about upon netting four thousand feet up in the air, trying to
understand Kurt when he spoke in English and to divine him
when he used German.

It was giddy work, but not nearly so giddy as a rather over-
nourished reader sitting in a warm room might imagine. Bert
found it quite possible to look down and contemplate the
wild sub-arctic landscape below, now devoid of any sign of
habitation, a land of rocky cliffs and cascades and broad
swirling desolate rivers, and of trees and thickets that grew
more stunted and scrubby as the day wore on. Here and
there on the hills were patches and pockets of snow. And
over all this he worked, hacking away at the tough and slippery
oiled silk and clinging stoutly to the netting. Presently they
cleared and dropped a tangle of bent steel rods and wires from

the frame, and a big chunk of silk bladder.   That was trying.
The airship flew up at once as this loose hamper parted.   It
seemed almost as though they were dropping all Canada.   The
stuff spread out in the air and floated down and hit and twisted
up in a nasty fashion on the lip of a gorge.   Bert clung like a
frozen monkey to his ropes, and did not move a muscle for
five minutes.

But there was something very exhilarating, he found, in
this dangerous work, and, above everything else, there was
the sense of fellowship.   He was no longer an isolated and
distrustful stranger among these others, he had now a common
object with them, he worked with a friendly rivalry to get
through with his share before them.   And he developed a great
respect and affection for Kurt, which had hitherto been only
latent in him.   Kurt with a job to direct was altogether admirable :   he was resourceful, helpful, considerate, swift.   He
seemed to be everywhere.   One forgot his pinkness, his light
cheerfulness of manner.   Directly one had trouble he was at
hand with sound and confident advice.   He was like an elder
brother to his men.

Altogether they cleared three considerable chunks of wreckage, and then Bert was glad to clamber up into the cabins
again and give place to a second squad.   He and his companions
were given hot coffee, and, indeed, even gloved as they were,
the job had been a cold one.   They sat drinking it and regarding each other with satisfaction.   One man spoke to Bert
amiably in German, and Bert nodded and smiled.   Through
Kurt, Bert, whose ankles were almost frozen, succeeded in
getting a pair of top-boots from one of the disabled men.

In the afternoon the wind abated greatly, and small infrequent snowflakes came drifting by.   Snow also spread more
abundantly below, and the only trees were clumps of pine and
spruce in the lower valleys.   Kurt went with three men into
the still intact gas-chambers, let out a certain quantity of gas
from them, and prepared a series of ripping panels for the
descent.   Also the residue of the bombs and explosives in the
magazine were thrown overboard and fell, detonating loudly
in the wilderness below.   And about four o'clock in the afternoon, upon a wide and rocky plain within sight of snow-
crested cliffs, the *Vaterland* ripped and grounded.

It was necessarily a difficult and violent affair, for the
Vaterland had not been planned for the necessities of a balloon.
The captain got one panel ripped too soon and the others not
soon enough.   She dropped heavily, bounced clumsily, and
smashed the hanging gallery into the forepart, mortally
injuring von Winterfeld, and then came down in a collapsing
heap after dragging for some moments.   The forward shield
and its machine gun tumbled in upon the things below.   Two
men were hurt badly—one got a broken leg and one was
internally injured—by flying rods and wires, and Bert was

pinned for a time under the side. When at last he got clear
and could take a view of the situation, the great black eagle
that had started so splendidly from Franconia six evenings
ago, sprawled deflated over the cabins of the airship and the
frost-bitten rocks of this desolate place and looked a most
unfortunate bird—as though some one had caught it and wrung
its neck and cast it aside. Several of the crew of the airship
were standing about in silence, contemplating the wreckage
and empty wilderness into which they had fallen. Others were
busy under the impromptu tent made by the empty gas-
chambers. The Prince had gone a little way off and was
scrutinising the distant heights through his field-glass. They
had the appearance of old sea cliffs ; here and there were
small clumps of conifers, and in two places tall cascades.
The nearer ground was strewn with glaciated boulders and
supported nothing but a stunted Alpine vegetation of compact
clustering stems and stalkless flowers. No river was visible,
but the air was full of the rush and babble of a torrent close
at hand. A bleak and biting wind was blowing. Ever and
again a snowflake drifted past. The springless, frozen earth
under Bert's feet felt strangely dead and heavy after the
buoyant airship.

§ 6

So it came about that that great and powerful Prince Karl
Albert was for a time thrust out of the stupendous conflict he
chiefly had been instrumental in provoking. The chances of
battle and the weather conspired to maroon him in Labrador,
and there he raged for six long days, while war and wonder
swept the world. Nation rose against nation and air-fleet
grappled air-fleet, cities blazed and men died in multitudes ;
but in Labrador one might have dreamt that, except for a little
noise of hammering, the world was at peace.

There the encampment lay ; from a distance the cabins,
covered over with the silk of the balloon part, looked like a gipsy's
tent on a rather exceptional scale, and all the available hands
were busy in building out of the steel of the framework a mast
from which the *Vaterland's* electricians might hang the long
conductors of the apparatus for wireless telegraphy that was
to link the Prince to the world again. There were times when
it seemed they would never rig that mast. From the onset
the party suffered hardship. They were not too abundantly
provisioned, and they were put on short rations, and for all
the thick garments they had, they were but ill-equipped against
the piercing wind and inhospitable violence of this wilderness.
The first night was spent in darkness and without fires. The
engines that had supplied power were smashed and dropped
far away to the south, and there was never a match among
the company. It had been death to carry matches. All the
explosives had been thrown out of the magazine, and it was

only towards morning that the bird-faced man whose cabin Bert had taken in the beginning confessed to a brace of duelling pistols and cartridges, with which a fire could be started. Afterwards the lockers of the machine gun were found to contain a supply of unused ammunition.

The night was a distressing one and seemed almost interminable. Hardly any one slept. There were seven wounded men aboard, and von Winterfeld's head had been injured and he was shivering and in delirium, struggling with his attendant and shouting strange things about the burning of New York. The men crept together in the mess room in the darkling, wrapped in what they could find, and drank cocoa from the fireless heaters and listened to his cries. In the morning the Prince made them a speech about Destiny, and the God of his Fathers, and the pleasure and glory of giving one's life for his dynasty, and a number of similar considerations that might otherwise have been neglected in that bleak wilderness. The men cheered without enthusiasm, and far away a wolf howled.

Then they set to work, and for a week they toiled to put up a mast of steel, and hang from it a gridiron of copper wires two hundred feet by twelve. The theme of all that time was work, work continually, straining and toilsome work, and all the rest was grim hardship and evil chances, save for a certain wild splendour in the sunset and sunrise, in the torrents and drifting weather, in the wilderness about them. They built and tended a ring of perpetual fires, gangs roamed for brushwood and met with wolves, and the wounded men and their beds were brought out from the airship cabins, and put in shelters about the fires. There old von Winterfeld raved and became quiet and presently died, and three of the other wounded sickened for want of good food, while their fellows mended. These things happened, as it were, in the wings; the central facts before Bert's consciousness were always firstly the perpetual toil, the holding and lifting, and lugging at heavy and clumsy masses, the tedious filing and winding of wires, and secondly, the Prince, urgent and threatening whenever a man relaxed. He would stand over them and point over their heads, southward into the empty sky. " The world there," he said in German, " is waiting for us ! Fifty centuries come to their Consummation." Bert did not understand the words, but he read the gesture. Several times the Prince grew angry ; once with a man who was working slowly, once with a man who stole a comrade's ration. The first he scolded and set to a more tedious task ; the second he struck in the face and ill-used. He did no work himself. There was a clear space near the fires, in which he would walk up and down, sometimes for hours together, with arms folded, muttering to himself of Patience and his destiny. At times these mutterings broke out into rhetoric, into shouts and gestures that would arrest the workers ; they would stare at him until they perceived that his blue eyes glared and his waving hand addressed itself always to the southward hills. On Sunday the work ceased for half an hour, and the Prince preached on faith and God's friendship for David, and afterwards they all sang : " Ein feste Burg ist unser Gott."

In an improvised hovel lay von Winterfeld, and all one morning he raved of the greatness of Germany. " Blut und Eisen ! " he shouted, and then, as if in derision, " Welt-Politik —ha, ha ! " Then he would explain complicated questions of policy to imaginary hearers, in low, wily tones. The other sick men kept still, listening to him. Bert's distracted attention would be recalled by Kurt. " Smallways, take that end. So ! "

Slowly, tediously, the great mast was rigged, and hoisted foot by foot into place. The electricians had contrived a catchment pool and a wheel in the torrent close at hand—for the little Mulhausen dynamo with its turbinal volute used by the telegraphists was quite adaptable to water driving, and on the sixth day in the evening the apparatus was in working order and the Prince was calling—weakly, indeed, but calling —to his air-fleet across the empty spaces of the world. For a time he called unheeded.

The effect of that evening was to linger long in Bert's memory. A red fire spluttered and blazed close by the electricians at their work, and red gleams ran up the vertical steel mast and threads of copper wire towards the zenith. The Prince sat on a rock close by, with his chin on his hand, waiting. Beyond and to the northward was the cairn that covered von Winterfeld, surmounted by a cross of steel, and from among the tumbled rocks in the distance the eyes of a wolf gleamed redly. On the other hand was the wreckage of the great airship and the men bivouacked about a second ruddy flare. They were all keeping very still, as if waiting to hear what news might presently be given them. Far away, across many hundreds of miles of desolation, other wireless masts would be clicking and snapping, and waking into responsive vibration. Perhaps they were not. Perhaps these throbs upon the ether wasted themselves upon a regardless world. When the men spoke, they spoke in low tones. Now and then a bird shrieked remotely, and once a wolf howled. All these things were set in the immense cold spaciousness of the wild.

§ 7

Bert got the news last, and chiefly in broken English, from a linguist among his mates. It was only far on in the night that the weary telegraphist got an answer to his calls, but then the messages came clear and strong. And such news it was !

" I say," said Bert at his breakfast, amidst a great clamour, " tell us a bit."

"All de vorlt is at vor!" said the linguist, waving his cocoa in an illustrative manner, "all de vorlt is at vor!"

Bert stared southward into the dawn. It did not seem so.

"All de vorlt is at vor! They haf burn' Berlin; they haf burn' London; they haf burn' Hamburg and Paris. Chapan hass burn' San Francisco. We haf mate a camp at Niagara. Dat is whad they are telling us. China has cot drachenflieger and luftschiffe beyont counting. All de vorlt is at vor!"

"Gaw!" said Bert.

"Yess," said the linguist, drinking his cocoa.

"Burnt up London, 'ave they? Like we did New York?"

"It wass a bombardment."

"They don't say anything about a place called Clapham, or Bun Hill, do they?"

"I haf heard noding," said the linguist.

That was all Bert could get for a time. But the excitement of all the men about him was contagious, and presently he saw Kurt standing alone, hands behind him, and looking at one of the distant waterfalls very steadfastly. He went up and saluted soldier-fashion. "Beg pardon, lieutenant," he said.

Kurt turned his face. It was unusually grave that morning. "I was just thinking I would like to see that waterfall closer," he said. "It reminds me—— What do you want?"

"I can't make 'ead or tail of what they're saying, sir. Would you mind telling me the news?"

"Damn the news," said Kurt. "You'll get news enough before the day's out. It's the end of the world. They're sending the *Graf Zeppelin* for us. She'll be here by the morning, and we ought to be at Niagara—or eternal smash—within eight and forty hours. . . . I want to look at that waterfall. You'd better come with me. Have you had your rations?"

"Yessir."

"Very well. Come."

And musing profoundly, Kurt led the way across the rocks towards the distant waterfall. For a time Bert walked behind him in the character of an escort; then as they passed out of the atmosphere of the encampment, Kurt lagged for him to come alongside.

"We shall be back in it all in two days' time," he said. "And it's a devil of a war to go back to. That's the news. The world's gone mad. Our fleet beat the Americans the night we got disabled, that's clear. We lost eleven—eleven airships certain, and all their aeroplanes got smashed. God knows how much we smashed or how many we killed. But that was only the beginning. Our start's been like firing a magazine. Every country was hiding flying-machines. They're fighting in the air all over Europe—all over the world. The Japanese and Chinese have joined in. That's the great fact. That's the supreme fact. They've pounced into our little quarrels. . . ."

The Yellow Peril was a peril after all! They've got thousands of airships. They're all over the world. We bombarded London and Paris, and the French and English have smashed up Berlin. And now Asia is at us all, and on the top of us all. . . . It's mania. China on the top. And they don't know where to stop. It's limitless. It's the last confusion. They're bombarding capitals, smashing up dockyards and factories, mines and fleets."

" Did they do much to London, sir ? " asked Bert.

" Heaven knows. . . . "

He said no more for a time.

" This Labrador seems a quiet place," he resumed at last. " I'm half a mind to stay here. Can't do that. No! I've got to see it through. I've got to see it through. You've got to, too. Everyone. . . . But why ? . . . I tell you—our world's gone to pieces. There's no way out of it, no way back. Here we are! We're like mice caught in a house on fire, we're like cattle overtaken by a flood. Presently we shall be picked up, and back we shall go into the fighting. We shall kill and smash again—perhaps. It's a Chino-Japanese air-fleet this time, and the odds are against us. Our turn will come. What will happen to you I don't know, but for myself, I know quite well; I shall be killed."

" You'll be all right," said Bert, after a queer pause.

" No! " said Kurt. " I'm going to be killed. I didn't know it before, but this morning, at dawn I knew it—as though I'd been told."

" 'Ow ? "

" I tell you I know."

" But 'ow *could* you know ? "

" I know."

" Like being told ? "

" Like being certain.

" I know," he repeated, and for a time they walked in silence towards the waterfall.

Kurt, wrapped in his thoughts, walked heedlessly, and at last broke out again. " I've always felt young before, Smallways, but this morning I feel old—old. So old! Nearer to death than old men feel. And I've always thought life was a lark. It isn't. . . . This sort of thing has always been happening, I suppose—these things, wars and earthquakes, that sweep across all the decency of life. It's just as though I had woke up to it all for the first time. Every night since we were at New York I've dreamt of it. . . . And it's always been so —it's the way of life. People are torn away from the people they care for ; homes are smashed, creatures full of life and memories and little peculiar gifts are scalded and smashed and torn to pieces, and starved and spoilt. London! Berlin! San Francisco! Think of all the human histories we ended in New York! . . . And the others go on again as though such things weren't possible. As I went on! Like animals! Just like animals."

He said nothing for a long time, and then he dropped out, " The Prince is a lunatic ! "

They came to a place where they had to climb, and then to a long peat level beside a rivulet. There a quantity of delicate little pink flowers caught Bert's eye. " Gaw ! " he said, and stooped to pick one. " In a place like this."

Kurt stopped and half turned. His face winced.

" I never see such a flower," said Bert. " It's so delicate."

" Pick some more if you want to," said Kurt.

Bert did so, while Kurt stood and watched him. " Funny 'ow one always wants to pick flowers," said Bert.

Kurt had nothing to add to that.

They went on again, without talking, for a long time.

At last they came to a rocky hummock, from which the view of the waterfall opened out. There Kurt stopped and seated himself on a rock. " That's as much as I wanted to see," he explained. " It isn't very like, but it's like enough."

" Like what ? "

" Another waterfall I knew."

He asked a question abruptly. " Got a girl, Smallways ? "

" Funny thing," said Bert, " those flowers, I suppose.—I was jes' thinking of 'er."

" So was I."

" *What* ! Edna ? "

" No. I was thinking of *my* Edna. We've all got Ednas, I suppose, for our imaginations to play about. This was a girl. But all that's past for ever. It's hard to think I can't see her just for a minute—just let her know I'm thinking of her."

" Very likely," said Bert, " you'll see 'er all right."

" No," said Kurt with decision, " I *know*.

" I met her," he went on, " in a place like this—in the Alps—Engstlen Alp. There's a waterfall rather like this one —a broad waterfall down towards Innertkirchen. That's why I came here this morning. We slipped away and had half a day together beside it. And we picked flowers. Just such flowers as you picked. The same, for all I know. And gentian."

" I know," said Bert ; " me and Edna—we done things like that. Flowers. And all that. Seems years off now."

" She was beautiful and daring and shy. Mein Gott ! . . . I can hardly hold myself for the desire to see her and hear her voice again before I die. Where is she ? . . . Look here, Smallways, I shall write a sort of letter—— And there's her portrait." He touched his breast pocket.

" You'll see 'er again all right," said Bert.

" No ! I shall never see her again. . . . I don't understand why people should meet just to be torn apart. But I know she and I will never meet again. That I know as surely as that the sun will rise, and that cascade come shining over the rocks after I am dead and done. . . . Oh ! It's all foolishness and haste and violence and cruel folly, stupidity and blundering hate and selfish ambition—all the things that men have done—all the things they will ever do. Gott ! Smallways, what a muddle and confusion life has always been —the battles and massacres and disasters, the hates and harsh acts, the murders and sweatings, the lynchings and cheatings. This morning I am tired of it all, as though I'd just found it out for the first time. I *have* found it out. When a man is tired of life I suppose it is time for him to die. I've lost heart, and death is over me. Death is close to me, and I know I have got to end. But think of all the hopes I had only a little time ago, the sense of fine beginnings ! . . . It was all a sham. There were no beginnings. . . . We're just ants in ant-hill cities, in a world that doesn't matter ; that goes on and rambles into nothingness. New York—New York doesn't even strike me as horrible. New York was nothing but an ant-hill kicked to pieces by a fool !

" Think of it, Smallways ; there's war everywhere ! They're smashing up their civilisation before they have made it. The sort of thing the English did at Alexandria, the Japanese at Port Arthur, the French at Casablanca, is going on everywhere. Everywhere ! Down in South America even they are fighting among themselves ! No place is safe—no place is at peace. There is no place where a woman and her daughter can hide and be at peace. The war comes through the air, bombs drop in the night. Quiet people go out in the morning, and see air-fleets passing overhead—dripping death—dripping death ! "

CHAPTER EIGHT

A WORLD AT WAR

§ 1

IT was only very slowly that Bert got hold of this idea that the whole world was at war, that he formed any image at all of the crowded countries south of these Arctic solitudes stricken with terror and dismay as these new-born aerial navies swept across their skies. He was not used to thinking of the world as a whole, but as a limitless hinterland of happenings beyond the range of his immediate vision. War in his imagination was something, a source of news and emotion, that happened in a restricted area called the Seat of War. But now the whole atmosphere was the Seat of War, and every land a cockpit. So closely had the nations raced along the path of research and invention, so secret and yet so parallel had been their plans and acquisitions, that it was within a few hours of the launching of the first fleet in Franconia

that an Asiatic Armada beat its westward way across, high
above, the marvelling millions in the plain of the Ganges.
But the preparations of the Confederation of Eastern Asia
had been on an altogether more colossal scale than the German.
" With this step," said Tan Ting-siang, " we overtake and
pass the West. We recover the peace of the world that these
barbarians have destroyed."

Their secrecy and swiftness and inventions had far sur-
passed those of the Germans, and where the Germans had
had a hundred men at work the Asiatics had ten thousand.
There came to their great aeronautic parks at Chinsi-fu and
Tsingyen, by the mono-rails that now laced the whole surface
of China, a limitless supply of skilled and able workmen,
workmen far above the average European in industrial efficiency. The news of the German World Surprise simply
quickened their efforts. At the time of the bombardment of
New York it is doubtful if the Germans had three hundred
airships altogether in the world ; the score of Asiatic fleets
flying east and west and south must have numbered several
thousand. Moreover, the Asiatics had a real fighting flying-
machine, the *Niaio* as it was called, a light but quite efficient
weapon, infinitely superior to the German drachenflieger.
Like that, it was a one-man machine, but it was built very
lightly of steel and cane and chemical silk, with a transverse
engine, and a flapping side wing. The aeronaut carried a gun
firing explosive bullets loaded with oxygen, and in addition,
and true to the best tradition of Japan, a sword. The riders
were Japanese, and it is characteristic that from the first it
was contemplated that the aeronaut should be a swordsman.
The wings of these fliers had bat-like hooks forward, by which
they were to cling to their antagonist's gas-chambers while
boarding him. These light flying-machines were carried with
the fleets, and also sent overland or by sea to the front with
the men. They were capable of flights of from two to five
hundred miles, according to the wind.

So, hard upon the uprush of the first German air-fleet,
these Asiatic swarms took to the atmosphere. Instantly
every organised Government in the world was frantically
and vehemently building airships and whatever approach to
a flying-machine its inventors had discovered. There was
no time for diplomacy. Warnings and ultimatums were tele-
graphed to and fro, and in a few hours all the panic-fierce
world was openly at war, and at war in the most complicated
way. For Britain and France and Italy had declared war
upon Germany and outraged Swiss neutrality ; India, at the
sight of Asiatic airships, had broken into a Hindoo insurrection in Bengal and a Mohammedan revolt hostile to this
in the North-West Provinces—the latter spreading like wild-
fire from Gobi to the Gold Coast—and the Confederation of
Eastern Asia had seized the oil wells of Burmah and was

impartially attacking America and Germany. In a week they were building airships in Damascus and Cairo and Johannesburg ; Australia and New Zealand were frantically equipping themselves. One unique and terrifying aspect of this development was the swiftness with which these monsters could be produced. To build an ironclad took from two to four years ; an airship could be put together in as many weeks. Moreover, compared with even a torpedo boat the airship was remarkably simple to construct : given the air-chamber material, the engines, the gas plant, and the design, it was really not more complicated and far easier than an ordinary wooden boat had been a hundred years before. And now from Cape Horn to Nova Zembla, and from Canton round to Canton again, there were factories and workshops and industrial resources.

And the German airships were barely in sight of the Atlantic waters, the first Asiatic fleet was scarcely reported from Upper Burmah, before the fantastic fabric of credit and finance that had held the world together economically for a hundred years strained and snapped. A tornado of realisation swept through every stock exchange in the world ; banks stopped payment, business shrank and ceased, factories ran on for a day or so by a sort of inertia, completing the orders of bankrupt and extinguished customers, then stopped. The New York Bert Smallways saw, for all its glare of light and traffic, was in the pit of an economic and financial collapse unparalleled in history. The flow of the food supply was already a little checked. And before the world-war had lasted two weeks—by the time, that is, that mast was rigged in Labrador —there was not a city or town in the world outside China, however far from the actual centres of destruction, where police and government were not adopting special emergency methods to deal with a want of food and a glut of unemployed people.

The special peculiarities of aerial warfare were of such a nature as to trend, once it had begun, almost inevitably towards social disorganisation. The first of these peculiarities was brought home to the Germans in their attack upon New York ; the immense power of destruction an airship has over the thing below, and its relative inability to occupy or police or guard or garrison a surrendered position. Necessarily, in the face of urban populations in a state of economic disorganisation and infuriated and starving, this led to violent and destructive collisions, and even where the air-fleet floated inactive above, there would be civil conflict and passionate disorder below. Nothing comparable to this state of affairs had been known in the previous history of warfare, unless we take such a case as that of a nineteenth-century warship attacking some large savage or barbaric settlement, or one of those naval bombardments that disfigure the history of Great

Britain in the late eighteenth century. Then, indeed, there had been cruelties and destruction that faintly foreshadowed the horrors of the aerial war. Moreover, before the twentieth century the world had had but one experience, and that a comparatively light one, in the Communist insurrection of Paris, 1871, of the possibilities of a modern urban population under warlike stresses.

A second peculiarity of airship war as it first came to the world that also made for social collapse, was the ineffectiveness of the early airships against each other. Upon anything below they could rain explosives in the most deadly fashion, forts and ships and cities lay at their mercy, but unless they were prepared for a suicidal grapple they could do remarkably little mischief to each other. The armament of the huge German airships, big as the biggest mammoth liners afloat, was one machine gun that could easily have been packed up on a couple of mules. In addition, when it became evident that the air must be fought for, the air-sailors were provided with rifles with explosive bullets of oxygen or inflammable substance, but no airship at any time ever carried as much in the way of guns and armour as the smallest gun-boat on the navy list had been accustomed to do. Consequently, when these monsters met in battle they manœuvred for the upper place or grappled and fought like junks, throwing grenades, fighting hand to hand in an entirely mediaeval fashion. The risks of a collapse and fall on either side came near to balancing in every case the chances of victory. As a consequence, and after their first experiences of battle, one finds a growing tendency on the part of the air-fleet admirals to evade joining battle and to seek rather the moral advantage of a destructive counter-attack.

And if the airships were too ineffective, the early drachenflieger were either too unstable, like the German, or too light, like the Japanese, to produce immediately decisive results. Later, it is true, the Brazilians launched a flying-machine of a type and scale that was capable of dealing with an airship, but they built only three or four, they operated only in South America, and they vanished from history untraceably in the time when world-bankruptcy put a stop to all further engineering production on any considerable scale.

The third peculiarity of aerial warfare was that it was at once enormously destructive and entirely indecisive. It had this unique feature, that both sides lay open to punitive attack. In all previous forms of war, both by land and sea the losing side was speedily unable to raid its antagonists' territory and the communications. One fought on a " front," and behind that front the winner's supplies and resources, his towns and factories and capital, the peace of his country, were secure. If the war was a naval one, you destroyed your enemy's battle fleet and then blockaded his ports, secured his coaling stations, and hunted down any stray cruisers that threatened your ports of commerce. But to blockade and watch a coastline is one thing, to blockade and watch the whole surface of a country is another, and cruisers and privateers are things that take long to make, that cannot be packed up and hidden and carried unostentatiously from point to point. In aerial war the stronger side, even supposing it destroyed the main battle fleet of the weaker, had then either to patrol and watch or destroy every possible point at which he might produce another and perhaps novel and more deadly form of flier. It meant darkening his air with airships. It meant building them by the thousand and making aeronauts by the hundred thousand. A small uninflated airship could be hidden in a railway shed, in a village street, in a wood ; a flying-machine is even less conspicuous.

And in the air are no streets, no channels, no point where one can say of an antagonist, " If he wants to reach my capital he must come by here." In the air all directions lead everywhere.

Consequently it was impossible to end a war by any of the established methods. A having outnumbered and overwhelmed B, hovers, a thousand airships strong, over his capital, threatening to bombard it unless B submits. B replies by wireless telegraphy that he is now in the act of bombarding the chief manufacturing city of A by means of three raider airships. A denounces B's raiders as pirates and so forth, bombards B's capital and sets off to hunt down B's airships, while B in a state of passionate emotion and heroic unconquerableness, sets to work amidst his ruins, making fresh airships and explosives for the benefit of A. The war became perforce a universal guerilla war, a war inextricably involving civilians and homes and all the apparatus of social life.

These aspects of aerial fighting took the world by surprise. There had been no foresight to deduce these consequences. If there had been, the world would have arranged for a Universal Peace Conference in 1900. But mechanical invention had gone faster than intellectual and social organisation, and the world, with its silly old flags, its silly unmeaning tradition of nationality, its cheap newspapers and cheaper passions and imperialisms, its base commercial motives and habitual insincerities and vulgarities, its race lies and conflicts, was taken by surprise. Once the war began there was no stopping it. The flimsy fabric of credit that had grown with no man foreseeing, and that had held those hundreds of millions in an economic interdependence that no man clearly understood, dissolved in panic. Everywhere went the airships dropping bombs, destroying any hope of a rally, and everywhere below were economic catastrophe, starving, workless people, rioting, and social disorder. Whatever constructive guiding intelligence there had been among the nations vanished in the pas-

sionate stresses of the time. Such newspapers and documents
and histories as survive from this period all tell one universal
story of towns and cities with the food supply interrupted
and their streets congested with starving unemployed ; of
crises in administration and states of siege, of provisional
Governments and Councils of Defence, and in the cases of
India and Egypt, insurrectionary committees taking charge,
of the re-arming of the population, of the making of batteries
and gun-pits, of the vehement manufacture of airships and
flying-machines.

One sees these things in glimpses, in illuminated moments,
as if through a driving reek of clouds, going on all over the
world. It was the dissolution of an age ; it was the collapse
of the civilisation that had trusted to machinery, and the
instruments of its destruction were machines. But while the
collapse of the previous great civilisation, that of Rome, had
been a matter of centuries, had been a thing of phase and
phase, like the ageing and dying of a man, this, like his killing
by railway or motor-car, was one swift, conclusive smashing
and an end.

§ 2

The early battles of the aerial war were no doubt determined by attempts to realise the old naval maxim, to ascertain
the position of the enemy's fleet and to destroy it. There
was first the battle of the Bernese Oberland, in which the
Italian and French navigables in their flank raid upon the
Franconian Park were assailed by the Swiss experimental
squadron, supported as the day wore on by German airships ;
and then the encounter of the British Winterhouse-Dunne
aeroplanes with three unfortunate Germans.

Then came the battle of North India, in which the entire
Anglo-Indian aeronautic settlement establishment fought for
three days against overwhelming odds, and was dispersed and
destroyed in detail.

And simultaneously with the beginning of that commenced
the momentous struggle of the Germans and Asiatics that
is usually known as the Battle of Niagara because of the
objective of the Asiatic attack. But it passed gradually into
a sporadic conflict over half a continent. Such German airships as escaped destruction in battle descended and surrendered to the Americans, and were remanned, and in the
end it became a series of pitiless and heroic encounters between
the Americans, savagely resolved to exterminate their enemies,
and a continually reinforced army of invasion from Asia
quartered upon the Pacific slope and supported by an immense
fleet. From the first the war in America was fought with implacable bitterness ; no quarter was asked, no prisoners were
taken. With ferocious and magnificent energy the Americans
constructed and launched ship after ship to battle and perish

against the Asiatic multitudes. All other affairs were sub-ordinate to this war, the whole population was presently living or dying for it. Presently, as I shall tell, the white men found in the Butteridge machine a weapon that could meet and fight the flying-machines of the Asiatic swordsmen.

The Asiatic invasion of America completely effaced the German-American conflict. It vanishes from history. At first it had seemed to promise quite sufficient tragedy in itself—beginning as it did in unforgettable massacre. After the destruction of central New York all America had risen like one man, resolved to die a thousand deaths rather than submit to Germany. The Germans grimly resolved upon beating the Americans into submission and, following out the plans developed by the Prince, had seized Niagara—in order to avail themselves of its enormous power works, expelled all its inhabitants and made a desert of its environs as far as Buffalo. They had also, directly Great Britain and France declared war, wrecked the country upon the Canadian side for nearly ten miles inland. They began to bring up men and material from the fleet off the east coast, stringing out to and fro like bees getting honey. It was then that the Asiatic forces appeared, and it was in their attack upon this German base at Niagara that the air-fleets of East and West first met and the greater issue became clear.

One conspicuous peculiarity of the early aerial fighting arose from the profound secrecy with which the airships had been prepared. Each power had had but the dimmest inkling of the schemes of its rivals, and even experiments with its own devices were limited by the needs of secrecy. None of the designers of airships and aeroplanes had known clearly what their inventions might have to fight ; many had not imagined they would have to fight anything whatever in the air, and had planned them only for the dropping of explosives. Such had been the German idea. The only weapon for fighting another airship with which the Franconian fleet had been provided, was the machine gun forward. Only after the fight over New York were the men given short rifles with deton-ating bullets. Theoretically, the drachenflieger were to have been the fighting weapon. They were declared to be aerial torpedo-boats, and the aeronaut was supposed to swoop close to his antagonist and cast his bombs as he whirled past. But indeed these contrivances were hopelessly unstable ; not one third in any engagement succeeded in getting back to the mother airship. The rest were either smashed up or grounded.

The allied Chino-Japanese fleet made the same distinction as the Germans between airships and fighting machines heavier than air, but the type in both cases was entirely different from the Accidental models, and—it is eloquent of the vigour with which these great peoples took up and bettered the European methods of scientific research—in almost every

particular the invention of Asiatic engineers. Chief among
these, it is worth remarking, was Mohini K. Chatterjee, a
political exile who had formerly served in the British-Indian
aeronautic park at Lahore.

The German airship was fish-shaped, with a blunted head ;
the Asiatic airship was also fish-shaped, but not so much on
the lines of a cod or goby as of a ray or sole. It had a wide,
flat underside, unbroken by windows or any opening except
along the middle line. Its cabins occupied its axis, with a
sort of bridge deck above, and the gas-chambers gave the
whole affair the shape of a gipsy's hooped tent, except that
it was much flatter. The German airship was essentially a
navigable balloon very much lighter than air ; the Asiatic
airship was very little lighter than air and skimmed through
it with much greater velocity if with considerably less stability.
They carried fore and aft guns, the latter much the larger,
throwing inflammatory shells, and in addition they had nests
for riflemen on both the upper and the under side. Light
as this armament was in comparison with the smallest gun-
boat that ever sailed, it was sufficient for them to outfight
as well as outfly the German monster airships. In action they
flew to get behind or over the Germans : they even dashed
underneath, avoiding only passing immediately beneath the
magazine, and then as soon as they had crossed let fly with
their rear gun, and sent flares or oxygen shells into the antagonist's gas-chambers.

It was not in their airships, but, as I have said, in their
flying-machines proper, that the strength of the Asiatics
lay. Next only to the Butteridge machine these were certainly
the most efficient heavier-than-air fliers that had ever appeared.
They were the invention of a Japanese artist, and they differed
in type extremely from the box-kite quality of the German
drachenflieger. They had curiously curved, flexible side wings,
more like *bent* butterflys' wings than anything else, and made
of a substance like celluloid and of brightly painted silk, and
they had a long humming-bird tail. At the forward corner
of the wings were hooks, rather like the claws of a bat, by
which the machine could catch and hang and tear at the walls
of an airship's gas-chamber. The solitary rider sat between
the wings above a transverse explosive engine, an explosive
engine that differed in no essential particular from those in
use in the light motor bicycles of the period. Below was a
single large wheel. The rider sat astride of a saddle, as in
the Butteridge machine, and he carried a large double-edged
two-handed sword in addition to his explosive bullet firing
rifle.

§ 3

One sets down these particulars and compares the points
of the American and German pattern of aeroplane and navi-

gable, but none of these facts were clearly known to any of those who fought in this monstrously confused battle above the American great lakes.

Each side went into action against it knew not what, under novel conditions and with apparatus that even without hostile attacks were capable of producing the most disconcerting surprises. Schemes of action, attempts at collective manœuvring necessarily went to pieces directly the fight began, just as they did in almost all the early ironclad battles of the previous century. Each captain then had to fall back upon individual action and his own devices ; one would see triumph in what another read as a cue for flight and despair. It is as true of the Battle of Niagara as of the Battle of Lissa that it was not a battle but a bundle of " battlettes " !

To such a spectator as Bert it presented itself as a series of incidents, some immense, some trivial, but collectively incoherent. He never had a sense of any plain issue joined, of any point struggled for and won or lost. He saw tremendous things happen, and in the end his world darkened to disaster and ruin.

He saw the battle from the ground, from Prospect Park and from Goat Island, whither he fled.

But the manner in which he came to be on the ground needs explaining.

The Prince had resumed command of his fleet through wireless telegraphy long before the *Zeppelin* had located his encampment in Labrador. By his direction the German air-fleet, whose advance scouts had been in contact with the Japanese over the Rocky Mountains, had concentrated upon Niagara and awaited his arrival. He had rejoined his command early in the morning of the twelfth, and Bert had his first prospect of the Gorge of Niagara while he was doing net drill outside the middle gas-chamber at sunrise. The *Zeppelin* was flying very high at the time and far below he saw the water in the gorge marbled with froth, and then away to the west the great crescent of the Canadian Fall shining, flickering, and foaming in the level sunlight, and sending up a deep incessant thudding rumble to the sky. The air-fleet was keeping station in an enormous crescent, with its horns pointing south-westward, a long array of shining monsters with tails rotating slowly, and German ensigns now trailing from their bellies aft of their Marconi pendants.

Niagara City was still largely standing then, albeit its streets were empty of all life. Its bridges were intact, its hotels and restaurants still flying flags and inviting sky signs, its power-stations running. But about it the country on both sides of the gorge might have been swept by a colossal broom. Everything that could possibly give cover to an attack upon the German position at Niagara had been levelled as ruthlessly as machinery and explosives could contrive ; houses blown up

and burnt, woods burnt, fences and crops destroyed. The
mono-rails had been torn up, and the roads in particular
cleared of all possibility of concealment or shelter. Seen from
above the effect of this wreckage was grotesque. Young
woods had been destroyed wholesale by dragging wires, and
the spoilt saplings, smashed or uprooted, lay in swathes like
corn after the sickle. Houses had an appearance of being
flattened down by the pressure of a gigantic finger. Much
burning was still going on, and large areas had been reduced
to patches of smouldering and sometimes still glowing black-
ness. Here and there lay the debris of belated fugitives, carts,
and dead bodies of horses and men ; and where houses had had
water supplies there were pools of water and running springs
from the ruptured pipes. In unscorched fields horses and
cattle fed peacefully. Beyond this desolated area the country-
side was still standing, but almost all the people had fled.
Buffalo was on fire to an enormous extent, and there were no
signs of any efforts to grapple with the flames.

Niagara City itself was being rapidly converted to the needs
of a military depot. A large number of skilled engineers had
already been brought from the fleet, and were busily at work
adapting the exterior industrial apparatus of the place to the
purposes of an aeronautic park. They had made a gas re-
charging station at the corner of the American Fall above
the funicular railway, and they were opening up a much larger
area to the south for the same purpose. Over the power houses
and hotels and suchlike prominent or important points, the
German flag was flying.

The *Zeppelin* circled slowly over this scene twice while
the Prince surveyed it from the swinging gallery ; it then
rose towards the centre of the crescent and transferred the
Prince and his suit, Kurt included, to the *Hohenzollern*, which
had been chosen as the flagship during the impending battle.
They were swung up on a small cable from the forward gallery,
and the men of the *Zeppelin* manned the outer netting as the
Prince and his staff left them. The *Zeppelin* then came about,
circled down and grounded in Prospect Park, in order to land
the wounded and take aboard explosives ; for she had come
to Labrador with her magazines empty, it being uncertain
what weight she might need to carry. She also replenished the
hydrogen in one of her forward chambers which had leaked.

Bert was detailed as a bearer and helped to carry the wounded
one by one into the nearest of the large hotels that faced the
Canadian shore. The hotel was quite empty except that there
were two trained American nurses and a negro porter, and
three or four Germans awaiting them. Bert went with the
Zeppelin's doctor into the main street of the place, and they
broke into a drug shop and obtained various things of which
they stood in need. As they returned they found an officer
and two men making a rough inventory of the available

material in the various stores. Except for them the wide,
main street of the town was quite deserted, the people had
been given three hours to clear out, and everybody, it seemed,
had done so. At one corner a dead man lay against the wall
—shot. Two or three dogs were visible up the empty vista,
but towards its river end the passage of a string of mono-rail
cars broke the stillness and the silence. They were loaded with
hose, and were passing to the trainful of workers who were
converting Prospect Park into an airship dock.

Bert pushed a case of medicine balanced on a bicycle taken
from an adjacent shop, to the hotel, and then he was sent to
load bombs into the *Zeppelin* magazine, a duty that called for
elaborate care. From this job he was presently called off by
the captain of the *Zeppelin*, who sent him with a note to the
officer in charge of the Anglo-American Power Company,
for the field telephone had still to be adjusted. Bert received
his instructions in German, whose meaning he guessed, and
saluted and took the note, not caring to betray his ignorance
of the language. He started off with a bright air of knowing
his way and turned a corner or so and was only beginning
to suspect that he did not know where he was going when his
attention was recalled to the sky by the report of a gun from
the *Hohenzollern* and celestial cheering.

He looked up and found the view obstructed by the houses
on either side of the street. He hesitated, and then curiosity
took him back towards the bank of the river. Here his view
was inconvenienced by trees, and it was with a start that he
discovered the *Zeppelin*, which he knew had still a quarter
of her magazines to fill, was rising over Goat Island. She
had not waited for her complement of ammunition. It occurred
to him that he was left behind. He ducked back among the
trees and bushes until he felt secure from any after-thought
on the part of the *Zeppelin's* captain. Then his curiosity to
see what the German air-fleet faced overcame him, and drew
him at last half-way across the bridge to Goat Island. From
that point he had nearly a hemisphere of sky and got his
first glimpse of the Asiatic airships low in the sky above the
glittering tumults of the Upper Rapids.

They were far less impressive than the German ships. He
could not judge the distance, and they flew edgeways to him,
so as to conceal the broader aspect of their bulk.

Bert stood there in the middle of the bridge, in a place
that most people who knew it remembered as a place populous
with sightseers and excursionists, and he was the only human
being in sight there. Above him, very high in the heavens,
the contending air-fleets manœuvred ; below him the river
seethed like a sluice towards the American Fall. He was
curiously dressed. His cheap blue serge trousers were thrust
into German airship rubber boots, and on his head he wore
an aeronaut's white cap that was a trifle too large for him.

He thrust that back to reveal his staring little Cockney face, still scarred upon the brow. " Gaw ! " he whispered.

He stared. He gesticulated. Once or twice he shouted and applauded.

Then at a certain point terror seized him and he took to his heels in the direction of Goat Island.

§ 4

For a time after they were in sight of each other, neither fleet attempted to engage. The Germans numbered sixty-seven great airships and they maintained the crescent formation at a height of nearly four thousand feet. They kept a distance of about one and a half lengths, so that the horns of the crescent were nearly thirty miles apart. Closely in tow of the airships of the extreme squadrons on either wing were about thirty drachenflieger ready manned, but these were too small and distant for Bert to distinguish.

At first, only what was called the Southern fleet of the Asiatics was visible to him. It consisted of forty airships, carrying altogether nearly four hundred one-man flying-machines upon their flanks, and for some time it flew slowly and at a minimum distance of perhaps a dozen miles from the Germans, eastward across their front. At first Bert could distinguish only the greater bulks, then he perceived the one-man machines as a multitude of very small objects drifting like motes in the sunshine about and beneath the larger shapes.

Bert saw nothing then of the second fleet of the Asiatics, though probably that was coming into sight of the Germans at the time, in the north-west.

The air was very still, the sky almost without a cloud, and the German fleet had risen to an immense height, so that the airships seemed no longer of any considerable size. Both ends of their crescent showed plainly. As they beat southward they passed slowly between Bert and the sunlight, and became black outlines of themselves. The drachenflieger appeared as little flecks of black on either wing of this aerial Armada.

The two fleets seemed in no hurry to engage. The Asiatics went far away into the east, quickening their pace and rising as they did so, and then tailed out into a long column and came flying back, rising towards the German left. The squadrons of the latter came about, facing this oblique advance, and suddenly little flickerings and a faint crepitating sound told that they had opened fire. For a time no effect was visible to the watcher on the bridge. Then, like a handful of snow-flakes, the drachenflieger swooped to the attack, and a multitude of red specks whirled up to meet them. It was to Bert's sense not only enormously remote but singularly inhuman. Not four hours since he had been on one of those very airships, and yet they seemed to him now not gas-bags carrying men, but strange sentient creatures that moved about and did things

with a purpose of their own. The flight of the Asiatic and
German flying-machines joined and dropped earthward,
became like a handful of white and red rose petals flung from
a distant window, grew larger, until Bert could see the overturned ones spinning through the air, and were hidden by
great volumes of dark smoke that were rising in the direction
of Buffalo. For a time they all were hidden, then two or three
white and a number of red ones rose again into the sky, like
a swarm of big butterflies, and circled fighting and drove
away out of sight again towards the east.

A heavy report recalled Bert's eyes to the zenith, and behold
the great crescent had lost its dressing and burst into a disorderly long cloud of airships ! One had dropped half-way
down the sky. It was flaming fore and aft, and even as Bert
looked it turned over and fell, spinning over and over itself
and vanished into the smoke of Buffalo.

Bert's mouth opened and shut, and he clutched tighter
on the rail of the bridge. For some moments — they seemed
long moments — the two fleets remained without any further
change, flying obliquely towards each other, and making
what came to Bert's ears as a midget uproar. Then suddenly
from either side airships began dropping out of alignment,
smitten by missiles he could neither see nor trace. The string
of Asiatic ships swung round and either charged into or over
(it was difficult to say from below) the shattered line of the
Germans, who seemed to open out to give way to them. Some
sort of manœuvring began, but Bert could not grasp its import.
The left of the battle became a confused dance of airships.
For some minutes up there the two crossing lines of ships
looked so close it seemed like a hand-to-hand scuffle in the
sky. Then they broke up into groups and duels. The descent
of German airships towards the lower sky increased. One of
them flared down and vanished far away in the north ; two
dropped with something twisted and crippled in their movements ; then a group of antagonists came down from the
zenith in an eddying conflict, two Asiatics against one German,
and were presently joined by another, and drove away eastward altogether with others dropping out of the German line
to join them. One Asiatic either rammed or collided with
a still more gigantic German, and the two went spinning
to destruction together. The northern squadron of Asiatics
came into the battle unnoted by Bert, except that the multitude of ships above seemed presently increased. In a little
while the fight was utter confusion, drifting on the whole to
the south-west against the wind. It became more and more
a series of group encounters. Here a huge German airship
flamed earthward with a dozen flat Asiatic craft about her,
crushing her every attempt to recover. Here another hung
with its crew fighting off the swordsmen from a swarm of
flying-machines. Here, again, an Asiatic aflame at either end

swooped out of the battle. His attention went from incident to incident in the vast clearness overhead ; these conspicuous cases of destruction caught and held his mind ; it was only very slowly that any sort of scheme manifested itself between those nearer, more striking episodes.

The mass of the airships that eddied remotely above was, however, neither destroying nor destroyed. The majority of them seemed to be going at full speed and circling upward for position, exchanging ineffectual shots as they did so. Very little ramming was essayed after the first tragic down-fall of rammer and rammed, and whatever attempts at boarding were made were invisible to Bert. There seemed, however, a steady endeavour to isolate antagonists, to cut them off from their fellows and bear them down, causing a perpetual sailing back and interlacing of these shoaling bulks. The greater numbers of the Asiatics and their swifter heeling movements gave them the effect of persistently attacking the Germans. Overhead, and evidently endeavouring to keep itself in touch with the works of Niagara, a body of German airships drew itself together into a compact phalanx, and the Asiatics became more and more intent upon breaking this up. He was grotesquely reminded of fish in a fish-pond struggling for crumbs. He could see puny puffs of smoke and the flash of bombs, but never a sound came down to him. . . .

A flapping shadow passed for a moment between Bert and the sun and was followed by another. A whirring of engines, click, clock, clitter clock, smote upon his ears. Instantly he forgot the zenith.

Perhaps a hundred yards above the water, out of the south, riding like Valkyries swiftly through the air on the strange steeds the engineering of Europe had begotten upon the artistic inspiration of Japan, came a long string of Asiatic swordsmen. The wings flapped jerkily, click, clock, clitter clock, and the machines drove up ; they spread and ceased, and the apparatus came soaring through the air. So they rose and fell and rose again. They passed so closely overhead that Bert could hear their voices calling to one another. They swooped towards Niagara City and landed one after another in a long line in a clear space before the hotel. But he did not stay to watch them land. One yellow face had craned over and looked at him, and for one enigmatical instant met his eyes. . . .

It was then the idea came to Bert that he was altogether too conspicuous in the middle of the bridge, and that he took to his heels towards Goat Island. Thence, dodging about among the trees, with perhaps an excessive self-consciousness, he watched the rest of the struggle.

§ 5

When Bert's sense of security was sufficiently restored for him to watch the battle again, he perceived that a brisk little fight was in progress between the Asiatic aeronauts and the German engineers for the possession of Niagara City. It was the first time in the whole course of the war that he had seen anything resembling fighting as he had studied it in the illustrated papers of his youth. It seemed to him almost as though things were coming right. He saw men carrying rifles and taking cover and running briskly from point to point in a loose, attacking formation. The first batch of aeronauts had probably been under the impression that the city was deserted. They had grounded in the open near Prospect Park and approached the houses towards the power-works before they were disillusioned by a sudden fire. They had scattered back to the cover of a bank near the water—it was too far for them to reach their machines again ; they were lying and firing at the men in the hotels and frame-houses about the power-works.

Then to their support came a second string of red flying-machines driving up from the east. They rose up out of the haze above the houses and came round in a long curve as if surveying the position below. The fire of the Germans rose to a roar, and one of those soaring shapes gave an abrupt jerk backwards and fell among the houses. The others swooped down exactly like great birds upon the roof of the power-house. They caught upon it, and from each sprang a nimble little figure and ran towards the parapet.

Other flapping bird-shapes came into this affair, but Bert had not seen their coming. A staccato of shots came over to him, reminding him of army manœuvres, of newspaper descriptions of fights, of all that was entirely correct in his conception of warfare. He saw quite a number of Germans running from the outlying houses towards the power-house. Two fell. One lay still, but the other wriggled and made efforts for a time. The hotel that was used as a hospital, and to which he had helped carry the wounded men from the *Zeppelin* earlier in the day, suddenly ran up the Geneva flag. The town that had seemed so quiet had evidently been concealing a considerable number of Germans, and they were now concentrating to hold the central power-house. He wondered what ammunition they might have. More and more of the Asiatic flying-machines came into the conflict. They had disposed of the unfortunate German drachenflieger and were now aiming at the incipient aeronautic park, the electric gas generators and repair stations which formed the German base. Some landed, and their aeronauts took cover and became energetic infantry soldiers. Others hovered above the fight, their men ever and again firing shots down at some chance exposure below. The firing came in paroxysms ; now there would be a watchful lull and now a rapid tattoo of shots, rising to a roar. Once or twice flying-machines, as they circled warily, came right overhead, and for a time Bert gave himself body and soul to cowering.

Ever and again a larger thunder mingled with the rattle and reminded him of the grapple of airships far above, but the nearer fight held his attention.

Abruptly something dropped from the zenith ; something like a barrel or a huge football.

CRASH ! It smashed with an immense report. It had fallen among the grounded Asiatic aeroplanes that lay among the turf and flower-beds near the river. They flew in scraps and fragments, turf, trees, and gravel leapt and fell ; the aeronauts still lying along the canal bank were thrown about like sacks, catspaws flew across the foaming water. All the windows of the hotel hospital that had been shiningly reflecting blue sky and airships the moment before became vast black stars. Bang !—a second followed. Bert looked up and was filled with a sense of a number of monstrous bodies swooping down, coming down on the whole affair like a flight of bellying blankets, like a string of vast dish-covers. The central tangle of the battle above was circling down as if to come into touch with the power-house fight. He got a new effect of airships altogether, as vast things coming down upon him, growing swiftly larger and larger and more overwhelming, until the houses over the way seemed small, the American rapids narrow, the bridge flimsy, the combatants infinitesimal. As they came down they became audible as a complex of shoutings and vast creakings and groanings and beatings and throbbings and shouts and shots. The fore-shortened black eagles at the fore-ends of the Germans had an effect of actual combat of flying feathers.

Some of these fighting airships came within five hundred feet of the ground. Bert could see men on the lower galleries of the Germans firing rifles ; could see Asiatics clinging to the ropes ; saw one man in aluminium diver's gear fall flashing headlong into the waters above Goat Island. For the first time he saw the Asiatic airships closely. From this aspect they reminded him more than anything else of colossal snowshoes ; they had a curious patterning in black and white, in forms that reminded him of the engine-turned cover of a watch. They had no hanging galleries, but from little openings on the middle line peeped out men and the muzzles of guns. So driving in long descending and ascending curves, these monsters wrestled and fought. It was like clouds fighting, like puddings trying to assassinate each other. They whirled and circled about each other, and for a time threw Goat Island and Niagara into a smoky twilight, through which the sunlight smote in shafts and beams. They spread and closed and spread and grappled and drove round over the rapids, and two miles away or more into Canada, and back over the Falls again. A German caught fire and the whole crowd broke away from her flare and rose about her dispersing, leaving her to drop towards Canada and blow up as she dropped. Then with renewed uproar the others closed again. Once from the men in Niagara City came a sound like an ant-hill cheering. Another German burnt, and one badly deflated by the prow of an antagonist, flopped out of action southward.

It became more and more evident that the Germans were getting the worst of the unequal fight. More and more obviously were they being persecuted. Less and less did they seem to fight with any object other than escape. The Asiatics swept by them and above them, ripped their bladders, set them alight, picked off their dimly seen men in diving clothes, who struggled against fire and tear with fire extinguishers and silk ribbons in the inner netting. They answered only with ineffectual shots. Thence the battle circled back over Niagara, and then suddenly the Germans, as if at a preconcerted signal, broke and dispersed, going east, west, north, and south, in open and confused flight. The Asiatics, as they realised this, rose to fly above them and after them. Only one little knot of four German and perhaps a dozen Asiatics remained fighting about the *Hohenzollern* and the Prince as he circled in a last attempt to save Niagara.

Round they swooped once again over the Canadian Fall, over the waste of waters eastward, until they were distant and small, and then round and back, hurrying, bounding, swooping towards the one gaping spectator.

The whole struggling mass approached very swiftly, growing rapidly larger, and coming out black and featureless against the afternoon sun and above the blinding welter of the Upper Rapids. It grew like a storm cloud, until once more it darkened the sky. The flat Asiatic airships kept high above the Germans and behind them, and fired unanswered bullets into their gas-chambers and upon their flanks ; the one-man flying-machines hovered and alighted like a swarm of attacking bees. Nearer they came and nearer, filling the lower heaven. Two of the Germans swooped and rose again, but the *Hohenzollern* had suffered too much for that. She lifted weakly, turned sharply as if to get out of the battle, burst into flames fore and aft, swept down to the water, splashed into it obliquely and rolled over and over and came down-stream rolling and smashing and writhing like a thing alive, halting and then coming on again, with her torn and bent propeller still beating the air. The bursting flames spluttered out again in clouds of steam. It was a disaster gigantic in its dimensions. She lay across the rapids like an island, like tall cliffs, tall cliffs that came rolling, smoking, and crumpling, and collapsing, advancing with a sort of fluctuating rapidity upon Bert. One Asiatic airship—it looked to Bert from below like three hundred yards of pavement—whirled back and circled two or three times over that great overthrow, and half a dozen crimson flying-machines danced for a moment like great midges in the sunlight before they swept on after their fellows. The rest of the fight had already gone over the island, a wild crescendo of shots and yells and smashing uproar. It was hidden from Bert now by the trees of the island, and forgotten by him in the nearer spectacle of the huge advance of the defeated German airship. Something fell with a mighty smashing and splintering of boughs unheeded behind him.

It seemed for a time that the *Hohenzollern* must needs break her back upon the Parting of the Waters, and then for a time her propeller flopped and frothed in the river and thrust the mass of buckling, crumpled wreckage towards the American shore. Then the sweep of the torrent that foamed down to the American Fall caught her, and in another minute the immense mass of deflating wreckage, with flames spurting out in three new places, had crashed against the bridge that joined Goat Island and Niagara City, and forced a long arm, as it were, in a heaving tangle under the central span. Then the middle chambers blew up with a loud report, and in another moment the bridge had given way and the main bulk of the airship, like some grotesque cripple in rags, staggered, flapping and waving flambeaux, to the crest of the Fall and hesitated there and vanished in a desperate suicidal leap.

Its detached fore-end remained jammed against that little island, Green Island it used to be called, which forms the stepping-stone between the mainland and Goat Island's patch of trees.

Bert followed this disaster from the Parting of the Waters to the bridge head. Then, regardless of cover, regardless of the Asiatic airship hovering like a huge house roof without walls above the Suspension Bridge, he sprinted along towards the north and came out for the first time upon that rocky point by Luna Island that looks sheer down upon the American Fall. There he stood breathless amidst that eternal rush of sound, breathless and staring.

Far below, and travelling rapidly down the gorge, whirled something like a huge empty sack. For him it meant—what did it not mean ?—the German air-fleet, Kurt, the Prince, Europe, all things stable and familiar, the forces that had brought him, the forces that had seemed indisputably victorious. And it went down the rapids like an empty sack and left the visible world to Asia, to yellow people beyond Christendom, to all that was terrible and strange !

Remote over Canada receded the rest of that conflict and vanished beyond the range of his vision. . . .

CHAPTER NINE

ON GOAT ISLAND

§ 1

THE whack of a bullet on the rocks beside him reminded him that he was a visible object and wearing at least portions of a German uniform. It drove him into the trees again, and for a time he dodged and dropped and sought cover like a chick hiding among reeds from imaginary hawks. " Beaten," he whispered. " Beaten and done for. . . . Chinese! Yellow chaps chasing 'em ! "

At last he came to rest in a clump of bushes near a locked-up and deserted refreshment shed within view of the American side. They made a sort of hole and harbour for him ; they met completely overhead. He looked across the rapids, but the firing had ceased now altogether and everything seemed quiet. The Asiatic aeroplane had moved from its former position above the Suspension Bridge, was motionless now above Niagara City, shadowing all that district about the power-house which had been the scene of the land fight. The monster had an air of quiet and assured predominance, and from its stern it trailed, serene and ornamental, a long, streaming flag, the red, black, and yellow of the great alliance, the Sunrise and the Dragon. Beyond, to the east, and at a much higher level, hung a second consort, and Bert, presently gathering courage, wriggled out and craned his neck to find another still airship against the sunset in the south.

" Gaw ! " he said. " Beaten and chased ! My Gawd ! "

The fighting, it seemed at first, was quite over in Niagara City, though a German flag was still flying from one shattered house. A white sheet was hoisted above the power-house, and this remained flying all through the events that followed. But presently came a sound of shots and then German soldiers running. They disappeared among the houses, and then came two engineers in blue shirts and trousers hotly pursued by three Japanese swordsmen. The foremost of the two fugitives was a shapely man, and ran lightly and well ; the second was a sturdy little man, and rather fat. He ran comically in leaps and bounds, with his plump arms bent up by his side and his head thrown back. The pursuers ran with uniforms and dark thin metal and leather headdresses. The little man stumbled, and Bert gasped, realising a new horror in war.

The foremost swordsman won three strides on him and was near enough to slash at him and miss as he spurted.

A dozen yards they ran, and then the swordsman slashed again, and Bert could hear across the waters a little sound like the moo of an elfin cow as the fat little man fell forward.

Slash went the swordsman and slash at something on the ground that tried to save itself with ineffectual hands " Oh, I carn't ! " cried Bert, near blubbering and staring with starting eyes.

The swordsman slashed a fourth time and went on as his fellows came up after the better runner. The hindmost swordsman stopped and turned back. He had perceived some movement perhaps ; but at any rate he stood, and ever and again slashed at the fallen body.

" Oo-oo ! " groaned Bert at every slash, and shrank closer into the bushes and became very still. Presently came a sound of shots from the town, and then everything was quiet, everything, even the hospital.

He saw presently little figures sheathing swords come out from the houses and walk to the debris of the flying machines the bomb had destroyed. Others appeared wheeling undamaged aeroplanes upon their wheels as men might wheel bicycles, and sprang into the saddles and flapped into the air. A string of three airships appeared far away in the east and flew towards the zenith. The one that hung low above Niagara City came still lower and dropped a rope ladder to pick up men from the power house.

For a long time he watched the further happenings in Niagara City as a rabbit might watch a meet. He saw men going from building to building to set fire to them, as he presently realised, and he heard a series of detonations from the wheel pit of the power-house. Some similar business went on among the works on the Canadian side. Meanwhile more and more airships appeared, and many more flying-machines, until at last it seemed to him nearly a third of the Asiatic fleet had reassembled. He watched them from his bush, cramped but immovable, watched them gather and range themselves and signal and pick up men, until at last they sailed away towards the glowing sunset, going to the great Asiatic rendezvous above the oil wells of Cleveland. They dwindled and passed away, leaving him alone, so far as he could tell, the only living man in a world of ruin and strange loneliness almost beyond describing. He watched them recede and vanish. He stood gaping after them.

" Gaw ! " he said at last, like one who rouses himself from a trance.

It was far more than any personal desolation and extremity that flooded his soul. It seemed to him indeed that this must be the sunset of his race.

§ 2

He did not at first envisage his own plight in any definite and comprehensible terms. Things had happened to him so much of late, his own efforts had counted for so little, that he had become passive and planless. His last scheme had been to go round the coast of England as a Desert Dervish giving refined entertainment to his fellow-creatures. Fate had quashed that. Fate had seen fit to direct him to other destinies, had hurried him from point to point, and dropped him at last upon this little wedge of rock between the cataracts. It did not instantly occur to him that now it was his turn to play. He had a singular feeling that all must end as a dream ends, that presently surely he would be back in the world of Grubb and Edna and Bun Hill, that this roar, this glittering presence of incessant water would be drawn aside as a curtain is drawn aside after a holiday lantern show, and old, familiar customary things reassume their sway. It would be interesting to tell people how he had seen Niagara. And then Kurt's words came into his head : " People torn away from the people they care for ; homes smashed, creatures full of life and memories and peculiar little gifts—torn to pieces, starved, and spoilt." . . .

He wondered, half incredulous, if that was indeed true. It was so hard to realise it. Out beyond there was it possible that Tom and Jessica were also in some dire extremity ? that the little greengrocer's shop was no longer standing open, with Jessica serving respectfully, warming Tom's ears in sharp asides, or punctually sending out the goods ?

He tried to think what day of the week it was, and found he had lost his reckoning. Perhaps it was Sunday. If so were they going to church—or were they hiding, perhaps, in bushes ? What had happened to the landlord, the butcher, and to Butteridge and all those people on Dymchurch beach ? something, he knew, had happened to London—a bombardment. But who had bombarded ? Were Tom and Jessica, too, being chased by strange brown men with long bare swords and evil eyes ? He thought of various possible aspects of affliction, but presently one phase ousted all the others. Were they getting much to eat ? The question haunted him, obsessed him.

If one was very hungry would one eat rats ?

It dawned upon him that a peculiar misery that oppressed him was not so much anxiety and patriotic sorrow as hunger. Of course he was hungry !

He reflected and turned his steps towards the little refreshment shed that stood near the end of the ruined bridge. " Ought to be somethin'—— "

He strolled round it once or twice, and then attacked the shutters with his pocket-knife, reinforced presently by a wooden stake he found conveniently near. At last he got a shutter to give, and tore it back and stuck in his head.

" Grub," he remarked, " anyhow. Leastways—— "

He got at the inside fastening of the shutter and had presently this establishment open for his exploration. He found several sealed bottles of sterilised milk, much mineral water,

two tins of biscuits and a crock of very stale cakes, cigarettes
in great quantity but very dry, some rather dry oranges, nuts,
some tins of canned meat and fruit, and plates and knives
and forks and glasses sufficient for several score of people.
There was also a zinc locker, but he was unable to negotiate
the padlock of this.

" Shan't starve," said Bert, " for a bit, anyhow." He sat
on the vender's seat and regaled himself with biscuits and
milk, and felt for a moment quite contented.

" Quite restful," he muttered, munching and glancing about
him restlessly, " after what I been through.

" Crikey ! *Wot* a day ! Oh ! *Wot* a day ! "

Wonder took possession of him. " Gaw ! " he cried : " What
a fight it's been ! Smashing up the poor fellers ! 'Eadlong !
The airships—the fliers and all. I wonder what happened
to the *Zeppelin* ? . . . And that chap Kurt—I wonder what
happened to 'im ? 'E was a good sort of chap was Kurt."

Some phantom of imperial solicitude floated through his
mind. " Injia," he said. . . .

A more practical interest arose.

" I wonder if there's anything to open one of these tins of
corned beef ? "

§ 3

After he had feasted, Bert lit a cigarette and sat meditative for a time. " Wonder where Grubb is," he said ; " I do
wonder that ! Wonder if any of 'em wonder about me ? "

He reverted to his own circumstances. " Dessay I shall
'ave to stop on this island for some time."

He tried to feel at his ease and secure, but presently the
indefinable restlessness of the social animal in solitude distressed him. He began to want to look over his shoulder,
and, as a corrective, roused himself to explore the rest of the
island.

It was only very slowly that he began to realise the peculiarities of his position, to perceive that the breaking down of
the arch between Green Island and the mainland had cut him
off completely from the world. Indeed, it was only when he
came back to where the fore-end of the *Hohenzollern* lay like
a stranded ship, and was contemplating the shattered bridge,
that this dawned upon him. Even then it came with no sort
of shock to his mind, a fact among a number of other extraordinary and unmanageable facts. He stared at the shattered
cabins of the *Hohenzollern* and its widow's garment of dishevelled silk for a time, but without any idea of its containing
any living thing ; it was all so twisted and smashed and
entirely upside down. Then for a while he gazed at the evening
sky. A cloud haze was now appearing and not an airship was
in sight. A swallow flew by and snapped some invisible victim.
" Like a dream," he repeated.

Then for a time the rapids held his mind. " Roaring. It keeps on roaring and splashin' always and always. Keeps on. . . ."

At last his interests became personal. " Wonder what I ought to do now ? "

He reflected. " Not an idee," he said.

He was chiefly conscious that a fortnight ago he had been in Bunhill with no idea of travel in his mind, and that now he was between the Falls of Niagara amidst the devastation and ruins of the greatest air fight in the world, and that in the interval he had been across France, Belgium, Germany, England, Ireland, and a number of other countries. It was an interesting thought and suitable conversation but of no great practical utility. " Wonder 'ow I can get orf this ? " he said. " Wonder if there is a way out ? If not . . . rummy ! "

Further reflection decided, " I believe I got myself in a bit of a 'ole coming over that bridge. . . ."

" Any'ow—got me out of the way of them Japanesy chaps. Wouldn't 'ave taken 'em long to cut *my* froat. No. Still——"

He resolved to return to the point of Luna Island. For a long time he stood without stirring, scrutinising the Canadian shore and the wreckage of hotels and houses and the fallen trees of the Victoria Park, pink now in the light of sundown. Not a human being was perceptible in that scene of headlong destruction. Then he came back to the American side of the island, crossed close to the crumpled aluminium wreckage of the *Hohenzollern* to Green Islet, and scrutinised the hopeless breach in the further bridge and the water that boiled beneath it. Towards Buffalo there was still much smoke, and near the position of the Niagara railway station the houses were burning vigorously. Everything was deserted now, everything was still. One little abandoned thing lay on a transverse path between town and road, a crumpled heap of clothes with sprawling limbs. . . .

" 'Ave a look round," said Bert, and taking a path that ran through the middle of the island he presently discovered the wreckage of the two Asiatic aeroplanes that had fallen out of the struggle that ended the *Hohenzollern*.

With the first he found the wreckage of an aeronaut too.

The machine had evidently dropped vertically and was badly knocked about amidst a lot of smashed branches in a clump of trees. Its bent and broken wings and shattered stays sprawled amidst new splintered wood, and its forepeak stuck into the ground. The aeronaut dangled weirdly head downward among the leaves and branches some yards away, and Bert only discovered him as he turned from the aeroplane. In the dusky evening light and stillness—for the sun had gone now and the wind had altogether fallen—this inverted yellow face was anything but a tranquillising object to discover suddenly a couple of yards away. A broken branch had run clean through the man's thorax, and he hung, so stabbed, looking limp and absurd. In his hand he still clutched, with the grip of death, a short, light rifle.

For some time Bert stood very still, inspecting this thing.

Then he began to walk away from it, looking constantly back at it.

Presently in an open glade he came to a stop.

" Gaw ! " he whispered, " I don' like dead bodies some'ow ! I'd almost rather that chap was alive."

He would not go along the path athwart which the China-man hung. He felt he would rather not have trees round him any more, and that it would be more comfortable to be quite close to the sociable splash and uproar of the rapids.

He came upon the second aeroplane in a clear, grassy space by the side of the streaming water, and it seemed scarcely damaged at all. It looked as though it had floated down into a position of rest. It lay on its side with one wing in the air. There was no aeronaut near it, dead or alive. There it lay abandoned, with the water lapping about its long tail.

Bert remained a little aloof from it for a long time looking into the gathering shadows among the trees, in the expectation of another Chinaman alive or dead. Then very cautiously he approached the machine and stood regarding its widespread vanes, its big steering wheel and empty saddle. He did not venture to touch it.

" I wish that other chap wasn't there," he said. " I do wish 'e wasn't there ! "

He saw, a few yards away, something bobbing about in an eddy that spun within a projecting head of rock. As it went round it seemed to draw him unwillingly towards it. . . .

What could it be ?

" Blow ! " said Bert. " It's another of 'em."

It held him. He told himself that it was the other aeronaut that had been shot in the fight and fallen out of the saddle as he strove to land. He tried to go away, and then it occurred to him that he might get a branch or something and push this rotating object out into the stream. That would leave him with only one dead body to worry about. Perhaps he might get along with one. He hesitated, and then with a certain emotion forced himself to do this. He went towards the bushes and cut himself a wand and returned to the rocks and clambered out to a corner between the eddy and the stream. By that time the sunset was over and the bats were abroad, and he was wet with perspiration.

He prodded the floating blue-clad thing with his wand, failed, tried again successfully as it came round, and as it went out into the stream it turned over, the light gleamed on golden hair, and—it was Kurt !

It was Kurt, white, and dead, and very calm. There was no mistaking him. There was still plenty of light for that.

The stream took him and he seemed to compose himself in its swift grip as one who stretches himself to rest. White-faced he was now, and all the colour gone out of him.

A feeling of infinite distress swept over Bert as the body swept out of sight towards the fall. "Kurt ! " he cried. " Kurt ! I didn't mean to ! Kurt ! don' leave me 'ere ! Don' leave me ! "

Loneliness and desolation overwhelmed him. He gave way. He stood on the rock in the evening light, weeping and wailing passionately like a child. It was as though some link that had held him to all these things had broken and gone. He was afraid like a child in a lonely room, shamelessly afraid.

The twilight was closing about him. The trees were full now of strange shadows. All the things about him became strange and unfamiliar with that subtle queerness one feels oftenest in dreams. " O God ! I carn' stand this," he said, and crept back from the rocks to the grass and crouched down, and suddenly wild sorrow for the death of Kurt, Kurt the brave, Kurt the kindly, came to his help, and he broke from whimpering to weeping. He ceased to crouch ; he sprawled upon the grass and clenched an impotent fist.

" This war," he cried, " this blarsted foolery of a war.

" O Kurt ! Lieutenant Kurt !

" I done," he said, " I done. I've 'ad all I want, and more than I want. The world's all rot, and there ain't no sense in it. The night's coming. . . . If 'E comes after me——. 'E can't come after me—'E can't ! . . .

" If 'E comes after me, I'll fro' myself into the water." . . .

Presently he was talking again in a low undertone.

" There ain't nothing to be afraid of reely. It's jest im- agination. Poor old Kurt—he thought it would happen. Prevision like. 'E never gave me that letter or tole me who the lady was. It's like what 'e said—people tore away from everything they belonged to—everywhere. Exactly like what 'e said. . . . 'Ere I am cast away thousand of miles from Edna or Grubb or any of my lot—like a plant tore up by the roots. . . . And every war's been like this, only I 'adn't the sense to understand it. Always. All sorts of 'oles and corners chaps 'ave died in. And people 'adn't the sense to understand, 'adn't the sense to feel it and stop it. Thought war was fine. My Gawd ! . . .

" Dear old Edna. She was a fair bit of all right—she was. That time we 'ad a boat at Kingston. . . .

" I bet—I'll see 'er again yet. Won't be my fault if I don't." . . .

§ 4

Suddenly, on the very verge of this heroic resolution, Bert became rigid with terror. Something was creeping towards him through the grass. Something was creeping and halting

and creeping again towards him through the dim, dark grass.
The night was electrical with horror. For a time everything
was still. Bert ceased to breathe. It could not be. No, it
was too small!

It advanced suddenly upon him with a rush, with a little
meawling cry and tail erect. It rubbed its head against him
and purred. It was a tiny, skinny little kitten.

" Gaw, Pussy! 'ow you frightened me ! " said Bert, with
drops of perspiration on his brow.

§ 5

He sat with his back to a tree stump all that night, holding
the kitten in his arms. His mind was tired, and he talked
or thought coherently no longer. Towards dawn he dozed.

When he awoke he was stiff but in better heart, and the
kitten slept warmly and reassuringly inside his jacket. And
fear, he found, had gone from amidst the trees.

He stroked the kitten, and the little creature woke up
to excessive fondness and purring. " You want some milk,"
said Bert. " That's what you want. And I could do with a
bit of brekker too."

He yawned and stood up, with the kitten on his shoulder,
and stared about him, recalling the circumstances of the
previous day, the gray, immense happenings.

" Mus' do something," he said.

He turned towards the trees, and was presently contemplating the dead aeronaut again. The kitten he held com-
panionably against his neck. The body was horrible, but
not nearly so horrible as it had been at twilight, and now the
limbs were limper and the gun had slipped to the ground
and lay half hidden in the grass.

" I suppose we ought to bury 'im, Kitty," said Bert, and
looked helplessly at the rocky soil about him. " We got to
stay on the island with 'im."

It was some time before he could turn away and go on
towards that provision shed. " Brekker first," he said, " anyhow," stroking the kitten on his shoulder. She rubbed his
cheek affectionately with her furry little face and presently
nibbled at his ear. " Wan' some milk, eh ? " he said and
turned his back on the dead man as though he mattered
nothing.

He was puzzled to find the door of the shed open, though
he had closed and latched it very carefully overnight, and
he found also some dirty plates he had not noticed before
on the bench. He discovered that the hinges of the tin locker
were unscrewed and that it could be opened. He had not
observed this overnight.

" Silly of me ! " said Bert. " 'Ere I was puzzlin' and whackin'
away at the padlock, never noticing." It had been used
apparently as an ice-chest, but it contained nothing now but

the remains of half a dozen boiled chickens some ambiguous substance that might once have been butter, and a singularly unappetising smell. He closed the lid again carefully.

He gave the kitten some milk in a dirty plate and sat watching its busy little tongue for a time. Then he was moved to make an inventory of the provisions. There were six bottles of milk unopened and one opened, sixty bottles of mineral water and a large stock of syrups, about two thousand cigarettes and upwards of a hundred cigars, nine oranges, two unopened tins of corned beef and one opened, two tins of biscuits and eleven hard cakes, a hatful of nuts and five large tins of Californian peaches. He jotted it down on a piece of paper. " 'Ain't much solid food," he said. " Still—— A fortnight, say !

" Anything might happen in a fortnight."

He gave the kitten a small second helping and a scrap of beef and then went down with the little creature running after him, tail erect and in high spirits, to look at the remains of 'the *Hohenzollern*. It had shifted in the night and seemed on the whole more firmly grounded on Green island than before. From it his eye went to the shattered bridge and then across to the still desolation of Niagara city. Nothing moved over there but a number of crows. They were busy with the engineer he had seen cut down on the previous day. He saw no dogs, but he heard one howling.

" We got to get out of this some'ow, Kitty," he said. " That milk won't last for ever—not at the rate you lap it."

He regarded the sluice-like flood before him. " Plenty of water," he said. " Won't be drink we shall want."

He decided to make a careful exploration of the island. Presently he came to a locked gate labelled " Biddle Stairs," and clambered over to discover a steep old wooden staircase leading down the face of the cliff amidst a vast and increasing uproar of waters. He left the kitten above and descended these, and discovered with a thrill of hope a path leading among the rocks at the foot of the roaring downrush of the Centre Fall. Perhaps this was a sort of way !

It led him only to the choking and deafening experience of the Cave of the Winds, and after he had spent a quarter of an hour in a partially stupefied condition flattened between solid rock and nearly as solid waterfall, he decided that this was after all no practicable route to Canada, and retraced his steps. As he reascended the Biddle Stairs, he heard what he decided at last must be a sort of echo, a sound of some one walking about on the gravel paths above. When he got to the top of the place was as solitary as before.

Thence he made his way, with the kitten skirmishing along beside him in the grass, to a staircase that led to a lump of projecting rock that enfiladed the huge green majesty of the Horseshoe Fall. He stood there for some time in silence.

" You wouldn't think," he said at last, " there was so much water. . . . This roarin' and splashin', it gets on one's nerves at last. . . . Sounds like people talking. . . . Sounds like people going about. . . . Sounds like anything you fancy."

He retired up the staircase again. " I s'pose I shall keep on goin' round this blessed island," he said drearily. " Round and round and round."

He found himself presently beside the less damaged Asiatic aeroplane again. He stared at it and the kitten smelt it. " Broke ! " he said.

He looked up with a convulsive start.

Advancing slowly towards him out from among the trees were two tall, gaunt figures. They were blackened and tattered and bandaged ; the hindmost one limped and had his head swathed in white, but the foremost one still carried himself as a Prince should do, for all that his left arm was in a sling and one side of his face scalded a livid crimson. He was the Prince Karl Albert, the War Lord, the " German Alexander," and the man behind him was the bird-faced man whose cabin had once been taken from him and given to Bert.

§ 6

With that apparition began a new phase of Goat Island in Bert's experience. He ceased to be a solitary representative of humanity in a vast and violent and incomprehensible universe, and became once more a social creature, a man in a world of other men. For an instant these two were terrible, then they seemed sweet and desirable as brothers. They, too, were in this scrape with him, marooned and puzzled. He wanted extremely to hear exactly what had happened to them. What mattered it, if one was a Prince and both were foreign soldiers, if neither perhaps had adequate English ? His native Cockney freedom flowed too generously for him to think of that, and surely the Asiatic fleets had purged all such trivial differences. " Ul-*lo* ! " he said, " 'ow did you get 'ere ? "

" It is the Englishman who brought us the Butteridge machine," said the bird-faced officer in German, and then in a tone of horror as Bert advanced, " Salute ! " and again louder, " *Salute !* "

" Gaw ! " said Bert, and stopped with a second comment under his breath. He stared and saluted awkwardly and became at once a masked defensive thing with whom co-operation was impossible.

For a time these two perfected modern aristocrats stood regarding the difficult problem of the Anglo-Saxon citizen, that ambiguous citizen who, obeying some mysterious law in his blood, would neither drill nor be a democrat. Bert was by no means a beautiful object, but in some inexplicable

way he looked resistent. He wore his cheap suit of serge,
now showing many signs of wear, and its loose fit made him
seem sturdier than he was ; above his disengaging face was
a white German cap that was altogether too big for him, and
his trousers were crumpled up his legs and their ends tucked
into the rubber highlows of a deceased German aeronaut.
He looked an inferior, though by no means an easy inferior,
and instinctively they hated him.

The Prince pointed to the flying-machine and said something in broken English that Bert took for German and failed
to understand. He intimated as much.

" Dummer Kerl ! " said the bird-faced officer from among
his bandages.

The Prince pointed again with his undamaged hand. " You
understan' dis drachenflieger ? "

Bert began to comprehend the situation. He regarded
the Asiatic machine. The habits of Bun Hill returned to
him. " It's a foreign make," he said ambiguously.

The two Germans consulted. " You are—an expert ? "
said the Prince.

" We reckon to repair," said Bert, in the exact manner of
Grubb.

The Prince sought in his vocabulary. " Is dat," he said,
" goot to fly ? "

Bert reflected, and scratched his chin slowly. " I got to
look at it," he replied. . . . " It's 'ad rough usage ! "

He made a sound with his teeth he had also acquired from
Grubb, put his hands in his trouser pockets and strolled back
to the machine. Typically Grubb chewed something, but
Bert could chew only imaginatively. " Three days' work in
this," he said, teething. For the first time it dawned on him
that there were possibilities in this machine. It was evident
that the wing that lay on the ground was disabled. The three
stays that held it rigid had snapped across a ridge of rock,
and there was also a strong possibility of the engine being
badly damaged. The wing hook on that side was also askew,
but probably that would not affect the flight. Beyond that
there probably wasn't much the matter. Bert scratched his
cheek again, and contemplated the broad sunlit waste of
the Upper Rapids. " We might make a job of this. . . You
leave it to me."

He surveyed it intently again, and the Prince and his
officer watched him. In Bun Hill Bert and Grubb had developed to a very high pitch among the hiring stock a method
of repair by substitution ; they substituted other bits of
other machines. A machine that was too utterly and obviously
done for even to proffer for hire had nevertheless still capital
value. It became a sort of quarry for nuts and screws and
wheels, bars and spokes, chain-links and the like ; a mine of ill-
fitting " parts " to replace the defects of machines still current.

And back among the trees was a second Asiatic aeroplane. The kitten caressed Bert's airship boats unheeded.

" Mend dat drachenflieger," said the Prince.

" If I do mend it," said Bert, struck by a new thought, " none of us ain't to be trusted to fly it."

" *I* vill fly it," said the Prince.

" Very likely break your neck," said Bert, after a pause.

The Prince did not understand him and disregarded what he said. He pointed his gloved finger to the machine and turned to the bird-faced officer with some remark in German. The officer answered and the Prince responded with a sweeping gesture towards the sky. Then he spoke—it seemed eloquently. Bert watched him and guessed his meaning. " Much more likely to break your neck," he said. " 'Owever. 'Ere goes."

He began to pry about the saddle and engine of the drachenflieger in a search for tools. Also he wanted some black oily stuff for his hands and face. For the first rule in the art of repairing as it was known to the firm of Grubb and Smallways, was to get your hands and face thoroughly and conclusively blackened. Also he took off his jacket and waistcoat and put his cap carefully to the back of his head in order to facilitate scratching.

The Prince and the officer seemed disposed to watch him, but he succeeded in making it clear to them that this would inconvenience him and that he had to " puzzle out a bit " before he could get to work. They thought him over, but his shop experience had given him something of the authoritative way of the expert with common men. And at last they went away. Thereupon he went straight to the second aeroplane, got the aeronaut's gun and ammunition and hid them in a clump of nettles close at hand. " That's all right," said Bert, and then proceeded to a careful inspection of the debris of the wings in the trees. Then he went back to the first aeroplane to compare the two. The Bun Hill method was quite possibly practicable if there was nothing hopeless or incomprehensible in the engine.

The Germans returned presently to find him already generously smutty and touching and testing knobs and screws and levers with an expression of profound sagacity. When the bird-faced officer addressed a remark to him he waved him aside with, " Nong comprong. Shut it ! It's no good."

Then he had an idea. " Dead chap back there wants burying," he said, jerking a thumb over his shoulder.

§ 7

With the appearance of these two men Bert's whole universe had changed again. A curtain fell before the immense and terrible desolation that had overwhelmed him. He was in a world of three people, a minute human world that nevertheless filled his brain with eager speculations and schemes and cunning ideas. What were they thinking of ? What did they think of him ? What did they mean to do ? A hundred busy threads interlaced in his mind as he pottered studiously over the Asiatic aeroplane. New ideas came up like bubbles in soda water.

"Gaw!" he said suddenly. He had just appreciated as a special aspect of this irrational injustice of fate that these two men were alive and that Kurt was dead. All the crew of the *Hohenzollern* were shot or burnt or smashed or drowned, and these two lurking in the padded forward cabin had escaped.

"I suppose 'e thinks it's 'is bloomin' Star," he muttered, and found himself uncontrollably exasperated.

He stood up, facing round to the two men. They were standing side by side regarding him. "It's no good," he said, "starin' at me. You only put me out." And then, seeing they did not understand, he advanced towards them, wrench in hand. It occurred to him as he did so that the Prince was really a very big and powerful and serene-looking person. But he said, nevertheless, pointing through the trees, " dead man ! "

The bird-faced man intervened with a reply in German.

"Dead man ! " said Bert to him. " There."

He had great difficulty in inducing them to inspect the dead Chinaman, and at last led them to him. Then they made it evident that they proposed that he, as a common person below the rank of officer, should have the sole and undivided privilege of disposing of the body by dragging it to the water's edge. There was some heated gesticulation, and at last the bird-faced officer abased himself to help. Together they dragged the limp and now swollen Asiatic through the trees, and after a rest or so—for he trailed very heavily—dumped him into the westward rapid. Bert returned to his expert investigation of the flying-machine at last with aching arms and in a state of gloomy rebellion. " Brasted cheek ! " he said. " One'd think I was one of 'is beastly German slaves !

" Prancing beggar ! "

And then he fell speculating what would happen when the flying-machine was repaired—if it could be repaired.

The two Germans went away again, and after some reflection Bert removed several nuts, resumed his jacket and vest, pocketed those nuts and his tools and hid the set of tools from the second aeroplane in the fork of a tree. " Right-o," he said, as he jumped down after the last of these precautions. The Prince and his companion reappeared as he returned to the machine by the water's edge. The Prince surveyed his progress for a time, and then went towards the Parting of the Waters and stood with folded arms gazing up-stream in profound thought. The bird-faced officer came up to Bert, heavy with a sentence in English.

" Go," he said with a helping gesture, " und eat."

When Bert got to the refreshment shed he found all tne food had vanished except one measured ration of corned beef and three biscuits. He regarded this with open eyes and mouth. The kitten appeared from under the vender's seat with an ingratiating purr. " Of course ! " said Bert. " Why ! where's your milk ? "

He accumulated wrath for a moment or so, then seized the plate in one hand, and the biscuits in another, and went in search of the Prince, breathing vile words anent " grub " and his intimate interior. He approached without saluting.

" 'Ere ! " he said fiercely. " Whad the devil's this ? "

An entirely unsatisfactory altercation followed. Bert expounded the Bun Hill theory of the relations of grub to efficiency in English, the bird-faced man replied with points about nations and discipline in German. The Prince, having made an estimate of Bert's quality and physique, suddenly hectored. He gripped Bert by the shoulder and shook him, making his pockets rattle, shouted something to him, and flung him struggling back. He hit him as though he was a German private. Bert went back, white and scared, but resolved by all his Cockney standards upon one thing. He was bound in honour to " go for " the Prince. " Gaw ! " he gasped, buttoning his coat.

" Now," cried the Prince, " vill you go ! " and then, catching the heroic gleam in Bert's eye, drew his sword.

The bird-faced officer intervened, saying something in German and pointing skyward.

Far away in the south-west appeared a Japanese airship coming fast towards them. Their conflict ended at that. The Prince was first to grasp the situation and lead the retreat. All three scuttled like rabbits for the trees, and ran to and fro for cover until they found a hollow in which the grass grew rank. There they all squatted within six yards of one another. They sat in this place for a long time, up to their necks in the grass and watching through the branches for the airship. Bert had dropped some of his corned beef, but he found the biscuits in his hand and ate them quietly. The monster came nearly overhead and then went away to Niagara and dropped beyond the power works. When it was near they all kept silence, and then presently they fell into an argument that was robbed perhaps of immediate explosive effect only by their failure to understand one another.

It was Bert began the talking, and he talked on, regardless of what they understood or failed to understand. But his voice must have conveyed his cantankerous intentions.

" You want that machine done," he said first, " you better keep your 'ands off me ! "

They disregarded that and he repeated it.

Then he expanded his idea, and the spirit of speech took

hold of him. " You think you got 'old of a chap you can kick
and 'it like you do your private soldiers—you're jolly well
mistaken. See ? I've 'ad about enough of you and your antics.
I been thinking you over, you and your war and your Empire,
and all the rot of it. Rot it is. It's you Germans made all the
trouble in Europe first and last. And all for nothin'. Jest silly
prancing ! Jest because you've got the uniforms and flags !
'Ere I was—I didn't want to 'ave anything to do with you. I
jest didn't care a 'eng at all about you. Then you gets 'old
of me—steal me practically—and 'ere I am, thousands of miles
away from 'ome and everything, and all your silly fleet smashed
up to rags. And you want to go on prancin' *now* ! Not if I
know it !

" Look at the mischief you done. Look at the way you
smashed up New York—the people you killed, the stuff you
wasted. Can't you learn ? "

" Dummer Kerl ! " said the bird-faced man suddenly, in a
tone of concentrated malignity, glaring under his bandages.
" Esel ! "

" That's German for silly ass ! I know. But who's the silly
ass—'im or me ? When I was a kid I used to read penny
dreadfuls about 'aving adventures and being a great c'mander
and all that rot. I stowed it. But what's 'e got in 'is 'ead ?
Rot about Napoleon, rot about Alexander, rot about 'is blessed
family and 'im and Gawd and David and all that. Any one who
wasn't a dressed-up silly fool of a Prince could 'ave told all
this was goin' to 'appen. There was us in Europe all at sixes
and sevens with our silly flags and our silly newspapers raggin'
us up against each other and keepin' us apart, and there was
China as solid as a cheese, with millions and millions of men
only wantin' a bit of science, and a bit of enterprise, to be as
good as all of us. You thought they couldn't get at you. And
then they got flying-machines. And bif !—'ere we are. Why,
when they didn't go on making guns and armies in China we
went and poked 'em up until they did. They 'ad to give us this
lickin' they've give us. We wouldn't be 'appy till they did.
And as I say, 'ere we are ! "

The bird-faced officer shouted to him to be quiet, and then
began conversation with the Prince.

" British citizen," said Bert. " You ain't obliged to listen,
but I ain't obliged to shut up." And for some time he continued
his dissertation upon Imperialism, militarism, and international
politics. But their talking put him out, and for a time he was
certainly merely repeating abusive terms, " prancin' nincom-
poops " and the like, old terms and new.

Then suddenly he remembered his essential grievance.
" 'Owever, look 'ere—'ere !—the thing I started this talk about
is where's that food there was in that shed ? That's what I
want to know. Where you put it ? "

He paused. They went on talking in German. He repeated

his question. They disregarded him. He asked a third time in a manner insupportably aggressive.

There fell a tense silence. For some seconds the three regarded one another. The Prince eyed Bert steadfastly, and Bert quailed under his eye. Slowly the Prince rose to his feet and the bird-faced officer jerked up beside him. Bert remained squatting.

" Be quaiat," said the Prince.

Bert perceived this was no moment for eloquence.

The two Germans regarded him as he crouched there. Death for a moment seemed near.

Then the Prince turned away and the two of them went towards the flying-machine.

" Gaw ! " whispered Bert, and then uttered under his breath one single word of abuse. He sat crouched together for perhaps three minutes, then he sprang to his feet and went off towards the Chinese aeronaut's gun hidden among the weeds.

§ 8

There was no pretence after that moment that Bert was under the orders of the Prince or that he was going on with the repairing of the flying-machine. The two Germans took possession of that and set to work upon it. Bert, with his new weapon, went off to the neighbourhood of Terrapin Rock, and there sat down to examine it. It was a short rifle with a big cartridge and nearly a full magazine. He took out the cartridges carefully and then tried the trigger and fittings until he felt sure he had the use of it. He reloaded carefully. Then he remembered he was hungry and went off, gun under his arm, to hunt in and about the refreshment shed. He had the sense to perceive that he must not show himself with the gun to the Prince and his companion. So long as they thought him un-armed they would leave him alone, but there was no knowing what the Napoleonic person might do if he saw Bert's weapon. Also he did not go near them because he knew that within him-self boiled a reservoir of rage and fear, that he wanted to shoot these two men. He wanted to shoot them, and he thought that to shoot them would be a quite horrible thing to do. The two sides of his inconsistent civilisation warred within him.

Near the shed the kitten turned up again, obviously keen for milk. This greatly enhanced his own angry sense of hunger. He began to talk as he hunted about, and presently stood still shouting insults. He talked of war and pride and Imperialism. " Any other Prince but you would have died with his men and his ship ! " he cried.

The two Germans at the machine heard his voice going ever and again amidst the clamour of the waters. Their eyes met and they smiled slightly.

He was disposed for a time to sit in the refreshment shed

waiting for them, but then it occurred to him that so he might get them both at close quarters. He strolled off presently to the point of Luna Island to think the situation out.

It had seemed a comparatively simple one at first, but as he turned it over in his mind its possibilities increased and multiplied. Both these men had swords—had either a revolver ?

Also if he shot them both he might never find the food !

So far he had been going about with this gun under his arm, and a sense of lordly security in his mind, but what if they saw the gun and decided to ambush him ? Goat Island is nearly all cover, trees, rocks, thickets, and irregularities.

Why not go and murder them both now ?

" I carn't," said Bert, dismissing that. " I got to be worked up."

But it was a mistake to get right away from them. That suddenly became clear. He ought to keep them under observation, ought to " scout " them. Then he would be able to see what they were doing, whether either of them had a revolver, where they had hidden the food. He would be better able to determine what they meant to do to him. If he didn't "scout" them, presently they would begin to " scout " him. This seemed so eminently reasonable that he acted upon it forthwith. He thought over his costume and threw his collar and the tell-tale aeronaut's white cap into the water far below. He turned his coat collar up to hide any gleam of his dirty shirt. The tools and nuts in his pockets were disposed to clank, but he rearranged them and wrapped some letters and his pocket-handkerchief about them. He started off circumspectly and noiselessly, listening and peering at every step. As he drew near his antagonists, much grunting and creaking served to locate them. He discovered them engaged in what looked like a wrestling match with the Asiatic flying-machine. Their coats were off, their swords laid aside, they were working magnificently. Apparently they were turning it round and were having a good deal of difficulty with the long tail among the trees. He dropped flat at the sight of them and wriggled into a little hollow, and so lay watching their exertions. Ever and again, to pass the time, he would cover one or other of them with his gun.

He found them quite interesting to watch, so interesting that at times he came near shouting to advise them. He perceived that when they had the machine turned round they would then be in immediate want of the nuts and tools he carried. Then they would come after him. They would certainly conclude he had them or had hidden them. Should he hide his gun and do a deal for food with these tools ? He felt he would not be able to part with the gun again now he had once felt its reassuring company. The kitten turned up and made a great fuss with him and licked and bit his ear.

The sun clambered to midday, and once that morning he

saw, though the Germans did not, an Asiatic airship very far to the south, going swiftly eastward.

At last the flying-machine was turned and stood poised on its wheel, with its hooks pointing up the Rapids. The two Germans wiped their faces, resumed jackets and swords, spoke and bore themselves like men who congratulated themselves on a good laborious morning. Then they went off briskly towards the refreshment shed, the Prince leading. Bert became active in pursuit ; but he found it impossible to stalk them quickly enough and silently enough to discover the hiding-place of the food. He found them when he came into sight of them again, seated with their backs against the shed, plates on knee, and a tin of corned beef and a plateful of biscuits between them. They seemed in fairly good spirits, and once the Prince laughed. At this vision of eating Bert's plans gave way. Fierce hunger carried him. He appeared before them suddenly at a distance of perhaps twenty yards, gun in hand. " 'Ands up ! " he said in a hard, ferocious voice.

The Prince hesitated, and then up went two pairs of hands. The gun had surprised them both completely.

" Stand up," said Bert. . . . " Drop that fork ! "

They obeyed again.

" What nex' ? " said Bert to himself. " 'Orf stage, I suppose. That way," he said. " Go ! "

The Prince obeyed with remarkable alacrity. When he reached the head of the clearing he said something quickly to the bird-faced man and they both, with an entire lack of dignity, *ran* !

Bert was struck with an exasperating afterthought.

" Gord ! " he cried with infinite vexation. " Why ! I ought to 'ave took their swords ! 'Ere ! "

But the Germans were already out of sight, and no doubt taking cover among the trees. Bert fell back upon imprecations, then he went up to the shed, cursorily examined the possibility of a flank attack, put his gun handy and set to work, with a convulsive listening pause before each mouthful on the Prince's plate of corned beef. He had finished that up and handed its gleanings to the kitten and he was falling-to on the second plateful, when the plate broke in his hand ! He stared, with the fact slowly creeping upon him that an instant before he had heard a crack among the thickets. Then he sprang to his feet, snatched up his gun in one hand and the tin of corned beef in the other, and fled round the shed to the other side of the clearing. As he did so came a second crack from the thickets, and something went *phwit !* by his ear.

He didn't stop running until he was in what seemed to him a strongly defensible position near Luna Island. Then he took cover, panting, and crouched expectant.

" They got a revolver after all ! " he panted. . . . " Wonder if they got two ? If they 'ave—Gord !—I'm done ! "

" Where's the kitten ? Finishin' up that corned beef, I
suppose. Little beggar ! "

§ 9

So it was that war began upon Goat Island. It lasted a
day and a night, the longest day and the longest night in
Bert's life. He had to lie close and listen and watch. Also
he had to scheme what he should do. It was clear now that
he had to kill these two men if he could, and that if they
could they would kill him. The prize was first food and then
the flying-machine and the doubtful privilege of trying to
ride it. If one failed one would certainly be killed, if one
succeeded one would get away somewhere over there. For a
time Bert tried to imagine what it was like over there. His
mind ran over possibilities, deserts, angry Americans, Japanese,
Chinese—perhaps Red Indians ! (Were there still Red Indians?)
" Got to take what comes," said Bert. " No way out of it
that I can see ! "
Was that voices ? He realised that his attention was wandering. For a time all his senses were very alert. The uproar of
the Falls was very confusing, and it mixed in all sorts of sounds,
like feet walking, like voices talking, like shouts and cries.
" Silly great catarac'," said Bert. " There ain't no sense in
it, fallin' and fallin'."
Never mind that now ! What were the Germans doing ?
Would they go back to the flying-machine ? They couldn't
do anything with it, because he had those nuts and screws
and the wrench and other tools. But suppose they found the
second set of tools he had hidden in the tree ! He had hidden
the things well, of course, but they *might* find them. One wasn't
sure, of course—one wasn't sure. He tried to remember just
exactly how he had hidden those tools. He tried to persuade
himself they were certainly and surely hidden, but his memory
began to play antics. Had he really left the handle of the
wrench sticking out, shining out at the fork of the branch ?
Ssh ! What was that ? Some one stirring in those bushes?
Up went an expectant muzzle. No ! Where was the kitten ?
No ! It was just imagination, not even the kitten.
The Germans would certainly miss and hunt about for the
tools and nuts and screws he carried in his pockets ; that was
clear. Then they would decide he had them and come for him.
He had only to remain still under cover, therefore, and he would
get them. Was there any flaw in that ? Would they take off
more removable parts of the flying-machine and then lie up
for him ? No, they wouldn't do that, because they were two
to one ; they would have no apprehension of his getting off
in the flying-machine, and no sound reason for supposing he
would approach it, and so they would do nothing to damage
or disable it. That, he decided, was clear. But suppose they
lay up for him by the food. Well, that they wouldn't do, because

they would know he had this corned beef ; there was enough
in this can to last, with moderation, several days. Of course,
they might try to tire him out instead of attacking him——

He roused himself with a start. He had just grasped the real
weakness of his position. He might go to sleep !

It needed but ten minutes under the suggestion of that idea
before he realised that he was going to sleep !

He rubbed his eyes and handled his gun. He had never
before realised the intensely soporific effect of the American
sun, of the American air, the drowsy, sleep-compelling uproar
of Niagara. Hitherto these things had on the whole seemed
stimulating. . . .

If he had not eaten so much and eaten it so fast, he would
not be so heavy. Are vegetarians always bright ? . . .

He roused himself with a jerk again.

If he didn't do something he would fall asleep, and if he fell
asleep it was ten to one they would find him snoring, and finish
him forthwith. If he sat motionless and noiseless he would
inevitably sleep. It was better, he told himself, to take even
the risks of attacking than that. This sleep trouble, he felt,
was going to beat him, must beat him in the end. They were all
right ; one could sleep and the other could watch. That, come
to think of it, was what they would always do ; one would do
anything they wanted done, the other would lie under cover
near at hand, ready to shoot. They might even trap him like
that. One might act as a decoy.

That set him thinking of decoys. What a fool he had been
to throw his cap away. It would have been invaluable on a
stick—especially at night.

He found himself wishing for a drink. He settled that for
a time by putting a pebble in his mouth. And then the sleep
craving returned.

It became clear to him he must attack.

Like many great generals before him, he found his baggage,
that is to say his tin of corned beef, a serious impediment to
mobility. At last he decided to put the beef loose in his pocket
and abandon the tin. It was not, perhaps, an ideal arrangement, but one must make sacrifices when one is campaigning.
He crawled perhaps ten yards, and then for a time the
possibilities of the situation paralysed him.

The afternoon was still. The roar of the cataract simply
threw up that immense stillness in relief. He was doing his
best to contrive the deaths of two better men than himself.
Also they were doing their best to contrive his. What, behind
this silence, were they doing ?

Suppose he came upon them suddenly and fired and missed ?

§ 10

He crawled, and halted listening, and crawled again until
nightfall, and no doubt the German Alexander and his

lieutenant did the same. A large scale map of Goat Island marked with red and blue lines to show these strategic movements would no doubt have displayed much interlacing, but as a matter of fact neither side saw anything of the other throughout that age-long day of tedious alertness. Bert never knew how near he got to them nor how far he kept from them. Night found him no longer sleepy, but athirst, and near the American Fall. He was inspired by the idea that his antagonists might be in the wreckage of the *Hohenzollern* cabins that was jammed against Green Island. He became enterprising, broke from any attempt to conceal himself, and went across the little bridge at the double. He found nobody. It was his first visit to those huge fragments of airship, and for a time he explored them curiously in the dim light. He discovered the forward cabin was nearly intact, with its door slanting downward and a corner under water. He crept in, drank, and then was struck by the brilliant idea of shutting the door and sleeping on it.

But now he could not sleep at all.

He nodded towards morning and woke up to find it fully day. He breakfasted on corned beef and water, and sat for a long time appreciative of the security of his position. At last he became enterprising and bold. He would, he decided, settle this business forthwith, one way or the other. He was tired of all this crawling. He set out in the morning sunshine, gun in hand, scarcely troubling to walk softly. He went round the refreshment shed without finding any one, and then through the trees towards the flying-machine. He came upon the bird-faced man sitting on the ground with his back against a tree, bent up over his folded arms, sleeping, his bandage very much over one eye.

Bert stopped abruptly and stood perhaps fifteen yards away, gun in hand ready. Where was the Prince ? Then, sticking out at the side of the tree beyond, he saw a shoulder. Bert took five deliberate paces to the left. The great man became visible, leaning up against the trunk, pistol in one hand and sword in the other, and yawning—yawning. You can't shoot a yawning man, Bert found. He advanced upon his antagonist with his gun levelled, some foolish fancy of " hands up ! " in his mind. The Prince became aware of him, the yawning mouth shut like a trap, and he stood stiffly up. Bert stopped, silent. For a moment the two regarded one another.

Had the Prince been a wise man he would, I suppose, have dodged behind the tree. Instead, he gave vent to a shout, and raised pistol and sword. At that, like an automaton, Bert pulled his trigger.

It was his first experience of an oxygen-containing bullet. A great flame spurted from the middle of the Prince, a blinding flare, and there came a thud like the firing of a gun. Something hot and wet struck Bert's face. Then through a whirl of blinding smoke and steam he saw limbs and a collapsing burst body fling themselves to earth.

Bert was so astonished that he stood agape, and the bird-faced officer might have cut him to the earth without a struggle. But, instead, the bird-faced officer was running away through the undergrowth, dodging as he went. Bert roused himself to a brief ineffectual pursuit, but he had no stomach for further killing. He returned to the mangled, scattered thing that had so recently been the great Prince Karl Albert. He surveyed the scorched and splashed vegetation about it. He made some speculative identifications. He advanced gingerly and picked up the hot revolver, to find all its chambers strained and burst. He became aware of a cheerful and friendly presence. He was greatly shocked that one so young should see so frightful a scene.

" 'Ere, Kitty," he said, " this ain't no place for you."

He made three strides across the devastated area, captured the kitten neatly, and went his way towards the shed, with her purring loudly on his shoulder.

" *You* don't seem to mind," he said.

For a time he fussed about the shed, and at last discovered the rest of the provisions hidden in the roof. " Seems 'ard," he said, as he administered a saucerful of milk, " when you get three men in a 'ole like this, they can't work together. But 'im and 'is princing was jest a bit too thick ! "

" Gaw ! " he reflected, sitting on the counter and eating, " What a thing life is ! 'Ere am I ; I seen 'is picture, 'eard 'is name since I was a kid in frocks. Prince Karl Albert ! And if any one 'ad tole me I was going to blow him to smithereens—there ! I shouldn't 'ave believed it, Kitty.

" That chap at Margit ought to 'ave tole me about it. All 'e tole me was that I got a weak chess.

" That other chap, 'e ain't going to do much. Wonder what I ought to do about 'im ? "

He surveyed the trees with a keen blue eye and fingered the gun on his knee. " I don't like this killing, Kitty," he said. " It's like Kurt said about being blooded. Seems to me you got to be blooded young. . . . If that Prince 'ad come up to me and said, ' Shake 'ands ! ' I'd 'ave shook 'ands. . . . Now 'ere's that other chap, dodging about ! 'E's got 'is 'ead 'urt already, and there's something wrong with his leg. And burns. Golly ! it isn't three weeks ago I first set eyes on 'im, and then 'e was smart and set up—'ands full of 'air-brushes and things, and swearin' at me. A regular gentleman ! Now 'e's 'arf-way to a wild man. What am I to do with 'im ? What the 'ell am I to do with 'im ? I can't let 'im 'ave that flying-machine ; that's a bit *too* good, and if I don't kill 'im 'e'll jest hang about this island and starve. . . .

" 'E's got a sword, of course." . . .

He resumed his philosophising after he had lit a cigarette.

" War's a silly gaim, Kitty. It's a silly gaim ! We common people—we were fools. We thought those big people knew what they were up to—and they didn't. Look at that chap ! 'E 'ad all Germany be'ind 'im, and what 'as 'e made of it ? Smeshin' and blunderin' and destroyin', and there 'e is ! Jest a mess of blood and boots and things ! Jest an 'orrid splash ! Prince Karl Albert ! And all the men 'e led and the ships 'e 'ad, the airships and the dragonfliers—all scattered like a paper-chase between this 'ole and Germany. And fightin' going on and burnin' and killin' that 'e started, war without end all over the world !

" I suppose I shall 'ave to kill that other chap. I suppose I must. But it ain't at all the sort of job I fancy, Kitty ! "

For a time he hunted about the island amidst the uproar of the waterfall looking for the wounded officer, and at last he started him out of some bushes near the head of Biddle Stairs. But as he saw the bent and bandaged figure in limping flight before him, he found his Cockney softness too much for him again : he could neither shoot nor pursue. " I carn't," he said, " that's flat. I 'aven't the guts for it ! 'E'll 'ave to go."

He turned his steps towards the flying-machine. . . .

He never saw the bird-faced officer again, nor any further evidence of his presence. Towards evening he grew fearful of ambushes and hunted vigorously for an hour or so, but in vain. He slept in a good defensible position at the extremity of the rocky point that runs out to the Canadian Fall, and in the night he woke in panic terror and fired his gun. But it was nothing. He slept no more that night. In the morning he became curiously concerned for the vanished man, and hunted for him as one might for an erring brother. " If I knew some German," he said, " I'd 'oller. It's jest not knowing German does it. You can't explain."

He discovered, later, traces of an attempt to cross the gap in the broken bridge. A rope with a bolt attached had been flung across and had caught in a fenestration of a projecting fragment of railing. The end of the rope trailed in the seething water towards the fall.

But the bird-faced officer was already rubbing shoulders with certain inert matter that had once been Lieutenant Kurt and the Chinese aeronaut and a dead cow, and much more uncongenial company, in the huge circle of the whirlpool two and a quarter miles away. Never had that great gathering place, that incessant, aimless, unprogressive hurry of waste and battered things, been so crowded with strange and melancholy derelicts. Round they went and round, and every day brought its new contributions, luckless brutes, shattered fragments of boat and flying-machine, endless citizens from the cities upon the shores of the great lakes above. Much came from Cleveland. It all gathered here, and whirled about indefinitely, and over it all gathered daily a greater abundance of birds.

CHAPTER TEN

THE WORLD UNDER THE WAR

§ I

BERT spent two more days upon Goat Island, and finished all his provisions except the cigarettes and mineral water, before he brought himself to try the Asiatic flying-machine.

Even at last he did not so much go off upon it as get carried off. It had taken only an hour or so to substitute wing stays from the second flying-machine and to replace the nuts he had himself removed. The engine was in working order, and differed only very simply and obviously from that of a contemporary motor bicycle. The rest of the time was taken up by a vast musing and delaying and hesitation. Chiefly he saw himself splashing into the rapids and whirling down them to the Fall, clutching and drowning, but also he had a vision of being hopelessly in the air, going fast and unable to ground. His mind was too concentrated upon the business of flying for him to think very much of what might happen to an indefinite-spirited Cockney without credentials who arrived on an Asiatic flying-machine amidst the war-infuriated population beyond.

He still had a lingering solicitude for the bird-faced officer. He had a haunting fancy he might be lying disabled or badly smashed in some way in some nook or cranny of the Island ; and it was only after a most exhaustive search that he abandoned that distressing idea. " If I found 'im," he reasoned the while, " what could I do wiv 'im ? You can't blow a chap's brains out when 'e's down. And I don' see 'ow else I can 'elp 'im."

Then the kitten bothered his highly developed sense of social responsibility. " If I leave 'er she'll starve. . . . Ought to catch mice for 'erself. . . . *Are* there mice ? . . . Birds ? . . . She's too young. . . . She's like me ; she's a bit too civilised."

Finally he stuck her in his side pocket, and she became greatly interested in the memories of corned beef she found there.

With her in his pocket, he seated himself in the saddle of the flying-machine. Big, clumsy thing it was—and not a bit like a bicycle. Still, the working of it was fairly plain. You set the engine going—*so* ; kicked yourself up until the wheel was vertical, *so*; engaged the gyroscope, *so*, and then —then—you just pulled up this lever.

Rather stiff it was, but suddenly it came over——

The big curved wings on either side flapped disconcertingly, flapped again, click, clock, click, clock, clitter-clock!

Stop! The thing was heading for the water; its wheel was in the water. Bert groaned from his heart and struggled to restore the lever to its first position. Click, clock, clitter-clock; he was rising! The machine was lifting its dripping wheel out of the eddies, and he was going up! There was no stopping now, no good in stopping now. In another moment, Bert, clutching and convulsive and rigid, with staring eyes and a face pale as death, was flapping up above the Rapids, jerking to every jerk of the wings, and rising, rising.

There was no comparison in dignity and comfort between a flying-machine and a balloon. Except in its moments of descent, the balloon was a vehicle of faultless urbanity; this was a buck-jumping mule, a mule that jumped up and never came down again. Click, clock, click, clock; with each beat of the strangely shaped wings it jumped Bert upward and caught him neatly again half a second later on the saddle. And while in ballooning there is no wind, since the balloon is a part of the wind, flying is a wild perpetual creation of, and plunging into, wind. It was a wind that above all things sought to blind him, to force him to close his eyes. It occurred to him presently to twist his knees and legs inward and grip with them, or surely he would have been bumped into two clumsy halves. And he was going up, a hundred yards high, two hundred, three hundred, over the streaming, frothing wilderness of water below—up, up, up. That was all right, but how presently would one go horizontally? He tried to think if these things did go horizontally. No! They flapped up and then they soared down. For a time he would keep on flapping up. Tears streamed from his eyes. He wiped them with one temerariously disengaged hand.

Was it better to risk a fall over land or over water—such water?

He was flapping up above the Upper Rapids towards Buffalo. It was at any rate a comfort that the Falls and the wild swirl of waters below them were behind him. He was flying up straight. That he could see. How did one turn?

He was presently almost cool, and his eyes got more used to the rush of air, but he was getting very high, very high. He tilted his head forwards and surveyed the country, blinking. He could see all over Buffalo, a place with three great blackened scars of ruin, and hills and stretches beyond. He wondered if he was half a mile high, or more. There were some people among some houses near a railway station between Niagara and Buffalo, and then more people. They went like ants busily in and out of the houses. He saw two motor-cars

gliding along the road towards Niagara City. Then far away
in the south he saw a great Asiatic airship going eastward.
" O Gord ! " he said, and became earnest in his ineffectual
attempts to alter his direction. But that airship took no
notice of him, and he continued to ascend convulsively. The
world got more and more extensive and map-like. Click, clock,
clitter-clock. Above him and very near to him now was a
hazy stratum of cloud.

He determined to disengage the wing clutch. He did so.
The lever resisted his strength for a time, then over it came,
and instantly the tail of the machine cocked up and the
wings became rigidly spread. Instantly everything was swift
and smooth and silent. He was gliding rapidly down the
air against a wild gale of wind, his eyes three-quarters shut. . . .

A little lever that had hitherto been obdurate now confessed
itself mobile. He turned it over gently to the right, and
whiroo !—the left wing had in some mysterious way given
at its edge, and he was sweeping round and downwards
in an immense right-handed spiral. For some moments he
experienced all the helpless sensations of catastrophe. He
restored the lever to its middle position with some difficulty,
and the wings were equalised again.

He turned it to the left and had a sensation of being spun
round backwards. " Too much ! " he gasped.

He discovered that he was rushing down at a headlong
pace towards a railway line and some factory buildings.
They appeared to be tearing up to him to devour him. He
must have dropped all that height. For a moment he had
the ineffectual sensations of one whose bicycle bolts downhill. The ground had almost taken him by surprise. " 'Ere ! "
he cried ; and then with a violent effort of all his being he
got the beating engine at work again and set the wings flapping.
He swooped down and up and resumed his quivering and pulsating ascent of the air.

He went high again, until he had a wide view of the pleasant
upland country of western New York State, and then made
a long coast down, and so up again, and then a coast. Then
as he came swooping a quarter of a mile above a village he
saw people running about, running away—evidently in relation to his hawk-like passage. He got an idea that he had
been shot at.

" Up ! " he said, and attacked that lever again. It came
over with remarkable docility, and suddenly the wings seemed
to give way in the middle. But the engine was still ! It had
stopped. He flung the lever back rather by instinct than
design. What to do ?

Much happened in a few seconds, but also his mind was
quick, he thought very quickly. He couldn't get up again,
he was gliding down the air ; he would have to hit something.

He was travelling at the rate of perhaps thirty miles an hour, down, down.

That plantation of larches looked the softest thing—mossy almost!

Could he get it? He gave himself to the steering. Round to the right—left!

Swirroo! Crackle! He was gliding over the tops of the trees, ploughing through them, tumbling into a cloud of green, sharp leaves and black twigs. There was a sudden snapping, and he fell off the saddle forward, a thud and a crashing of branches. Some twigs hit him smartly in the face. . . .

He was between a tree-stem and the saddle, with his leg over the steering lever and, so far as he could realise, not hurt. He tried to alter his position and free his leg, and found himself slipping and dropping through branches with everything giving way beneath him. He clutched, and found himself in the lower branches of a tree beneath the flying-machine. The air was full of a pleasant, resinous smell. He stared for a moment motionless, and then very carefully clambered down branch by branch to the soft needle-covered ground below.

" Good business," he said, looking up at the bent and tilted kite-wings above.

" I dropped soft! "

He rubbed his chin with his hand and meditated. " Blowed if I don't think I'm a rather lucky fellow! " he said, surveying the pleasant, sun-bespattered ground under the trees. Then he became aware of a violent tumult at his side. " Lord! " he said, " you must be 'arf smothered," and extracted the kitten from his pocket-handkerchief and pocket. She was twisted and crumpled and extremely glad to see the light again. Her little tongue peeped between her teeth. He put her down, and she ran a dozen paces and shook herself and stretched and sat up and began to wash.

" Nex'? " he said, looking about him, and then with a gesture of vexation, " Desh it! I ought to 'ave brought that gun! "

He had rested it against a tree when he had seated himself in the flying-machine saddle.

He was puzzled for a time by the immense peacefulness in the quality of the world, and then he perceived that the roar of the cataract was no longer in his ears.

§ 2

He had no very clear idea of what sort of people he might come upon in this country. It was, he knew, America. Americans, he had always understood, were the citizens of a great and powerful nation, dry and humorous in their manner, addicted to the use of the bowie-knife and revolver, and in the habit of talking through the nose like Norfolk, and saying

" allow " and " reckon " and " calculate," after the manner of
the people who live on the New Forest side of Hampshire.
Also they were very rich, had rocking-chairs, and put their feet
at unusual altitudes, and they chewed tobacco, gum, and
other substances with untiring industry. Commingled with
them were cowboys, Red Indians, and comic, respectful niggers.
This he had learnt from the fiction in his public library. Beyond
that he had learnt very little. He was not surprised, therefore,
when he met armed men.

He decided to abandon the shattered flying-machine. He
wandered through the trees for some time, and then struck a
road that seemed to his urban English eyes to be remarkably
wide but not properly " made." Neither hedge nor ditch nor
curved distinctive footpath separated it from the woods, and
it went in that long, easy curve which distinguishes the tracks
of an open continent. Ahead he saw a man carrying a gun
under his arm, a man in a soft black hat, a blue blouse, and
black trousers and with a round, fat face quite innocent of
goatee. This person regarded him askance and heard him
speak with a start.

" Can you tell me whereabouts I am at all ? " asked Bert.

The man regarded him, and more particularly his rubber
boots, with sinister suspicion. Then he replied in a strange,
outlandish tongue that was, as a matter of fact, Czech. He
ended suddenly at the sight of Bert's blank face with " Don't
spik English."

" Oh ! " said Bert. He reflected gravely for a moment, and
then went his way.

" Thenks," he said as an afterthought. The man regarded
his back for a moment, was struck with an idea, began an
abortive gesture, sighed, gave it up, and went on also with a
depressed countenance.

Presently Bert came to a big wooden house standing casually
among the trees. It looked a bleak, bare box of a house to
him, no creeper grew on it, no hedge nor wall nor fence parted
it off from the woods about it. He stopped before the steps
that led up to the door, perhaps thirty yards away. The place
seemed deserted. He would have gone up to the door and
rapped, but suddenly a big black dog appeared at the side and
regarded him. It was a huge, heavy-jawed dog of some unfamiliar breed, and it wore a spike-studded collar. It did not
bark nor approach him, it just bristled quietly and emitted a
single sound like a short, deep cough.

Bert hesitated and went on.

He stopped thirty paces away and stood peering about him
among the trees. " If I 'aven't been and lef' that kitten," he
said.

Acute sorrow wrenched him for a time. The black dog came
through the trees to get a better look at him and coughed that
well-bred cough again. Bert resumed the road.

" She'll do all right," he said. . . . " She'll catch things. . . .

" She'll do all right," he said presently, without conviction. But if it had not been for the black dog he would have gone back.

When he was out of sight of the house and the black dog, he went into the woods on the other side of the way and emerged after an interval trimming a very tolerable cudgel with his pocket-knife. Presently he saw an attractive looking rock by the track and picked it up and put it in his pocket. Then he came to three or four houses, wooden like the last, each with an ill-painted white veranda (that was his name for it) and all standing in the same casual way upon the ground. Behind, through the woods, he saw pigsties and a rooting black sow leading a brisk, adventurous family. A wild-looking woman with sloe black eyes and dishevelled black hair sat upon the steps of one of the houses nursing a baby, but at the sight of Bert she got up and went inside, and he heard her bolting the door. Then a boy appeared among the pigsties, but he would not understand Bert's hail.

" I suppose it is America ! " said Bert.

The houses became more frequent down the road, and he passed two other extremely wild and dirty-looking men without addressing them. One carried a gun and the other a hatchet, and they scrutinised him and his cudgel scornfully. Then he struck a cross-road with a mono-rail at its side, and there was a notice board at the corner with " Wait here for the cars." " That's all right, any'ow," said Bert. " Wonder 'ow long I should 'ave to wait ? " It occurred to him that in the present disturbed state of the country the service might be interrupted, and as there seemed more houses to the right than the left he turned to the right. He passed an old negro. " 'Ullo ! " said Bert. " Goo'-morning ! "

" Good-day, sah ! " said the old negro in a voice of almost incredible richness.

" What's the name of this place ? " asked Bert.

" Tanooda, sah ! " said the negro.

" Thenks," said Bert.

" Thank *you*, sah ! " said the negro overwhelmingly.

Bert came to houses of the same detached, unwalled, wooden type, but adorned now with enamelled advertisements partly in English and partly in Esperanto. Then he came to what he concluded was a grocer's shop. It was the first house that professed the hospitality of an open door, and from within came a strangely familiar sound. " Gaw ! " he said, searching in his pockets. " Why ! I 'aven't wanted money for free weeks ! I wonder if I——Grubb 'ad most of it. Ah ! " He produced a handful of coins and regarded it ; three pennies, sixpence, and a shilling. " That's all right," he said, forgetting a very obvious consideration.

He approached the door, and as he did so a compactly built,

gray-faced man in shirt sleeves appeared in it and scrutinised him and his cudgel. " Mornin'," said Bert. " Can I get anything to eat 'r drink in this shop ? "

The man in the door replied, thank Heaven, in clear, good American. " This, sir, is not A shop, it is A store."

" Oh ! " said Bert, and then, " Well, can I get anything to eat ? "

" You can," said the American in a tone of confident encouragement, and led the way inside.

The shop seemed to him by his Bun Hill standards extremely roomy, well lit, and unencumbered. There was a long counter to the left of him, with drawers and miscellaneous commodities ranged behind it, a number of chairs, several tables and two spittoons to the right, various barrels, cheeses, and bacon up the vista, and beyond, a large archway leading to more space. A little group of men was assembled round one of the tables, and a woman of perhaps five-and-thirty leant with her elbows on the counter. All the men were armed with rifles, and the barrel of a gun peeped above the counter. They were all listening idly, inattentively, to a cheap, metallic-toned gramophone that occupied a table near at hand. From its brazen throat came words that gave Bert a qualm of home-sickness, that brought back in his memory a sunlit beach, a group of children, red-painted bicycles, Grubb and an approaching balloon :—

> Ting-a-ling-a-ting-a-ling-a-ting-a-ling-a-tang
> What price hairpins now ?

A heavy-necked man in a straw hat, who was chewing something, stopped the machine with a touch, and they all turned their eyes on Bert. And all their eyes were tired eyes.

" Can we give this gentleman anything to eat, mother, or can we not ? " said the proprietor.

" He kin have what he likes," said the woman at the counter, without moving, " right up from a cracker to a square meal." She struggled with a yawn, after the manner of one who has been up all night.

" I want a meal," said Bert, " but I 'aven't very much money. I don't want to give mor'n a shillin'."

" Mor'n a *what* ? " said the proprietor sharply.

" Mor'n a shillin'," said Bert, with a sudden disagreeable realisation coming into his mind.

" Yes," said the proprietor, startled for a moment from his courtly bearing, " but what in hell *is* a shilling ? "

" He means a quarter," said a wise-looking, lank young man in riding gaiters.

Bert, trying to conceal his consternation, produced a coin. " That's a shilling," he said.

" He calls A store A shop," said the proprietor, " and he

wants A meal for A shilling. May I ask you, sir, what part of America you hail from ? "

Bert replaced the shilling in his pocket as he spoke. " Niagara," he said.

" And when did you leave Niagara ? "

" 'Bout an hour ago."

" Well," said the proprietor, and turned with a puzzled smile to the others. " Well ! "

They asked various questions simultaneously.

Bert selected one or two for reply. " You see," he said, " I been with the German air-fleet. I got caught up by them, sort of by accident, and brought over here."

" From England ? "

" Yes—from England. Way of Germany. I was in a great battle with them Asiatics, and I got lef' on a little island between the Falls."

" Goat Island ? "

" I don' know what it was called. But any'ow I found a flying-machine and made a sort of fly with it and got here."

Two men stood up with incredulous eyes on him. " Where's the flying-machine ? " they asked ; " outside ? "

" It's back in the woods here—'bout 'arf a mile away."

" Is it good ? " said a thick-lipped man with a scar.

" I come down rather a smash——"

Everybody got up and stood about him and talked confusingly. They wanted him to take them to the flying-machine at once.

" Look 'ere," said Bert, " I'll show you—only I 'aven't 'ad anything to eat since yestiday—except mineral water."

A gaunt, soldierly-looking young man with long, lean legs in riding gaiters and a bandolier, who had hitherto not spoken, intervened now on his behalf in a note of confident authority. " That's aw right," he said. " Give him a feed, Mr. Logan— from me. I want to hear more of that story of his. We'll see his machine afterwards. If you ask me, I should say it's a remarkably interesting accident had dropped this gentleman here. I guess we requisition that flying-machine—if we find it—for local defence."

§ 3

So Bert fell on his feet again, and sat eating cold meat and good bread and mustard and drinking very good beer, and telling in the roughest outline and with the omissions and inaccuracies of statement natural to his type of mind, the simple story of his adventures. He told how he and a " gentleman friend " had been visiting the seaside for their health, how a " chep " came along in a balloon and fell out as he fell in, how he had drifted to Franconia, how the Germans had seemed to mistake him for some one and had " took him prisoner " and brought him to New York, how he had been to Labrador and back, how he had got to Goat Island and found himself there alone. He omitted the matter of the Prince and the Butteridge aspect of the affair, not out of any deep deceitfulness, but because he felt the inadequacy of his narrative powers. He wanted everything to seem easy and natural and correct, to present himself as a trustworthy and understandable Englishman in a sound mediocre position, to whom refreshment and accommodation might be given with freedom and confidence.

When his fragmentary story came to New York and the battle of Niagara they suddenly produced newspapers which had been lying about on the table, and began to check him and question him by these vehement accounts. It became evident to him that his descent had revived and roused to flames again a discussion, a topic, that had been burning continuously, that had smouldered only through sheer exhaustion of material during the temporary diversion of the gramophone, a discussion that had drawn these men together, rifle in hand, the one supreme topic of the whole world, the War and the methods of the War. He found any question of his personality and his personal adventures falling into the background, found himself taken for granted, and no more than a source of information. The ordinary affairs of life, the buying and selling of everyday necessities, the cultivation of the ground, the tending of beasts, was going on as it were by force of routine, as the common duties of life go on in a house whose master lies under the knife of some supreme operation. The overruling interest was furnished by those great Asiatic airships that went upon incalculable missions across the sky, the crimson-clad swordsmen who might come fluttering down demanding petrol or food, or news. These men were asking, all the continent was asking, " What are we to do ? What can we try ? How can we get at them ? " Bert fell into his place as an item, ceased even in his own thoughts to be a central and independent thing.

After he had eaten and drunken his fill and sighed and stretched and told them how good the food seemed to him, he lit a cigarette they gave him and led the way, with some doubts and trouble, to the flying-machine amidst the larches. It became manifest that the gaunt young man, whose name, it seemed, was Laurier, was a leader both by position and natural aptitude. He knew the names and characters and capabilities of all the men who were with him, and he set them to work at once with vigour and effect to secure this precious instrument of war. They got the thing down to the ground deliberately and carefully, felling a couple of trees in the process, and they built a wide, flat roof of timbers and tree boughs to guard their precious find against its chance discovery by any passing Asiatics. Long before evening they had an engineer from the next township at work upon it, and they were casting lots among the seventeen picked men who wanted to take it for its first flight. And Bert found his kitten and carried it back to Logan's store and handed it with earnest admonition to Mrs. Logan. And it was reassuringly clear to him that in Mrs. Logan both he and the kitten had found a congenial soul.

Laurier was not only a masterful person and a wealthy property owner and employer—he was president, Bert learnt with awe, of the Tanooda Canning Corporation—but he was popular and skilful in the arts of popularity. In the evening quite a crowd of men gathered in the store and talked of the flying-machine and of the war that was tearing the world to pieces. And presently came a man on a bicycle with an ill-printed newspaper of a single sheet which acted like fuel in a blazing furnace of talk. It was nearly all American news ; the old-fashioned cables had fallen into disuse for some years, and the Marconi stations across the ocean and along the Atlantic coastline seemed to have furnished particularly tempting points of attack.

But such news it was.

Bert sat in the background—for by this time they had gauged his personal quality pretty completely—listening. Before his staggering mind passed strange, vast images as they talked, of great issues at a crisis, of nations in tumultuous march, of continents overthrown, of famine and destruction beyond measure. Ever and again, in spite of his efforts to suppress them, certain personal impressions would scamper across the weltering confusion, the horrible mess of the exploded Prince, the Chinese aeronaut upside down, the limping and bandaged bird-faced officer blundering along in miserable and hopeless flight. . . .

They spoke of fire and massacre, of cruelties and counter cruelties, of things that had been done to harmless Asiatics by race-mad men, of the wholesale burning and smashing up of towns, railway junctions, bridges, of whole populations in hiding and exodus. " Every ship they've got is in the Pacific," he heard one man exclaim. " Since the fighting began they can't have landed on the Pacific Slope less than a million men. They've come to stay in these States, and they will—living or dead."

Slowly, broadly, invincibly, there grew upon Bert's mind realisation of the immense tragedy of humanity into which his life was flowing ; the appalling and universal nature of the epoch that had arrived ; the conception of an end to security and order and habit. The whole world was at war and it could not get back to peace, it might never recover peace.

He had thought the things he had seen had been exceptional, conclusive things, that the besieging of New York and the battle of the Atlantic were epoch-making events between long years of security. And they had been but the first warning impacts of universal cataclysm. Each day destruction and hate and disaster grew, the fissures widened between man and man, new regions of the fabric of civilisation crumbled and

gave way. Below, the armies grew and the people perished ;
above, the airships and aeroplanes fought and fled, raining
destruction.

It is difficult, perhaps, for the broad-minded and long perspective reader to understand how incredible the breaking
down of the scientific civilisation seemed to those who actually
lived at this time, who in their own persons went down in that
debacle. Progress had marched, as it seemed, invincible about
the earth, never now to rest again. For three hundred years
and more the long, steadily accelerated diastole of Europeanised
civilisation had been in progress : towns had been multiplying,
populations increasing, values rising, new countries developing ;
thought, literature, knowledge unfolding and spreading. It
seemed but a part of the process that every year the instruments of war were vaster and more powerful, and that armies
and explosives outgrew all other growing things. . . .

Three hundred years of diastole, and then came the swift
and unexpected systole, like the closing of a fist. They could
not understand it was a systole. They could not think of it as
anything but a jolt, a hitch, a mere oscillatory indication of the
swiftness of their progress. Collapse, though it happened all
about them, remained incredible. Presently some falling mass
smote them down, or the ground opened beneath their feet.
They died incredulous. . . .

These men in the store made a minute, remote group under
this immense canopy of disaster. They turned from one little
aspect to another. What chiefly concerned them was defence
against Asiatic raiders swooping for petrol or to destroy weapons
or communications. Everywhere levies were being formed at
that time to defend the plant of the railroads day and night
in the hope that communication would speedily be restored.
The land war was still far away. A man with a flat voice distinguished himself by a display of knowledge and cunning. He
told them all with confidence just what had been wrong with
the German drachenflieger and the American aeroplanes, just
what advantage the Japanese fliers possessed. He launched
out into a romantic description of the Butteridge machine and
riveted Bert's attention. " I *see* that," said Bert, and was
smitten silent by a thought. The man with the flat voice talked
on, without heeding him, of the strange irony of Butteridge's
death. At that Bert had a little twinge of relief—he would never
meet Butteridge again. It appeared Butteridge had died
suddenly, very suddenly.

" And his secret, sir, perished with him ! When they came
to look for the parts—none could find them. He had hidden
them all too well."

" But couldn't he tell ? " asked the man in the straw hat.
" Did he die so suddenly as that ? "

" Struck down, sir. Rage and apoplexy. At a place called
Dymchurch in England."

" That's right," said Laurier. " I remember a page about it in the Sunday *American*. At the time they said it was a German spy had stolen his balloon."

" Well, sir," said the flat-voiced man, " that fit of apoplexy at Dymchurch was the worst thing—ab-so-lutely the worst thing that ever happened to the world. For if it had not been for the death of Mr. Butteridge——"

" No one knows his secret ? "

" Not a soul. It's gone. His balloon, it appears, was lost at sea, with all the plans. Down it went, and they went with it." Pause.

" With machines such as he made we could fight these Asiatic fliers on more than equal terms. We could outfly and beat down those scarlet humming-birds wherever they appeared. But it's gone, it's gone, and there's no time to reinvent it now. We got to fight with what we got—and the odds are against us. *That* won't stop us fightin'. No ! but just think of it ! "

Bert was trembling violently. He cleared his throat hoarsely.

" I say," he said, " look here, I——"

Nobody regarded him. The man with the flat voice was opening a new branch of the subject. " I allow——" he began.

Bert became violently excited. He stood up. He made clawing motions with his hands. " I say ! " he exclaimed, " Mr. Laurier. Look 'ere—I want—about that Butteridge machine——"

Mr. Laurier, sitting on an adjacent table, with a magnificent gesture, arrested the discourse of the flat-voiced man. " What's *he* saying ? " said he.

Then the whole company realised that something was happening to Bert : either he was suffocating or going mad. He was spluttering, " Look 'ere ! I say ! 'Old on a bit ! " and trembling and eagerly unbuttoning himself.

He tore open his collar and opened vest and shirt. He plunged into his interior and for an instant it seemed he was plucking forth his liver. Then as he struggled with buttons on his shoulder they perceived this flattened horror was in fact a terribly dirty flannel chest-protector. In another moment Bert, in a state of irregular décolletage, was standing over the table displaying a sheaf of papers.

" These ! " he gasped. " These are the plans ! . . . You know ! Mr. Butteridge—his machine ! What died ! I was the chap that went off in that balloon ! "

For some seconds every one was silent. They stared from these papers to Bert's white face and blazing eyes, and back to the papers on the table. Nobody moved. Then the man with the flat voice spoke.

" Irony ! " he said, with a note of satisfaction. " Real right-down Irony ! *When it's too late to think of making 'em any more !* "

They would all no doubt have been eager to hear Bert's story over again, but it was at this point that Laurier showed his quality. " No, *sir*," he said, and slid from off his table.

He impounded the dispersing Butteridge plans with one comprehensive sweep of his arm, rescuing them even from the expository fingermarks of the man with the flat voice, and handed them to Bert. " Put those back," he said, " where you had 'em. We have a journey before us."

Bert took them.

" Whar ? " said the man in the straw hat.

" Why, sir, we are going to find the President of these States and give these plans over to him. I decline to believe, sir, we are too late."

" Where is the President ? " asked Bert weakly in the pause that followed.

" Logan," said Laurier, disregarding that feeble inquiry, " you must help us in this."

It seemed only a matter of a few minutes before Bert and Laurier and the storekeeper were examining a number of bicycles that were stowed in the hinder room of the store. Bert didn't like any of them very much. They had wood rims, and an experience of wood rims in the English climate had taught him to hate them. That, however, and one or two other objections to an immediate start were overruled by Laurier. " But where *is* the President ? " Bert repeated as they stood behind Logan while he pumped up a deflated tyre.

Laurier looked down on him. " He is reported in the neighbourhood of Albany—out towards the Berkshire Hills. He is moving from place to place and, as far as he can, organising the defence by telegraph and telephone. The Asiatic air-fleet is trying to locate him. When they think they have located the seat of government they throw bombs. This inconveniences him, but so far they have not come within ten miles of him. The Asiatic air-fleet is at present scattered all over the Eastern States, seeking out and destroying gas works and whatever seems conducive to the building of air-ships or the transport of troops. Our retaliatory measures are slight in the extreme. But with these machines—— Sir, this ride of ours will count among the historical rides of the world ! "

He came near to striking an attitude.

" We shan't get to him to-night ? " asked Bert.

" No, sir ! " said Laurier. " We shall have to ride some days, sure ! "

" I suppose we can't get a lift on a train—or anything ? "

" No, sir ! There's been no transit by Tanooda for three

days. It is no good waiting. We shall have to get on as well as we can."

" Startin' now ? "

" Starting now ! "

" But 'ow about—— We shan't be able to do much to-night."

" May as well ride till we're fagged and sleep then. So much clear gain. Our road is eastward."

" Of course——" began Bert, with memories of the dawn upon Goat Island, and left his sentence unfinished.

He gave his attention to the more scientific packing of the chest-protector, for several of the plans flapped beyond his vest.

§ 5

For a week Bert led a life of mixed sensations. Amidst these fatigue in the legs predominated. Mostly he rode, rode with Laurier's back inexorably ahead, through a land like a larger England, with bigger hills and wider valleys, larger fields, wider roads, fewer hedges, and wooden houses with commodious piazzas. He rode. Laurier made inquiries, Laurier chose the turnings, Laurier doubted, Laurier decided. Now it seemed they were in telephonic touch with the President ; now something had happened and he was lost again. But always they had to go on, and always Bert rode. A tyre was deflated. Still he rode. He grew saddle sore. Laurier declared that unimportant. Asiatic flying ships passed overhead, the two cyclists made a dash for cover until the sky was clear. Once a red Asiatic flying-machine came fluttering after them, so low they could distinguish the aeronaut's head. He followed them for a mile. Now they came to regions of panic, now to regions of destruction, here people were fighting for food, here they seemed hardly stirred from the countryside routine. They spent a day in a deserted and damaged Albany. The Asiatics had descended and cut every wire and made a cinder-heap of the Junction, and our travellers pushed on eastward. They passed a hundred half-heeded incidents, and always Bert was toiling after Laurier's indefatigable back. . . .

Things struck upon Bert's attention and perplexed him, and then he passed on with unanswered questionings fading from his mind.

He saw a large house on fire on a hill-side to the right, and no man heeding it. . . .

They came to a narrow railroad bridge and presently to a mono-rail train standing in the track on its safety feet. It was a remarkably sumptuous train, the Last Word Trans-Continental Express, and the passengers were all playing cards or sleeping or preparing a picnic meal on a grassy slope near at hand. They had been there six days. . . .

At one point ten dark-complexioned men were hanging in a string from the trees along the roadside. Bert wondered why. . . .

At one peaceful-looking village where they stopped off to get Bert's tyre mended and found beer and biscuits, they were approached by an extremely dirty little boy without boots, who spoke as follows,—

" Deyse been hanging a Chink in dose woods ! "

" Hanging a Chinaman ? " said Laurier.

" Sure. Der sleuths got him rubberin' der railroad sheds ! "

" Oh ! "

" Dose guys done wase cartridges. Deyse hung him and dey pulled his legs. Deyse doin' all der Chinks dey can fine dat weh ! Dey ain't takin' no risks. All der Chinks dey can fine."

Neither Bert nor Laurier made any reply, and presently, after a little skilful expectoration, the young gentleman was attracted by the appearance of two of his friends down the road, and shuffled off, whooping weirdly. . . .

That afternoon they almost ran over a man shot through the body and partly decomposed, lying near the middle of the road, just outside Albany. He must have been lying there for some days. . . .

Beyond Albany they came upon a motor-car with a tyre burst and a young woman sitting absolutely passive beside the driver's seat. An old man was under the car trying to effect some impossible repairs. Beyond, sitting with a rifle across his knees, with his back to the car, and staring into the woods, was a young man. The old man crawled out at their approach and still on all fours accosted Bert and Laurier. The car had broken down overnight. The old man said he could not understand what was wrong, but he was trying to puzzle it out. Neither he nor his son-in-law had any mechanical aptitude. They had been assured this was a fool-proof car. It was dangerous to have to stop in this place. His party had been attacked by tramps and had had to fight. It was known they had provisions. He mentioned a great name in the world of finance. Would Laurier and Bert stop and help him ? He proposed it first hopefully, then urgently, at last in tears and terror.

" No ! " said Laurier inexorably. " We must go on ! We have something more than a woman to save. We have to save America ! "

The girl never stirred. . . .

Once they passed a madman singing. . . .

At last they found the President hiding in a small saloon upon the outskirts of a place called Pinkerville on the Hudson, and gave the plans of the Butteridge machine into his hands.

CHAPTER ELEVEN

THE GREAT COLLAPSE

§ 1

AND now the whole fabric of civilisation was bending and giving, and dropping to pieces and melting in the furnace of the war. The stages of the swift and universal collapse of the financial and scientific civilisation with which the twentieth century opened followed each other very swiftly, so swiftly that upon the fore-shortened page of history they seem altogether to overlap. To begin with, one sees the world nearly at a maximum of wealth and prosperity. To its inhabitants indeed it seemed also at a maximum of security. When now in retrospect the thoughtful observer surveys the intellectual history of this time, when one reads its surviving fragments of literature, its scraps of political oratory, the few small voices that chance has selected out of a thousand million utterances to speak to later days, the most striking thing of all this web of wisdom and error is surely that hallucination of security. To men living in our present world state, orderly, scientific and secured, nothing seems so precarious, so giddily dangerous, as the fabric of the social order with which the men of the opening of the twentieth century were content. To us it seems that every institution and relationship was the fruit of haphazard and tradition and the manifest sport of chance, their laws each made for some separate occasion and having no relation to any future needs, their customs illogical, their education aimless and wasteful. Their method of economic exploitation indeed impresses a trained and informed mind as the most frantic and destructive scramble it is possible to conceive ; their credit and monetary system resting on an unsubstantial tradition of the worthiness of gold, seems a thing almost fantastically unstable. And they lived in planless cities, for the most part dangerously congested, their rails and roads and population were distributed over the earth in the wanton confusion ten thousand irrelevant considerations had made. Yet they thought confidently that this was a secure and permanent progressive system, and on the strength of some three hundred years of chancy and irregular improvement answered the doubter with, " Things always *have* gone well. We'll worry through ! "

But when we contrast the state of man in the opening of the twentieth century with the condition of any previous period in his history, then perhaps we may begin to understand something of that blind confidence. It was not so much a reasoned confidence as the inevitable consequence of sustained good fortune. By such standards as they possessed, things *had* gone amazingly well for them. It is scarcely an exaggeration to say that for the first time in history whole populations found themselves regularly supplied with more than enough to eat, and the vital statistics of the time witness to an amelioration of hygienic conditions rapid beyond all precedent, and to a vast development of intelligence and ability in all the arts that make life wholesome. The level and quality of the average education had risen tremendously ; and at the dawn of the twentieth century comparatively few people in Western Europe or America were unable to read or write. Never before had there been such reading masses. There was wide social security. A common man might travel safely over three-quarters of the habitable globe, could go round the earth at a cost of less than the annual earnings of a skilled artisan. Compared with the liberality and comfort of the ordinary life of the time, the order of the Roman Empire under the Antonines was local and limited. And every year, every month, came some new increment to human achievement, a new country opened up, new mines, new scientific discoveries, a new machine !

For those three hundred years, indeed, the movement of the world seemed wholly beneficial to mankind. Men said, indeed, that moral organisation was not keeping pace with physical progress, but few attached any meaning to these phrases, the understanding of which lies at the basis of our present safety. Sustaining and constructive forces did indeed for a time more than balance the malign drift of chance and the natural ignorance, prejudice, blind passion, and wasteful self-seeking of mankind.

The accidental balance on the side of Progress was far slighter and infinitely more complex and delicate in its adjustments than the people of that time suspected ; but that did not alter the fact that it was an effective balance. They did not realise that this age of relative good fortune was an age of immense but temporary opportunity for their kind. They complacently assumed a necessary progress towards which they had no moral responsibility. They did not realise that this security of progress was a thing still to be won or lost, and that the time to win it was a time that passed. They went about their affairs energetically enough, and yet with a curious idleness towards those threatening things. No one troubled over the real dangers of mankind. They saw their armies and navies grow larger and more portentous ; some of their ironclads at the last cost as much as their whole annual expenditure upon advanced education ; they accumulated explosives and the machinery of destruction ; they allowed their national traditions and jealousies to accumulate ; they contemplated a steady enhancement of race hostility as the races drew closer without concern or understanding, and they permitted the growth in their midst of an evil-spirited press, mercenary and unscrupulous, incapable of good and powerful for evil. Their State had practically no control over the press at all. Quite heedlessly they allowed this touch-paper to lie at the door of their war magazine for any spark to fire. The precedents of history were all one tale of the collapse of civilisations, the dangers of the time were manifest. One is incredulous now to believe they could not see.

Could mankind have prevented this disaster of the War in the Air ? An idle question that, as idle as to ask could mankind have prevented the decay that turned Assyria and Babylon to empty deserts or the slow decline and fall, the gradual social disorganisation, phase by phase, that closed the chapter of the Empire of the West ! They could not, because they did not, they had not the will to arrest it. What mankind could achieve with a different will is a speculation as idle as it is magnificent. And this was no slow decadence that came to the Europeanised world ; those other civilisations rotted and crumbled down, the Europeanised civilisation was, as it were, blown up. Within the space of five years it was altogether disintegrated and destroyed. Up to the very eve of the War in the Air one sees a spacious spectacle of incessant advance, a world-wide security, enormous areas with highly organised industry and settled populations, gigantic cities spreading gigantically, the seas and oceans dotted with shipping, the land netted with rails and open ways. Then suddenly the German air-fleets sweep across the scene, and we are in the beginning of the end.

§ 2

This story has already told of the swift rush upon New York of the first German air-fleet and of the wild, inevitable orgy of inconclusive destruction that ensued. Behind it a second air-fleet was already swelling at its gasometers when England and France and Spain and Italy showed their hands. None of these countries had prepared for aeronautic warfare on the magnificent scale of the Germans, but each guarded secrets, each in a measure was making ready, and a common dread of German vigour and that aggressive spirit Prince Karl Albert embodied, had long been drawing these powers together in secret anticipation of some such attack. This rendered their prompt co-operation possible, and they certainly co-operated promptly. The second aerial power in Europe at this time was France ; the British, nervous for their Asiatic empire, and sensible of the immense moral effect of the airship upon half-educated populations, had placed their aeronautic parks in North India, and were able to play but a subordinate part in the European conflict. Still, even in England they had nine or ten big navigables, twenty or thirty smaller ones, and a variety of experimental aeroplanes. Before the fleet of Prince Karl Albert had crossed England, while Bert was still surveying Manchester in bird's-eye view, the diplomatic exchanges were going on that led to an attack upon Germany. A heterogeneous collection of navigable balloons of all sizes and types gathered over the Bernese Oberland, crushed and burnt the twenty-five Swiss airships that unexpectedly resisted this concentration in the battle of the Alps, and then, leaving the Alpine glaciers and valleys strewn with strange wreckage, divided into two fleets and set itself to terrorise Berlin and destroy the Franconian Park, seeking to do this before the second air-fleet could be inflated.

Both over Berlin and Franconia the assailants with their modern explosives effected great damage before they were driven off. In Franconia twelve fully distended and five partially filled and manned giants were able to make head against, and at last, with the help of a squadron of drachen-flieger from Hamburg, defeat and pursue the attack and to relieve Berlin, and the Germans were straining every nerve to get an overwhelming fleet in the air, and were already raiding London and Paris when the advance fleets from the Asiatic air-parks, the first intimation of a new factor in the conflict, were reported from Burmah and Armenia.

Already the whole financial fabric of the world was stagger-ing when that occurred. With the destruction of the American fleet in the North Atlantic, and the smashing conflict that ended the naval existence of Germany in the North Sea, with the burning and wreckage of billions of pounds' worth of property in the four cardinal cities of the world, the fact of the hopeless costliness of war came home for the first time, came like a blow in the face, to the consciousness of mankind. Credit went down in a wild whirl of selling. Everywhere appeared a phenomenon that had already in a mild degree manifested itself in preceding period of panics ; a desire to *secure and hoard gold* before prices reached bottom. But now it spread like wild-fire, it became universal. Above was visible conflict and destruction ; below something was happening far more deadly and incurable to the flimsy fabric of finance and commercialism in which men had so blindly put their trust. As the airships fought above, the visible gold supply of the world vanished below. An epidemic of private cornering and universal distrust swept the world. In a few weeks, money, except for depreciated paper, vanished into vaults, into holes, into the walls of houses, into ten million hiding-places. Money vanished and at its disappearance trade and industry came to an end. The economic world staggered and fell dead. It was like the stroke of some disease ; it was like the water vanishing out of the blood of a living creature ; it was a sudden, universal coagulation of intercourse. . . .

And as the credit system, that had been the living fortress

of the scientific civilisation, reeled and fell upon the millions it had held together in economic relationship, as these people, perplexed and helpless, faced this marvel of credit utterly destroyed, the airships of Asia, countless and relentless, poured across the heavens, swooped eastward to America and westward to Europe. The page of history becomes a long crescendo of battle. The main body of the British-Indian air-fleet perished upon a pyre of blazing antagonists in Burmah ; the Germans were scattered in the great battle of the Carpathians ; the vast peninsula of India burst into insurrection and civil war from end to end, and from Gobi to Morocco rose the standards of the " Jehad." For some weeks of warfare and destruction it seemed as though the Confederation of Eastern Asia must needs conquer the world, and then the jerry-built " modern " civilisation of China, too, gave way under the strain. The teeming and peaceful population of China had been " westernised " during the opening years of the twentieth century with the deepest resentment and reluctance ; they had been dragooned and disciplined under Japanese and European influence into an acquiescence with sanitary methods, police controls, military service, and a wholesale process of exploitation against which their whole tradition rebelled. Under the stresses of the war their endurance reached the breaking point. China rose in incoherent revolt, and the practical destruction of the central government at Pekin by a handful of British and German airships that had escaped from the main battles rendered that revolt invincible. In Yokohama appeared barricades, the black flag, and the social revolution. With that the whole world became a welter of conflict.

So that a universal social collapse followed, as it were a logical consequence, upon world-wide war. Wherever there were great populations, great masses of people found themselves without work, without money, and unable to get food. Famine was in every working-class quarter in the world within three weeks of the beginning of the war. Within a month there was not a city anywhere in which the ordinary law and social procedure had not been replaced by some form of emergency control, in which fire-arms and military executions were not being used to keep order and prevent violence. And still in the poorer quarters, and in the populous districts, and even here and there already among those who had been wealthy, famine spread.

§ 3

So what historians have come to call the Phase of the Emergency Committees sprang from the opening phase and from the phase of social collapse. Then followed a period of vehement and passionate conflict against disintegration ; everywhere the struggle to keep order and to keep fighting went on. And at the same time the character of the war altered through the replacement of the huge gas-filled airships by flying-machines as the instruments of war. So soon as the big fleet engagements were over, the Asiatics endeavoured to establish in close proximity to the more vulnerable points of the countries against which they were acting, fortified centres from which flying-machine raids could be made. For a time they had everything their own way in this, and then, as this story has told, the lost secret of the Butteridge machine came to light, and the conflict became equalised and less conclusive than ever. For these small flying-machines, ineffectual for any large expedition or conclusive attack, were horribly convenient for guerilla warfare, rapidly and cheaply made, easily used, easily hidden. The design of them was hastily copied and printed in Pinkerville, and scattered broadcast over the United States, and copies were sent to Europe, and there reproduced. Every man, every town, every parish that could, was exhorted to make and use them. In a little while they were being constructed not only by governments and local authorities, but by robber bands, by insurgent committees, by every type of private person. The peculiar social destructiveness of the Butteridge machine lay in its complete simplicity. It was nearly as simple as a motor-bicycle. The broad outlines of the earlier stages of the war disappeared under its influence, the spacious antagonism of nations and empires and races vanished in a seething mass of detailed conflict. The world passed at a stride from a unity and simplicity broader than that of the Roman Empire at its best, to a social fragmentation as complete as the robber-baron period of the Middle Ages. But this time, for a long descent down gradual slopes of disintegration, comes a fall like a fall over a cliff. Everywhere were men and women perceiving this, and struggling desperately to keep, as it were, a hold upon the edge of the cliff.

A fourth phase follows. Through the struggle against Chaos, in the wake of the Famine, came now another old enemy of humanity—the Pestilence, the Purple Death. But the war does not pause. The flags still fly. Fresh air-fleets rise, new forms of airship, and beneath their swooping struggles the world darkens —scarcely heeded by history.

It is not within the design of this book to tell that further story, to tell how the War in the Air kept on through the sheer inability of any authorities to meet and agree and end it, until every organised government in the world was as shattered and broken as a heap of china beaten with a stick. With every week of those terrible years history becomes more detailed and confused, more crowded and uncertain. Not without great and heroic resistance was civilisation borne down. Out of the bitter social conflict below rose patriotic associations, brotherhoods of order, city mayors, princes, provisional committees, trying to establish an order below and to keep the sky above. The double effort destroyed them. And as the exhaustion of the mechanical resources of civilisation clears the heavens of airships at last altogether, Anarchy, Famine, and Pestilence are discovered triumphant below. The great nations and empires have become but names in the mouths of men. Everywhere there are ruins and unburied dead, and shrunken, yellow-faced survivors in a mortal apathy. Here there are robbers, here vigilance committees, and here guerilla bands ruling patches of exhausted territory, strange federations and brotherhoods form and dissolve, and religious fanaticisms begotten of despair gleam in famine-bright eyes. It is a universal dissolution. The fine order and welfare of the earth have crumpled like an exploded bladder. In five short years the world and the scope of human life have undergone a retrogressive change as great as that between the age of the Antonines and the Europe of the ninth century. . . .

§ 4

Across this sombre spectacle of disaster goes a minute and insignificant person for whom perhaps the readers of this story have now some slight solicitude. Of him there remains to be told just one single miraculous thing. Through a world darkened and lost, through a civilisation in its death agony, our little Cockney errant went and found his Edna ! He found his Edna !

He got back across the Atlantic partly by means of an order from the President and partly through his own good luck. He contrived to get himself aboard a British brig in the timber trade that put out from Boston without cargo, chiefly, it would seem, because its captain had a vague idea of " getting home " to South Shields. Bert was able to ship himself upon her mainly because of the seamanlike appearance of his rubber boots. They had a long, eventful voyage, they were chased, or imagined themselves to be chased, for some hours by an Asiatic ironclad, which was presently engaged by a British cruiser. The two ships fought for three hours, circling and driving southward as they fought, until the twilight and the cloud-rift of a rising gale swallowed them up. A few days later Bert's ship lost her rudder and mainmast in a gale. The crew ran out of food and subsisted on fish. They saw strange airships going eastward near the Azores, and landed to get provisions and repair the rudder at Teneriffe. There they found the town destroyed, and two big liners, with dead still aboard, sunken in the harbour. From there they got canned food and material for repairs, but their operations were greatly impeded by the hostility of a band of men amidst the ruins of the town, who sniped them and tried to drive them away.

At Mogador they stayed and sent a boat ashore for water, and were nearly captured by an Arab ruse. Here, too, they got the Purple Death aboard, and sailed with it incubating in their blood. The cook sickened first, and then the mate, and presently every one was down and three in the forecastle were dead. It chanced to be calm weather, and they drifted helplessly and indeed careless of their fate backwards towards the Equator. The captain doctored them all with rum. Nine died altogether, and of the four survivors none understood navigation ; when at last they took heart again and could handle a sail they made a course by the stars roughly northward and were already short of food once more when they fell in with a petrol-driven ship from Rio to Cardiff, shorthanded by reason of the Purple Death and glad to take them aboard. So, at last after a year of wandering, Bert reached England. He landed in bright June weather, and found the Purple Death was there just beginning its ravages.

The people were in a state of panic in Cardiff and many had fled to the hills, and directly the steamer came to the harbour she was boarded and her residue of food impounded by some unauthenticated Provisional Committee. Bert tramped through a country disorganised by pestilence, foodless, and shaken to the very base of its immemorial order. He came near death and starvation many times, and once he was drawn into scenes of violence that might have ended his career. But the Bert Smallways who tramped from Cardiff to London vaguely " going home," vaguely seeking something of his own that had no tangible form but Edna, was a very different person from the Desert Dervish who was swept out of England in Mr. Butteridge's balloon a year before. He was brown and lean and enduring, steady-eyed and pestilence-salted, and his mouth, which had once hung open, shut now like a steel trap. Across his brow ran a white scar that he had got in a fight on the brig. In Cardiff he had felt the need of new clothes and a weapon, and had, by means that would have shocked him a year ago, secured a flannel shirt, a corduroy suit and a revolver and fifty cartridges from an abandoned pawnbroker's. He also got some soap and had his first real wash for thirteen months in a stream outside the town. The Vigilance bands that had at first shot plunderers very freely were now either entirely dispersed by the plague, or busy between town and cemetery in a vain attempt to keep pace with it. He prowled on the outskirts of the town for three or four days, starving, and then went back to join the Hospital Corps for a week, and so fortified himself with a few square meals before he started eastward.

The Welsh and English countryside at that time presented the strangest mingling of the assurance and wealth of the opening twentieth century with a sort of Düreresque mediae-valism. All the gear, the houses and mono-rails, the farm hedges and power cables, the roads and pavements, the signposts and advertisements of the former order were still for the most part intact. Bankruptcy, social collapse, famine and pestilence, had done nothing to damage these ; it was only to the great capitals and ganglionic centres, as it were, of the State, that positive destruction had come. Any one dropped suddenly into the country would have noticed very little difference. He would have remarked first, perhaps, that all the hedges needed clipping, that the roadside grass grew rank, that the road-tracks were unusually rainworn, and that the cottages by the wayside seemed in many cases shut up, that a telephone wire had dropped here, and that a cart stood abandoned by the wayside. But he would still find his hunger whetted by the bright assurance that Wilder's Canned Peaches were excellent, or that there was nothing so good for the breakfast table as Gobbles's Sausages. And then suddenly would come the Düreresque element ; the skeleton of a horse, or some crumpled mass of rags in the ditch, with gaunt, extended feet and a yellow, purple-blotched skin and face, or what had been a face, gaunt and glaring and devastated. Then here would be a field that had been ploughed and not sown, and here a field of corn carelessly trampled by beasts, and here a hoarding torn down across the road to make a fire.

Then presently he would meet a man or a woman, yellow-faced and probably negligently dressed and armed—prowling for food. These people would have the complexions and eyes and expressions of tramps or criminals, and often the clothing of prosperous middle-class or upper-class people. Many of these would be eager for news, and willing to give help and even scraps of queer meat, or crusts of gray and doughy bread in return for it. They would listen to Bert's story with avidity, and attempt to keep him with them for a day or so. The virtual cessation of postal distribution and the collapse of all newspaper enterprise had left an immense and aching gap in the mental life of this time. Men had suddenly lost sight of the ends of the earth and had still to recover the rumour-spreading habits of the Middle Ages. In their eyes, in their bearing, in their talk, was the quality of lost and deoriented souls.

As Bert travelled from parish to parish and from district to district, avoiding as far as possible those festering centres of violence and despair, the larger towns, he found the condition of affairs varying widely. In one parish he would find the large house burnt, the vicarage wrecked, evidently in violent conflict for some suspected and perhaps imaginary store of food, un-buried dead everywhere, and the whole mechanism of the com-munity at a standstill. In another he would find organising forces stoutly at work, newly-painted notice boards warning off vagrants, the roads and still cultivated fields policed by armed men, the pestilence under control, even nursing going on, a store of food husbanded, the cattle and sheep well guarded, and a group of two or three justices, the village doctor or a farmer, dominating the whole place ; a reversion, in fact, to the autonomous community of the fifteenth century. But at any time such a village would be liable to a raid of Asiatics or Africans or suchlike air-pirates, demanding petrol and alcohol or provisions. The price of its order was an almost intolerable watchfulness and tension. Then the approach to the confused problems of some larger centre of population and the presence of a more intricate conflict would be marked by roughly smeared notices of " Quarantine " or " Strangers Shot," or by a string of decaying plunderers dangling from the telephone poles at the roadside. About Oxford big boards were put on the roofs warning all air wanderers off with the single word, " Guns."

Taking their risks amidst these things, cyclists still kept abroad, and once or twice during Bert's long tramp powerful motor-cars containing masked and goggled figures went tearing past him. There were few police in evidence, but ever and again squads of gaunt and tattered soldier-cyclists would come drifting along, and such encounters became more frequent as he got out of Wales into England. Amidst all this wreckage they were still campaigning. He had had some idea of resorting to the workhouses for the night if hunger pressed him too closely, but some of these were closed and others converted into temporary hospitals, and one he came up to at twilight near a village in Gloucestershire stood with all its doors and windows open, silent as the grave, and, as he found to his horror by stumbling along evil-smelling corridors, full of unburied dead.

From Gloucestershire Bert went northward to the British aeronautic park outside Birmingham, in the hope that he might be taken on and given food, for there the Government, or at any rate the War Office still existed as an energetic fact, concentrated amidst collapse and social disaster upon the effort to keep the British flag still flying in the air, and trying to brisk up mayor and mayor and magistrate and magistrate in a new effort of organisation. They had brought together all the best of the surviving artisans from that region, they had provisioned the park for a siege, and they were urgently building a larger type of Butteridge machine. Bert could get no footing at this work : he was not sufficiently skilled, and he had drifted to Oxford when the great fight occurred in which these works were finally wrecked. He saw something, but not very much, of the battle from a place called Boar Hill. He saw the Asiatic squadron coming up across the hills to the south-west, and he saw one of their airships circling southward again chased by two aeroplanes, the one that was ultimately overtaken, wrecked and burnt at Edge Hill. But he never learnt the issue of the combat as a whole.

He crossed the Thames from Eton to Windsor and made his way round the south of London to Bun Hill, and there he found his brother Tom, looking like some dark, defensive animal in the old shop, just recovering from the Purple Death, and Jessica upstairs delirious, and, as it seemed to him, dying grimly. She raved of sending out orders to customers, and

scolded Tom perpetually lest he should be late with Mrs.
Thompson's potatoes and Mrs. Hopkins' cauliflower, though all
business had long since ceased and Tom had developed a quite
uncanny skill in the snaring of rats and sparrows and the
concealment of certain stores of cereals and biscuits from
plundered grocers' shops. Tom received his brother with a sort
of guarded warmth.

"Lor!" he said, "it's Bert. I thought you'd be coming
back some day, and I'm glad to see you. But I can't arst you
to eat anything, because I 'aven't got anything to eat. . . .
Where you been, Bert, all this time?"

Bert reassured his brother by a glimpse of a partly-eaten
Swede, and was still telling his story in fragments and paren-
theses, when he discovered behind the counter a yellow and
forgotten note addressed to himself. "What's this?" he said,
and found it was a year-old note from Edna. "She came 'ere,"
said Tom, like one who recalls a trivial thing, "arstin' for you
and arstin' us to take 'er in. That was after the battle and
settin' Clapham Rise afire. I was for takin' 'er in, but Jessica
wouldn't 'ave it—and so she borrowed five shillings of me quiet
like and went on. I dessay she's tole you——"

She had, Bert found. She had gone on, she said in her note,
to an aunt and uncle who had a brickfield near Horsham. And
there at last, after another fortnight of adventurous journeying,
Bert found her.

§ 5

When Bert and Edna set eyes on one another they stared
and laughed foolishly, so changed they were, and so ragged and
surprised. And then they both fell weeping.

"Oh! Bertie, boy!" she cried. "You've come—you've
come!" and put out her arms and staggered. "I told 'im.
He said he'd kill me if I didn't marry him."

But Edna was not married, and when presently Bert could
get talk from her she explained the task before him. That little
patch of lonely agricultural country had fallen under the power
of a band of bullies led by a chief called Bill Gore, who had
begun life as a butcher boy and developed into a prize-fighter
and a professional "sport." They had been organised by a
local nobleman of former eminence upon the turf, but after a
time he had disappeared, no one quite knew how, and Bill had
succeeded to the leadership of the countryside, and had
developed his teacher's methods with considerable vigour.
There had been a strain of advanced philosophy about the local
nobleman, and his mind ran to "improving the race" and
producing the Over-Man, which in practice took the form of
himself especially and his little band in moderation marrying
with some frequency. Bill followed up this idea with an
enthusiasm that even trenched upon his popularity with his
followers. One day he had happened upon Edna tending her

pigs, and had at once fallen a-wooing with great urgency among
the troughs of slush. Edna had made a gallant resistance, but
he was still vigorously about and extraordinarily impatient.
He might, she said, come at any time ; and she looked Bert in
the eyes. They were back already in the barbaric stage when a
man must fight for his love.

And here one deplores the conflicts of truth with the
chivalrous tradition. One would like to tell of Bert sallying
forth to challenge his rival, of a ring formed and a spirited
encounter, and Bert by some miracle of pluck and love and
good fortune winning. But indeed nothing of the sort occurred.
Instead, he reloaded his revolver very carefully, and then sat
in the best room of the cottage by the derelict brickfield, looking
anxious and perplexed, and listening to talk about Bill and his
ways, and thinking, thinking. Then suddenly Edna's aunt,
with a thrill in her voice, announced the appearance of that
individual. He was coming with two others of his gang through
the garden gate. Bert got up, put the woman aside, and looked
out. They presented remarkable figures. They wore a sort of
uniform of red golfing jackets and white sweaters, football
singlets and stockings and boots, and each had let his fancy
play about his headdress. Bill had a woman's hat full of cock's
feathers, and all had wild, slouching cowboy brims.

Bert sighed and stood up, deeply thoughtful, and Edna
watched him, marvelling. The women stood quite still. He
left the window, and went out into the passage rather slowly,
and with the careworn expression of a man who gives his
mind to a complex and uncertain business. "Edna!" he
called, and when she came he opened the front door.

He asked very simply, and pointing to the foremost of the
three, "That 'im ? . . . Sure ?" . . . and being told that it
was, shot his rival instantly and very accurately through the
chest. He then shot Bill's best man much less tidily in the head,
and then shot at and winged the third man as he fled. The
third gentleman yelped, and continued running with a comical
end-on twist.

Then Bert stood still meditating with the pistol in his hand,
and quite regardless of the women behind him.

So far things had gone well.

It became evident to him that if he did not go into politics
at once he would be hanged as an assassin, and accordingly,
and without a word to the women, he went down to the village
public-house he had passed an hour before on his way to Edna,
entered it from the rear, and confronted the little band of ambiguous roughs, who were drinking in the tap-room and discussing
matrimony and Bill's affections in a facetious but envious
manner, with a casually held but carefully reloaded revolver,
and an invitation to join what he called, I regret to say, a
"Vigilance Committee" under his direction. "It's wanted
about 'ere, and some of us are gettin' it up." He presented

himself as one having friends outside, though indeed he had no friends at all in the world but Edna and her aunt and two female cousins.

There was a quick but entirely respectful discussion of the situation. They thought him a lunatic who had tramped into this neighbourhood ignorant of Bill. They desired to temporise until their leader came. Bill would settle him. Some one spoke of Bill.

" Bill's dead," said Bert. " I jest shot 'im. We don't need reckon with '*im*. 'E's shot, and a red-'aired chap with a squint, '*e's* shot. We've settled up all that. There ain't going to be no more Bill, ever. 'E'd got wrong ideas about marriage and things. It's 'is sort of chap we're after."

That carried the meeting.

Bill was perfunctorily buried, and Bert's Vigilance Committee (for so it continued to be called) reigned in his stead.

That is the end of this story so far as Bert Smallways is concerned. We leave him with his Edna to become squatters among the clay and oak thickets of the Weald, far away from the stream of events. From that time forth life became a succession of peasants' encounters, an affair of pigs and hens and small needs and little economies and children, until Clapham and Bun Hill and all the life of the Scientific Age became to Bert no more than the fading memory of a dream. He never knew how the War in the Air went on, nor whether it still went on. There were rumours of airships going and coming, and of happenings Londonward. Once or twice their shadows fell on him as he worked, but whence they came or whither they went he could not tell. Even his desire to tell died out for want of food. At times came robbers and thieves, at times came diseases among the beasts and shortness of food, once the country was worried by a pack of boar-hounds he helped to kill ; he went through many inconsecutive, irrelevant adventures. He survived them all.

Accident and death came near them both ever and again, and passed them by ; and they loved and suffered and were happy, and she bore him many children—eleven children— one after the other, of whom only four succumbed to the necessary hardships of their simple life. They lived and did well, as well was understood in those days. They went the way of all flesh, year by year.

THE EPILOGUE

IT happened that one bright summer's morning exactly thirty years after the launching of the first German air-fleet, an old man took a small boy to look for a missing hen through the ruins of Bun Hill and out towards the splintered pinnacles of the Crystal Palace. He was not a very old man; he was, as a matter of fact, still within a few weeks of sixty-three, but constant stooping over spades and forks and the carrying of roots and manure, and exposure to the damps of life in the open air without a change of clothing, had bent him into the form of a sickle. Moreover, he had lost most of his teeth, and that had affected his digestion, and through that his skin and temper. In face and expression he was curiously like that old Thomas Smallways who had once been coachman to Sir Peter Bone, and this was just as it should be, for he was Tom Smallways the son, who formerly kept the little greengrocer's shop under the straddle of the mono-rail viaduct in the High Street of Bun Hill. But now there were no greengrocer's shops, and Tom was living in one of the derelict villas hard by that unoccupied building site that had been and was still the scene of his daily horticulture. He and his wife lived upstairs, and in the drawing and dining-rooms, which had each French windows opening on the lawn, and all about the ground floor generally, Jessica, who was now a lean and lined and baldish but still very efficient and energetic old woman, kept her three cows and a multitude of gawky hens.

These two were part of a little community of stragglers and returned fugitives, perhaps a hundred and fifty souls of them altogether, that had settled down to the new condition of things after the Panic and Famine and Pestilence that followed in the wake of the War. They had come back from strange refuges and hiding-places and had squatted down among the familiar houses and begun that hard struggle against nature for food which was now the chief interest of their lives. They were by sheer preoccupation with that a peaceful people, more particularly after Wilkes, the house agent, driven by some obsolete dream of acquisition, had been drowned in the pool by the ruined gasworks for making inquiries into title and displaying a litigious turn of mind. (He had not been murdered, you understand, but the people had carried an exemplary ducking ten minutes or so beyond its healthy limits.)

This little community had returned from its original habits of suburban parasitism to what no doubt had been the normal life of humanity for nearly immemorial years, a life of homely economies in the most intimate contact with cows and hens

and patches of ground, a life that breathes and exhales the
scent of cows and finds the need for stimulants satisfied by
the activity of the bacteria and vermin it engenders. Such
has been the life of the European peasant from the dawn of
history to the beginning of the Scientific Era, so it was the
large majority of the people of Asia and Africa had always
been wont to live. For a time it had seemed that by virtue
of machines and scientific civilisation, Europe was to be
lifted out of this perpetual round of animal drudgery, and
that America was to evade it very largely from the outset.
And with the smash of the high and dangerous and splendid
edifice of mechanical civilisation that had arisen so marvellously, back to the land came the common man, back to the
manure.

The little communities, still haunted by ten thousand
memories of a greater state, gathered and developed almost
tacitly a customary law and fell under the guidance of a
medicine man or a priest. The world rediscovered religion
and the need of something to hold its communities together.
At Bun Hill this function was entrusted to an old Baptist
minister. He taught a simple but adequate faith. In his
teaching a good principle called the Word fought perpetually
against a diabolical female influence called the Scarlet Woman
and an evil being called Alcohol. This Alcohol had long since
become a purely spiritualised conception deprived of any
element of material application ; it had no relation to the
occasional finds of whisky and wine in Londoners' cellars
that gave Bun Hill its only holidays. He taught this doctrine
on Sundays, and on week-days he was an amiable and kindly
old man, distinguished by his quaint disposition to wash
his hands, and if possible his face, daily, and with a wonderful
genius for cutting up pigs. He held his Sunday services in the
old church in the Beckenham Road, and then the country-
side came out in a curious reminiscence of the urban dress
of Edwardian times. All the men without exception wore
frock coats, top hats and white shirts, though many had no
boots. Tom was particularly distinguished on these occasions
because he wore a top hat with gold lace about it and a green
coat and trousers that he had found upon a skeleton in the
basement of the Urban and District Bank. The women,
even Jessica, came in jackets and immense hats extravagantly
trimmed with artificial flowers and exotic birds' feathers—of
which there were abundant supplies in the shops to the north—
and the children (there were not many children, because a
large proportion of the babies born in Bun Hill died in a few
days' time of inexplicable maladies) had similar clothes cut
down to accommodate them ; even Stringer's little grandson
of four wore a large top hat.

That was the Sunday costume of the Bun Hill district, a
curious and interesting survival of the genteel traditions of

the Scientific Age. On a week-day the folk were dingily and curiously hung about with dirty rags of housecloth and scarlet flannel, sacking, curtain serge and patches of old carpet, and went either bare-footed or on rude wooden sandals. These people, the reader must understand, were an urban population sunken back to the state of a barbaric peasantry, and so without any of the simple arts a barbaric peasantry would possess. In many ways they were curiously degenerate and incompetent. They had lost any idea of making textiles, they could hardly make up clothes when they had material, and they were forced to plunder the continually dwindling supplies of the ruins about them for cover. All the simple arts they had ever known they had lost, and with the breakdown of modern drainage, modern water supply, shopping, and the like, their civilised methods were useless. Their cooking was worse than primitive. It was a feeble muddling with food over wood fires in rusty drawing-room fireplaces ; for the kitcheners burnt too much. Among them all no sense of baking or brewing or metal-working was to be found.

Their employment of sacking and such-like coarse material for work-a-day clothing, and their habit of tying it on with string and of thrusting wadding and straw inside it for warmth, gave these people an odd, " packed " appearance, and as it was a week-day when Tom took his little nephew for the hen-seeking excursion, so it was they were attired.

" So you've really got to Bun Hill at last, Teddy," said old Tom, beginning to talk, and slackening his pace as soon as they were out of range of old Jessica. " You're the last of Bert's boys for me to see. Wat I've seen, young Bert I've seen, Sissie and Matt, Tom what's called after me, and Peter. The traveller people brought you along all right, eh ? "

" I managed," said Teddy, who was a dry little boy.

" Didn't want to eat you on the way ? "

" They was all right," said Teddy. " And on the way near Leatherhead we saw a man riding on a bicycle."

" My word ! " said Tom, " there ain't many of those about nowadays. Where was he going ? "

" Said he was going to Dorking if the High Road was good enough. But I doubt if he got there. All about Burford it was flooded. We came over the hill, uncle—what they call the Roman Road. That's high and safe."

" Don't know it," said old Tom. " But a bicycle ! You're sure it was a bicycle ? Had two wheels ? "

" It was a bicycle right enough."

" Why ! I remember a time, Teddy, when there was bicycles no end, when you could stand just here—the road was as smooth as a board then—and see twenty or thirty coming and going at the same time, bicycles and moty bicycles, moty cars, all sorts of whirly things."

" No ! " said Teddy.

" I do. They'd keep on going by all day—'undreds and 'undreds."

" But where was they all going ? " asked Teddy.

" Tearin' off to Brighton—you never seen Brighton, I expect—it's down by the sea, used to be a moce 'mazing place—and coming and going from London."

" Why ? "

" They did."

" But why ? "

" Lord knows why, Teddy. They did. Then you see that great thing there like a great big rusty nail sticking up higher than all the houses, and that one yonder, and that, and how something's fell in between 'em among the houses. They was parts of the mono-rail. They went down to Brighton, too, and all day and night there was people going, great cars as big as 'ouses full of people."

The little boy regarded the rusty evidences across the narrow, muddy ditch of cow-droppings that had once been a High Street. He was clearly disposed to be sceptical, and yet there the ruins were ! He grappled with ideas beyond the strength of his imagination.

" What did they go for ? " he asked ; " all of 'em ? "

" They 'ad to. Everything was on the go those days—everything."

" Yes, but where did they come from ? "

" All round 'ere, Teddy, there was people living in those 'ouses, and up the road more 'ouses and more people. You'd hardly believe me, Teddy, but it's Bible truth. You can go on that way for ever and ever, and keep on coming on 'ouses, more 'ouses, and more. There's no end to 'em. No end. They get bigger and bigger." His voice dropped as though he named strange names. " It's *London*," he said.

" And it's all empty now and left alone. All day it's left alone. You don't find 'ardly a man, you won't find nothing but dogs and cats after the rats until you get round by Bromley and Beckenham, and there you find the Kentish men herding swine. (Nice rough lot they are, too !) I tell you that so long as the sun is up it's as still as the grave. I been about by day—orfen and orfen." He paused.

" And all those 'ouses and streets and ways used to be full of people before the War in the Air and the Famine and the Purple Death. They used to be full of people, Teddy, and then came a time when they was full of corpses, when you couldn't go a mile that way before the stink of 'em drove you back. It was the Purple Death 'ad killed 'em every one. The cats and dogs and 'ens and vermin caught it. Everything and every one 'ad it. Jest a few of us 'appened to live. I pulled through and your aunt, though it made 'er lose 'er 'air. Why, you find the skeletons in the 'ouses now. This way we been into all the 'ouses and took what we wanted and buried moce of the people, but up that way, Norwood way, there's 'ouses with the glass in the windows still, and the furniture not touched—all dusty and falling to pieces—and the bones of the people lying, some in bed, some about the 'ouse, jest as the Purple Death left 'em five-and-twenty years ago. I went into one—me and old Higgins las' year—and there was a room with books, Teddy— you know what I mean by books, Teddy?"

"I seen 'em. I seen 'em with pictures."

"Well, books all round, Teddy, 'undreds of books, beyond rhyme or reason, as the saying goes, green-mouldy and dry. I was for leavin' 'em alone—I was never much for reading— but ole Higgings he must touch 'em. 'I believe I could read one of 'em *now*,' 'e says.

"'Not it,' I says.

"'I could,' 'e says, laughing, and takes one out and opens it.

"I looked, and there, Teddy, was a cullud picture, oh, so lovely! It was a picture of women and serpents in a garden. I never see anything like it.

"'This suits me,' said old Higgins, 'to rights.'

"And then kind of friendly he gave the book a pat——"

Old Tom Smallways paused impressively.

"And then?" said Teddy.

"It all fell to dus'. White dus'!" . . . He became still more impressive. "We didn't touch no more of them books that day. Not after that."

For a long time both were silent. Then Tom, playing with a subject that attracted him with a fatal fascination, repeated. "All day long they lie—still as the grave."

Teddy took the point at last. "Don't they lie o' nights?" he asked.

Old Tom shook his head. "Nobody knows, boy, nobody knows."

"But what could they do?"

"Nobody knows. Nobody ain't seen to tell—not nobody."

"Nobody?"

"They tell tales," said old Tom. "They tell tales, but there ain't no believing 'em. I gets 'ome about sundown, and keeps indoors, so I can't say nothing, can I? But there's them that thinks some things and them as thinks others. I've 'eard it's unlucky to take clo'es off of 'em unless they got white bones. There's stories——"

The boy watched his uncle sharply. "*Wot* stories?" he said.

"Stories of moonlight nights and things walking about. But I take no stock in 'em. I keeps in bed. If you listen to stories—Lord! You'll get afraid of yourself in a field at midday."

The little boy looked round and ceased his questions for a space.

" They say there's a 'og man in Beck'n'am what was lost in
London three days and three nights. 'E went up after whisky
to Cheapside, and lorst 'is way among the ruins and wandered.
Three days and three nights 'e wandered about and the streets
kep' changing so's 'e couldn't get 'ome. If 'e 'adn't remembered
some words out of the Bible 'e might 'ave been there now. All
day 'e went and all night—and all day long it was still. It was
as still as death all day long, until the sunset came and the
twilight thickened, and then it began to rustle and whisper
and go pit-a-pat with a sound like 'urrying feet."

He paused.

" Yes," said the little boy breathlessly. " Go on. What
then ? "

" A sound of carts and 'orses there was, and a sound of cabs
and omnibuses, and then a lot of whistling, shrill whistles,
whistles that froze 'is marrer. And directly the whistles began
things begun to show, people in the streets 'urrying, people
in the 'ouses and shops busying themselves, moty-cars in the
streets, a sort of moonlight in all the lamps and winders.
People, I say, Teddy, but they wasn't people. They was the
ghosts of them that was overtook, the ghosts of them that used
to crowd those streets. And they went past 'im and through
'im and never 'eeded 'im, went by like fogs and vapours,
Teddy. And sometimes they was cheerful and sometimes they
was 'orrible, 'orrible beyond words. And once 'e come to a
place called Piccadilly, Teddy, and there was lights blazing like
daylight, and ladies and gentlemen in splendid clo'es crowding
the pavement, and taxi-cabs follering along the road. And as
'e looked, they all went evil—evil in the face, Teddy. And
it seemed to 'im suddenly *they saw 'im*, and the women began
to look at 'im and say things to 'im—'orrible—wicked things.
One come very near 'im, Teddy, right up to 'im, and looked
into 'is face—close. And she 'adn't got a face to look with,
only a painted skull, and then 'e see they was all painted skulls.
And one after another they crowded on 'im saying 'orrible
things, and catchin' at 'im and threatenin' and coaxing 'im, so
that 'is 'eart near left 'is body for fear." . . .

" Yes," gasped Teddy in an unendurable pause.

" Then it was he remembered the words of Scripture and
saved himself alive. ' The Lord is my 'Elper,' 'e says, ' therefore I will fear nothing,' and straight away there came a cock-
crowing and the street was empty from end to end. And after
that the Lord was good to 'im and guided 'im 'ome."

Teddy stared and caught at another question. " But who
was the people," he asked, " who lived in all these 'ouses ?
What was they ? "

" Gent'men in business, people with money—leastways we
thought it was money till everything smashed up, and then
seemingly it was jes' paper—all sorts. Why, there was 'undreds
of thousands of them. There was millions. I've seen that 'I

Street there regular so's you couldn't walk along the pavements, shoppin' time, with women and people shoppin'.''

" But where'd they get their food and things ? "

" Bort 'em in shops like I used to 'ave. I'll show you the place, Teddy, 's we go back. People nowadays 'aven't no idee of a shop—no idee. Plateglass winders—it's all Greek to them. Why, I've 'ad as much as a ton and a 'arf of petaties to 'andle all at one time. You'd open your eyes till they dropped out to see jest what I used to 'ave in my shop. Baskets of pears 'eaped up, marrers, apples and pears, d'licious great nuts.'' His voice became luscious—" Benanas, oranges.''

" What's Benanas ? " asked the boy, " and Oranges ? "

" Fruits they was. Sweet, juicy, d'licious fruits. Foreign fruits. They brought them from Spain and N' York and places. In ships and things. They brought 'em to me from all over the world, and I sold 'em in my shop. *I* sold 'em, Teddy ! Me what goes about now with you, dressed up in old sacks and looking for lost 'ens. People used to come into my shop, great beautiful ladies like you'd 'ardly dream of now, dressed up to the nines, and say, ' Well, Mr. Smallways, what you got 'smorning ? ' and I'd say, ' Well, I got some very nice C'nadian apples,' or p'raps I got custed marrers. See ? And they'd buy 'em. Right off they'd say, ' Send me some up.' Lord ! what a life that was. The business of it, the bussel, the smart things you saw, moty-cars going by, kerridges, people, organ-grinders, German bands. Always something going past—always. If it wasn't for those empty 'ouses I'd think it all a dream.''

" But what killed all the people, uncle ? " asked Teddy.

" It was a smash up," said old Tom. " Everything was going right until they started that War. Everything was going like clockwork. Everybody was busy and everybody was 'appy and everybody got a good square meal every day.'' He met incredulous eyes. " Everybody," he said firmly. " If you couldn't get it anywhere else, you could get it in the workhuss, a nice 'ot bowl of soup called skilly, and bread better'n any one knows 'ow to make now, reg'lar *white* bread, gov'ment bread.''

Teddy marvelled, but said nothing. It made him feel deep longings that he found it wisest to fight down.

For a time the old man resigned himself to the pleasures of gustatory reminiscence. His lips moved. " Pickled Sammin!" he whispered, " an' vinegar. . . . Dutch cheese, *Beer !* A pipe of terbakker.''

" But *'ow* did the people get killed ? " asked Teddy presently.

" There was the War. The War was the beginning of it. The War banged and flummocked about, but it didn't really *kill* many people. But it upset things. They came and set fire to London and burnt and sank all the ships there used to be in the Thames—we could see the smoke and steam for weeks—and they threw a bomb into the Crystal Palace and made a bust-up, and broke down the rail lines and things like that. But as for killin' people, it was just accidental if they did. They killed each other more. There was a great fight all hereabout one day, Teddy—up in the air. Great things bigger than fifty 'ouses, bigger than the Crystal Palace —bigger, bigger than anything, flying about up in the air and whacking at each other and dead men fallin' off 'em. T'riffic ! But it wasn't so much the people they killed as the business they stopped. There wasn't any business doin', Teddy, there wasn't any money about, and nothin' to buy if you 'ad it."

" But 'ow did the people get *killed* ? " said the little boy in the pause.

" I'm tellin' you, Teddy," said the old man. " It was the stoppin' of business come nex'. Sudden, some'ow, there didn't seem to be any money. There was cheques—there was a bit of paper written on, and they was jes' as good as money —jes' as good if they came from customers you knew. Then all of a sudden they wasn't. I was lef' with three of 'em and two I'd given change. Then it got about that five-pun' notes were no good, and then the silver sort of went off. Gold you couldn't get for love or—anything. The banks in London 'ad got it, and the banks was all smashed up. Everybody went bankrup'. Everybody was thrown out of work. Everybody ! "

He paused, and scrutinised his hearer. The small boy's intelligent face expressed hopeless perplexity.

" That's 'ow it 'appened," said old Tom. He sought for some means of expression. " It was like stoppin' a clock," he said. " Things were quiet for a bit, deadly quiet, except for the airships fighting about in the sky, and then people begun to get excited. I remember my lars' customer, the very lars' customer that ever I 'ad. He was a Mr. Moses Gluckstein, a city gent, and very pleasant and fond of sparrow-grass and chokes, and 'e cut in—there 'adn't been no customers for days—and began to talk very fast, offerin' me for anything I 'ad, anything, petaties or anything, its weight in gold. 'E said it was a little speculation 'e wanted to try. 'E said it was a sort of bet reely, and very likely 'e'd lose ; but never mind that, 'e wanted to try. 'E always 'ad been a gambler, 'e said. 'E said I'd only got to weigh it out and 'e'd give me 'is cheque right away. Well, that led to a bit of a argument, perfectly respectful it was, but a argument about whether a cheque was still good, and while 'e was explaining there comes by a lot of these here unemployed with a great banner they 'ad for every one to read—every one could read those days—" We want Food." Three or four of 'em suddenly turns and comes into my shop.

" ' Got any food ? ' says one.

" ' No,' I says, ' not to sell. I wish I 'ad. But if I 'ad

I'm afraid I couldn't let you have it. This gent, 'e's been offerin' me—— '

" Mr. Gluckstein tried to stop me, but it was too late.

" ' What's 'e been offerin' you ? ' says a great big chap with a 'atchet ; ' what's 'e been offerin' you ? ' I 'ad to tell.

" ' Boys,' 'e said, ' 'ere's another feenancier ! ' and they took 'im out there and then, and 'ung 'im on a lam'pose down the street. 'E never lifted a finger to resist. After I tole on 'im 'e never said a word. . . . "

Tom meditated for a space. " First chap I ever sin 'ung ! " he said.

" 'Ow old was you ? " asked Teddy.

" 'Bout thirty," said old Tom.

" Why ! I saw free pig-stealers 'ung before I was six," said Teddy. " Father took me because of my birfday being near. Said I ought to be blooded. . . . "

" Well, you never saw no one killed by a moty-car, any'ow," said old Tom after a moment of chagrin. " And you never saw no dead men carried into a chemis' shop."

Teddy's momentary triumph faded. " No," he said, " I 'aven't."

" Nor won't. Nor won't. You'll never see the things I've seen, never. Not if you live to be a 'undred. . . . Well, as I was saying, that's how the Famine and Riotin' began. Then there was strikes and Socialism, things I never did 'old with, worse and worse. There was fightin' and shootin' down, and burnin' and plunderin'. They broke up the banks up in London and got the gold. But they couldn't make food out of gold. 'Ow did *we* get on ? Well, we kep' quiet. We didn't interfere with no one and no one didn't interfere with us. We 'ad some old 'tatoes about, but mocely we lived on rats. Ours was a old 'ouse, full of rats, and the famine never seemed to bother 'em. Orfen we got a rat. Orfen. But moce of the people who lived hereabouts was too tender stummicked for rats. Didn't seem to fancy 'em. They'd been used to all sorts of fallals, and they didn't take to 'onest feeding, not till it was too late. Died rather.

" It was the famine began to kill people. Even before the Purple Death come along they was dying like flies at the end of the summer. 'Ow I remember it all ! I was one of the first to 'ave it. I was out seein' if I mightn't get 'old of a cat or somethin', and then I went round to my bit of ground to see whether I couldn't get up some young turnips I'd forgot, and I was took something awful. You've no idee the pain, Teddy —it doubled me up pretty near. I jes' lay down by that there corner, and your aunt come along to look for me and dragged me 'ome like a sack.

" I'd never 'ave got better if it 'adn't been for your aunt. ' Tom,' she says to me, ' you got to get well,' and I 'ad to. Then *she* sickened. She sickened, but there ain't much dyin' about your aunt. ' Lor ! ' she says, ' as if I'd leve you to go muddlin' along alone ! ' That's what she says. She's got a tongue 'as your aunt. But it took 'er 'air off—and arst though I might, she's never cared for the wig I got 'er—orf the old lady what was in the vicarage garden.

" Well, this 'ere Purple Death—it jes' wiped people out, Teddy. You couldn't bury 'em. And it took the dogs and the cats, too, and the rats and 'orses. At last every 'ouse and garden was full of dead bodies. London way you couldn't go for the smell of them, and we 'ad to move out of the 'I Street into that villa we got. And all the water run short that way. The drains and underground tunnels took it. Gor' knows where the Purple Death come from ; some say one thing and some another. Some said it come from eatin' rats and some from eatin' nothing. Some say the Asiatics brought it from some 'I place, Thibet, I think, where it never did nobody much 'arm. All I know is it come after the Famine. And the Famine come after the Penic, and the Penic come after the War."

Teddy thought. " What made the Purple Death ? " he asked.

" 'Aven't I tole you ! "

" But why did they 'ave a Penic ? "

" They 'ad it."

" But why did they start the War ? "

" They couldn't stop themselves. 'Aving them airships made 'em."

" And 'ow did the War end ? "

" Lord knows if it's ended, boy," said old Tom. " Lord knows if it's ended. There's been travellers through 'ere— there was a chap only two summers ago—say it's goin' on still. They say there's bands of people up north who keep on with it, and people in Germany and China and 'Merica and places. 'E said they still got flying-machines and gas and things. But we 'aven't seen nothin' in the air now for seven years, and nobody 'asn't come nigh of us. Last we saw was a crumpled sort of airship going away—over there. It was a littleish-sized thing and lop-sided, as though it 'ad something the matter with it."

He pointed, and came to a stop at a gap in the fence, the vestiges of the old fence from which, in the company of his neighbour, Mr. Stringer, the milkman, he had once watched the South of England Aero Club's Saturday afternoon ascents. Dim memories, it may be, of that particular afternoon returned to him.

" There, down there, where all that rus' looks so red and bright, that's the gasworks."

" What's gas ? " asked the little boy.

" Oh, a hairy sort of nothin' what you put in balloons to make 'em go up. And you used to burn it till the 'lectricity come."

The little boy tried vainly to imagine gas on the basis of these particulars. Then his thoughts reverted to a previous topic.

" But why didn't they end the War ? "

" Obstinacy. Everybody was getting 'urt, but everybody was 'urtin' and everybody was 'igh-spirited and patriotic, and so they smeshed up things instead. They jes' went on smeshin'. And afterwards they jes' got desp'rite and savige."

" It ought to 'ave ended," said the little boy.

" It didn't ought to 'ave begun," said old Tom. " But people was proud. People was la-dy-da-ish and uppish and proud. Too much meat and drink they 'ad. Give in—not them ! And after a bit nobody arst 'em to give in. Nobody arst 'em. . . . "

He sucked his old gums thoughtfully, and his gaze strayed away across the valley to where the shattered glass of the Crystal Palace glittered in the sun. A dim, large sense of waste and irrevocable lost opportunities pervaded his mind. He repeated his ultimate judgment upon all these things, obstinately, slowly, and conclusively, his final saying upon the matter.

" You can say what you like," he said, " it didn't ought ever to 'ave begun."

He said it simply—somebody somewhere ought to have stopped something, but who or how or why were all beyond his ken.